NEW ARRIVALS IN BYLAND CRESCENT

An absolutely heartbreaking and unputdownable historical family saga

BILL KITSON

The Cowgill Family Saga Book 4

Joffe Books, London
www.joffebooks.com

First published in Great Britain in 2023

Cover art by Jarmila Takač

ISBN: 978-1-83526-309-9

Dedicated to Laurence Gordon Kitson, my father.

His work for the Wool Control during World War II provided the basis for Sonny Cowgill's exploits.

PART ONE: 1959–1960

How clear, how lovely bright,
How beautiful to sight
Those beams of morning play;
How heaven laughs out with glee
Where, like a bird set free,
Up from the eastern sea
Soars the delightful day.

To-day I shall be strong,
No more shall yield to wrong,
Shall squander life no more;
Days lost, I know not how,
I shall retrieve them now;
Now I shall keep the vow
I never kept before.

Ensanguining the skies
How heavily it dies
Into the west away;
Past touch and sight and sound
Not further to be found,
How hopeless under ground
Falls the remorseful day.

How clear, how lovely bright.
A E Houseman

CHAPTER ONE

In Byland Crescent, Scarborough, the Victorian house had been home to a large contingent of the Cowgill family since 1897, but now in 1959, that number had declined sharply. As the family occupancy dwindled, so the need for household staff diminished. For the past few years, Jenny Cowgill had shared the household duties with her mother-in-law, Rachael, since Jenny's mother who had been the cook/housekeeper had died, and their elderly butler had retired. With fifty percent of the current residents absent, Jenny's work was reduced to catering for her husband Mark and their daughter Susan.

She looked round the large kitchen, remembering the day she arrived as a young girl with her widowed mother. The house was always busy — weekend visitors and evening soirees were the height of her youth. As was her developing friendship with the only child in the house, Mark Cowgill. They attended the same school, and played together, before they grew and married. How things had changed. Through the kitchen window she could see the old stables and coach house, now converted to her father-in-law's carpentry workshop and garages.

Now, recalling the lively parties of the past, she was trying to plan a much quieter Christmas. She had filled the teapot and was wondering whether to begin baking, when her thought processes were interrupted by the click of the letter box. Glad of the distraction, she walked to the hall to collect the post.

Jenny smiled. The phrase "feast or famine" had an ironic significance as she stared at the two letters and the postcard in her hand. She and Mark had been waiting for weeks to get news of Mark's father and mother, Sonny and Rachael, who they believed were en route to America following a visit to Crete. They were equally keen to know where their son Andrew was. His previous communication had been from Rome, the second destination in what his grandmother laughingly referred to as "a latter-day Grand Tour". Judging by the images of the Eiffel Tower on the postcard, he had reached Paris.

Jenny returned to the kitchen. It would be pointless to let her tea go cold, when she could drink it while catching up on the family news. She began with the postcard, posted weeks earlier, judging by the date. Andrew had assumed, correctly, that Jenny would be the one to read it. *'Hi Mum, hope you, Dad and the Noise box are OK.'* Jenny smiled at the insulting reference to his younger sister and her habit of playing pop music on her radio at high volume. *'I'm about to set off for Madrid,'* the message continued, *'and I'll spend some time there, before going to Barcelona, Granada, Seville and finally to Ibiza, where I'll visit your friend and her daughter.'*

Coincidentally, the next item Jenny picked up was from the friend Andrew had referred to, Carmen Diaz. Mark and Jenny had met Carmen in Spain in 1936 when they fought alongside her during the Spanish Civil War. Now, as Jenny read the contents of Carmen's letter, she felt overwhelmed with sorrow. Carmen had survived so much tragedy during the conflict when her husband and daughter were killed by Nationalist troops. But her life had taken an upward turn following the birth of another child, fathered by her lover, a fellow guerrilla fighter. The daughter, born in the hillside camp, and delivered by Jenny, had been named Consuela Genoveva. Consuela was Spanish for 'consolation'. The baby's other name, Genoveva, was a close equivalent to Jennifer, in honour of Jenny, whom Carmen had come to think of as almost a sister.

It was concerning Consuela that the major part of the letter focussed. Following previous correspondence, in which Carmen had revealed that her daughter, like Mark and Jenny's son Andrew, was hoping to become involved in the emerging technology industry, Carmen had gone into further detail.

Her daughter's best hope of study and advancement rested on her ability to go to Great Britain, at the time the leading light in such industries. However, because of Carmen's shady past, she had grave reservations about the authorities being willing to grant permission for Consuela to leave the country without documentation.

In a previous letter, Jenny had offered to accommodate Consuela should she be able to get to England. Carmen thanked her for this, but now she had other, far more worrying, concerns. Although she had concealed this from her daughter, Carmen had been increasingly worried about her own health. Now, having consulted a specialist, she had been forced to tell Consuela the unacceptable news. Carmen was suffering from cancer. '*I have only a few months to live*,' she ended by saying, '*and I fear for Consuela's safety, alone and unprotected, after I have gone. Nevertheless*,' she ended by telling Jenny, '*we look forward to meeting Andrew and will ensure he is cared for during his visit*.'

Jenny sat for a moment, deeply saddened at the news from her friend. When she had recovered her composure, and anxious to get more positive news, she turned to the final item of post, an envelope bearing a Greek stamp. The handwriting was that of Jenny's mother-in-law. Jenny and Mark had assumed his parents would already be in Texas, where they were going to stay with Mark's sister Frances and her husband Henry. Clearly they had not begun this leg of their journey yet. When Jenny read the letter, the cause of the delay became clear.

In the first paragraph Rachael expressed her love, and that of her husband, Sonny, for the family members at home. But as Jenny absorbed the contents of the following paragraphs her concentration intensified. It was some time before she reached the end of the eight-page letter. Jenny wasn't aware of the passage of time until she took a drink of her tea, which by then was cold. She grimaced slightly and began to read the letter again.

The purpose of Sonny and Rachael's visit to Crete had been to find the resting place of their younger son Billy. He had been listed as missing, believed killed following the withdrawal of Allied troops in 1941. Now, it seemed that their quest, which Sonny had referred to as a pilgrimage, had been successful. In fact, they had achieved far more than they could have hoped for — so much so that they were planning to remain on the island until January. Jenny's eyes filled with tears as she read the reason for prolonging their stay.

Billy Cowgill, it seemed, was regarded as a hero by the inhabitants of several villages in the Cretan mountains. His action, which had resulted in his death, had saved the lives of his colleagues and a number of resistance fighters. '*New Year's Day is devoted to* Agios Vassili *(St Basil)*' Rachael wrote, '*and that name is the Greek equivalent of Billy.*'

The saint's day was marked by the villagers in celebrating the life and sacrifice of the young British soldier, and on learning that his parents were among them, the residents had invited them to be guests of honour on this special occasion.

Rachael had ended her letter by asking Mark and Jenny to contact Frances in Texas, advise her of the delay, and explain the reason. Jenny folded the letter, deciding the best way to do that would be by telegram, but that could wait until Mark returned home that evening.

Jenny decided to phone Mark's office in Bradford to pass on the news, then she would start baking.

Mark was sales director at what had been the family business, originally Haigh Ackroyd & Cowgill, now the UK subsidiary of an Australian company, Fisher Springs Pty. Jenny's phone call, however, was abortive as she was told he had gone to visit a client. She left a message for him to phone back and began preparing her ingredients.

Jenny's thoughts centred on the contents of Rachael's letter. She hoped that on learning her son's death had not been in vain, Rachael might at last be able to rid herself of the burden of guilt she had carried for many years. Her angry outburst on discovering that Billy had enlisted had led to a split within the family. Billy's younger sister Elizabeth, who hero-worshipped him, had blamed her parents for the schism and, to a lesser extent, for his death.

When Elizabeth had been co-opted in her teens into a team of code-breakers, she had sworn never to return to Byland Crescent. She had cut all ties with the family, vowing to have nothing more to do with them, other than what appeared to be an obligatory card at Christmas.

Jenny was in the midst of rolling out pastry for mince pies when the doorbell rang. On answering it she saw two police officers standing outside. A cold frisson of fear ran down her spine as the senior of them asked, 'Mrs Cowgill?'

'Yes, that's me,' she agreed, all the while thinking, was this some awful news, about one of the family? Her fear multiplied, and was barely lessened when he glanced down at his occurrence book.

The officer looked puzzled. 'Mrs Rachael Cowgill?'

'No, I'm her daughter-in-law. What's this about?'

'We need to speak to Mrs Rachael Cowgill.' The officer glanced down at his notebook again before adding, 'or Mr Mark Cowgill? Are either of them available?'

'Mark is my husband.' Jenny noticed the confusion on the officer's face. 'I'm sorry, you mean his father, Mark Senior. Everyone calls him Sonny. But I'm afraid they're away. They're abroad, and they're not expected back for some months. Would you mind telling me what this is about?'

'I think it would be better if we come inside.'

Jenny stood aside for them to pass. Once inside the grand hallway, the senior officer explained, but what he told her failed to shed much light on the reason they were there.

'We have been asked to contact Mr or Mrs Cowgill because there has been an accident.'

'What sort of accident, and to whom?'

'I'm afraid that's all we know. We were asked to come here by the police force in London, because a member of your family is in hospital there. They didn't give us any further details beyond a telephone number on which to speak to them. They seemed to take it for granted that your parents-in-law would know what it was about.'

Jenny found this totally incomprehensible. 'I'm sorry. I think there has been a mistake. We don't have any members of our family either living in, or working near, London. Nor, to the best of my knowledge, do any of them ever visit the capital. Added to which, I think all our relatives can be accounted for, so perhaps you've been sent on a fool's errand. I know Cowgill isn't the most common surname but there must be other families bearing it. Maybe this is about one of their relatives.'

The officer disagreed. 'The phone number I've been given belongs to Special Branch. They aren't prone to making that sort of error, especially with something as important as this.'

'I think I should telephone my husband and see if he can shed any light on the mystery, although I doubt whether he knows any more than me. He's at work in Bradford, but when I tried to speak to him earlier he was unavailable. If you care to wait I'll call him again. If he's in the office, he'll most likely want to speak to you.'

Mark's initial reaction was a comparable if not greater degree of astonishment, which continued up to the point when the police officer told him that the message had been delivered on behalf of Special Branch.

Mark thanked the officer and said he would attend to it on his return home, before asking to speak to his wife. The officers left, and after a few seconds' silence, Mark said, 'I think there's only one person they could be referring to. It must be Lizzie.'

'Elizabeth? Your sister? But she isn't in London or anywhere near there. The few cards we've had from her in recent years are from around the Bristol area.'

'There's nobody else it could be. Think about it, Jenny. Think about what she got conscripted into during the war. Why else would Special Branch be involved? Anyway, I'm setting off home straight away, then we'll call that number.'

The only problem with Mark's theory was that getting information out of Special Branch was like trying to extract blood from a stone. As he pointed out later, that was probably because they were only used to collecting information rather than distributing it. After a long, drawn-out process, Mark had not only to prove his own identity, but that of his parents and his siblings, and then explain why his parents were not contactable.

'They've gone to try and find the place where my brother, William, died during the war, and hopefully, make sure he is properly buried,' Mark told him.

'Where exactly are they? Do you know?'

'Somewhere in the mountains of southern Crete, or so we believe.'

Strangely it was only this piece of information that satisfied the officer, following which he divulged what he knew, even if that was very little. 'Your sister, Elizabeth Hannah, is in hospital, but I'm afraid it's too early to tell you how serious her injuries are. I think the best course of action would be for you to travel to London and visit her. All I can say at this point is that your sister was attacked and robbed. She was stabbed several times. We're still not certain why she was in the location where she was found, and we've had to wait for her to regain consciousness before we can question her. Needless to say, apart from any personal considerations, we're also concerned that the apparent motive might only serve as a distraction, and the real reason for the attack might be to do with the work she is involved in. I feel sure you'll understand that.'

'Actually,' Mark told him, 'that's not true, because I haven't the faintest idea what you're talking about. Let me explain. Owing to circumstances beyond either my control or Lizzie's, I haven't spoken to my sister since 1939. That's partly because I was away during the war, during which time she got co-opted to work in some secret government department. As she had a big disagreement with our parents, she no longer keeps in touch, so I have no idea what she does for a living these days — or rather,' he added, 'I didn't until a moment ago. But what you've just told me suggests she might still be involved in something clandestine.'

The officer's tone relaxed slightly as he said, 'Perhaps it would be best if you were to travel to London as soon as possible. If you phone this number and give us your travel plans we will have someone meet you from the train and take you to the hospital.' With that he ended the call, leaving Mark still baffled.

Mark explained to Jenny, 'Allied to the code-breaking unit Lizzie was conscripted into, and the fact that Special Branch are getting hot under the collar about the possible reason for what happened, all I can think is that she must still be working for the government or something. Reading between the lines of what that guy inferred, I think they're worried the motive for the attack might be down to her work. One thing for certain, the only way to find out is by doing what he suggested and travelling down to London. I'll have to play by their rules, though, because he didn't even tell me what hospital Lizzie is in.'

Faced with the potentially bad news concerning his sister, Jenny was reluctant to reveal the contents of the letters she'd received that morning. Mark knew her too well to be deceived, and demanded to know what she was concealing.

'We've had a letter from your mother and father. Part of it was a bit distressing, but not as harrowing as the news from Carmen.'

'Are Mum and Dad all right?'

'They're fine, but they're remaining on Crete longer than we expected. They've found Billy's grave and discovered a lot about how he died.' Jenny told him the rest of their news, before adding, 'I actually think their stay on Crete will be good for them.'

'I'll read that later. What was Carmen's news?'

Jenny told him, adding, 'Carmen's main concern, apart from her own health, is about Consuela's welfare. I believe she still worries about her part in the Civil War coming to light, and the knock-on effect on her daughter. I wish there was some way we could help, but I suspect that if we did try, even if it was possible, our actions might cause more problems.'

'What did you have in mind?'

'I was thinking we should try to bring Consuela to England, but I doubt she would get a passport, and even applying for one could be difficult given their circumstances. Carmen has in effect been in hiding for over twenty years. Revealing her personal details might trigger an alert in official circles.'

'I see what you mean. It's a bit of an impasse, I'd say. We're so fortunate living here, and having British citizenship as a safeguard following our involvement. I'm not sure we can do anything to help, apart from offering our hopes and prayers for them. In the meantime, I've a trip to sort out.'

CHAPTER TWO

Organizing the visit to London was by no means straightforward. Mark first had to ensure his absence from work would be covered, and to figure out a way to get the news of what had happened to his mother and father. Oddly — or so he thought at the time — it was Jessica Binks, who had taken his father's place as managing director, who provided the solution to both problems. During the war she had headed a covert research facility and had many contacts. In doing so, she gave Mark both contact information and advice that helped him get the cooperation he needed, and prevented him making a serious mistake.

'In the first instance, don't worry about work, that's easily covered. And, you might think your parents are out of reach but that's not so. Wherever they are, be it in Crete or anywhere in Greece, there will be a British Consulate not too far away. Because of the relatively few foreign visitors, they should be able to track Sonny and Rachael down easily if it becomes essential. But I wouldn't try to get word to them yet, or to your other sister in the US. What you should do is find out exactly how bad Elizabeth's injuries are and then make a judgement. There's no point in scaring them unnecessarily if the problem's not as bad as it seems. Also, if they've already left Crete it might be better to tell Frances first and then she can pass the news on when they reach America.' Jessica paused for a moment then added, 'If your contacts prove difficult, try dropping the name Edrith Pointon and see if that makes them more cooperative.'

'Who is he?'

'He was the head of the government section I worked for during the war, but if you tell anyone, I shall deny it. If he's still involved, which he might well be, because he won't be of retiring age yet, he'll most likely be near the top of the tree in departments concerned in covert activities.'

'You mean such as espionage.'

'You said that, not me.' Jessica laughed. 'And I'm not going to confirm — or deny it.'

That, as Mark and Jenny agreed, was both sensible advice, and more potential assistance than they could have bargained for.

Next morning, having given Special Branch his travel details, Mark waited on Scarborough station for the local train to York, where he would catch the express to London King's Cross. Once he reached the capital he had been instructed to wait by the telephone box adjacent to the station newspaper kiosk. Following which, he would be approached by a Special Branch officer and taken to the hospital to see Elizabeth.

Jenny commented, 'If it needed anything to convince me you were correct, that Lizzie is still working for the government, those arrangements prove it. They could have just told you which hospital and ward to visit.'

* * *

After alighting at King's Cross, Mark had barely taken up his position when he was accosted by a stranger, a man of about his own age. Even as he was agreeing that he was indeed Mr Mark Cowgill, he assessed the man's attire and demeanour, both of which proclaimed him to be a minor official of some sort.

'I have a car waiting outside the concourse to take you to the hospital.'

Although the man had requested confirmation of his identity, Mark noticed that the man didn't furnish his own name, so he asked for some identification. To the officer's consternation, Mark took the warrant card from his hand and examined it carefully before returning it. 'You can't be too careful,' he pointed out. 'Now, can you tell me how my sister is?'

'I'm afraid not. I've only been asked to meet you and ensure you arrive at the hospital safely. When you get there one of my colleagues will take over from me.'

When they reached the man's car he opened the boot for Mark to stow his suitcase and then drove the short distance to his destination. As he pulled up outside the main entrance, he told Mark, 'Take the stairs to the first floor, then turn towards ward six. My colleague will be watching for your arrival and will brief you.'

'How will he recognize me?'

The officer smiled slightly. 'The suitcase should be sufficient proof.'

It was only when Mark reached the door leading to the ward that his patience was rewarded. 'Mr Cowgill, I'm Inspector Jackson.' The man proffered his hand.

As Mark shook it, he asked, 'What can you tell me about my sister's condition?'

'Although we were very concerned to begin with, especially as she has been kept sedated for quite some time, I'm pleased to report that she is now awake and able to answer questions.'

'Hang on. I thought the attack happened a couple of days ago? How come we weren't informed earlier?'

'It was a difficult decision, and we had to rely on the doctors' prognosis before we made it. Once they told us she was out of danger there seemed little point in worrying you unnecessarily. There was nothing you could have done to help Elizabeth until she regained consciousness.'

Mark was furious. He glared at the man. 'What you mean is that you wanted to question her about the motive behind the attack before informing her relatives. I hope you got the information you needed! I wonder what some of the more radical newspapers would make of your behaviour.'

Jackson winced slightly at the acid tone in Mark's voice, but told him, 'Please don't do anything like that. It appears that it was purely a robbery. There have been a few such instances in that area recently. Elizabeth was in town for a meeting before she set off to walk back to her hotel. Unfortunately, there has been a lot of freezing fog in the past few weeks and she took a wrong turning in the dark, which is why she ended up where she did.'

'What injuries does she have?'

'She was stabbed three times — once in her side, damaging a lung, and twice in her back. The knife entered near her spine. The bruising and swelling is severe and has put pressure on her spinal cord. From what the surgeons told me, they will not know the full extent of the damage until the bruising subsides.' Jackson paused before delivering the next piece of news, news that was more traumatic than Mark could have imagined. 'It is possible that Elizabeth will never walk again.'

Mark was still trying to come to terms with these horrific implications when he was ushered into a private room. A patient was lying flat on a bed, her face contorted by a spasm of pain as the nurses were changing her dressings. Mark waited until they left, before looking towards his sister. When he had last seen Elizabeth she was twelve years old, and he struggled to identify the woman who was staring at him in equal perplexity, until recognition dawned.

If she was pleased to see her older brother it was certainly not apparent, either from her expression or her opening words. 'They sent you, did they? Couldn't even be bothered to come themselves. Really caring, my parents. If that's how little I mean to them I'm surprised they took the trouble to send anyone. So I reckon you've had a wasted journey.'

She turned her head away and Mark guessed this was to hide the tears he had seen in her eyes.

'I see you're still as bitter as ever, Lizzie, and still jumping to conclusions without any facts. That saddens me, because I was going to say how nice it was to see you, even in such horrible circumstances. The reason I came, the reason Mum and Dad didn't visit you, is because they don't know what happened to you. We thought you were living, and presumably working, somewhere in the West Country.'

Elizabeth turned and stared at him for a moment before asking, 'Why don't they know what happened? Didn't Special Branch tell them?'

'They couldn't, because Mum and Dad are not in England at present. Given time I might be able to get in touch with them, but it won't be easy. I thought it best to see how things are rather than frighten them unnecessarily.'

There was another silence as Elizabeth tried to assimilate what Mark had told her. 'I don't understand,' she admitted eventually. 'Surely you must have some idea where they are.'

'Until a couple of days ago I thought they were probably in the middle of the Atlantic, on their way to Texas.' Mark could tell from her expression that none of this made any sense whatsoever to Elizabeth. He explained why their parents had gone to Crete and why they intended to go to Texas.

Elizabeth frowned. 'I assume Fran must be our sister Frances, but who's Henry? And what kids are you talking about?'

'Sorry, I keep forgetting how long you've been out of touch. Henry is Fran's husband. They met during the war when he was serving with the USAF stationed in England — Dad calls him Hank the Yank. They got married and went to live in Texas where his family own a cattle ranch. They have two children, a boy and a girl.'

Elizabeth sighed, and Mark found her next comment deeply saddening. 'Why don't you tell me all the news, everything I've missed while I've been away?'

They talked for almost half an hour before the nurse re-entered the room and demanded he leave and let her patient get some rest. Before he went, Mark promised to return the following day. He paused before asking, 'Have the medics told you the extent of your injuries?'

'You mean have they told me I'm possibly going to be a helpless cripple for the rest of my life? Yes, but I wasn't sure you were aware of the fact.'

Mark ignored the bitterness in her voice. 'Crippled you might be, but helpless — never. That just isn't in your nature.' He bent over and kissed her on the forehead. 'See you tomorrow, Lizzie.'

Elizabeth smiled, the first time Mark had seen her do this, as she replied, 'You don't have to make an appointment, I'm not going anywhere.'

Mark was surprised to find the Special Branch officer waiting in the corridor outside the room. 'I've made a reservation for you at a nearby hotel,' Jackson told him. 'It's clean, comfortable and convenient. The food's not bad either,' he added with a smile.

Mark couldn't resist the temptation to test the officer out. 'Is it expensive?' he asked.

Jackson looked surprised. 'I didn't think that would be an issue.'

'It isn't,' Mark said, pointedly. 'But I wanted to see how in-depth your investigation into Elizabeth's family has been. Obviously, judging by your reply, I'd say it was fairly thorough, which confirms other theories of mine.'

'Very astute of you, but don't read too much into it. Such procedure is fairly standard in my department.'

'There's a word for that statement round our way,' Mark told him. 'It's connected to the waste product of male cattle.'

Jackson smiled slightly, but stated, 'I was told you knew nothing of your sister's occupation until we contacted you, but now I'm beginning to wonder how true that was.'

'Perfectly true, because the last time I spoke to Lizzie she was barely a teenager. Obviously my parents told me about her being seconded to work in code-breaking during the war. But I'd no idea she continued working in the intelligence sector afterwards — not until you lot got so agitated about the motive for the assault on her. That meant she had to be the recipient of information that's classified by the Official Secrets Act, and you were concerned that the attack was to do with unauthorised access to such information.'

Jackson's reply was a thinly disguised compliment. 'That was a bit like listening to Sherlock Holmes, only with a Yorkshire accent.'

CHAPTER THREE

That evening, during Mark's telephone conversation with Jenny, he placed strong emphasis on the family rift, and his hope that this traumatic experience might present them with the opportunity to heal it along with the physical wounds Elizabeth had suffered. 'Once she'd got over her bitterness and anger, we had a long chat and by the end of it I think she was coming round to a more balanced judgement. Can you believe it, though, she actually thought Mum and Dad couldn't be bothered to come to London and they'd sent me instead.'

He heard Jenny's shocked exclamation.

'I know. It's difficult to credit, but that's what she believed. This has obviously been a festering sore in Lizzie's mind and her outlook on life for almost twenty years. Even now, she still finds it hard to forgive Mum for what she said to Billy when he joined up, so it was some comfort when I mentioned why they've gone to Crete. What we have to do is build on this more positive attitude and strengthen Lizzie's bonds with the family. That's going to be vital. Otherwise the atmosphere at home will be intolerably bad. The situation will be difficult enough to manage anyway, at least to begin with. Hopefully things might ease when we've become accustomed to the changes we're going to have to make.'

The last part of Mark's comments baffled Jenny. 'How do you mean? Are you saying that Lizzie's planning to come back to live in Byland Crescent?'

'To be honest, I think it's her only option, Jenny.' It was only then that Mark revealed the extent of Elizabeth's injuries and the doctors' prognosis, adding, 'So in view of Mum and Dad's absence, I think it's up to me to take charge of the situation — or to put it another way, for you and me to take control. Before we start making any plans though, I'd like you to come down to London — and bring Suzie with you. Once we're all here we can begin to assess the situation properly.'

'If I came to London I'd have to bring Suzie along anyway. I can't leave her alone here. Can't we do everything over the phone? Making arrangements and organizing transport, I mean.'

'I thought by introducing her to Suzie, the niece she didn't know existed, we could remind Lizzie of all the things she's missed during her self-imposed exile. I had a good example of how far we've been from her thoughts when I was talking about Mum and Dad's visit to Crete. I said Andrew had gone with them, and Lizzie had to ask me who Andrew is. I think it shocked her when I reminded her he is our son. She'd obviously forgotten. She was also really taken aback when I told her about Fran marrying Hank. My thought is that we should use all the tools at our disposal to persuade Lizzie to return to the fold.'

Jenny approved of Mark's thinking, but disguised it by taking mock umbrage. 'So you think of Suzie and me as tools, do you? What do you have us down as, a pair of hammers, a couple of screwdrivers, or something worse?'

Mark hastened to reassure her that he was speaking purely figuratively. While she accepted his apology, Jenny was smiling complacently, aware that her expression couldn't be detected over the telephone. She was surprised, therefore, when Mark added, 'And you can wipe that smug grin off your face, Jennifer Cowgill. You know very well I adore you as much as ever.'

Towards the end of their conversation they debated the wisdom, or otherwise, of telling Frances about this shock development, but eventually decided to leave matters in abeyance. 'If Fran knows the situation she'd be duty-bound to tell Mum and Dad, and they'd want to come straight home. I think it would be wiser to wait until we know how things are going to pan out,' Jenny suggested. 'If Lizzie doesn't agree to your idea they'd miss out on spending time with Fran and the grandchildren, and all for no reason.'

Mark agreed, telling Jenny he'd been thinking on the same lines. But that was only natural, as their minds had always been in perfect harmony.

* * *

Although he was extremely fond of his sister, Mark realized that his affection was for a young girl, a being who no longer existed except in his memory. Of the adult Elizabeth he had no knowledge of her likes and dislikes, of her way of life, nothing apart from a sketchy knowledge of the world of espionage that had become her profession. Having little awareness of her personality made it difficult to approach her and put forward the scheme he and Jenny had discussed.

He decided to leave any mention of the future until such time as he had the backup and distraction of his wife and daughter to counter any adverse reaction. The delay was a matter of tactics rather than cowardice, and Mark carefully avoided any mention of what lay ahead for Elizabeth.

This was easily achieved, because when he arrived at the hospital he was met by the surgeon in charge of her case. He told him that the previous day's visit, and a second by an officer from Special Branch, had caused a mild setback in Elizabeth's recovery, to such an extent that he had deemed it necessary to sedate her. 'This is a temporary measure and I am doing it as a precaution, so if you find her less responsive than yesterday, please don't be alarmed.'

Mark nodded. 'While I've got you alone, without Elizabeth hearing, can you clarify the long-term prognosis? I was told she might never be able to walk again. Is that your reading of the situation?'

'She will need a wheelchair, but it is also possible she might make a partial, if not full, recovery. I'm afraid there is a lot we don't yet understand about injuries such as your sister sustained. All I can say is you should give her every chance by utilising such things as specialist physiotherapy sessions.'

Despite the doctor's encouraging words Mark was relieved when Jenny and Susan joined him a couple of days later. Without previous experience of Elizabeth's condition, both Jenny and Susan were shocked by the listless, apathetic reaction of the patient lying in the bed. Even taking into account the devastating news of her incapacity, and the bleak outlook of her future, Elizabeth seemed despondent, careless of whether her condition would improve or not. This, Jenny thought, represented a danger signal, one that they could not ignore, but how to achieve a more positive attitude was a question neither she nor Mark could answer.

When they touched on the subject of Sonny and Rachael's trip to Crete, Jenny was surprised by Elizabeth's reaction. 'I'm surprised they bothered. Mother virtually threw Billy out of the house when he told her he'd enlisted. My father spent a lot of his time away, making money out of other people's suffering.'

'What on earth are you talking about?' Jenny asked, her voice sharp with irritation.

'Those business trips he went on. He was away for days, sometimes weeks on end. He wasn't even at home when we got the news about Billy being killed.'

Mark was about to refute that idea, but Jenny beat him to it. Her irritation had turned to downright anger, and the fury in her voice made Elizabeth wince.

'You are talking absolute rubbish. Where did you get the idea that your father was away on business? Don't you know what he was doing? Did nobody tell you where he was when the news of Billy's death came through?'

There was no response, so Jenny continued, 'He was appointed to the Wool Control as an appraiser, which meant he had to inspect bales of wool as they were offloaded at various ports throughout the country. The ships carried no documentation, which meant he had to sample the contents of every bale. That was a highly dangerous task. He was in Southampton when the city was bombed, and when we got the news about Billy he was in the East End of London working at the docks. In case you don't remember, that was right in the middle of the Blitz. Your father wasn't making money. He was doing his bit to serve his country, and was probably at more risk than a fair number of soldiers. So don't let me hear you talking such nonsense ever again.'

It was clear from both Mark and Susan's expressions that they were shocked by the way Jenny had reacted with such fury. Mark was proud of his wife's defence of her in-laws, while Susan sat wide-eyed, staring at her mother.

Elizabeth begged Jenny's forgiveness.

'It isn't my forgiveness you need; it's the terrible injustice you've done your parents. Yes, I know Rachael overreacted when Billy enlisted and said things she regretted, but that doesn't mean she didn't care. She was concerned for Mark away on active service because she knew how dangerous the work his unit was likely to be given might be. And because, unlike you, she knew exactly what your father was doing and the risks involved. She was terrified of facing the same situation as during the First World War when Sonny was missing all those years. I think the time is long overdue for reconciliation, but that decision is one that only you can make. I guess you've blamed your mother for Billy's death all these years.'

Jenny could see by Elizabeth's expression that she was right and pressed home her point. 'That is totally unfair, Lizzie. Billy would have died whether your mother had said what she did or not. Putting the blame on her is wrong, and you should accept that.'

* * *

Although Mark and Jenny were prepared to try and talk Elizabeth into returning to Byland Crescent once she was released from hospital, they had no idea how to achieve their objective, but fortunately, even as they were puzzling over the right approach, their daughter Susan accomplished the act of persuasion for them. Later, when she mulled over the outcome, Jenny wondered if her sister-in-law had subconsciously identified herself with her young niece, who, although now on the verge of her teenage years, Elizabeth had never met. She had also been taken aback when, on their second visit, Susan had more or less commandeered the conversation and taken control of the discussion regarding Elizabeth's future.

Once the usual pleasantries had been exchanged there followed a brief discussion on the subject of Susan's educational progress, and this gave her the opportunity to introduce the touchy subject her parents had been avoiding.

After a short, slightly awkward silence, Susan took the bull by the horns. 'Mum and Dad are going to talk to you about coming back to live in Byland Crescent, but they haven't mentioned it yet because they're scared you'll refuse. Before you do that, can I ask why I've never met you? I've heard the story about how you fell out with Grandma, but that all happened before I was born. I never got chance to meet my Uncle Billy, and my Auntie Frances got married and went to live in America when I was only a few weeks old. That means I've been left with just Mum and Dad plus my older brother — and believe me, Andy's not all sweetness and light. All I knew about you was an occasional mention, plus a photograph of you that Grandpa keeps in his study. I think it would be terrific if you were to come and live with us — especially if you're a fan of Elvis Presley.'

There was a long pause before Elizabeth replied, and when she did so it was an oblique acceptance of her niece's plea. 'I'm not sure if you'd be that keen once you got to know me better, Susan. I can be very irritable and grumpy at times. Also, I'm sorry to disappoint you but I've always preferred Buddy Holly to Elvis. And although I've been considering whether to return to Scarborough, I'm not sure if I'd be welcome. Apart from anything else there's the practical side to consider. Byland Crescent isn't exactly convenient for someone who is going to be confined to a wheelchair.'

Mark interrupted, keen to provide a practical solution to the mobility issue and to demonstrate their support. 'Don't talk daft, of course you'd be welcome, Lizzie. As for the house, Jenny and I have a couple of ideas that we think would work. Do you remember George, our butler? When he retired Mum and Dad didn't think it necessary to replace him. That means the butler's pantry and his rooms are standing idle. It wouldn't take much work to have them converted into a bathroom, bedroom and a sitting room for if you need privacy, or even a nurse. Once you're on site, we can examine other ways of making life easier for you.'

Not to be outdone by her husband and daughter, Jenny pitched in. 'What do you think, Lizzie? I know it's a rare event, but I think Mark's had a really bright idea, so will you put the past behind you and come home?'

Jenny's final word destroyed the last remnants of Elizabeth's composure. She looked from her sister-in-law to her brother, and finally to her niece, as tears flowed unchecked down her cheeks. After another long silence she managed to speak, and although her voice was muffled by emotion, the answer was as clear as a clarion call. 'Yes, I will come home, if only to get the chance to spend time with my lovely niece — but no nurse!' she said, emphatically. 'I just hope Mum and Dad don't kick me out.'

'They won't do that, Lizzie,' Jenny told her. 'When they were planning to go to Crete, Mum told me they were going to make peace with Billy and she wished above all else she could do the same with you. Unfortunately, we didn't think to bring the letter they sent recently, because if you read it, I think you'll understand them better.'

* * *

As Mark and Jenny were preparing for their next visit to the hospital, Mark realized there was one matter that had not been discussed, the question of Elizabeth's job. Mark wondered how that would be affected and determined to broach the subject when they reached the hospital. He was aware that it could be a cause of concern but there was one aspect of her work that hadn't occurred to him and this caused a degree of difficulty at first.

On learning what he was referring to, Elizabeth's initial reaction surprised him. 'I'm afraid I'm forbidden by the Official Secrets Act from discussing my employment with anyone, even members of my own family.'

Mark thought for a moment before replying. 'That's OK, I'll phone that guy from Special Branch, Jackson I think his name was — and if he won't help, I'll ask to be put in touch with Edrith Pointon.'

Elizabeth stared at her brother, shock at his mention of the name rendering her speechless for several seconds. Eventually she stammered, 'H-how do you . . . ? Where did you get his name from?'

'I'm afraid I can't divulge my sources.' Mark grinned. 'Official Secrets Act, you know.'

'Mark, stop tormenting Lizzie, it isn't fair,' Jenny chided him.

'I will, as long as she promises to be more cooperative.' He acquiesced and added, 'I was given his name by someone who used to work for him.'

Elizabeth relented a little. 'The problem is I don't know how I stand with regard to my job. Somebody's supposed to come and talk to me about it, but they haven't turned up yet.'

'Would you prefer to continue whatever it was you were doing?'

'I would, but I don't see how that's going to be possible if I come back to live in Scarborough.'

'Why don't you see if you can get a transfer to Irton Moor?'

For the second time in five minutes Elizabeth was at a loss for words, and once again it was the extent of Mark's knowledge that left her bereft of the power of speech. 'What do you mean?' she managed, eventually.

'Come off it, Lizzie, it didn't take a genius to work things out. You've been sending Christmas cards for years bearing a Bristol postmark. Bristol is only just down the road from Cheltenham. The set-up there is called GCHQ, isn't it? And they have a station on Irton Moor, just outside Scarborough.'

Elizabeth stared at her brother for several moments, and then signalled her capitulation by turning to Jenny and saying, 'He's quite intelligent at times, isn't he?'

'He has his moments,' Jenny agreed. 'Few and far between, I grant you, but they do happen.'

Elizabeth smiled at Mark. 'Thank you, that's a really good idea. All I have to do now is to convince my employers. If I can't persuade them, I guess I'll have to retire and find something else to do.'

'In that case, I suggest Jenny and I should go back to Scarborough tomorrow or the day after. I know school will be breaking soon for the Christmas holiday but Susan should be there until that time. We can make a start on the house alterations. I also have to report in at work, but I'll come back next weekend if that's OK with you. Hopefully by then you'll have some idea of what your future at work holds, and in the meantime we can keep in touch by phone, if they allow you to use one in here.'

Jenny brought up another problem they hadn't discussed. 'The other thing we must talk about before we go is what to tell Mum and Dad if they contact us.'

'Why do we need to tell them anything?' Mark asked. 'If they got to know what's happened here they would be bound to cut their visit short and come hurrying back, worried stiff, and if they do that, what good would it achieve?'

They looked at Elizabeth, who pondered the question for a few minutes before giving her verdict. 'I'm with Mark on this. Like he said, this could be their one and only chance, and I wouldn't want to be responsible for them missing out on time with Fran. The only reservation I have is how they're going to react when they *do* come home and find you've knocked the house about.'

'I wouldn't worry about that, Lizzie. Look at it this way. Our grandparents bought Byland Crescent, then Dad inherited it after they died, and once he and Mum are gone it'll belong to us anyway. When that happens we'll be able to make all the alterations we want, so why not now? As the changes are for your comfort and convenience I can't see them objecting, can you?'

CHAPTER FOUR

At around the same time as Mark was heading for London, his son Andrew was booking into a small hotel in Ibiza Town, having arrived on the island a few hours earlier. He had decided to travel onto his destination, the village of San Juan Bautista, the following day.

Having deposited his rucksack in his hotel room, Andrew decided it was time to explore. The sun had already set and it was almost dark when he emerged from the hotel entrance. He hadn't eaten since breakfast on the mainland that morning and satisfying his hunger was a priority.

The old town was a maze of narrow streets and alleyways. It was sometimes easier to get lost than to remain on course, as Andrew soon discovered. Although he attempted to follow the directions given by the hotel receptionist he missed his way, not once but twice. On the second occasion, he was trying to find his way back to what passed for a main road when he encountered an incident that caused him to stop — and to act. He could never have imagined the dramatic and far-reaching consequences of what to him was a purely reflex action.

Andrew had turned a corner, passing a butcher's shop, long closed at this late hour, when he heard scuffling sounds and a stifled scream. Peering into the near darkness, he saw two figures in a doorway. One was clearly a woman, despite her features being obscured by a heavy black veil. She was struggling fiercely as she attempted to escape the unwelcome attention of a man.

As he spoke, Andrew was grateful for his linguistic ability. 'Is this man bothering you, senorita?'

The woman bit her attacker's hand, freeing it from her mouth as she pleaded, 'Please, please, help me, senor!'

Her assailant glanced over his shoulder. 'Go away. I am Diego Cortes, son of Gustavo Cortes, and this woman is mine. Disappear, if you know what's good for you.'

As the names meant absolutely nothing to Andrew, the threat was meaningless. His reply was in highly colloquial and extremely coarse Spanish. It owed nothing to his tutors, rather to an irate Madrid taxi driver who had sworn at a motorcyclist. '*Tomar por culo*,' Andrew said loudly.

The action he suggested was physically impossible, the instruction extremely insulting. Cortes retained his hold on the woman with one hand, turned and struck out with the other.

Fortunately there was still sufficient light in the alley for Andrew to see the glint of the knife blade. During his school years he had attended karate classes in Scarborough, and had also benefitted from his father's instruction in unarmed combat. Mark Cowgill, a former commando, told his son, 'I am teaching you this in the hope you will never have to use these skills.'

Andrew moved swiftly to one side and seconds later, after a flurry of movement and some indistinct sounds, Diego Cortes, son of Gustavo Cortes, was lying on the stone floor of the alley. He was barely conscious, temporarily blind in one eye and his right arm was broken.

Ignoring him, Andrew gave a small bow and asked, 'Can I escort you to safety, senorita? Are you hurt?'

'No. But please, I must go home. Would you go with me to where the bus stops?'

'How do we get there? I'm a stranger in town and I've already got lost twice.'

She knew he was a stranger by his accent, which wasn't Ibicencan. 'I will show you.'

He offered his arm and together they emerged from the network of alleyways onto the main street. Anyone passing would have taken them for lovers, judging by the way she was clinging to him.

Fifteen minutes later, as they were waiting for the bus to arrive, she attempted to thank him and also warned him to be wary. 'That animal who attacked me, his father is a very high-ranking official. They could cause big trouble for you if they discover who you are.'

Andrew laughed. 'Don't worry about me. I'm not a local, so his threats are empty ones. What about you, though? He might try something like that again.'

'I will try to avoid coming into town again.'

'I take it you know the animal?'

'Yes, he has been trying to force his attention on me for some while, but recently things have changed and he thought this was his opportunity. If he does try again, it will be the last time, I promise.' There was a pause before she added, 'I will keep a gun by my side always. Now, here is my bus. Thank you again for your help, senor.'

With that, she turned and boarded the bus, which pulled away and was soon lost to view.

The distraction meant that it was very late when Andrew finally got to assuage his hunger. As he dined in one of the many kerbside restaurants, he reflected on the incident and on the woman he'd rescued. She was young, no more than his own age, he guessed. That much was obvious by her voice. He wondered what she looked like without the heavy veil that masked her features. He ceased his speculation, knowing it was highly unlikely that he'd ever meet her again.

Late the following morning, Andrew boarded a bus for his journey to the north of the island. It was lunchtime when he knocked on the door of a small casita that corresponded to the address his mother had given him. There was a short delay as bolts were slid back, the key in the lock turned and only then did the door open as far as the chain would allow. Andrew heard a gasp of surprise or alarm, before a voice from inside demanded angrily, 'What do *you* want?'

The tone of voice, half fearful, half angry, and the way she asked the question puzzled him, but he told the unseen occupant, 'My name is Andrew Cowgill. I'm sorry to disturb you, but I'm looking for Senora Carmen Diaz.'

The door opened wide, revealing the most beautiful young woman he had ever seen. In addition to her stunning looks, Andrew noticed her eyes were reddened, as if she had been crying. He was astonished as the girl grabbed his arm and pulled him inside, slammed the door shut, and embraced him, kissing him on the cheek as she whispered, 'Thank you, Andrew, thank you, thank you, thank you.'

It was nothing like he'd experienced before. The platonic hugs of the female members of his family couldn't compare to this encounter. He could feel every inch of the girl's body pressed tightly against his, the curve of her breasts and the warmth of her body making him almost dizzy.

After a few seconds she released him, much to his disappointment. As she looked at him, she smiled slightly and said, 'You don't recognize me, do you?'

'I don't, because if we had met before, I would definitely remember you.'

The compliment and the sincerity in his voice made her blush slightly. 'I am Consuela Diaz, and you are wrong, we *have* met. We met last night, in Ibiza Town, when you rescued me from that beast.'

'That was you? I couldn't see your face because of the veil.'

Consuela's expression changed to one of deep sadness. 'I wear that outside, in respect for my mother. You cannot have known, because you have been travelling for so long, but my mother died three weeks ago. I was in town completing some official forms yesterday.'

Andrew was shocked. 'I am truly sorry. I heard so much about her from my parents. They told me of her beauty and great courage, and it would have been a privilege to meet her. Your mother invited me to stay, but obviously that isn't possible now.'

'Why is it not possible?'

'I don't think it would be proper, without anyone else here.'

Consuela shook her head. 'That does not bother me. Please will you stay here as arranged? I do not want to be alone, and if you are beside me I will feel safe and protected.'

As she spoke, she removed his rucksack from his shoulders, then turned and replaced the chain and bolts on the door. Andrew wondered briefly if this was to keep intruders out or to keep him in. He hoped it was the latter, and was surprised by the idea.

Later, as they sat in the tiny cottage kitchen nursing cups of strong coffee, Andrew insisted she call him Andy, then asked what she intended to do now her mother had gone. 'I don't know, I have nowhere to go. But I cannot remain here on Ibiza because I am terrified of that beast Cortes and his amigos.' She smiled, and put her hand on his, which did something strange to his blood pressure. 'Or at least I was terrified of him until now, but if you are with me, I know you will protect me.'

For the next week they remained locked inside the casita. During that time, Andrew helped Consuela with tidying her mother's effects. They were nearing the end of that task before the subject was touched on again.

They had paused from their labours when he asked, somewhat reluctant to broach the subject again, 'Have you given any thought to what you will do when you've sorted everything out here? What about this house, for example?'

'I have a second cousin who lives in Santa Eulalia. He is a fisherman, and his wife runs a house where people come to stay. I could give this casita to them so they can rent it to visitors, on the understanding that if it ever becomes safe for me to return it will revert to me.'

'That still leaves the problem of where you should go in the meantime.' As he was speaking, he stared at Consuela, entranced by her beauty. His suggestion was immediate, instinctive. 'Why not come to England with me? You'll be safe there.'

'I would love to do that, but it is not possible. I have no passport, no birth certificate. Without papers I would not be able to leave Spain or to enter England.'

There it was again, back to square one. The problem seemed insoluble.

Later, after Andrew had ventured out to visit the small shop in the village, their only source of supplies, he returned with the shopping and walked into the tiny kitchen, where he saw Consuela standing alongside the sink. She was holding a small brooch, tears rolling unchecked down her face.

'Consuela, please don't cry.' He moved across the room and put his arms round her, holding her in a comforting embrace.

She clung to him and slowly, her tears ceased. She explained why she'd been crying. 'I was packing some of Mama's personal items when I saw this. It was her favourite, given to her by my father, who I never met. Then I realized I am now totally alone.'

Their closeness, the warmth of her body, her head resting against his shoulder, was beginning to make Andrew feel uncomfortable. To avoid Consuela noticing the effect she was having on him, he loosened his grip, stepped away a short distance, using his handkerchief to wipe the tears from her cheeks. 'Don't worry, Consuela, we'll figure a way to get you off the island to somewhere safe. Then you can begin a new life, free from danger, and eventually the sadness will abate.'

Consuela looked at him for a long moment and then smiled. There was something in that smile he found perturbing, but he couldn't place what it was.

Next morning, as they were eating breakfast, Andrew mentioned the idea he had dreamed up in the middle of the night. He said it casually, his tone noncommittal. 'I've thought of a way for you to get to England.'

Consuela looked at him, hope in her eyes as she asked, 'You have?'

He told her, and she stared at him in disbelief.

'Marry you!' This man, an almost complete stranger, had already done so much for her, now he was apparently prepared to go much further. 'Andy, I cannot ask you to do this thing.'

'I don't see why not. I've even worked out how we can manage it.'

'How can I possibly agree to something like that — and even if I did, are you sure it will be possible?' Was she mad, even considering his crazy idea? And if so, was it the madness of desperation that allowed her to entertain such an outlandish scheme — or was it something completely different?

She listened as he explained and agreed, albeit only to part of his plan. 'When you speak to your cousin about the house, ask him to ferry us to the mainland in his fishing boat. There you'll be at least a little safer than on the island. Then we simply catch a train to Madrid, and if you agree, we can activate part two.'

'I will happily go with the first part, but I need to think about the other.' Consuela laid her hand on his, the touch sending shivers of delight up his spine. 'Even if it comes to nothing, Andy, I will always cherish the thought that you would consider doing such a thing for me.'

She smiled, a secretive smile that was clearly for him alone, and had Andy's heart turning somersaults. 'If I get to England I will have to speak English all the time, so perhaps we should speak English now, so I can increase my vocabulary and improve my pronunciation. Your Spanish doesn't need improving. You even know how to swear.' She giggled. 'I don't know where you learned that, but I'm sure telling Cortes to stick his thing up his backside couldn't have been taught at your school.'

Andy laughed. 'No, my tutor was an angry taxi driver in Madrid.' He paused, before returning to the main theme of their conversation. 'The other thing you will need is somewhere to stay in England.'

Consuela looked surprised. 'You haven't been told about that? It was all arranged by your parents and my mother before she passed away. If I can somehow reach England, I've been invited to live with your family in Scarborough. Did I pronounce that correctly?'

'I didn't know anything about that,' Andrew admitted. 'But it's without doubt the best news I've heard for a long time. And yes, your pronunciation was perfect.' He wanted to add, 'like everything about you,' but his nerve failed him. There was one other thing he wanted to tell Consuela, but decided then and there was not the correct opportunity to do so. He had not known her anywhere near long enough to say what was in his mind. Her courage when faced with her attacker, her steadfastness in a time of deep tragedy, and her stunning beauty had caused him to fall head over heels in love with her. Even in his wildest dreams, he couldn't believe that she would be interested in him, not in the way he yearned for her.

Whether he would have plucked up courage enough to declare his interest in her he didn't know, for at that moment Consuela announced, 'I've just realized. Today is *La Día de Navidad*, how do you say it?'

'Christmas Day,' Andrew told her.

'Normally I would go to mass, but I dare not leave the casita in case Cortes is nearby. We should celebrate, however. I will prepare a special meal and you must be in charge of the wine, from *La Rioja*.'

The meal was excellent, the wine superb, and when they retired for the night, Consuela paused by the door to Andy's room. 'Thank you for making this day better than I could have hoped,' she told him, then leaned forward and kissed him gently.

It wasn't until the early hours of Boxing Day that he fell asleep, the memory of that kiss and Consuela's beautiful dark eyes causing his insomnia.

CHAPTER FIVE

Their escape from Ibiza, the voyage to the mainland, and the train journey to the Spanish capital passed without incident, save a severe case of seasickness Andrew suffered during the crossing. This was, as Consuela's cousin told him, a common occurrence, caused by the choppy waters often encountered during the winter months. Andrew's discomfort wasn't eased in the slightest by this information.

Whatever he had expected from the dawn of a new decade, hanging over the side of a fishing boat wasn't something he would have considered. It was only when they had been ashore for a few hours that he began to feel better. During the time of his suffering, Consuela had been alongside him, holding his hand, trying to comfort him. It didn't help at the time, but later, he remembered her anxiety. Her actions and obvious concern for his welfare cheered him slightly.

When they reached the mainland she held grave reservations about his scheme. It called for a commitment like no other. 'Is there no other way than for us to get married?' she asked.

'None whatsoever, but in case you are worried that I will hold you to everything that follows a couple's wedding, please take my word that I will treat it as purely a marriage of convenience. I wish it weren't so, but you have my assurance that I will not overstep the bounds.'

Consuela stared at him for a moment, mulling over his last sentence, and then remembered his obvious arousal when he'd embraced her in the casita. Almost as if it was someone else speaking, she said, 'In that case I accept. What happens next?'

'We go into the British Embassy, and no doubt they will interview us about the application we must make.' He paused. 'That's where the difficult bit comes in. We must speak and act like lovers. I don't mean simply holding hands. I also mean the way we look at one another, the way we speak, every tiny gesture.'

'Is this playacting necessary?'

'It might be, because I'm not prepared to take the chance of them turning you down. These people have to safeguard British interests, so they are trained to watch out for people trying to cheat the system. I believe there are many such attempts made to gain entry to the British Isles. The question is, will you be able to carry off the deception? It will be easy for me. All I have to do is look at you, and everyone will know for certain that I am truly and deeply in love with you.'

Consuela blushed slightly, but fortunately Andrew didn't see her secretive little smile. However, the apparent sincerity in her voice excited him, momentarily, until he reprimanded himself, certain it was no more than wishful thinking.

'I will have no difficulty convincing them that I love you, Andy.'

They entered the British Embassy and Andrew explained how Consuela had been born during the Civil War and had no documentation, causing their dilemma. A junior diplomat was summoned, who proved to be as helpful as possible. His belief that the young couple were truly in love with each other might possibly have been the result of Andrew's instructions to Consuela prior to entering the embassy building.

However, their initial interview gave them little encouragement that the plan would prove successful. The junior diplomat merely noted the details and asked them to return two days later. There was something he needed to check. Once they had left, the man picked up the phone and spoke to his superior. Had Andrew known the gist of their conversation, he would have been extremely worried. It was only when they returned and were told that matters were in hand, and given instructions for a further visit, that the concern eased, if only marginally.

Four weeks later, at the end of January, Andrew and Consuela arrived in England. After a long train journey, conducted for the most part in companionable silence, they arrived in Scarborough late in the evening, and took a taxi for the short drive to Byland Crescent.

* * *

Mark, Jenny, and Suzie were watching television. 'Did you lock the door?' Jenny asked.

'Yes, of course I did. Why do you ask?'

'Because I thought I heard it close.'

'Shush,' Suzie said. 'You're spoiling the programme.'

Having deposited their luggage at the foot of the stairs, Andrew puzzled briefly over the presence of some building materials and tools. He left Consuela seated in the hall, uncertain of her welcome, opened the sitting-room door, and walked in.

'Happy New Year! Hi, Mum, hi, Dad, hello, Noise box,' he greeted his kinfolk.

Mark and Jenny jumped to their feet.

'Andrew! Oh my goodness. Why didn't you let us know you were on your way?' Jenny asked, as she hugged her son.

'There wasn't time. Sit down, please. I'm afraid I have some extremely sad news for you.' He paused, noting their expressions and the tension he had caused. 'I'm sorry to tell you your friend Carmen passed away.'

He allowed the news to sink in. His mother turned to Mark, her distress apparent. Then he explained, 'And because Consuela was having problems and it was unsafe for her to remain in Ibiza, I brought her back with me, as you had agreed with her mother.'

He turned, stepped into the hall, gave Consuela a reassuring smile, grasped her hand, and drew her into the room. 'Allow me to introduce Consuela, or, to give her full name, Senora Consuela Genoveva Diaz-Cowgill.'

There was a long, stunned silence before Mark and Jenny demanded an explanation.

Susan sat wide-eyed. 'Wow!' was all she could say.

The long description of what had occurred in Ibiza ended with both the bride and groom stressing, perhaps a little too forcibly to be convincing, that it had been purely a marriage of convenience. They said this more than once, emphasizing that it was a desperate measure, carried out solely to allow Consuela to escape the danger that threatened had she remained.

Two of their three listeners were taken in by this narrative. However, Jenny noticed that throughout their explanation, Andrew had been holding Consuela's hand. This attention was obviously not unwelcome, judging by the way she was returning his grip, and the way the Spanish girl looked adoringly at her husband.

Later, as Mark was telling Andrew about the reason for the building work being carried out, and the attack on Elizabeth, Jenny seized the opportunity for a quiet talk with Consuela.

Jenny was extremely concerned by the news of the marriage. Knowing that Consuela would have been brought up in the Catholic tradition which forbids divorce, she believed Andrew had forfeited his right to a proper union where love was present. However, when she listened to what Consuela had to say, those fears were allayed.

After Consuela went into greater detail about how Andrew had rescued her, using his skill to overpower her attacker, Jenny smiled. 'You don't think of your child being able to do such things. And you say he didn't know who you were until he arrived at your house?'

'That's right, and as soon as he heard about Mama, he wanted to stay elsewhere, until I persuaded him to stay. It was comforting not to be alone, and to know there was someone to protect me, if the need arose. He helped me sort out my mother's possessions, and then told me the plan for us to escape to England. I couldn't believe it when he suggested we should get married. I'd only known him for such a short time.'

'How did he persuade you to agree?'

'It wasn't difficult, even though it was almost accidental. He told me, "I will treat it as purely a marriage of convenience. I wish it weren't so, but you have my assurance that I will not overstep the bounds". By then I was already in love with him, so I was happy to agree. I hope you're not angry about this.'

Jenny hugged her. 'Don't even think that way.' She held her for a while, as she whispered something that made Consuela stare in amazement.

As Mark and Jenny were locking up downstairs, Andrew escorted Consuela to her bedroom on the first floor. He pointed across the landing. 'That's my room, so if you need anything, just come and ask.'

Five minutes later, Andrew had stripped down to his underpants when the door opened. As Consuela walked swiftly across to him, Andrew stared, entranced by her beauty and her divine figure, only partly concealed by the flimsy negligee she was wearing. 'You told me to come here if I need anything, so here I am.'

He turned away, trying to disguise the effect Consuela's presence was having on him. She put her hand on his shoulder, bringing him back to face her. She moved closer, so their bodies were touching. She gasped with delight at the effect her caress was having and whispered, 'You are all I need, Andreas, *mi querida*. When I agreed to marry you, it had nothing to do with me coming to England. It was purely because I love you and want to spend my life with you, wherever that takes us. I want it to be a complete union, but your mother told me you are too much of a gentleman to force your attention upon me after making that promise. She also said that if I needed to be with you, I would have to show you how much I want you, and I would have to come to you.'

Consuela stepped away and removed her negligee. By that point, her words and the accompanying actions were too much for Andrew to resist, even had he wanted to.

When Mark and Jenny reached the first floor, on their way to their room, Mark paused on the landing, hearing a variety of sounds that seemed to emanate from his son's room. 'What is that noise?' he asked.

Jenny's reply was little louder than a whisper, 'That, Mark, is the sound of a marriage being consummated.'

'I thought they said it was a marriage of convenience?'

'It is, extremely convenient.' Jenny saw Mark's puzzled frown and explained, 'I see they fooled you as easily as they fooled those embassy officials in Madrid. Ignore what they told you about it being a way for Consuela to reach safety. It's obvious they're deeply in love with one another.'

Much later, as Andrew and Consuela were lying together, she murmured, 'I never imagined making love could be as good as that.'

Andrew knew Consuela had been a virgin. 'Neither did I,' he admitted.

Consuela sat up in bed, staring at him in surprise. 'You have never been with a woman before?'

'No, because I hadn't found anyone I wanted. Not until you opened the casita door, then everything changed.'

Consuela realized that her love for Andrew had banished her sorrow. Now, she felt she belonged and had someone who cared about her. She vowed to do everything in her power to make his future a happy one. 'I think we have some catching up to do, don't you?'

His response was silent, but totally positive.

The newly augmented Cowgill family gathered for breakfast the following morning, a process extended by two members who seemed reluctant to leave their room. As the newlyweds entered the breakfast kitchen, Mark greeted them. 'Did you sleep well?' he asked, his face a mask of innocence.

'Mark, behave yourself,' Jenny reprimanded him. 'Don't answer that,' she instructed her son and daughter-in-law. 'It's your father's idea of humour. Unfortunately, he hasn't realized yet he's the only one who thinks his jokes are funny.'

* * *

One of the joys of her new life that Consuela had not anticipated was that of her location with Scarborough's proximity to the sea. Though she had enjoyed the ocean on her trips to Santa Eulalia, she had never lived so close to it before. The difference between the normally calm waters of the Mediterranean and the wilder, more tempestuous North Sea could not have been greater, and this enhanced the pleasure she got from taking long walks along the promenade.

During their walks, Consuela learned more about her husband, and with that deeper knowledge her love for him grew. She also used their time together to discover more about his family background, something she was keen to learn. She questioned him about his ancestors. 'All I really know,' Consuela said, by way of introducing the subject, 'is what my mother told me about your mother and father.'

'Mum and Dad went to Spain to fight, but from what I was told they didn't get much chance, apart from a few skirmishes.' Andy smiled. 'Maybe that's as well, otherwise I might not be here. Soon after they returned to England the Second World War started. Dad was a commando and got wounded right at the end of it. Mum was a bit annoyed though.'

'Why, because your father got wounded?'

He laughed. 'No, she was angry because she wasn't allowed to enlist and fight the enemy alongside Dad like she did in Spain. I grew up thinking of my father as a hero, but now I've learned more about my Uncle Billy, from Grandmother's letter, I know he was even more heroic. I said just now that I wouldn't be here if anything had happened to Mum and Dad in Spain, but neither would Uncle Billy, Aunt Fran or Aunt Lizzie if Grandpa had been killed, as everyone believed for a long time.'

'I don't understand. Why did everyone think your grandfather was dead?'

Andy explained about Sonny's ordeal at the end of World War One, being posted missing, believed killed, and then his return after hostilities ended. 'It was particularly bad for my great-grandfather, Albert. He received a telegram informing him his son had died. That brought on a stroke which killed him. He believed he'd lost his last remaining hope for the future.'

'What does that mean?'

'My great-grandfather, Albert Cowgill, married Hannah Ackroyd, and eventually became owner of the wool merchants in Bradford. They had five children, but one died of consumption when she was nine years old. His older son became involved with one of the housemaids — they eloped and were never heard of again. Another was a lesbian and cast out — she was killed serving as a nurse during the war. Great-grandpa also fell out with his other daughter, something to do with business and her husband, so my grandpa, Sonny, was all he had left of a big family.'

'That's terrible. It makes you wonder how they coped with all the scandal and tragedy.'

Andy chuckled. 'If you want scandal, you haven't heard the worst of it yet. One of Grandpa's cousins got hanged.'

'I don't understand.'

'In Britain, the punishment for murder, or other capital crimes, is death by hanging, using a rope known as the hangman's noose.'

'Ah, I see. In Spain they use the garrotte, which has the same effect, I guess.'

'You mean they finish up equally dead?'

Although Consuela smiled at Andrew's joke she was keen to understand the circumstances. 'What did your relative do wrong?'

'Clarence Barker, he was a really nasty piece of work. He shot a British officer during World War One — somebody saw him do it, and after the war they blackmailed him. So he stole a lot of money from our family business to pay the extortioner, and then later shot him, unaware the blackmailer had left a letter giving all the facts.'

'And I thought my family tragedies were the worst imaginable, but I believe yours are equally poignant.'

'I only learned a little, and that was from what my mum told me. I think she was being a bit protective, to be honest.'

'Did she tell you my mother shot her daughter?'

'What? That doesn't make sense. I've seen every inch of your beautiful body and there isn't a single bullet hole on it.'

Consuela smiled, but with little evidence of humour. 'This happened before I was born. Mother lived on the mainland, and early in the Civil War the town was attacked by Franco's troops. They killed her husband and son, then . . .' she paused, overcome with emotion. 'Then they raped her eight-year-old daughter before one stuck his bayonet in her, ripping her wide open. Then a stranger came in. He shot the soldiers and Mother took his pistol from him and ended her daughter's suffering.'

Andy saw how distressed Consuela was and put his arms around her, trying to console her. Several passers-by smiled knowingly, misinterpreting the reason for the embrace. After a few moments, he pulled away slightly, a puzzled expression on his face. 'If your mother told you her husband had been killed a few years before you were born, then who is your father?'

'I have no idea. He was known to everyone as *La Trompetista*. All Mother told me is he was a great hero, who fought alongside her during the Civil War. She believed he must have died, because she lost contact with him. Apparently, he wasn't aware she was expecting me when he was called away. The only fact I know for certain is that he was English.'

As they were strolling arm in arm along the seafront heading past the tiny harbour towards North Bay, Andy broached the subject of their future together, albeit in a roundabout manner.

At the time he began speaking their plans were non-existent, but his suggestion made it possible to begin planning their path in life. 'As I see it, we have similar skills. Let's start with the basics. How many languages do you speak? I know your Spanish is pretty good,' he added with a grin. Her answer surprised and pleased him.

'As well as Castilian Spanish and English, which you know of, I am also fluent in French, Italian, German, Portuguese and of course Catalan. Why are you asking?'

'I have much the same, except for the last two you mentioned, plus a fair amount of Greek, Latin and Russian. My idea is we could go to college and broaden our range of linguistic skills. That way we could obtain work as teachers or translators. That was one part of my idea. The alternative is to develop our talent for tinkering.'

'What does this mean, "tinkering"? I thought a tinker was a person who mended pots and pans.'

'That was the old definition, but it isn't too far from what I have in mind. I'm thinking about the enjoyment we get from working with electrical and mechanical devices. If we learn more about them we could set up a workshop where we could repair appliances. Nowadays, in addition to radios and vacuum cleaners there are refrigerators, washing machines and television sets. The number of these is increasing rapidly, so we're looking at a growing market, where someone with the ability to repair items of that sort will be in great demand. If we get in on the ground floor I think we could do pretty well out of it.

'When I went to town yesterday, I bumped into a guy I went to school with, and we got chatting. He told me he was taking evening classes at the Institute, and they've just opened new premises on Lady Edith's Drive, very modern,' he explained. 'When he mentioned some of the subjects available I wondered if they do electrical engineering, and if that's so, we could attend them together, instead of studying languages, if you want.'

'Are you planning to enrol?'

'I think so. What do you think?'

'I'd like that a lot. That sounds good in theory, but I think setting up a workshop such as you suggested could prove very expensive. Wouldn't we have to borrow a lot of money to begin a business like that, with no guarantee of success?'

'You're right, but I'm not thinking of going to a bank for the money. My old man and my grandfather are rolling in money, and I'm fairly confident they would lend us what we need. They might even give us it.'

Consuela agreed to think about his ideas. In truth, they both appealed to her. One thing for certain, she knew life with Andy was never going to be boring. Before long, though, other considerations regarding their future came into play.

* * *

A week after Andrew and Consuela's surprise arrival at Byland Crescent, Andrew's twelve-year-old sister sought her mother's advice — or reassurance. Susan Cowgill cared for her brother's welfare, even if she hid it extremely well. She also liked what she'd seen of his bride. However, there was one aspect of the married couple's behaviour that troubled Susan, and it was this she consulted Jenny about.

'Mum, I need to talk to you. It's about Andy and Consuela.'

'What about them?'

'I don't like telling tales, especially about my brother, but I'm sure they're doing something really bad.'

Jenny was alarmed by Susan's allegation and demanded to know what she meant. Susan looked around, as if she expected to see one or other of the guilty couple standing behind her, before revealing what she suspected was going on. 'Mum, I think they're taking LSD.'

Jenny stared at her daughter, taken aback by this outrageous claim. 'What on earth makes you think they're taking drugs, Suzie?'

'It's the way they're behaving — it isn't at all normal. They don't talk to anyone, even each other, and they don't listen. Time and again I've asked them things and got no reply. Sometimes I repeat my question a couple of times, but it's like they've gone deaf. And they're always tired, even in the morning. They yawn ever so often, and on a couple of occasions I've gone into the lounge in the afternoon and found them fast asleep on the sofa. That can't be right, because they go to bed early, even before me, and they don't get up until after everyone else. When they do come downstairs it's almost as if they're sleepwalking half the time.'

Jenny fought against the urge to laugh. She explained, as tactfully as possible, that when people get married, they need time to themselves, and are preoccupied getting to know one another really well, to the exclusion of everyone else. 'Don't fret, Suzie, it will pass. They'll be back to normal before too long, you'll see.'

She had tried to phrase her reply in a way that protected what she believed was Susan's innocence, so she was shocked by her daughter's response. 'Is that what it's all about? You're telling me all that weird behaviour is nothing more than the result of non-stop rumpy-pumpy?'

Jenny looked horrified. 'Where did you get that expression from, young lady?'

'School.'

'That is not a term I want to hear, OK?'

'Yes, Mum.'

'But . . . er . . . yes, you could put it like that, but I'd rather you used a more polite, less vulgar way of expressing yourself.'

Jenny had one other concern regarding the married couple, and shared this with her husband, only to discover that Mark had already thought about it — and acted on it. 'Do you think we ought to tell Andy and Consuela that they are related?'

'I was wondering about that, so I went to the library and looked into it. We know Consuela's father is Josh Jones, a distant cousin of mine. According to the graph I read, Andy and Consuela are second cousins. I don't believe that's breaking any consanguinity laws, especially when you think that Queen Elizabeth and Prince Philip are third cousins.

'Apart from that, there's one overriding factor which as far as I'm concerned rules out telling them anything about the relationship. If we were to reveal it, we would also have to explain how we know the identity of Consuela's father, and I don't believe that would be wise, do you?'

As usual, Mark was right, Jenny reflected. Not that she would have dreamed of telling him so.

CHAPTER SIX

By the end of February, Elizabeth's doctors had given her the all-clear. Her wounds had healed and she was deemed fit enough to leave hospital. Arrangements had been made for her to continue physiotherapy sessions in Scarborough, to begin rebuilding her wasted muscles.

In other areas of Elizabeth's life, her long-term future had also been discussed, although this news was not to be divulged beyond the bounds of her family. She telephoned Byland Crescent to inform them of her impending release.

The alterations needed to provide suitable accommodation were almost finished. Mark had arrived home one evening to find Jenny with dustpan in hand, muttering to herself about the quantity of dust.

'You've only yourself to blame,' he'd told her. 'If you'd allowed Father to reinstate some of the household staff after the war, you wouldn't need to do this.'

Jenny rounded on him. 'Are you telling me that my mother and I didn't make a good job of it before she died? And now, neither is your mother?'

He'd taken her in his arms. 'Of course not. Mother isn't getting any younger, and this house is far too big for you alone to manage. I'm going to speak to Father when they return.'

A few days earlier, Mark and Jenny had received a letter from Sonny and Rachael. This was postmarked from Texas, although it had been somewhat delayed in transit, as Jenny discovered when she read the date on the letter. It seemed that Sonny and Rachael would be arriving home during the second week of April.

'The news means we've time to get Lizzie back here and settled in before they return, so I think the sooner we get her installed the better.'

'I agree,' Jenny replied, 'but I have one big concern and that's the mode of transport. I don't think it would do her much good travelling all that way by train, knowing how some of those carriages bounce around. In fact it might set her recovery back, which is the last thing we want.'

'That's a good point, Jenny. Has anyone got an alternative, though?'

'What about Grandpa's old banger?' Andrew suggested.

Although Mark grinned at his son's description of Sonny's car, he thought the idea was a good one. 'You're right, Andy. If we take the Bentley and bring her back in that, she'll be far more comfortable. Not only has the Bentley got luxury seating, but if she was getting tired or in pain we could pull over and let her rest for a while, even break the journey with an overnight stop if necessary.'

One problem none of them had foreseen until almost the very last minute was that of access to the property for a wheelchair.

'How is Lizzie going to be able to get in and out of the house? She certainly won't be able to manage the steps, and I don't think she'll take very kindly to someone picking her up and manhandling her.'

Of all those involved in the meeting it was Consuela, surprisingly, who was quick to come up with a solution. 'Would it be possible to build a ramp for the rear entrance?'

'Andy, your wife is a treasure,' Mark said. 'I'll get onto the builders first thing tomorrow morning and ask them to pop back and install one.'

* * *

A week later, Mark and Jenny set off for London. After an overnight stay in an hotel close to the hospital, they went to collect their passenger for the journey home. Jenny was given the task of bringing Lizzie from the building to the adjacent car park.

As Lizzie looked at the luxurious limousine, she asked her brother, 'Where did you nick this from?'

Mark grinned. 'I *borrowed* it from the old man. Dad loves his Bentley, and as it hasn't been used much since they went on their travels, I thought it was time it had an outing.'

'Oh yes, I'd forgotten how much Dad loved the Bentley. He was quite peeved when petrol rationing came in because he had to put it in mothballs owing to the amount it used.'

Once Lizzie was safely ensconced in the back seat, her comfort ensured by the provision of a pair of cushions and a travelling rug, Mark loaded the wheelchair into the spacious boot and they set off to travel north.

During the journey, Lizzie explained, 'The hospital is sending my file to Scarborough. I've to report to the hospital for regular check-ups and physiotherapy sessions,' — Lizzie grimaced — 'and won't that be fun.'

Jenny sympathized, then quizzed her sister-in-law about her flat and her possessions. The only luggage Lizzie had was the overnight bag she had taken to her hotel on arrival in London.

'Have you given any thought as to how you'll get the rest of your clothing and other things to Scarborough from, er, Bristol?' Mark asked.

Lizzie grinned. 'Good try, Mark — Cheltenham actually. No, to be honest, I haven't as yet. In the beginning, my priority was trying to stay alive, and more recently, an urgent desire never to taste hospital food ever again.' She smiled as she added, 'I know that sounds a bit ungrateful after everything they did for me, but you have to try the food before you can appreciate how bad it is.'

She thought for a few moments. 'I suppose I'll have to make arrangements for someone to go and collect all the stuff from my flat, and my Beetle.'

'You drive a Volkswagen?' Mark laughed.

Lizzie rolled her eyes and sighed. 'I also have to give notice to my landlord. There are lots of things I haven't considered until now. I need to arrange for my bank account to be transferred to a Scarborough branch. Until I can organize that I won't be able to access my money, so I'll be the proverbial poor relation.'

Mark glanced in the rear-view mirror. 'Don't worry about brass, Lizzie. I can always lend you a few bob to tide you over.'

Jenny looked scornfully at her husband, before telling Lizzie, 'What he means is, we'll provide whatever money you need. A few bob indeed!'

They were nearing the outskirts of Malton, on the last leg of the journey, when Mark came up with a potential solution to Lizzie's problems. 'Why don't we ask the newlyweds to go to Cheltenham?' he said, out of the blue.

Jenny and Lizzie were only half awake, their senses lulled by the comfort and warmth of the Bentley. 'What are you babbling on about, Mark?' Jenny turned to Lizzie and told her, 'Sometimes your brother talks in riddles.'

'I can't help it if my audience is too dim to take in the meaning of a simple sentence first time round,' Mark responded. 'I was puzzling over Lizzie's problems and I thought it would be a good idea to ask the newlyweds to help. They could go on the train, stay at Lizzie's place, pack her belongings, and bring them back in her car. At the same time they could give notice to her landlord, visit her bank, and deliver a letter from Lizzie instructing them to transfer her account.'

'That's not a bad idea — for you,' Jenny retorted. 'What do you think, Lizzie? At least that way you wouldn't have a complete stranger messing about with your stuff. I know I'd far prefer it if I knew it was a woman, and a member of my family to boot, who was handling things like my underwear.'

'I think that would be nice. I've been looking forward to meeting Consuela.'

Mark was astonished by this statement. 'Hold on a minute, how did you know about Consuela? I don't think we've mentioned her.'

'When I was in hospital, one of my colleagues came to visit. They'd received word from our embassy in Madrid about someone called Andrew Cowgill who gave his address as Byland Crescent in Scarborough. The man was seeking help to marry a girl with no papers, and permission to bring his Spanish bride to England. He gave me the name of the prospective bride, and that tallied with your story about your adventures during the Spanish Civil War, plus Andrew visiting Ibiza. So I ordered him to ensure they got all the help they needed.'

'You ordered him?' Mark asked, taken aback.

Lizzie just smiled.

Jenny returned to Mark's original suggestion, and when Lizzie agreed, Jenny, seeing the complacent smile on her husband's face, asked him, 'Are you sure you're feeling OK, Mark? That's two good ideas you've had so far this year, and we're only in the middle of March.'

* * *

As she settled into her new surroundings, Lizzie got to know and like those of her relatives she had never met before. She vaguely remembered Andy, but only as a small boy, not the handsome and confident young man he had become. She also furthered her new acquaintance with her niece Susan, their friendship enhanced by a mutual love of pop music. It was her nephew's wife, however, whom Lizzie took to her heart almost from the moment of their first meeting.

Admittedly, given the assistance she had provided for the newlyweds, Lizzie had a vested interest in them. Despite that, she was surprised how quickly she and Consuela bonded, a rapport that enabled her to feel comfortable with Mark's plan for the couple to go to Cheltenham, acting as her agents.

Another part of Lizzie's reassessment of her new situation came via her adjustment to life in a wheelchair. This was softened by the way she had been taken back into the bosom of her family, whose every effort ensured she was cared for to the best of their ability. She hoped this would continue, but had serious misgivings if it would do so when her parents returned from America.

She expressed her reservations one evening over dinner, only to receive a mild reprimand from her brother. 'I know you're supposed to be a brain-box, Lizzie, with all your deciphering and linguistic skills, but sometimes you do talk a load of hogwash.'

Elizabeth blinked in surprise. She hadn't told anyone of her ability to speak and read a variety of languages — it was part of her secret life she was bound not to reveal. 'Now why do you suppose I can speak other languages, Mark?'

His smile broadened. 'It didn't take much to work it out, Lizzie, it isn't exactly rocket science. The fact that you've ostensibly been employed by GCHQ, presumably as a senior officer, not as a cleaner, is a big clue. I assume deciphering encoded messages from the other side of the Iron Curtain would require linguistic skills. I don't think for one minute that the Kremlin is generous enough to send them out in English — neither were the Germans during the war.'

Lizzie accepted that, along with her tacit acknowledgement of his deductive ability. 'Why did you say I talk hogwash?'

'Because Mum and Dad have never stopped loving you — regardless of your long-term sulk. Through all the years you were away they missed you and worried about your wellbeing, despite the annual card they received from you. They will be overjoyed when they come back and find you here.'

Remembering the curt messages on the cards she had sent, Lizzie felt guilty at what Mark referred to as her 'long-term sulk'.

* * *

As soon as Andy and Consuela had completed the task of rescuing her belongings, and settling matters in Cheltenham, Lizzie's next priority was to contact Scarborough Hospital for her continued treatment. She had one concern — that being transport to and from her weekly physiotherapy sessions. She mentioned her dilemma to Mark and Jenny.

'For the time being, I think we'll have to rely on taxis,' Mark told her. 'The only driver here will be Andrew. I'll be at work in Bradford during the week, and the Bentley isn't insured for Andy to drive . . . not that his grandfather would allow it.'

'Taxis will be very expensive over a long period of time,' Lizzie pointed out.

'Maybe so, but only as a temporary measure. That will give us time to find a suitable car for Andy, one that will give you the comfort you'll need after a gruelling session with a physiotherapist.' Mark grinned. 'I should know. I had to undergo the ordeal after being wounded. One of the guys renamed the medic as a physio-terrorist.'

Lizzie was shocked by her brother's idea. 'You can't go to all that expense,' she protested.

'Why not? The money isn't important. All that matters is ensuring you make a full recovery,' Jenny told her. 'I think Mark's excelled himself this time. It's the best way to deal with the problem. The only doubt you might have is Andy's driving skills, because although he passed his test, the only vehicle he's driven regularly was a tank while he was doing his National Service. And Mark's right, the only time his grandfather will allow Andy near his Bentley is when he wants it cleaning.'

This further evidence of their caring nature touched Lizzie deeply. Her only remaining reservation, despite Mark's censure, was regarding her parents' reaction to her return.

The doubts she harboured resurfaced when a telegram from Sonny and Rachael arrived, announcing their planned return in two weeks' time.

* * *

Lizzie visited Scarborough Hospital for her first meeting with the specialist. Having taken X-rays, he examined the images, informing Lizzie that the injuries looked to be improving, and told her, 'We have a long way to go, so from now on, I will place you in the care of my assistant, who will also liaise with the physiotherapist in charge of your exercise programme. I will be available should anything untoward happen, and I am happy to say my deputy is an extremely able physician.'

He buzzed through to his secretary. 'Please ask Dr Richardson to join us, will you?'

A few seconds later the door opened and Lizzie saw her new mentor for the first time. He appeared to be about her own age, and was rather good-looking, she thought. The specialist performed the introductions, and Dr Richardson shook her hand. Lizzie barely heard his reassurance that he would take great care of her, because she was staring into his deep blue eyes. Later, during the taxi ride home, Lizzie decided she would enjoy being cared for by Dr Richardson. Those blue eyes were really something.

Nor did her opinion waver after her first physiotherapy session. She had just arrived in the treatment room when the door opened and Dr Richardson entered. The exercise programme had been designed specifically to cater for her needs, and the physiotherapist explained, 'Dr Richardson is here to oversee the procedure and ensure everything runs smoothly.'

When the session ended, Richardson pushed her chair as Lizzie went towards the exit. 'Why don't we go for a cup of tea while you're waiting for the taxi?' he suggested. 'It will be a good opportunity to discuss the future treatment.'

Curiously, that subject didn't arise as they drank tea and chatted. Dr Richardson, who suggested she call him Gil, short for Gilbert, was more interested in the way she'd come by the injury, and seemed to want to know more about her.

'If you want me to call you Gil, you should call me Lizzie.' She smiled. 'I was in London for a business meeting and I took a wrong turning in the fog. I was attacked and robbed.'

'What sort of business are you in?'

'I'm sorry, I can't tell you,' Lizzie responded.

'Why not?'

'I'm not allowed to talk about my work to anyone, even you. It's a shame, because the Official Secrets Act is a bit of a barrier to getting to know people better.'

'I quite understand, Lizzie.' Gil put his hand on hers, patting it sympathetically as he spoke. 'I have the same problem.'

Lizzie was baffled. Seeing her puzzled frown, he explained, 'Imagine going to a swish cocktail party and having someone asking how you'd spent your day. Telling them you'd been conducting a rectal examination of a man with haemorrhoids isn't likely to be a great conversational gambit. Apart from that, I'm bound by patient confidentiality.'

Lizzie giggled slightly at his joke, but was happy the secrecy element had been bypassed. As they continued to talk, she realized he was still holding her hand. Although she guessed this was not part of a normal doctor–patient relationship, she did not object. Neither did she object when he assisted her to her taxi.

As she returned home, Lizzie wondered where, if at all, their relationship would end. She was surprised when she reached Byland Crescent to learn that her travelling for the day hadn't quite ended. As she slid out of the taxi into her wheelchair, she wondered who the other car outside the house belonged to. Seconds later, Lizzie's brother and nephew emerged, accompanied by a stranger.

Mark performed the introductions. The car salesman had brought along a vehicle for her to ride in while Andy took it for a test drive. Lizzie looked at it for several seconds, before telling her brother, 'This is almost as big as the Bentley. Will Andy be comfortable driving it?'

'That's not a problem, Auntie Liz. I actually took my driving lessons in an identical car to this.'

Twenty-five minutes later, the deal completed, the salesman handed over the keys and log book. Andy was now the owner of an Austin Westminster saloon car.

CHAPTER SEVEN

As Sonny and Rachael travelled home on the train from London to Scarborough, they reflected on their recent epic adventure. 'I'm glad we went, for so many reasons,' Rachael said.

'I agree. I will always remember the Cretan people we met. The hospitality they extended to us, taking us into their homes as if we were family, and the way they continue to celebrate our son is like a warm glow in my heart.'

Rachael could not resist the impulse to tease him. 'That's probably indigestion from the copious amounts of raki you consumed every evening after dinner.' She turned the topic to another facet of their travels. 'It was wonderful to see Fran and Hank, to know how happy they are, and to meet the grandchildren. All in all, it's been a wonderful journey, but now I'm glad we'll soon be home.'

'I don't suppose much will have changed while we've been away,' Sonny remarked.

'I'm not so sure about that,' Rachael responded, surprising Sonny.

'Have you any particular reason for saying that?'

'A couple of reasons, actually. Jenny promised to drop us a line, care of Fran, to update us on events at home and in the UK. That letter never arrived, so I'm beginning to wonder if it was ever sent. It could be that Jenny has forgotten, but that's most unlike her.'

'Well, it's possible the letter got lost in transit.'

'I suppose so. Anyway, I assume Andy will be back home by now. I'm sure he'll have some stories to tell of his travels.'

'It was probably nothing more than a lot of sightseeing. Talking about what happened when he went to Italy, France and Spain must be the verbal equivalent of someone showing you a load of boring holiday photos.'

When the travellers emerged onto the platform at Scarborough, their son was waiting, alongside a porter with a trolley, ready to take their luggage. Having greeted his parents, Mark fended off their questions, simply telling them everything at home was fine, and everyone was well. He was glad the distance from the station to Byland Crescent was short, otherwise he felt certain they would have tried to worm the secrets out of him. He didn't want to spoil the surprise, so he played dumb, mentioning nothing more than business matters, in which Sonny, as group chairman, was naturally interested.

Mark brought the Bentley to a halt, telling his parents, 'You go ahead. I'll park the jalopy round the back and offload your luggage mountain.'

As they climbed the steps, the door swung open, held by their grandson, who announced, somewhat in the manner of a butler, 'Welcome home, Grandpa and Grandma Cowgill, please enter your residence.'

Sonny and Rachael hugged Andy, before they did as instructed, but they had only taken a couple of steps into the hallway when they stopped dead in their tracks, frozen into speechless immobility. Four females were positioned in the hall, the first, their daughter-in-law Jenny, with their granddaughter Susan alongside. It took a few seconds for them to identify the young woman seated in a wheelchair.

Rachael was first to react. 'Elizabeth?' She turned to Sonny, who was staring at his daughter and looked just as bewildered.

The words came tumbling from Rachael's mouth as she darted forward and hugged her daughter. 'Elizabeth,

Elizabeth my darling, is it really you? Oh, what has happened? Why are you in that wheelchair?'

'I'm OK, honest. I'm getting better every day. I was injured in London, but I'm improving all the time.'

Lizzie returned her mother's embrace, holding onto her with one hand, her other arm around her father, as tears rolled down their faces.

Jenny suggested they move to the sitting room where they could talk, while she and Consuela headed to the kitchen to make tea, grabbing Susan by the arm, insisting she helped.

'But, Mum, it only takes one person to make tea,' she protested. 'I want to hear.'

'You already know the story. Grandpa and Grandma need time to understand exactly what has been happening.' She turned to Andy. 'Would you take Lizzie through, and then you and your father can take the luggage upstairs,' she said pointedly.

In the privacy of the sitting room, Lizzie explained what had happened, and how Mark and Jenny had insisted she return to Byland Crescent. 'I hope you don't mind.'

'Mind? Don't be silly, of course we don't mind. We've missed you so much. You know this is your home as much as it is ours. Does this mean you are here to stay? I mean are you going to live here full-time?' She gazed at her daughter affectionately. 'I do hope so.'

'Yes, Mum. If you'll have me?'

'No problem, Lizzie darling. But how do you manage the steps?'

Jenny had entered the room, pushing the tea trolley, once the sole province of the butler.

'That's OK, we've made a few alterations to the house to accommodate Lizzie's needs,' she told them.

'And what about her nurse?' Sonny asked, looking at the strikingly beautiful young woman standing behind Jenny.

Mark and Andy had just entered, and both Sonny and Rachael were astonished when everyone started to laugh.

Andrew took Consuela's hand. 'Sorry, Grandpa, I should have introduced you earlier, but everyone was too busy weeping buckets. Allow me to introduce Consuela Diaz, more commonly known round here as Consuela Cowgill — my wife.'

Rachael embraced, and Sonny shook hands with, Consuela. Before Sonny rounded on his daughter-in-law. 'I hope you haven't got any other surprises in store for us. I'm not sure my heart will stand up to much more.' He smiled. 'And to think that on the way back from London I suggested everything here would be just as we'd left it. How wrong I was — and how delighted I am to have been proved wrong.'

'I promise that's everything, Dad — or at least everything I can think of,' Jenny reassured him.

The joy of the reunion became more serious later, when the assembled family members listened to Sonny and Rachael's account of their stay on Crete. They did this seated on either side of Lizzie's wheelchair, their hands clutching hers as they told of Billy's heroic action, and the reverence in which he was held by the Cretan people.

'I will always regret that Billy and I parted in anger,' Rachael told her, 'but I acknowledge that even if I had given him my blessing to enlist, his life would still have ended that fateful day. However, I rejoice, as I think we all must, that by his brave sacrifice, Billy saved so many lives.'

Later still, Rachael and Sonny listened with growing fascination as Andy described what had happened in Ibiza. As with Andy's parents, Sonny and Rachael assumed the marriage was merely one of convenience, but Andy corrected this misapprehension. 'I suggested the marriage for that reason,' he told them, 'but I was already in love with Consuela. Then I found out she loved me too. We weren't sure we'd get away with it at the British Embassy in Madrid, but luckily Aunt Lizzie intervened on our behalf.'

His grandparents both looked confused, but decided it was wiser not to ask.

* * *

Over the coming months, life began to settle into a routine at Byland Crescent. Mark travelled daily on the train to the office, Sonny, as chairman, would accompany him once a month for meetings. Lizzie continued with her physiotherapy sessions, ferried around by Andy. Consuela would help Jenny and Rachael with the housework or take Lizzie out in her chair round the shops, or along the seafront for fresh air. In the evenings Andy and Consuela attended the technical college, training in basic electronics, to add to their existing skills. It was from this that one weekend Andy asked for a private meeting with his father and grandfather.

After dinner the three men assembled in Sonny's study, where Andy put forward his business idea. 'When Consuela and I finish the course at the tech, we are both confident that we will have the necessary skills to start our own business.'

He noted the expressions on the others' faces and tried to explain. 'We are both competent and, we believe, capable of operating a small repair shop here in town. Our tutor told me we are two of the brightest students he's had. During her walks out with Lizzie, Consuela spotted a small shop premises which is to let, and we thought it might be suitable, so we, er, went for a look.' He tried to sound positive. 'It's situated just off the main street, consists of two rooms, originally a sales area and stockroom at the rear, ideal as a workroom. There's also an upstairs room which would do for storage. Initially, I would do the repairs, with Consuela's help when required. She will run the shop, where we can sell small electrical items, and she can run adverts and things, while we get established. I, that is, we, wondered if you two might be prepared to back us — financially, I mean.'

Andy wasn't sure if he was digging himself into a hole or not.

His grandfather looked him up and down. 'And that is your business proposal?' he asked.

'Er, yes,' he said, trying to sound more confident than he felt.

'Do you have any set-up figures for us?'

'Here you are.' He passed them a sheet of paper on which was listed the rent and running costs, the required tools and equipment, and anything else the young couple could think of, including a nominal figure for stock.

'And you think this is sufficient to set up a repair shop?' his father asked.

Andy nodded.

'Then, tell me,' Sonny asked, 'as investors, what will our return be?'

Andy looked like a rabbit caught in the headlights. He hadn't thought of this. 'I, um, I, er, think we might be able to pay you back, eventually,' he stammered.

'I can't bear this any longer,' Mark said.

Andy stared at both men as they started to laugh, and watched with relief as his grandfather took his chequebook from the desk drawer.

* * *

When Sonny and Mark returned to the sitting room, they were surprised to find Rachael, not for the first time, asleep in her chair. Jenny put her fingers to her lips to signal for silence, and Lizzie waved her hands, shooing them, instructing them to leave. She wheeled herself forward into the hall and asked them to close the door.

Sonny was concerned. 'Is your mother ill?'

Lizzie looked at her father. 'No, Dad, she's not ill, she's exhausted. Running around all day with Jenny, looking after us lot, cleaning and cooking — and I'm no help,' she said in frustration, slapping her hands on the arms of her chair. 'Consuela helps when she can, but this house is too big for them to manage. Jenny has coped since her mother died, and Mother isn't young anymore. We had servants before the war, so what's wrong with now?' Having voiced her opinion, Lizzie shut up.

'And what would you suggest I do?' Sonny asked.

Mark answered him. 'Lizzie's right, Dad, and I've been meaning to speak to you since you got home from Texas. While you, Mum and Andy were away, there were only three of us here and Jenny could cope, but I promised her I would talk to you about getting some household help when everyone returned. And now there are eight of us.'

'I see. Well, we'd better have a conference tomorrow and see what we can do. I'm off to wake your mother, and take her up to bed.'

* * *

The next morning, Sonny requested all the family gather in the sitting room. 'I want to talk to you all. It has been brought to my attention that things are not as they should be within this house, and for that reason, I am not happy.'

Only Mark and Lizzie had a clue as to what their father was referring.

Sonny turned to his daughter-in-law. 'Jenny, you joined this household with your mother, who was employed as cook.' Jenny nodded. 'Now I am delighted that you are a member of the family, but that does not mean that you should have taken your mother's place in the kitchen.'

He turned to his wife. 'Rachael, my dear, what do you do in the house?'

'I do what I can to help Jenny, with the cooking and cleaning, making beds, sorting the laundry, etcetera.'

Sonny nodded. 'In the past, to cater for this establishment, we had a butler, a cook and a number of housemaids to service the house and the family's needs, a family no greater than it is now. I appreciate the changes brought about by modern-day inventions, but I still think it is unfair to ask Jenny and Rachael to do all the work, albeit with a little help from Consuela, plus odd bits from the male side of the family. And why don't we, a family of our standing in this town, have staff now?'

'I'm sorry, darling, but you didn't want any after the war. You said we were managing very well without,' Rachael reminded him.

'Ah, yes, well, perhaps I did. But we are not managing now. There are eight of us, and perhaps in the future there may be more.' He smiled at Consuela as he spoke.

Mark interrupted, 'I agree with Father, and I appreciate that everyone concerned is fit and well at present, but what if that changes? What if one of us is ill? Or more of us want to take an extended holiday? I'd like to take Jenny abroad to visit other parts of the world. Apart from our one trip to Spain — and that wasn't exactly a vacation, we've never been out of this country.'

Sonny nodded his agreement. 'And I think we should avoid employing young, highly attractive girls. That happened once before, and it ended up with her eloping with my brother.' He waited until their laughter subsided, and ended by saying, 'So I want to know what you need in terms of staff, and I want them employed — soon. I will increase the household budget accordingly.'

'Now that's a turn-up,' Mark said. 'A Yorkshireman spending more money, willingly.' He smiled. 'As long as you're not expecting us to start dressing for dinner again,' he added, to more laughter.

CHAPTER EIGHT

It was decided to advertise at the Labour Exchange for a cook and a housekeeper, neither of which were to be live-in positions. They would also employ a charlady to help with the heavier work.

After several interviews conducted by Rachael and Jenny, candidates with the right credentials either required accommodation or could command much higher salaries at the hotels in town. Others were discounted because of their perceived unsuitability.

On a Saturday morning, Jenny greeted two women sent by the Labour Exchange. The older of them introduced herself and her sister. 'My name is Sarah Clough, and this is my sister, Mary. I'm sorry this had to be on a Saturday, but we are both from out of town. We work in London.'

Jenny invited them in and introduced herself and Rachael. 'Perhaps the best way would be to explain exactly what we need and then you can tell us if you're interested.'

Having given the women a brief summary of the house, its permanent residents plus regular visitors, Jenny glanced at Rachael, who took the lead.

'I should tell you we have also advertised for extra help, four hours daily, five mornings a week, and we also utilise a laundry service. Is there anything else you need to know before we continue?'

Sarah glanced at her sister before replying. 'Much of what you described is more Mary's concern than mine. As a chef, my only brief is to know people's likes and dislikes, or any dietary restrictions necessary.'

Rachael and Jenny looked at Mary, who spoke for the first time. 'I am currently head of housekeeping in charge of a large hotel, so nothing you've told me presents the slightest problem. If I were to be employed here, I would appreciate the extra help in a house this size. That would enable me to help my sister, if necessary, in the kitchen, and with the assistance of another person I could ensure the standard throughout the house would be maintained.'

'In that case, why not tell us more about yourselves?'

Once again it was Sarah who spoke. 'We were both born in Scarborough, and named in honour of Winston Churchill's daughters. Luckily, we were both girls, otherwise we'd probably have been saddled with the name Randolph.'

Jenny and Rachael smiled at what was clearly a family joke, but listened intently as Sarah continued. 'I trained at the local cookery school, and then worked as sous chef in several hotels in Yorkshire, before I got my current position.' She named the London hotel where she was employed.

After a moment's stunned silence, Rachael asked, 'Why do you want to leave such a prestigious job?'

'The main reason is our mother, who is over seventy years old. After our father passed away three years ago, mother's health has been steadily deteriorating. Physically, she's well for her age, but her mental state is a huge concern. We need to be near her, so we can be on hand if anything untoward happens. We also believe it will be good for her state of mind when she's no longer alone in the house with only her memories.'

Sarah glanced at her sister, a clear invitation for Mary to add her story. 'My career followed similar lines to Sarah's. I worked in hotels in Edinburgh, Newcastle, Birmingham and London. Whenever I return home, I realize how much I miss Scarborough, so when Sarah suggested we come back here full-time, I was happy to go along with it.'

'I don't see us being able to match the sort of salaries you are getting in London,' Rachael told them, bluntly.

This time it was Mary who responded. 'The money isn't an overriding factor. We'd be doing what we both enjoy, in a town we love, and we'd also be able to care for Mum.'

'How far would you have to travel on a daily basis?' Jenny asked.

Sarah chuckled, and pointed to the window. 'If you look carefully, you'll just be able to see the roof of Mum's house. We'd only be a couple of streets away.'

Later, Rachael and Jenny reported to the family, who had been given strict instructions to stay well clear of the sitting room during the interview. Their endorsement of the Clough sisters was enthusiastic, with only one proviso, which Rachael outlined. 'We've made it clear we'll need satisfactory references from their current employers, but given they've both been employed there for five years or more, that shouldn't be a problem. Subject to those, we've agreed for them to start in five weeks' time, when they've worked their notice and have returned to Scarborough. When they are here, I suggested that Mary helps with the interviews for her assistant.'

Sonny asked, 'I suppose that means you've had to agree to pay them both a fancy salary?'

'It isn't that bad, and Mary said she would need a charlady for fewer hours, so we saved some money there,' Jenny protested, before Rachael told him, 'Don't be such a miserable old skinflint.'

* * *

Before the Clough sisters took up their positions, a spell of hot, dry weather had enabled Consuela to respond to an appeal made to her by her father-in-law. Having spent time in Spain during the Spanish Civil War, Mark and Jenny had developed a liking for the local food — one dish in particular. During the course of an evening meal, Mark turned to Consuela and asked her if she knew the recipe for paella, such as her mother had once cooked for him and Jenny.

'Yes, of course, why do you ask?'

'I thought it might be fun to cook it outdoors sometime this summer. As I remember, the main ingredients are fish, chicken and vegetables, and we're not short of any of those.'

'That's a good idea, Mark,' Rachael agreed. 'I've heard about paella, but never tasted it.'

'As I recall, it's quite complicated,' Jenny added. 'So we'll all pitch in and lend a hand.'

It was the end of July before they were able to have the meal, which became a celebration, following the end of Susan's summer term. Her school reports had arrived, and Susan, it seemed, had excelled in almost every subject her parents considered important. Mark, however, could not resist the temptation to tease his daughter. 'You'd better brush up on your mathematics,' he told her, 'especially if you're determined to become a lawyer, so that you'll be able to add up enormous sums, because all legal bills are huge.'

* * *

Securing the services of the Clough sisters had been one thing, ensuring their work lived up to the required standard was another. However, within weeks of them starting at Byland Crescent, Jenny and Rachael were pleased to confirm both Sarah's culinary skills and Mary's scrupulous attention to the cleanliness of the house more than met expectations.

'I agree,' Mark commented, 'the food is excellent, and I've been surprised by how quickly my shirts get washed and ironed. Mary has got the laundry service tamed. I wore a blue one last Monday and then put it in the laundry basket. When I opened my wardrobe on Friday, the shirt was hanging on the rail.'

'Yes,' Jenny commented, 'she asked me if I could arrange a set pick-up day on Tuesdays, so she has a schedule to work to for changing beds etcetera. She also recommended an alternative company to the one we've been using, saying they would provide a better service.'

'More expense,' Sonny groaned.

'Actually, they are more reasonably priced now we have a regular agreement with them, in effect, a contract.'

'And,' Rachael continued, 'Sarah's asked if she can extend the range of the menus, and wanted to know if there was anything she should avoid. I told her not to put porridge in front of Mark because he'd probably throw it at her.'

Mark grimaced. 'The so-called chef at our training camp served the squaddies porridge day in, day out for the three months we were there. Either I always got the burned offerings from the bottom of the pan or he used a flame-thrower to prepare it. I was almost relieved when I got called to active service.'

Sonny smiled at his wife. 'I know you and Jenny have coped admirably over the years, but now you can both take time for yourselves. And, looking forward, as much as I have enjoyed Christmas in the past, this year I will be able to spend it with you, as you and Jenny won't be permanently in the kitchen.'

'I know it's a little early to ask, but speaking of Christmas, would anyone object if I invite Gil Richardson, my doctor?' Lizzie asked. 'He lives alone and has no family.'

'Of course not,' her mother replied. 'He seems a very amiable young man.'

With that the other women in the room all gave each other a knowing look.

* * *

Consuela was looking out of the window at the autumn sunshine and was reminded of the day she cooked the paella, and what had followed. It had been only natural for her to try to ensure everything was perfect, so she had sent Andy on a quest to find the most fitting accompaniment to the food. After several failures, he had eventually returned triumphant, bearing a box containing six bottles of Rioja.

The wine had served its purpose in more ways than one, Consuela remembered with a smile. Not only did it complement the food, but the indulgence had caused Andy to become slightly inebriated. This in turn had made him even more amorous than usual. The hectic night of passion that followed had been yet more evidence of their feelings for each other.

Consuela stopped her recollections and glanced at the calendar on the wall beside the desk they shared for their studies. After a few seconds, she began to smile and walked slowly downstairs. She discovered Andy in his grandfather's workshop, where he had been helping Sonny by lifting several lengths of timber into position.

'Andy, I need to speak with you,' she told him, before leading him outside. When they were alone, she asked, 'Do you remember when I made that paella?'

'Of course, it was delicious.' Andy glanced at the now overcast sky. 'You're not thinking of repeating it, surely? It isn't exactly the weather for outdoor dining.'

'That isn't why I asked. You remember afterwards? When we went to bed?'

Andy grinned. 'I certainly do.'

'As I remember, you said it was a magical night.' She smiled and took his hands. 'That was true in more ways than you could have guessed. I think we will always remember that night. Even if we forget, there will be a permanent reminder for us.'

It was several seconds before Andy caught her meaning. 'Are you trying to tell me . . . ? Do you mean . . . ?'

'Yes, Andy, I'm trying to tell you we're going to have a baby.'

'Are you sure?'

'I've suspected for several weeks, but now I am sure.'

That evening, as they were sitting down for their meal, Andy looked at Consuela, who nodded as if in agreement with something he'd said. He then told everyone, 'I think you should know that we might be having a celebration somewhere around next April or May.'

There was a puzzled silence for a few seconds until Jenny caught her son's meaning. She put down her cutlery. 'Am I right in assuming that I'm soon going to become a grandmother?'

'That's right, Ma.'

Jenny rushed from her seat to hug both Andy and Consuela.

Lizzie had noticed that Consuela was the only adult who hadn't partaken of the wine that evening. She, along with Susan, was drinking orange juice. On hearing that her suspicions about the cause of Consuela's abstinence were accurate, Lizzie congratulated her and Andy. Remarking, 'I suppose I'd better get used to being called Great-aunt Lizzie.'

'If you think that's bad,' Rachael retorted, seeing Lizzie's comical grimace, 'Great-grandmother is far worse.'

* * *

As the family observed the Christmas morning ritual of opening presents, there was a surprise item, the label addressed to 'Andy, Consuela and ?'. When they opened it, the contents proved to be a tiny matinee coat plus a pair of baby's bootees.

As they stared in admiration at them, Jenny explained, 'I knitted those on the wooden needles Mark made for me in Spain. Both Andy and Suzie got items I made using those needles, but they weren't the first members of our family to wear my homemade garments.'

She turned to her daughter-in-law and smiled. 'That honour was yours, Consuela. When your mother was expecting you, we were trapped in a logging camp high in the mountains, cut off all winter by heavy snow. To provide something warm for you, I knitted three outfits and two pairs of bootees.'

'Yes,' Mark remarked, 'and she destroyed old sweaters to get the wool.'

Seeing Consuela was all but overcome with emotion, Andy attempted to lighten the moment. Holding up the garment, he told his mother, 'That was a bit short-sighted, don't you think, Ma? What if we have twins, or even triplets?'

'Give me chance,' Jenny replied once the laughter had died down. 'I've only known about the baby for a few weeks. With four months or so to go, I can certainly have enough ready for the big day.'

Later, over their Christmas dinner, the subject came up again. Susan introduced it by asking Consuela if she and Andy had given any thought to a name for the baby.

'Actually, we have,' Andy told her. 'And Consuela has already decided on the name, or names, but I'll let her explain.'

'I want names that will represent my origins as well as Andy's. However, I don't know much about my male ancestors, but if the baby turns out to be a boy, there is one that will tie in my Spanish roots and the Cowgill family tree. I would like to call my son Santiago.'

She turned to Sonny and explained, 'Santiago, which translates into English as Saint James, is the patron saint of Spain, and I believe you had an older brother who was also named James, so I thought this would be appropriate.'

'We decided to stick to the English version though,' Andy added. 'Because that would avoid the inevitable teasing he would get at school if the other boys knew his name was Santiago.'

'That's all very well if the baby's a boy, but what if it's a normal human being, a girl?' Susan asked.

'If we have a daughter, we propose to call her Angela Carmen. Carmen was my mother's name and Angela means angel, which for us she will be.' She paused. 'And we would like Lizzie to be the child's godmother.'

Lizzie gasped aloud. 'You want me to be your daughter's sponsor?' She turned to Gil Richardson sitting alongside her. 'Did you hear that? Me, a godmother!'

Gil smiled. 'I'm sure you could cope.'

'Actually, Lizzie, we would be pleased if you accept the role whether the child is a boy or a girl,' Andy told her.

'I will be honoured, and I will ensure I fulfil that position diligently,' Lizzie promised.

They raised their glasses in a toast to the future member of the Cowgill family.

CHAPTER NINE

At the dawn of 1960, when Lizzie's future was being decided, and plans made for her homecoming, many thousands of miles away in Australia at the headquarters of Fisher Springs Pty, Luke Fisher was heading for home.

Luke's father, James Cowgill, had left England in 1898 with Alice Fisher, a housemaid at Byland Crescent, vowing never to return, having quarrelled bitterly with his father, Albert Cowgill, about his and Alice's relationship. In doing so, they had severed their connection with the British branch of the family. Following their marriage James changed his surname to Fisher. Although Albert spent a long time having searches made for his son, the couple were never found. The only contact James had, via a London solicitor, was with his sister Constance and his grandfather — his surname, location and profession never revealed.

Eventually, James and Alice forged Fisher Springs Pty, an increasingly successful business empire and had extended their scope of operations to become a multi-faceted corporation. Under the cloak of anonymity, they invested in Sonny's ailing companies in Bradford, which now provided income for their hitherto estranged relatives.

Although Luke Fisher and Mark Cowgill were cousins, neither of them was aware of their relationship.

The only people aware of the family connection were Patrick Finnegan, formerly a director of Fisher Springs, and his wife Louise. After the sudden deaths of James, Alice and their daughter Mary in a devastating house fire, the Finnegans had taken in the Fisher children and raised them with their own. Now that Louise had also died, Patrick was the only survivor of those in the know.

* * *

Luke Fisher had married outspoken Isabella Finnegan in 1948, and now headed Fisher Springs. Following Bella's successful completion of a correspondence course in business studies and another in accountancy, she had commenced work alongside her husband. Despite Luke's wish for Bella to begin work in a management role she had refused his offer, opting instead for a far more junior post. 'I want to start at the bottom and work my way up and across,' she'd told him.

'What do you mean by up and across?'

'I want to learn the business at every level of operation, and by moving from one part of the group to another, I can gauge the performance and needs of each individual sector. That way, not only will I gain experience, but by familiarising myself with how each division operates I'll be able to make better judgements on the way forward, if you decide to promote me, and only then if my performance is judged solely on merit, not the fact that I'm sleeping with the owner.'

Luke had accepted Bella's suggestion, delighted by her pragmatic attitude to the career she intended to pursue. As he pondered the development he hoped that in the not-too-distant future Bella would join him in the Fisher Springs boardroom, replicating the scenario of his father and mother, who had founded the company and steered it on its road to success.

Bella's attitude to her future was a typical example of her down-to-earth, occasionally blunt way of viewing the world around her, and was part of her nature that had entranced him from the word go. Talking over the day's events had already become a habit, one Luke had suggested from the beginning. 'We can use the journey home each day to discuss what's happened at the office. That way we'll be able to leave work behind when we get home. Once we're through the door, there won't be much chance to discuss things anyway, not with the ankle-biters creating a rumpus.'

Bella had accepted Luke's idea, conscious that their three children would demand almost all their attention until bedtime. The arrangement seemed to be working fine for the moment, but before too long, they would have more than enough problems to contend with.

Luke had just ended a board meeting of Fisher Springs. The other directors were Josh Jones, Luke's second-in-command, and Elliot Finnegan, the group's research and development executive. Although Elliot was Luke's brother-in-law, his position within the company had little to do with their relationship. He had progressed through the ranks purely on merit. He had spent time in Bradford learning the UK side of the business and their methods, ensuring the entire company worked in harmony.

When Luke left the boardroom and returned to his office, he was mildly surprised to find one of the group's employees waiting for him. He closed the door, put his arms around her, and kissed her. After a few seconds he released her, saying, 'This is a pleasant surprise. What brings you away from the coal face?'

Bella Fisher looked at her husband sternly. 'I hope you don't greet all your colleagues that way.'

'I'd like to see the expression on Josh's face if I did.'

Bella smiled briefly, but told him, 'The reason I deserted my post is because I've had an urgent message from home. Nanny took a call from the headmaster of Jimmy's school.'

Although Luke and Bella's children were old enough for them to dispense with the services of a nanny, they had retained her to act as their housekeeper. With both parents working this was a pivotal role in the management of the household, and had the advantage that the children knew the woman and respected her authority.

'What's the little devil been up to this time?'

'Nothing. And he's not so little nowadays. He's tall and strongly built for a lad of his age. I know technically he's still a junior, but he'll be twelve years old in a couple of weeks.'

'Has there been an accident? Is Jimmy crook?'

'Apparently, he has taken a knock while out on the rugby field. He's not badly hurt but he needs to go home. Anyway, we should pick him up soon but it will mean leaving work early, so I thought I should come and ask your permission, sir.'

Luke smiled wryly. 'I don't think the day will ever dawn when you need my permission to do anything. We'll set off in ten minutes, if that's OK?'

'Yes, boss, whatever you say.'

Luke put his arms around her again. 'It's a long time until we get home, so I'd better have another of these.'

A minute passed before he released her from his embrace. As she turned to leave, Bella told him, 'Taking advantage of your employees like that is extremely naughty, Mr Fisher. Mind you,' she added, 'it was quite enjoyable. So get your car keys and hurry up.'

Luke saluted and was still smiling, long after the door closed behind her.

* * *

Jimmy Fisher was feeling sorry for himself. He had a headache and although his mother insisted he should rest in his room, he was frustrated he'd been unable to finish the rugby game. He lay back on his bed and listened. He could hear his ten-year-old sister Robyn practising her violin. Normally it would not bother him as she played well, but now it seemed to grate on him. Then there was his younger brother Saul.

The eight-year-old was a pain, in every aspect of the word. Jimmy sighed and buried his head beneath his pillow.

There was a gentle knock on his room door and it opened slightly. 'How are you feeling?' his mother asked, concern on her face.

'Dodgy. Nanny gave me some pills and I think they've helped a bit.'

His mother smiled. 'Have you looked in the mirror?'

'Why?'

'That black eye is going to be a real beaut tomorrow.'

'Really?' He jumped from the bed to look in the mirror.

Well maybe the headache was worth it after all. He had a great trophy for his efforts on the field.

'If you don't feel too good tomorrow, you can stay home with Nanny or, if you like, we can drop you at the Finnegans' on our way into the office. I'm sure Grandad will be pleased to see you.'

'No chance. I want the guys to see this at its best,' he said, pointing at his eye.

* * *

Retired from Fisher Springs Pty, Patrick Finnegan's health had been declining for over three years. Now, with a similar degradation of his mental powers, he still had long periods during which he was capable of rational thought. During one of those, he pondered memories from the distant past, most of which centred around Louise, his late wife. One recollection in particular was of their visit to England as representatives of Fisher Springs, undertaken when their daughter Bella was still only an infant. They were to meet with the UK element of the company. Prior to that journey, Patrick and Louise had become the repositories of the closely guarded secret regarding the Fisher family, and their English counterparts, the Cowgills. Now, many years hence, Patrick knew he was the only remaining holder of the information. Added to which, Sonny Cowgill was the sole representative of the generation it concerned.

Patrick remembered the early days and the occasion when James Fisher had revealed the surprising facts behind his and his wife Alice's past. At the time, it had been deemed advisable to keep the relationship hidden, but now, with everyone else who would have been affected by the news having died, Patrick decided it was the appropriate moment to reveal the truth. He believed it prudent to make the revelation while he was still able.

Following Luke and Bella's later visit to Britain, Patrick knew Luke had always considered there to be a great affinity with Sonny Cowgill, and had puzzled from time to time about how that could be. What Patrick had to tell him would resolve the mystery, and would perhaps draw the two arms of the family back together again.

With this in mind, Patrick spoke with Dottie, Luke's sister, who was married to Patrick's elder son Elliot, all living at the Finnegan family home. 'I need to discuss something with Luke,' Patrick told her. 'Will you ask him to come over as soon as he has a minute to spare? And it would be as well if you were here at the same time, as this is something that concerns you as well.'

That evening Dottie spoke to Elliot. 'I tried the office but couldn't reach Luke. It's obviously something important to your dad. I believe it's been weighing on his mind for quite a while. Don't ask me what it's about though, because I've no idea.'

'I'll tell him as soon as they're back,' Elliot told her. 'Luke and Bella are away touring some of the subsidiaries, then they're planning to visit the vineyard and talk to Gianni about future plans before they return. One thing for certain, they'll be back for Christmas.'

* * *

Such was Dottie's concern about the decline in her father-in-law's health that a few weeks later, she prevailed on her husband Elliot to send a telegram to his brother Finlay, now living and working in America. Finlay responded, telling them he would make arrangements immediately.

'I just hope he gets here in time,' Dottie told Elliot. 'The way your dad's condition has gone downhill over the past few weeks, it could be a close-run thing.'

The weeks before Finlay arrived seem to drag for Dottie, as her concern grew. She put any thoughts she had regarding the coming Christmas firmly from her mind. She had the children to think about, and the party she and Elliot usually held, but these could wait. Eventually, Finlay, accompanied by his fiancée, a stunning blonde with a deep tan and a rich mid-western American drawl, reached the homestead. They spent several hours with their father, in short sessions to avoid overtiring him.

A week later, Luke and Bella arrived home and were informed by their housekeeper that they were needed at Patrick's home. They travelled the short distance, and had just set foot on the veranda when Dottie burst out of the front door, her face a mask of tears. 'It's too late,' she wailed. 'I'm so sorry, Bella. Your father died five minutes ago.'

PART TWO: 1961–1962

I look for life in death,
for health in sickness,
for freedom in prison,
a way out from the impasse,
and loyalty in the Judas.
But my destiny, from which I would
never expect anything good,
has decreed with the Gods
that, since I ask for the impossible
they won't even give me the possible.

Miguel de Cervantès

CHAPTER TEN

If the decade had started well for the Cowgill family in England, the Fisher family in Australia couldn't have had a worse beginning to 1961. Luke and Bella were still shocked by the death of Bella's father.

Luke was impressed with the efficiency and consideration that had obviously gone into the planning of the funeral. Organization of an event that would draw a large gathering of mourners could not have been easy, but everything went smoothly, the preparations ensuring there was a separate space for those closest to the deceased, enabling them to grieve in privacy. Before they entered the church, Luke commented on this to Dottie.

'That's down to Eli,' she replied, using the pet name she had for her husband Elliot. 'Sadly, as Patrick's health had been declining slowly for ages, Eli had plenty of time to think the eventuality through, and plan everything.'

As the cortege followed the coffin, Finlay's fiancée held his hand as they walked into church, providing all the comfort and solace she could, seemingly oblivious to the admiring glances from a good many male members of those assembled.

Also amongst the close family was Luke Fisher's sister-in-law Amelia, widow of Luke's brother, Philip, accompanied by her daughter Clare. Clare was also the recipient of a good many interested inspections, both because of her undoubted good looks, but also her attire. Having reached the age of twenty-two, Clare Fisher had joined the State Police Force, and had donned her uniform to attend such a formal event as this.

Once the service and interment were over, family members and close friends attended the funeral tea. Watching proceedings, Luke Fisher remembered the title of a James Joyce book he had read while serving in the Royal Air Force during World War Two, but decided to remain silent. To refer to the event as *Finnegans Wake* would hardly be appropriate. If Elliot had organized the funeral to perfection, Dottie had more than matched it with the excellence of the food provided via caterers.

At such occasions people catch up with those they have not seen for a while, and this was certainly no exception. At one point, Luke had called for silence and read out a telegram received from the directors of Fisher Springs UK. In it, they recognized the invaluable contribution made over many years by Patrick, and the close, harmonious relationship he had fostered within the group. The message ended with deep condolences extended to Patrick's family. This effusive tribute from a group of people who were not only strangers to most of the mourners, but were also based many thousands of miles away, was evidence of how highly Patrick was regarded, and the extent of his influence worldwide. In some way, it lifted the spirits of those who heard it, and went some way to expiating their grief.

* * *

Several years earlier on the return leg of their round-the-world trip, Luke and Bella had met Finlay's girlfriend, Nancy, very briefly. Bella was particularly pleased that her younger brother was in a settled relationship. During their conversation now, Nancy revealed a surprising fact, one that caused her listeners to stare in astonishment.

'You actually got married? When did that happen?'

'It was a week before we got the phone call about Mr Finnegan. We'd been planning it for a long time. We intended to let you know, but then we received the sad news.'

After congratulations and hugs, Bella asked, 'I remember from his letters Finn was upset at having to leave you when he transferred to New York. How did you meet up again?'

Nancy grinned. 'I decided I didn't want to lose touch, so I followed him. I rented an apartment and got a job as secretary in the law firm where Finn works. He got quite a surprise when he found me in the office.'

Nancy smiled, as she continued, 'Finn was obviously not going to force the issue. So I told him I'd been trying to get a ticket for the Metropolitan Opera. They were performing *Aida*, and I was real keen to watch it, but they'd sold out.'

'Finn always loved opera. He used to get in trouble with Mum and Dad for playing it too loud on our gramophone,' Bella told her.

'I knew that. A couple of days later, Finn handed me a pair of complimentary tickets. I asked how he'd managed it. He told me about a client he'd helped with a tricky case, and the man owed him a favour. I knew the case because I'd handled the files, so I was aware the guy was a volunteer working on the admin staff at the Met, so he was happy to help.'

Nancy smiled. 'Naturally, I asked Finn if he would escort me. We went, it was great, and that's where our relationship began. Now we're real happy together, and I guess I've you to thank for that, Luke.'

Luke was puzzled. 'What do you mean?'

'Finn told me about the kidnapping when he was a child, and how you saved his life. He'll be in your debt forever — and so will I. He was convinced he was going to die. He said that when he was older, he became determined to live up to the standard you set. He's now highly thought of at work, and I happen to know he's being considered for a partnership,' — she glanced round as if she would be overheard — 'but don't tell him I said that. As it's reckoned to be one of the top law firms in New York, that's some accolade, believe me. A top-class attorney like Finn can command a huge salary, but that doesn't enter his thinking. He takes on a good few pro bono cases, because he's more interested in seeing justice done than the bottom line, and I reckon that's a measure of his character. And that's why I love him so much.'

* * *

As Finn and Nancy were scheduled to return to New York in a couple of days' time, the end of the day involved the family lawyer giving the reading of Patrick Finnegan's will. The estate was divided between his three children. With his usual commendable foresight, Patrick had ensured the monetary section of the will had amounts set aside for all his grandchildren's futures. Patrick's shareholding in Fisher Springs Pty was divided equally between his daughter Bella and his son Elliot. Elliot also inherited the family home. In doing so, Patrick had taken into account that Bella, along with her husband Luke, was already a majority shareholder in the group. The adjustment resulted in Finlay receiving the lion's share of the cash, which had been invested in a range of banks and financial institutions.

All three recipients agreed that their father had been scrupulously fair and just in the apportionment of his assets. That left no room for feelings of resentment, a major achievement when the large amount involved was taken into account.

During the reading, all the children were being entertained in the garden by Luke's fellow director, Englishman Josh Jones, and his Austrian wife, Astrid, accompanied by their daughter, two-year-old Daisy Emily. Prior to the war, Josh had been recruited as a linguistic specialist in the SOE, Special Operations Executive, and later sent overseas on covert operations, where he met Astrid.

'This marks the end of an epoch at Fisher Springs,' Josh told Astrid. 'A success story that began with Luke's father and mother.'

'Was Mr Finnegan involved with Fisher Springs from the beginning?'

'No, apparently they brought him in as the result of a takeover. Patrick worked for one of the banks, and when the Fishers realized his ability, they offered him a seat at the table, so to speak. Sadly, I never had the good fortune to meet James and Alice, but from what I've been given to understand, they were outstandingly good at recognizing talent, and they were extremely clever at exploiting it to the best advantage for all concerned.'

'What does that mean?'

'They believed a man or woman work far better when they're being properly recompensed for their efforts. They also believed that people will be far more careful with money when it's their own, and that policy has paid off handsomely. They did it by ensuring their executives were also shareholders in the companies they controlled, making them almost self-employed.'

'Luke is about the same age as you — does that mean he was a late addition to the family?'

'No, Luke is one of seven children. Dottie is a couple of years younger than him, and sadly, they are the only ones left now. James and Alice were killed in a dreadful fire that destroyed their homestead. It was built on the land they owned where they had their sheep station in the early days. Luke's sister Mary also died. In fact, had it not been for Luke's outstanding courage, all his family would have perished that night, plus Bella, who was staying with them.'

'How dreadful. It must have been a terrible ordeal for those who survived, knowing they'd lost their loved ones. Whereabouts was the house?'

He pointed along the river at the bottom of the large garden to an extensive property in the far distance.

'But that's where Luke and Bella live. You said it was destroyed.'

'True, but after the war Luke had it rebuilt. I think the happy memories he and Bella have created there might have helped erase the grim reminders of the earlier tragedy.'

'Sometimes, Josh, you can be really romantic. Usually that's because you want your way with me, but occasionally it's quite spontaneous.'

CHAPTER ELEVEN

Sonny and Mark were in Bradford, attending the annual general meeting of Fisher Springs (UK) Ltd. Although business had been good for the group previously, with profit and loss accounts for all member companies showing healthy surpluses, the figures presented by their finance director Paul Sugden at this meeting showed some increasingly worrying trends.

Paul had predicted a year ago the possible onset of a recession, which, combined with a tendency for many firms to indulge in over-trading, would lead to a potential for bad debts. It gave him little satisfaction, when presenting the latest set of trading figures, to confirm the accuracy of his earlier forecasts over the past year. Despite two of the group's divisions — the insurance and pharmaceutical companies — continuing to make profits, losses had been incurred in the chemical and textile arms, outweighing the gains.

The cause, as Sugden reported, was the demise of three customers, whose directors had been forced to call in the receivers, and from there to go into liquidation, resulting in their unsecured creditors getting only a minute fraction of the money owed to them. 'The distribution from the two companies that have thus far been wound up, after the banks have been paid off, will be less than two shillings in the pound,' Sugden told his fellow directors, 'and I anticipate no greater sum from the third.'

The act of liquidation, which Sonny Cowgill, the group chairman, referred to as 'company suicide', had hit Fisher Springs even harder than Sugden had anticipated. 'Luckily, we're still cash positive, as a result of pulling our horns in prior to the recession. But I regret to say there are worrying signs from one or two more of our clients, whose payment date of outstanding invoices is lengthening. The need for vigilance over these, and other accounts, is greater than ever, as is the requirement for extremely careful buying and selling strategies.'

'You mentioned something to me last week that I think we should also all be aware of,' managing director Jessica Binks suggested. 'I think you referred to it as phoenix trading, didn't you?'

'That's right, Jessica, and it's already happened to a couple of our smaller customers, plus others I've heard of who aren't on our books.'

'What on earth is that?' Sonny asked.

'Let me explain why I invented the term phoenix trading. Suppose Company A goes into receivership. Soon afterwards, a new company is formed and commences trading, sometimes even approaching the receivers appointed to dispose of Company A's assets and offering to buy these. The new company has one great advantage over Company A in that it has none of its liabilities.'

'Who owns the new company?' David Lyons, head of the pharmaceutical branch, asked.

'In the example I've quoted, the directors were the same as those responsible for the failure of the original company.'

'That is an extremely underhand trading practice. Is it legal?' Sonny asked.

'Sadly, unless someone brings in new legislation, or an amendment to the current laws, there is nothing to stop this happening. If you think what I've described so far is devious, there's even worse. One of these companies actually approached us. When our salesman came to me asking me what credit terms I could offer them, I instructed him to tell them to take a running jump.' Sugden smiled wryly. 'I think I spoilt his day.'

'And you named it phoenix trading, because one company rises from the ashes of the other?' Mark asked. 'A highly appropriate name, I'd say.'

Paul nodded agreement and continued, 'I've also made notes of our slow-paying customers, and I find it amusing, in a dark sort of way.' He passed sheets of paper to each of his colleagues. 'The worst offenders on that list are those who complained loudest about our change in invoicing policy. That's because they now have to pay interest on money they owe us that's been outstanding for longer than sixty days.'

Sugden paused before adding another word of caution. 'Although the results from our insurance division continue to be satisfactory, I've seen a recent increase in claims from both the private and commercial sectors that concern me. I believe we ought to issue an instruction to all our assessors to scrutinise closely any claim in excess of a hundred and fifty pounds.'

'Do you think those claims are spurious?' Jessica asked.

'Put it this way, I think the increase in numbers is a bit suspicious, given the current economic situation. I'm not saying we should deny such claims outright, merely ensure where possible they are absolutely genuine. I heard a joke the other day, which sadly I didn't find all that amusing. It was a conversation between two businessmen. The first sympathized with the other over the fire that had damaged his premises. The second one replied, "Shush, it doesn't happen until tomorrow."'

Although they smiled, Sugden's colleagues realized that for such an event to be joked about, the situation must be quite common.

* * *

As they rode the train back to Scarborough, Mark and Sonny reflected on the recent meeting. 'It looks as if we're in for a bumpy ride over the next few years, Dad,' Mark suggested.

'That's true, but the group has weathered worse storms on more than one occasion, both before the war and more recently, and at least on this occasion, unlike the previous ones, we're well prepared.'

'Because we've got substantial cash reserves, you mean?'

'That's certainly one aspect of it, but I was thinking more of the personnel heading our organization. Paul Sugden in particular has emerged as an outstanding policymaker, who has the gift of being able to anticipate the market in advance of it shifting, and provides us with the means to act. I reckon it must be one of the luckiest accidents of all time the day that bale of wool almost fell on Bella Fisher and her son, when the Fishers visited the UK arm of the business. When Paul saved them that day, he was trying to get an interview with us. I don't think anyone could have envisaged what an input he would have on our company's success.'

Sonny thought for a moment. 'There is yet another aspect to what I was thinking, and that is, no matter how good those policies Paul dreams up are, they would be meaningless without people to implement them. Jessica, David and you, also have key roles to play. That gives me confidence that our small team of executives will ensure the group emerges from this recession in a strong enough state to take full advantage of the recovery.'

'You're sure that will happen — the recovery, I mean?'

'I'm confident of it, because I've experienced it. I read somewhere of an economic theory, with a lot of supporting evidence, that suggests periods of boom and bust follow a definite cycle. The trick is being able to recognize when one part of that cycle ends and the other begins, and I don't think there are many people better equipped to spot those signs than Paul and our other board members.'

One item that had definitely not been discussed during the board meeting was the question of staff recruitment.

Although there was no outright ban in place on hiring new employees, there was a tacit understanding that this would have to wait until trading conditions improved.

The needs of one department within the group, however, could not be ignored, and this was the sole topic for discussion at a private meeting later that day between Jessica Binks and Paul Sugden. It was Jessica who raised the issue that had been troubling her. 'This is all piling a lot of extra work on your shoulders, Paul,' she suggested. 'And to be honest, I don't know how you've coped. What really worries me is that if things get worse before they improve, it might all prove too much for you.'

'You're right. It has been difficult. And some of the things I ought to have dealt with have had to be shelved. They are sitting there until I can free myself from other matters that are more important or urgent.'

'Can you see a way round it?'

'Short of working a twenty-four-hour day, seven days a week, there is no way round it.'

'There is one alternative. Taking on another member of staff, one extra person would be a major help to you. I know we are not hiring at the moment, but I think this is important enough to make an exception. The problem is going to be finding someone of the right calibre.'

Paul thought for a moment. 'Actually, there is someone, a person whose work ethic I know, and who is qualified, loyal, trustworthy and highly intelligent. But I'm reluctant to put them forward, because of who they are.'

Jessica stared at her colleague in surprise. 'You'd better tell me who this paragon of virtue is, and why you're so hesitant in recommending them.'

'I reckon Sally would be ideal for the job.'

'Sally? Your wife?' She paused, studying him thoughtfully. 'That actually sounds like a really good idea. We all know and like Sally, and I'm certain she'll be extremely efficient. Why don't you go ahead and ask her. I'll make sure the rest of the board know the idea has my complete approval.'

'I'll do that, as long as you're happy with the arrangement.'

'I can't think of anyone better, although I do have one small concern.' Jessica was smiling as she said this.

'What's your reservation?'

'How do you think Sally will put up with taking orders from you?'

Sugden grinned. 'Probably much the same as always, which means she'll end up running the show.'

Paul's final statement clinched the argument as far as Jessica was concerned. She was all in favour of having another strong-minded, decisive woman on board.

'It will be a week or so before she could start,' Paul added. 'Because at the moment she's supervising the redecoration of our house.' He paused and then said, 'Damn, that means I'll be in trouble when I get home tonight. I was supposed to talk to Sonny about one of the things Sally no longer needs, but I clean forgot. Now it'll have to wait until I see him again.'

* * *

When Mark and his father reached Byland Crescent, they discovered their family in the sitting room. They were clustered around Mark's sister, who was in her wheelchair.

'What's going on here?' Sonny asked.

'Stand there and watch,' Rachael ordered the newcomers. 'OK, Lizzie, show them what you can do.'

Mark and Sonny did as they were told, and were rewarded when Lizzie pushed down firmly on the wheelchair armrests and rose to her feet slowly, with Rachael and Jenny supporting her by her arms.

Consuela hovered protectively in front of her, and Susan stood behind the wheelchair as Lizzie took a faltering step forward. Susan immediately brought the wheelchair forward, allowing Lizzie to sit down.

Rachael explained, 'Lizzie showed us once before you arrived. Isn't that marvellous? We think it's a great step forward, in both senses of the word.'

'I'll say it is. How long have you been able to do that?' Sonny asked his daughter.

'I'm now much stronger as a result of that torture regime the physiotherapist dreamed up for me. Several weeks ago, he thought it was time to see if I could support my weight. I stood up using the parallel bars with help from two of the staff. And strangely enough, when I try to move forward on the bars, it becomes a bit easier and less painful. Now, with practice, it's even better.'

Sonny's delight was obvious by his broad smile. 'That's wonderful news. Why didn't you tell us?'

'I wanted to wait until I was sure. I had to know I could succeed first — the therapist warned me it could take time. I'm being discharged from the hospital and I'll be having therapy sessions at home from now on with Dr Richardson. There's more news too, Dad. Sit down and I'll tell you.'

Sonny took a seat facing her, and Lizzie continued, 'I've decided I'm not going to return to my old job. They've offered me a retirement package on health grounds and I've decided to accept it.'

'I see. So what will you do with your time? You've such an active mind you'd soon be bored sitting here all day.'

'That depends on how fully I recover. Hopefully, if my condition improves sufficiently, I'd like to go for a teaching job at one of the local schools.'

'What will you teach?'

'Modern Languages, principally European ones, and if there's sufficient demand, some of the Arabic tongues as a backup.'

Sonny blinked with surprise. 'Have you the necessary qualifications?'

'I have degrees in the Romance languages, plus I speak Russian, German and some of the Nordic languages. I can also read, write and speak Latin and Ancient Greek, and know enough Arabic to ask for a coffee in Cairo, or tea in Tunis.'

Sonny realized his daughter had the power to astound him. 'Goodness me, that's really impressive. Where did you learn all that?'

'Some of them were taught in-house, as part of my training, the others I learned via correspondence courses and at night school. Even if I don't get fit enough to teach in a school, I thought I could hold classes in my rooms here, if that's OK with you and Mum. You know I've already got two pupils, although that's on a pro-rata basis.'

'We'd have no problems with that. Would we, Sonny?' Rachael said.

'This is your home, Elizabeth. You can do as you wish.'

'What did you mean by the pro-rata basis?' Suzie asked.

'Now that Andy and Consuela have got their business up and running, they dismissed the idea of taking linguistics at college, so I'm teaching them. But they're also teaching me. Andy's Greek is far better than mine, so he's helping me improve, and in exchange, I'm teaching him Russian. He knows the basics, but that's about all. I'm doing something similar with Consuela, who also wants to learn Russian, and by way of reward she's teaching me Catalan.' Lizzie smiled, and her father asked what was amusing her.

'It's Andy's definition of Catalan. He said Catalan is to Spanish what Welsh is to English — totally incomprehensible.'

Jenny and Rachael both noticed Lizzie's demeanour, which was cheerfully upbeat. Their speculation on the cause for this was wholly accurate, which they later discussed when they were alone.

'I think Lizzie's fallen for that good-looking doctor, and what's more, I think his interest in her might be more than simply professional.'

'What makes you say that?' Rachael asked.

'Lizzie has just told us Gil plans to visit here every week to help with her physiotherapy.' Jenny grinned, and raised her eyebrows.

Rachael frowned, slightly puzzled. 'Yes, but that's purely professional interest now she won't be attending the hospital, surely?'

'Not likely! Lizzie told me, when he first asked if he could call on her at home, he stressed that his visits would also be personal as he wants to get to know her better. He's already told her he could have signed her off sooner.'

'Gosh, that's a turn-up for the book.'

Now both sets of eyebrows were raised.

CHAPTER TWELVE

Some weeks later, as Mark and his father were travelling to Bradford, he asked, 'Do you have any idea what this meeting is about?'

'Not really,' Sonny replied, 'all Jessica told me was it had something to do with another of Paul Sugden's brainwaves.'

When they reached the office, Mark and Sonny found the other directors already in the boardroom, drinking tea as they waited for the travellers. 'We ought to get a samovar in here,' Mark joked.

'It wouldn't be the first drinks dispenser in this room,' Sonny told him. 'Your grandfather had a drinks cabinet installed, but when I saw what sort of condition his over-indulgence caused, I had it removed.'

'You always were a spoilsport, Dad.'

'Now we're all here, let's get started,' Jessica suggested, clearly concerned the verbal sparring match would deteriorate into a squabble, albeit an amicable one. 'Paul, would you care to tell us what happened, and your reason for requesting this meeting.'

'I got a phone call from the receivers who have been called in to handle the winding up of one of our clients,' Sugden told them. 'The account isn't a large one, certainly not big enough to hurt us. But when I realized who the client was I became alarmed, because they have always been one of the most prompt at paying their bills.'

Sugden paused and glanced at his colleagues, who were paying close attention as he continued, 'I was concerned that if one of our best customers had gone to the wall, the overall economic situation must have worsened far more rapidly and deeply than we anticipated. However, when I did a little more digging, courtesy of the receiver passing on some information, I found out the underlying cause of the receivership. That sparked off an idea as to how we might be able to protect ourselves — and our clients — from the same thing happening in future.'

'What was the reason for our client going belly-up?' Sonny asked.

'They suffered a huge bad debt, which made it impossible for them to continue trading. A customer they dealt with had failed, and that debt represented too great a share of their turnover for them to recover. Obviously, from what I could gather, they either weren't aware of or ignored the eighty/twenty rule.'

'Pardon my ignorance, but what on earth is the eighty/twenty rule? I've certainly never heard of it, and by the expression on their faces, neither have the others,' Jessica said a trifle waspishly.

'It's a recommended trading practice. By spreading your business over a wider range of customers, this allows you to keep their debt to you within manageable limits. Then, if one of them went bust, you wouldn't have to follow suit. Simply put, you don't put more than eighty per cent of your turnover with less than twenty per cent of your client base. That's good for businesses, bad for receivers,' Sugden added with a grin.

'Like preventing a domino effect,' Mark suggested.

'Exactly, and that's where I believe if we implement the scheme I have in mind we can both protect ourselves, and at the same time provide a rich income source for one of our divisions.'

'That sounds promising, Paul, would you care to explain?' Jessica prompted him.

'I think we should consider taking out bad debt insurance, and not only do it ourselves but encourage our customers to do likewise, even offering them it as part of our long-term dealings with them. More than that, I think we should make it clear to them that without such insurance, either with ourselves, or another company, it would restrict the amount we could sell to them. If we do so, monitoring it prudently and using our insurance division wherever possible, we will benefit via the insurance premiums the clients pay.'

'Won't that simply be shifting the potential bad debt from one part of the group to another?' David Lyons asked.

'Hopefully not, David, although that's a very good point. Avoiding such a situation is where the prudent monitoring I mentioned comes in. If we agree a sensible strategy beforehand, we will be able to assess each client, giving them a credit rating allied to their performance and liquidity. Then, once we've built up a portfolio, our insurance division can act in the same way that bookmakers do.'

'What does that mean?' Jessica wanted to know. 'You've lost me again.'

'If a bookmaker finds he has taken too many bets on a particular horse, he passes some of them off to another bookie. I believe it's known as "laying off the bet". Likewise, insurers with too many potential claims from one sector of their portfolio can pass a chunk of the liabilities from those policies to another company.'

'What percentage of a potential bad debt will they cover?'

'That's a very good question, Mark, and to be honest I haven't looked into it yet. I didn't want to spend time taking the idea further until I gauged your reaction to it. If you're in agreement with the general principle, I can always get my new assistant to check out the nuts and bolts and perhaps prepare a report for our next meeting.'

Sugden's colleagues smiled at his reference to his wife Sally, but listened attentively as he continued, 'Whatever your reaction to the scheme is, I have one other suggestion I'd like the board to consider.'

'Two in one day, Paul? My word, you have been busy,' Sonny teased him.

'Actually, one leads almost directly to the other. I think we ought to consider appointing Harry Barnes onto the main board. Harry's done a great job since he was appointed managing director of the insurance division following our takeover bid, and I think he's earned the promotion. I also believe his advice at sessions such as this will be invaluable, with or without the implementation of the bad-debt insurance scheme.'

Although Sugden's fellow directors were aware of Harry Barnes' commercial track record, and approved of his business acumen, as demonstrated by the insurance division's success, they knew little or nothing about his personal circumstances. In this respect, it seemed, Barnes was somewhat of a mystery man, who apparently guarded his privacy from his colleagues and employers alike.

Mark Cowgill was first to declare his opinion. 'I agree with both of Paul's suggestions, but I believe we should check out Harry's background more thoroughly before issuing the invitation. We inherited him when we took over the insurance company, and I guess we assumed that any such checks had already been made, but we know little more about him now than we did on day one. I agree he's done a first-class job, but further than that, we seem to be at a loss. On the one hand, I respect a man's right to privacy, but as an employer I feel it would be irresponsible not to take the necessary safeguards, as we have always done, before appointing someone to such a prestigious position.'

After some discussion, Jessica suggested they should take a break. 'Let's reconvene this afternoon, once we've all had chance to mull over Paul's suggestions. In the meantime, we've got a business to run, so we'd be well advised to clear our desks as well as our minds before we take this any further.

Let's regroup at three o'clock, and before then I'll dig out Harry Barnes' personnel file and see if that can give us more of an insight into his way of life.'

When they dispersed, Paul seized the opportunity to buttonhole Sonny. 'There's something I should have spoken to you about last time we met, but I forgot until too late.' He paused and smiled ruefully. 'So I got my head in my hands from Sally. This isn't about business, it's a personal matter, so maybe it would be as well if Sally tells you, as she knows more about it than me.'

'OK, let's deal with it now, shall we.' Sonny was mystified as to the nature of the personal matter. When they reached Sally's office, however, the reason soon became clear.

'When we bought your sister Connie's house in Cecil Avenue, her daughter Marguerite included an item in the sale she told us brought back too many memories for her to keep it. It's an oil painting of a landscape scene in Nidderdale. She didn't explain why, so I managed to contact the artist, whose work is now quite collectable. Her name is Eleanor Rhodes, and she told me your sister Ada commissioned it as a wedding present for Connie and Michael. The painting is beautiful, but it doesn't fit with the new decor, so rather than simply send it for auction, I thought it better to ask you if you would like it for Byland Crescent. I don't want any money for it, but I thought it would be a nice present to thank you for all your kindness to us.'

Sonny was saddened by the memory of his sister, Ada, who had been Eleanor Rhodes' lover, but recognized the generosity of Sally's idea. 'Let me phone Rachael and see what she thinks,' he told her. 'And thank you for your consideration.'

Sonny phoned home and told Rachael about the offer regarding the painting, with no clear idea how she would react to the idea of it coming to Byland Crescent.

'I remember it from when we used to visit Connie and Michael,' Rachael said. 'It's a lovely scene. I think it would be nice to bring it here. In a sense, it would be almost like bringing your sister home. I think we should accept the offer.

How much does she want for the painting? I understand Eleanor Rhodes' landscapes are quite collectable nowadays.'

'Sally told me she and Paul would not accept any money for it. She said it was a gift, to express their gratitude for our kindness to them over the years. The only question I have is where would we be able to display such a work of art?'

'I don't know yet, I haven't had time to think it over. Leave it to me and Jenny to figure out. Between us we'll find a place to show it off to best effect.'

* * *

When the meeting resumed, Jessica touched on the subject that had been raised by Paul Sugden. 'I had a look in Harry Barnes' personnel file,' she began. 'The file lists his parents, both deceased, but there are no siblings, no mention of a wife or girlfriend. In the space reserved for next of kin there is simply a dash. The references taken up when he applied for a job in the insurance division were excellent, and were verified prior to him being offered the post. I don't see any reason why we can't offer him the promotion.'

Jessica's suggestion was approved unanimously.

Mark then changed the subject. 'Dad and I have been talking about Paul's other idea.'

'You mean the bad debt insurance scheme? Did you come to any firm conclusion?' Jessica asked.

'We did agree that Paul's idea makes excellent sense, providing the price doesn't outweigh the benefits. It might cost us a packet in premiums, but that would be more than recouped should one of our customers, even the smaller ones, go to the wall.'

'That's good news, because David and I also discussed it and we're both up for it.'

'Is that the sort of thing you use as pillow talk?'

Mark grinned at Jessica's response, which took the form of the sound popularly known as blowing a raspberry, or a Bronx cheer.

Jessica's final comment emphasized her ability as a man manager. 'Before we implement the bad debt insurance scheme, I believe we ought to wait for Harry to come on board. He's going to be the one to spearhead the plan, so we need to know his opinion.'

There was no hesitation in agreeing to speak to Harry Barnes.

* * *

In Byland Crescent, Jenny was in the kitchen talking to Sarah, the cook, when she heard a sound. She listened. Consuela was upstairs resting, Andy was at the repair shop, and his grandmother, now with free time to fill, had taken a liking to the local Women's Institute. Jenny heard it again — it was her name being called. She realized the possible significance as she ran though the hall and up the stairs, calling, 'I'm coming.' She found Consuela, laid on the bed, grimacing in pain.

Taking her hand, she told her not to panic. 'I'm here, everything will be fine. How long have you had pains?'

'All morning, but I thought I might be wrong.'

Jenny waited for more contractions, timing them on her wristwatch. 'Well, I might have delivered you, but this time the professionals can have the pleasure of delivering my grandchild.' She smiled reassuringly, before she opened the wardrobe and removed the overnight bag, packed ready for the birth. She sat alongside Consuela, wishing Rachael would return soon.

Sarah knocked on the door and opened it slightly. 'Can I come in?'

'Er, yes, please do,' Jenny replied.

'Can I help? I don't have any experience of this but if there's anything you need. Cup of tea, perhaps?'

Consuela tried to laugh but a fresh bout of pain prevented her.

Jenny smiled. 'I don't think that will be necessary, but would you mind phoning Andy? The number for the shop is alongside the phone in the hall.'

Moments later Sarah returned. 'I spoke to a lady called Nora. She said Mr Cowgill is out on a home repair. She will pass the message as soon as he returns.' She looked at Consuela. 'I do hope things go well for you, but, if you don't need me, I'll go back downstairs and watch for Mrs Cowgill coming home.' With that, she left the room, a trifle hurriedly.

'I don't think Sarah wanted to stay,' Consuela said.

'I think you're right, but now, young lady, I think you should be leaving as well.'

It was twenty minutes after Jenny had called for an ambulance, and knew that the mother-to-be was in safe hands, that a car screeched to a halt outside.

Jenny met Andy at the door, reassuring him all was well. He turned, dived back into the car, and headed for the hospital, where he spent the next few hours pacing the halls and corridors. After, to him, what seemed like days, Consuela gave birth to the first member of a new generation to reside in Byland Crescent. James (Santiago) Cowgill announced his arrival with a series of bloodcurdling screams, but fortunately, for most of his relatives, these were delivered in the maternity ward of Scarborough Hospital.

CHAPTER THIRTEEN

Lizzie had already become immensely attracted to Gil, and that feeling had been strengthened by their weekly meetings at Byland Crescent.

As Lizzie rested following her exercises she said, 'One of the nurses told me there had been a lot of speculation as to why you never seemed to take any interest in girls.'

'It's simply that I haven't met any girls who attracted me. That was until I met you. Once I started to get to know you, I realized how different you are. You have a bubbly, lively personality. If I was attracted initially by your looks, it was your lovely nature that made me fall for you, and I'm definitely falling in love with you.'

Before Lizzie could protest, if she had been going to, Gil lifted her onto his knee, put his arms around her, and began to kiss her.

Lizzie drew away slightly, looked into his eyes, and smiled. 'I've been wanting you to do that for quite a while.'

'Oh, good,' Gil replied. 'Shall I do it again?'

Her reply, 'Yes please,' was muffled by his lips against hers.

After several minutes, Lizzie asked, 'Where do we go from here?'

'If you decide you want a future together, as much as me, I'd like us to take that route, but only when you're absolutely certain. I've seen too many relationships fail because they were entered into on the spur of the moment, without due thought to the consequences. I wouldn't want that to happen to us, because much as I want us to be together, I also want us to remain together.'

Lizzie put her arms round his neck, still looking into his eyes, and smiled. 'I like that idea.'

* * *

Sonny was on the point of leaving the house, heading for the former stable block at the rear that had long since been converted to his carpentry workshop. He paused by the door to Lizzie's rooms, distracted from his purpose. Lizzie was seated with her back to him, her crutches were propped against another chair, and she was reading an old magazine. The headline of the article caught Sonny's eye.

He tapped on the door. 'Why the interest in that old news, Lizzie?'

She glanced up and smiled. 'The guy who wrote this article knew what he was talking about, which, believe me, is somewhat unusual for a journalist writing about this sort of thing. "The U-2 incident", as he calls it, that happened last year, certainly increased tension between Russia and America.'

'U-2, that's the American spy plane the Russians shot down, isn't it?'

'Correct, Dad, and according to what this guy wrote, the Russians retrieved some highly damaging photographic evidence from the plane's wreckage that allegedly shows the pilot was carrying out covert surveillance on their military installations. My guess would be he was doing so at the behest of the CIA.'

'Forgive my ignorance, but what is the CIA?'

Lizzie smiled, but with little evidence of humour. 'Central Intelligence Agency. And their stated purpose is to collect overt information about countries worldwide. That is a thinly disguised cloak for their espionage activities. They not only spy on other countries, they are also proactive in stirring up trouble in places where the rulers' policies clash with American interests, or propping up unsteady regimes that are friendly to the USA. What concerned me at the time was how the Russians would react. One thing for certain, they wouldn't have been happy about it.'

'That might be so. But what could they do?'

'For a start, they put this pilot, Gary Powers, on trial for espionage. It was a show trial, because the Russian authorities, guided by the KGB,' Lizzie paused and smiled at her father, 'that's the Russian equivalent of the CIA, had already decided he'd be found guilty, and sentenced to a term of imprisonment. They would also probably have decided on the length of his sentence. That's all rather immaterial, because he'll no doubt be used as a bargaining chip.'

'What does that mean?'

'Gary Powers will probably be exchanged for one of the Russian agents currently being detained in the West.'

'Are there many of them?'

The apparent innocence of Sonny's question failed to deceive his daughter. She shook her head in mock pity as she replied, 'Nice try, Dad, but you know I couldn't reveal anything of that nature, even if I was in possession of such sensitive information.'

Sonny thought for a moment. 'When your lot recruit spies, do they try and find out if they talk in their sleep?'

'What on earth makes you think I know anything like that?'

'Come off it, Lizzie, there's no way you're simply a code-breaker or translator. The trouble your people went to after you were attacked shows they were deeply concerned about your level of knowledge, and the fear that the motive was to obtain information.'

'How did you work all that out?'

'I didn't, your brother did. He was also very angry at not being told about your injuries until after they'd decided there were no security issues. He actually threatened them with exposure.'

Lizzie was touched by this evidence of Mark's concern, and to change the subject, asked what her father had meant about spies talking in their sleep.

'It concerned your distant cousin, Josh Jones. You wouldn't know, but he used to be an agent before and during the war.' Although Lizzie was fully aware of Josh Jones and his exploits, she feigned ignorance. 'He was undercover somewhere in Europe, passing himself off as a German, and the girl he was sleeping with heard him talking in his sleep — in English!'

That, however, was something Lizzie didn't know. 'Really? That sounds fascinating. What happened next?'

'I don't know. Josh wouldn't tell me anything else.' Sonny grinned. 'Official Secrets Act, you know. All I can tell you is that Josh went back after the war, married the girl, and they now live in Australia. He works at Fisher Springs. I recommended him as, following his wartime exploits, he had no employment references.'

Sonny was about to open the kitchen door when he had another thought. 'Is Dr Richardson due today?'

Lizzie blushed, but answered boldly, 'Yes, but only briefly. He's on duty this afternoon.'

'That man is highly conscientious, taking such an interest in a patient he only treated for a short time.'

'He wants to help me recover sufficiently to dispense with my wheelchair entirely, that's all.'

'What a shame. And there I was thinking he'd taken a fancy to you.'

Lizzie's cheeks were bright red by now. 'I don't know where you got that idea from.'

'I can't think of many patients who invite their doctor to Christmas dinner as you did last year. Your excuse that he would have been alone, and it was only to show your gratitude, didn't fool any of us. Of course, it might have been the passionate kiss he gave you as he was leaving a few days ago. I wasn't spying on you — there are enough spies in this house,' he said with a grin. 'I was crossing the landing and happened to glance down into the hallway. I didn't see you protesting too much.'

She remained silent, mainly because she couldn't think of anything to say. Sonny smiled at her and said, 'I'll stop teasing you, I promise. And it does my heart good to see you so happy, Lizzie. Long may it continue.'

After her father had left, Lizzie reflected on the many secrets she could have revealed during her conversation with him. Although she had accepted that her immediate family knew her to be involved in counter-espionage, she had assumed they would believe she held a low-level position, which was far from the truth. She was certain, despite Mark and her father's deductions, that they could have no idea as to how senior her rank was. That had been the reason the attack on her had caused such panic among her colleagues. They might have worried that the assault had been an attempt to kidnap and extract information, but one thing was for certain — there was no way she could have revealed anything by talking in her sleep like her cousin Josh had done. Even if she did talk in her sleep, there was definitely nobody to hear what she said. Lizzie smiled quietly as she wondered if that would continue to be so as she and Gil became closer. The idea both surprised and pleased her.

She wondered idly who had replaced her at work and was now receiving the daily briefings from the head of her department, her immediate boss. She wasn't concerned that the right choice had been made, for she was well aware how excellent a judge of character Edrith Pointon was. After a while, she ceased thinking about work and concentrated on Gil's impending visit. That was a far more interesting topic.

* * *

In Byland Crescent, Christmas Day 1961 saw a household gathering that went some way towards matching the splendid occasions of the past. Baby James, completely unaware of the occasion, had entertained everyone with his first attempt at crawling, much to the delight of not only his parents, but both his grandparents and great-grandparents. With more seats at the festive table than for many years, the resident family members had been augmented by three others, for whom it would be their first formal meal in the Cowgill residence.

In addition to Gilbert Richardson, now officially acknowledged within the family as Lizzie's boyfriend, there were two other newcomers, as Rachael and Jenny had extended an invitation towards their husbands' fellow directors. Paul and Sally Sugden declined as they would be entertaining Sally's parents. Jessica Binks and David Lyons had been pleased to accept.

Sonny had passed on the invitation to Jessica. 'We've plenty of room, and cooking for two extra isn't going to be a chore for our cook.' He then added, 'The more the merrier as far as we're concerned.'

The feast created by Sarah was worthy of the occasion. When the main course had been eaten, now without maids, Mark and Jenny carried the crockery through to the kitchen as had become the custom over the years. Rachael insisted the washing up, which she would do, should wait until the meal was over, when Sarah and Mary had both left. The two women were instructed to take with them sufficient food for their festive meal with their mother.

When everyone declared they had eaten sufficient, Rachael co-opted one assistant to help in the kitchen. Her choice for this task surprised many members of her family. The only exceptions to this were Jenny and Consuela, who knew Rachael's secret agenda in choosing Gil for the job.

As Rachael commenced washing the soup dishes, with Gil alongside her drying them, she talked frankly to him about his relationship with her daughter. 'Lizzie is a good, highly intelligent and passionate woman, but she is also extremely vulnerable. I'm speaking emotionally, not physically. I have evidence of that in her reaction in her early teens to my argument with her brother Billy, when he enlisted. He died during the Second World War. Lizzie didn't forgive me for that, and we have only recently become reconciled some twenty years later. I'm telling you this as background, because I don't want you to feel we're being over-protective. The one thing I will not tolerate is for Lizzie to get hurt.'

'I assume you're implying you don't want *me* to hurt Lizzie, and I can assure you that isn't going to happen. I love Lizzie too deeply to do anything that would upset her. You could claim it was love at first sight. I admit that at first it was pure physical attraction, but when I spoke with her and got to know her better, everything changed.'

'Thank you for sharing that with me, Gil, it is a great comfort to know you care so much for her. However, there is one thing you must do before we go any further.'

Gil looked at her, puzzled. 'What's that?'

'Help me tackle the rest of these dishes before the water goes cold.'

* * *

In Australia, Christmas was a time of deep contentment for Josh Jones, his wife Astrid and their daughter Daisy. Being a Yorkshireman, after the Christmas meal, Josh told Astrid, 'I never realized how costly it could be to buy presents for a child.'

Astrid gave her husband a long, slightly ironical stare before telling him, 'Make the most of it, Mr Scrooge, because it'll be doubly expensive next Christmas.'

It took a couple of seconds before the penny dropped. Josh put down his wine glass. 'Does that mean you're pregnant?'

'It certainly does.'

'Well, bless my soul, how did that happen?'

Astrid chuckled. 'We went upstairs into our bedroom, took our clothes off, got into bed and then you—'

Josh interrupted hastily, 'Yes, I know how it works. I was taken aback, that's all. Well, this is really wonderful news — what better gift could I ask for?' He scooped Daisy up and tickled her, making the infant giggle. 'How about that, Daisy love? You're going to have a little brother or sister, someone for you to boss around.'

'You'll have to tell Luke you'll need some time off when the baby comes. How do you think he'll react?'

He put the still giggling Daisy on the floor and took Astrid in his arms. 'I'd better check with him now and see what he thinks,' he said, and headed for the phone.

Astrid shook her head, smiled, and removed the empty wine glass out of Daisy's reach. The case of wine they had received from the Fishers was minus a bottle, and Astrid wasn't drinking.

At the Fisher homestead the party was in full swing, the ringing of the phone could hardly be heard above the sound of excited children. The noise from the impromptu game of cricket being played on the lawn filtered onto the veranda. Dottie and Elliot were there with all the family, adding to the atmosphere. Their only sad moment was when they raised their glasses to absent friends.

The housekeeper answered the phone and called Luke, who responded to Josh's greeting, concerned there was a problem.

'I've just got my Christmas present,' Josh told him.

Luke, who had also been sampling wine from his own vineyard, laughed. 'Do I need to hear this?'

'Not that. Well, I suppose it's relevant,' Josh replied. 'Anyhow, I haven't actually got it yet.'

'Why's that?'

'I can't have it until the summer.'

Luke was getting a little confused. 'You said you've got your present.'

'That's right, I'm having a baby.'

'Congratulations!' Luke said, heartily, before he replaced the receiver and returned to the party.

'Who was that?' Bella asked, watching her husband slump into his chair, grinning.

'It was Josh. He phoned to tell me he's pregnant.'

'Really? Well I'm sure he'll make a damn good mother,' Bella replied, to the laughter of the others.

CHAPTER FOURTEEN

Once the festivities were over, life at Byland Crescent soon returned to normal, but only for a few days. It was early Friday evening on 12 January 1962 when a phone call from Jessica Binks brought disturbing news from Bradford.

Mark answered the phone. He listened to what Jessica had to tell him, agreed with her summary of the situation and the action required, before going to relay the information to the other members of the family, who were about to sit down to dinner.

'I think it would be wise for us to forego our visits to the office for the time being,' he told his father.

Sonny looked at him, puzzled, his perplexity increasing as Mark continued. 'I know you only go there once in a blue moon nowadays, but even those trips would be better postponed until we get a clearer picture of the situation in Bradford. The same goes for me too,' he added.

'Why aren't you going to work?' Jenny asked.

'The call was from Jessica Binks. She's just read something extremely disturbing in the T and A. It came as quite a shock to her, as it did to me.'

'What is the T and A?' Consuela asked.

Mark smiled at his daughter-in-law. 'I'm sorry, I keep forgetting you're a stranger in these parts. T and A is local slang. It's short for the *Telegraph and Argus*, which is Bradford's local newspaper. The main story grabbing the headlines in today's edition is a report that two people have died from smallpox.'

There was a prolonged, stunned silence as everyone absorbed the shocking news. Eventually, Sonny remarked, 'I thought that smallpox had been eradicated in Great Britain?'

'That might well have been the case,' Rachael responded, 'but nowadays, with much higher levels of international travel, there is a far greater risk of someone who hasn't been vaccinated picking up the disease elsewhere and bringing it into this country.'

Given her background in the nursing profession, nobody argued with her disturbing summary of the situation.

'Jessica suggested it would be much safer for Dad and I to stay well clear of Bradford. Let's be fair, it's much easier these days, because if there is anything really urgent to deal with, we can discuss it over the phone.'

* * *

There was a long, tense wait until the middle of February before the outbreak was officially declared over. By that time, one of the directors stranded in Scarborough had come to a decision, which he confided to his wife before travelling to Bradford for the first board meeting of the year.

Having greeted his colleagues and expressed his relief that they had come through the epidemic unscathed, Sonny continued, 'My period away from the office has enabled me to take a look into the future. I am approaching my seventieth birthday, which I will celebrate later this year, and I intend to mark that milestone by taking full retirement. That means I will relinquish my post as chairman and resign from the board of directors.'

Jessica turned to Mark. 'Did you know about this?'

'Certainly not! He never tells me anything. On the way here all he talked about was football, Bradford City in particular. Back home, if I need to know what time it is I have to ask my mother. I only hope he told her what he's planning, if only to give her warning that he's going to be in her way, full-time!'

Ignoring his son's less than flattering remarks, Sonny told the others, 'To be fair, the post of chairman of this group is little more than a sinecure anyway. The companies within it are so well run that all the chairman does is act as a figurehead. The way I see it, you could select a new chairman from among the five of you without causing them undue stress or weakening the executive strength. In fact, the more I think about it, that would be the best solution. However, if you want time to consider the options available to you, I'd be happy to delay my departure for a while. I would also recommend advising Luke Fisher and his colleagues down under of my intention.'

* * *

In Australia, Luke Fisher had been delighted the previous year when he'd received the trading results from the auditors. The performance of Fisher Springs Pty had been the best for many years. With wool prices at almost a record high, and every sector of the Australian economy booming, the group he controlled, with fingers in almost every pie, had taken full advantage of the excellent trading conditions. As Luke had examined the figures in detail, he'd got further satisfaction from noting that every sector had contributed to the profits, with most divisions achieving record results.

If there were danger signals in the cause of these remarkable figures, the euphoria they caused blinded Luke and his fellow directors to them. To be fair to the Fisher Springs board members, their auditors had also failed to point these out. Blinkered vision is easy when all you can see is precisely what you want to be there. Nor was it only in the confines of the Fisher Springs boardroom and their auditors' offices that such ominous signs were ignored.

Added fuel to the fire of economic woes came from a balance of payments crisis, putting additional pressure on the already troubled exchange rate. It was a desperate situation, requiring desperate measures to rectify it. Fortunately, before it was too late to apply a healing remedy within Fisher Springs, Luke and Bella discussed the matter at home. The outcome became a crucial factor within the group's defence mechanism against the crisis sweeping the nation.

'I've been looking through every newspaper and trade publication issued over the past eighteen months that I could get my hands on,' Luke told her. 'I've been checking the financial statistics as and when they appear, and I've also been examining our purchasing policy in the manufacturing division. What I've discovered is a bit disturbing, to put it mildly. However, I'm not certain whether I'm drawing the correct conclusions, or whether I'm reading too much into the figures, so I'd value your opinion on what I've found.'

'Have you run these past Josh and Elliot?' Bella asked, indicating the mound of paperwork on their dining table.

Luke shook his head. 'No, I wanted to hear what you think before I dump it on them.'

'OK, bung the paperwork across here, put the kettle on and I'll make a start. Looking at this lot, it might take a gallon of tea, if not more, to get through it.'

The next couple of hours passed predominantly in silence, punctuated by occasional requests from Bella for clarification on some points, or demands for more tea, before she eventually delivered her verdict.

'Although this is purely guesswork, as I haven't seen sufficient evidence to back up my theory, I'm prepared to hazard a guess that the root cause is down to the removal of import restrictions in 1960, combined with sweeping price increases here at home.'

'How did you arrive at that conclusion?'

'I can see in these figures a vast increase in the purchase of imported raw materials, and, without any change in the mark-up percentage, a huge array of price rises. If our group statistics are representative of the nation as a whole, I'd say we're riding for a fall.'

'That's more or less the same conclusion that I reached, but now the next step is to decide how to counteract such potentially dangerous conditions. My first thought is to consult with our UK colleagues, who have already put a raft of severe controls in place.' Luke paused before delivering his bombshell. 'I propose to deliver these statistics and my deductions from them at a board meeting tomorrow. I'd like you to attend that meeting.' He smiled and then added, 'I'd also like you to attend all subsequent board meetings.'

'Is that permitted? I thought only directors could attend without special dispensation.'

'That's correct, so you'd better become an executive director.'

* * *

When Luke's co-directors, Elliot Finnegan and Josh Jones, entered the boardroom the next day they were surprised to find Bella seated alongside her husband. Nor was Bella's presence there the only shock they were to receive.

They had anticipated the board meeting to be a run-of-the-mill event, but what followed was far from ordinary.

'I've asked Bella to sit in on today's meeting for two reasons,' Luke informed them. 'The first is to provide in-depth background to the huge amount of statistical information you are about to receive, and the second is to ratify my proposal for Bella to become a full-time board member of Fisher Springs and all subsidiary companies. This group has always been a family business, from the day my parents started it, and even when they took Patrick on board he soon became a family member. That's by no means the primary reason I want Bella as a director. She is shrewd, incisive and has a special insight for identifying potential problems, and providing solutions to them. Apart from all that, she's far better-looking than either of you two.'

Elliot and Josh were happy to agree to Luke's suggestion, and with Bella now officially a director, Luke was able to turn to the major item on the agenda. 'The folder in front of you contains a summary of research I've been carrying out both within the group and across the whole of Australia. It covers the past eighteen months and I want you to study the information carefully, ask whatever questions occur to you, and form your own conclusions. Once you've let us know what those impressions are, Bella and I will see if they match ours.'

Luke paused and turned to his wife. 'As the most recently elected board member, you are in charge of refreshments.'

Bella stared at her husband, before retorting, 'And I suppose you'll be maintaining your role as Work Avoidance Officer.'

Any attempt by Luke to retaliate was thwarted by the laughter from Elliot and Josh.

It was lunchtime, and several rounds of drinks, before Elliot and Josh finished their read-through of the statistical mountain. Luke suggested they take a break, gather their thoughts, and recommence the meeting after they'd eaten.

Once they reassembled, Luke asked Josh to lead off.

'These figures are disturbing,' Josh began, 'not only the ones from within the group but the bigger picture as well. I reckon we're heading for trouble.' He outlined his reasons for reaching that conclusion, echoing almost exactly the assumptions Luke and Bella had made.

Luke then turned to Elliot, who told him, 'I'm in total agreement with Josh, and the question I've been asking myself is, how can we prevent the situation from getting out of hand?'

'Bella and I have a potential solution. It's a very tough policy that might upset a lot of people, but I think the dire circumstances call for it. We believe we ought to adopt a similar strategy to that being used by our colleagues in the UK. The credit squeeze seems to have already hit their economy hard, so it shows the foresight their board displayed in taking the initiative to avoid potential disaster. With your agreement, I intend to cable them as a matter of urgency, to ask them for the nuts and bolts of their policy shift, so we can employ those we believe to be necessary here.'

Having drafted the telegram to their British subsidiary, Luke reviewed the contents and then added another section. When he was satisfied with the result he passed it over to Bella, who was now sharing his office, originally his parents'. After reading it through, she questioned him about the final paragraph.

'This bit' — she pointed at the paper — 'asking Paul Sugden to predict the way the economy might go is putting him on the spot, isn't it? He can't have much idea about conditions here, apart from what you've told him, which isn't a lot to go on.'

'That's true, but we've experienced Paul's forward thinking on several occasions, and his ideas have both saved, and earned, the whole group a ton of money, so there's nobody whose opinion I value more.'

'What if he gets it wrong this time?'

'That's a possibility, I admit, but I certainly won't hold it against him, even if it costs us money. It would take an economic disaster to put a hole in the profits Paul has earned for us by his innovative thinking.'

Having sent the telegram, Luke waited with growing impatience for the reply. When it hadn't arrived after two weeks, he voiced his disquiet. 'I hope there's nothing wrong over in England. They've never taken this long to respond before.'

'Remember, they have an outbreak of smallpox, Luke. I'm sure we would have heard if there was a problem. They may not even be in the office. But my guess is that Paul's weighing up the situation carefully before replying. If anything, that's a good sign, because it shows he's gathering all the facts and indicators he can, in order to deliver a well-thought-out assessment.'

Bella's reaction quelled Luke's impatience and a few days later, the reply arrived. The lengthy cable, as with all such communications, was in cipher, using the Bentley's code that had been the standard since Fisher Springs began trading. That meant a further delay for Luke until his secretary had deciphered it.

Luke and Bella studied the prognosis Sugden had provided. The telegram opened with a cautionary note that echoed Bella's earlier comments. '*Please bear in mind my opinion has been formed without in-depth knowledge of the state of the Australian economy.*' Paul explained in detail his reasoning, and the actions taken by the UK subsidiary of Fisher Springs, and the possible repercussions on the Australian economy as a whole.

'The big question is what are we to do about it?' Bella asked. 'Do we reject Paul's thesis as being too extreme and risk the repercussions, or pull our horns in and chance missing out on some lucrative profits?'

'Whichever route we choose, it's a decision that must be made by the full board, so let's get the others involved and try to work out our strategy in the face of this doomsday scenario.'

He suggested that all parties should be given sufficient time to consider the ramifications in depth. 'Let's all sleep on it and reconvene tomorrow morning.'

Next day they were of one mind, and the unanimous decision was to employ the strict disciplinary policies already in place in Britain as a template.

'This is going to put a brake on the group's expansion plans,' Luke suggested. 'That's primarily your department, Elliot. Have you anything in the pipeline that can't be halted? I'm thinking of contractual obligations we can't get out of without it costing us money.'

'There are a couple of acquisitions that are nearing completion. However, there's nothing in writing, so we can simply inform them the deal is off the table until further notice.' Elliot smiled wryly. 'Knowing the state of their finances, if half of what Paul Sugden forecasts is accurate, we might be able to pick them up for a song from the receivers.'

Luke turned to Josh and told him, 'I'll leave it to you to investigate the latest idea that Sugden mentioned, this bad-debt insurance.'

The plan would be put in place for a trial period. By the end of which, any measures the Treasury put in place would indicate the wisdom or otherwise of the scheme.

'When we've prepared a suitable policy I suggest we send a copy to Britain,' Bella proposed. 'I think that's the least we can do to show our appreciation and support.'

With the scheme up and running, the directors held a further meeting to discuss developments. The main topic for consideration was the recent budgetary announcement from the Treasury. 'The provisions of this prove the wisdom of the measures we've put in place,' Josh Jones commented. 'I think we're as prepared as possible for the potentially rocky economic conditions ahead.'

His colleagues agreed, but Bella went one further. 'It proves something else, too,' she said. 'It demonstrates the accuracy of Paul Sugden's predictions. Each and every clause in the Treasury statement mirrors those Paul put forward, almost exactly. I think we owe him a huge debt of gratitude.'

'We also owe one to Sonny Cowgill,' Luke said. 'I've had word from the UK that he plans to retire this year. He's been with the company since he left school, in the days of Haigh Ackroyd and Cowgill, excluding the war years of course. Did anyone realize he's almost seventy years old?'

'If we find out when that's to be, we should acknowledge it with a gift,' Bella suggested.

CHAPTER FIFTEEN

As March of 1962 drew to a close, there was little to indicate how radically things were about to change for at least one member of those resident in Scarborough.

Lizzie Cowgill's physical condition had improved dramatically. She was now reliant solely on a walking stick. When her father presented it to her, he said, 'This stick was bought originally for your grandfather, but sadly he didn't get much opportunity to use it. It has been gathering dust in a cupboard ever since. With luck, you won't need to use it for long, because your health is improving so rapidly.'

'I think much of that improvement is Gil's doing,' Rachael suggested.

Mark winked at his sister. 'Yes, and who knows, he might have more exercises up his sleeve for you to take part in with him — like dancing the horizontal tango.'

Lizzie blushed furiously as Jenny and Rachael castigated Mark for his lewd comment. Even if his suggestive comment came true, Lizzie knew there was no chance of that happening in the immediate future.

Until the end of May, Gil was on a residential tutorial that would enhance his status within the medical profession.

He was several hundred miles away from Scarborough — and from Lizzie.

Although she missed him more than she had thought possible, Lizzie took solace from the brevity of their separation, and hoped their relationship might enter a new dimension following his return, and perhaps then Mark's insinuation might come to pass.

A visitor who arrived in Byland Crescent towards the latter part of April put paid to any such aspirations.

Rachael tapped on Lizzie's door. 'There is someone here to see you,' her mother announced. 'An older gentleman. He said he was an old friend. When I asked his name, he told me it was Smith.'

Lizzie stared at her mother, astounded by the identity of her visitor. 'Did he say what he wanted?'

'No, he simply asked to speak with you.'

'OK, I'll come through.'

When Lizzie walked into the sitting room, employing the walking stick, her boss, Edrith Pointon, was standing by the window. Although she hadn't seen him in over three years, she was shocked to see how much that relatively short period of time seemed to have aged him.

'I see the code names haven't changed,' she said, as she invited him to take a seat, before closing the door.

Having answered his questions about her recovery and level of fitness, Lizzie waited, confident there was much more to the visit than to enquire about her health. When he did introduce the topic, the reason came as a complete, and unwelcome, surprise.

She listened intently as Pointon outlined developments that were threatening the stability of east/west relationships. 'The situation between America and Russia has been worsening over several years, as you know, and events such as the U-2 spy plane incident are only the tip of the iceberg, I'm afraid. With matters deteriorating almost day by day, I've been made aware of something in the very near future that could well tip the balance. There are a lot of seemingly trivial occurrences that would appear irrelevant to outsiders, ones hardly worthy of media attention, but the cumulative effect is very serious.'

After citing several instances, Pointon went on to present his conclusions. 'It is my belief, and one shared by many of my senior colleagues, that unless we deploy every asset available, this situation will become uncontrollable. Measures must be taken to alter the course of events. We are like a ship heading inexorably for the rocks, and unless the officers can muster every crew member to effect a change of direction, that collision will undoubtedly take place, with the consequent loss of life.'

He paused before adding one final, even grimmer foreboding. 'We are faced with an unprecedented threat, that of an all-out nuclear conflict, a war that will annihilate many millions of people, here in Britain, America, Russia and elsewhere. If such an event came to pass, one of the prime targets for Russian missiles will be our communications hub, which owing to the proximity to Irton Moor, and the new development being constructed at Fylingdales, will place this beautiful resort in extreme danger.'

Pointon took a deep breath. 'To prevent such a disaster, we need everyone with the capability to analyse and react to each development to forecast potential consequences, and put forward counter-measures that would prevent such a catastrophe. Three members of your team, ones you recruited many years ago, have been brought out of retirement, and I am here to ask you to reconsider your decision to leave the service, if only until such time as the situation is resolved — one way or another.'

Although Lizzie had merely said she would think it over, as he was leaving, Edrith Pointon was confident that he would soon be able to rely on the services of his most trusted assistant. There was one trump card he thought would sway her in the decision-making process, and he had left it until he was on the point of departure to play that card. His offer for Lizzie to take over, to head the department following his retirement, was, he felt certain, an offer too good for her to resist — providing any of them were still alive.

* * *

Although the family tried to discover the identity and reason for the mystery man's visit, they were unsuccessful. Mark came closest, when he urged her, 'Come on, Dizzy Lizzie, tell us what was so important the head of MI5 came all the way from Whitehall just to see my nutty sister.'

'I didn't say he was head of MI5.'

'All I can guess is it's to do with your retirement package, so where's the gold watch?'

'OK, he was from work.' She glared at her brother. 'And now, I don't know if I am going to retire. I thought so, but that was when I was confined to a wheelchair. Now I'm not so sure, because things have changed, so I'm thinking it over.'

Despite Lizzie's strict adherence to the Official Secrets Act, one of her actions directly after the visit outlined to the rest of the family that this had been no routine call. It was only a few days later, when Lizzie enlisted Jenny and Consuela's assistance, that the gravity of matters became apparent. 'There's something I need to check, and I'm not certain I can do it on my own. Although I can manage the staircase, there is something I want to do, but I don't want to undo all the good work by having an accident.'

'What is it you're thinking of doing?' Jenny asked.

'I want to go down to the cellar, and there's no handrail. I need someone with me in case I can't make it on my own.'

'What on earth for?'

'I need to check something, that's all. At least this time I won't bump into a pig — at least I hope not.'

Consuela stared at her, wondering if Lizzie was losing her mind, but Jenny began to laugh. 'Good heavens, I'd forgotten all about that.'

'Lucky you. I had nightmares about it for years.'

Jenny glanced sideways. 'I think we ought to explain to Consuela what we're talking about. At the moment she's beginning to wonder if we've both gone barmy.'

Lizzie smiled at Consuela, and told her, 'The incident happened in the early part of the war, when I was about twelve years old. Dad was a member of a pig club. Clubs were set up by the Ministry of Food, to help combat food shortages. Although rationing was severe, there was still not enough to go round, so people were encouraged to grow their own vegetables, where possible, or keep hens, and in some cases club together to sponsor a pig that was expecting a litter. When the sow farrowed, the Ministry would take all but one of the young ones, leaving the spare one to grow and be divided between the club members.

'Once the animal had been slaughtered, it had to hang for about a week, or ten days, prior to butchering. Our cellar was chosen as the most suitable place to store it. Unfortunately,' — Lizzie glared at her sister-in-law, who grinned, knowing what was coming — 'nobody had the good manners to warn me it was down there. So when I was sent downstairs to collect some eggs, I got the shock of my life when I came face to face with an enormous pig.'

'It scared the living daylights out of her,' Jenny added, clearly enjoying the memory. 'And I reckon some of the residents of Byland Crescent thought her screams were a new form of air raid siren being tested.'

The strategy they adopted for descent involved Jenny walking backwards with extreme caution, preceding Lizzie. Consuela was one step behind her, holding on to a strong belt around Lizzie's waist. Slowly but surely, the trio made it safely to the bottom.

'OK, Lizzie, what prompted the urgent need for us to risk life and limb visiting this place?' Jenny asked.

Lizzie smiled wryly. 'You might have been closer than you think when you mentioned "life and limb", Jenny. Let me have a closer look at this salubrious apartment.'

Her companions were bemused as they watched Lizzie inspect the walls, the floor and the ceiling, paying particular attention to the two long, shallow windows near to the roof on one side of the building. The exterior surface of the windows would be at ground level or thereabouts. 'Those will have to go,' Lizzie muttered, but gave no explanation for her odd comment.

Eventually, she declared herself satisfied. 'I think it's a long way from ideal, but it's the best option open to us, given the time span available. It will take a fair amount of effort, but it might work.'

Jenny and Consuela renewed their appeals for enlightenment, but Lizzie asked them to remain patient for a few hours. 'I think it would be better for everyone, except Suzie, to hear what I have to say. We'll leave it until tonight, shall we?' With that, Lizzie mounted the cellar steps, this time with both women behind her.

* * *

That evening, ensuring Suzie was occupied elsewhere, the family gathered in the sitting room. Lizzie said, 'I'm sure you'll all have heard about my strange expedition to the cellar by now. Before I explain why, I want you all to promise me you won't repeat a word of what I'm about to tell you.'

She looked at her father and brother. 'I'm particularly concerned that you don't say anything at the office, Dad, Mark. Will you both give me your word on this?'

'OK, Lizzie, but you'd better explain soon, because everyone in this room apart from me thinks you've gone bonkers. Of course, I've known you were bonkers for years,' Mark added.

Lizzie smiled at her brother's insult, but her expression became serious. 'I know we used the cellar as an air raid shelter during the war, and it was perfectly adequate. However, after I carried out my inspection today, I realized that it is no longer fit for purpose with advances in weaponry over the years. We are now faced with far deadlier, more powerful armaments than we were then. My suggestion for dealing with this would be to strengthen the walls and ceilings, block up the windows, and put other measures in place, such as an enclosed ventilation system. If we do that, the cellar will serve as a temporary shelter.' She paused, unsure how they would react to her final statement. 'In effect — a nuclear bunker.'

She waited while the family, all staring at her aghast, absorbed the terrible implications of the word "nuclear".

'I said a temporary measure, because there is no way in the event of a nuclear explosion it would serve as anything but a short-term solution. If the occupants of the cellar survive such a blast, they will only be able to stay there for a very short time, so they will need to make a plan beforehand to enable them to escape to somewhere free of contamination from radiation.'

Every member of the family stared at Lizzie, dumbfounded by her statement. Eventually, it was her brother who correctly identified the source of her concern. 'I take it you believe there is a possibility of such an awful event happening? And my guess is that you've reached that conclusion as a result of the conversation with your visitor?'

'I wish I could explain, but I'm unable to do that. In fact, I shouldn't have said anything, but I couldn't simply walk away without forewarning those I care about.'

Lizzie paused, and took a deep breath before continuing, the emotion of the moment threatening to overcome her. 'What is more distressing for me is I have decided I must return to work. I cannot say for how long or where I will be stationed, because both those factors are beyond my control. I must do my duty, because that is the only way I know to try and keep the ones I love safe.'

Once again it was Mark who identified the root of Lizzie's concern and the reason for her decision. 'Russia? Why would Britain be on Nikita Khrushchev's hit list? Unless there is more to those stories that we read in the press, or other things going on we haven't heard about.'

Lizzie stared at her brother for a moment. 'I can't reveal anything I was told, Mark. Either one of your theories could be correct, but I couldn't confirm, or deny, such information. All I will say is sometimes you're a heck of a lot more intelligent than you look. Mind you,' she added with a flash of her old humour, 'that wouldn't be difficult.'

Her barbed comment brought a few smiles, but it was Sonny who summed up their situation, bringing the sobriety of the meeting into focus. 'I am immensely proud of you, Lizzie. Your choice to separate yourself from those you love, and who care for you, is very noble. I think it is similar in many respects to the heartrending quandary faced by young men and women at the outbreak of two world wars. They were prepared to sacrifice the life they knew when faced with an uncertain future, and your rejoining the ranks is an equally heroic act.

'I think all we can do is wait, hope and pray. Though I wonder if it might be best for the younger members of the family to move inland for a while where they'll be in a less sensitive area. I remember the hundreds of thousands of children who were evacuated from the big cities at the outbreak of World War Two. Many of them would have been killed in air raids had they remained in their homes. I'm particularly concerned for Andy, Consuela and baby James, plus Suzie. I think they should be out of harm's way.'

Andy glanced at Consuela before answering, 'We're not going anywhere. I can't speak for Suzie, but this is our home, and if it means we perish here, so be it. Let's not panic. No matter how bad things seem at present, I reckon they'll have to get much worse before someone is stupid enough to press the red button. In any case,' he added, with a flash of humour, 'how would you old folks get to sleep without Suzie's gentle lullabies to soothe us?'

One of the grimmest reminders of how close the potential disaster was came via a phrase that became widely used throughout Britain. The 'four-minute warning' referred to the time between an alert of incoming missiles and impact. The alarm would be via sirens, radio and television.

Later, when Mark and Jenny were alone, she asked, 'What should we do if the worst does happen? From what

I've read, that four-minute warning might not be sufficient for us to reach the cellar, if we're upstairs for instance.'

'If things get that bad, we could always go to bed and make love for one last time.'

Jenny thought this over for a moment and then asked, 'OK, but what should we do for the other three minutes?'

CHAPTER SIXTEEN

The following morning, before departing for Bradford, Mark sought out Lizzie and assured her he would reveal nothing of the previous night's disclosure. 'One more thing,' he added, as he turned to leave, 'despite all the teasing, I hope you know I love and respect you. See you tonight, Dizzy Lizzie.'

That was by no means the only emotionally torn conversation Lizzie had that day. As they were drinking their mid-morning cup of tea, Rachael asked Lizzie, 'When are you planning on leaving?'

Her mother's question, and the obvious concern in her voice, moved Lizzie, and it was a few seconds before she was able to reply. 'The day after tomorrow. I'm going by train. I would have taken the car, but I'm not confident of driving the distance.'

'I thought you didn't know where you were to be sent?'

'I don't — all I was told was to report to headquarters.'

'That sounds a bit daft. What if you get all the way to London and they send you back to Filey, or Whitby?'

'It does seem absurd, but I doubt that will be the case. I'll most likely be in London for the time being, then maybe somewhere else, either here in England or abroad. It all depends how things go.'

If Lizzie was upset about the thought of leaving, Jenny's question proved even more distressing. 'What about Gil? Are you going to tell him what's going on?'

'I've thought about it, but I'm going to write him a letter explaining things as best I can. I'll leave it with you, Mum, so you can give it to him when you see him, if that's OK?'

'Of course.' Rachael reached across and patted Lizzie's hand.

'Isn't that dodging the issue, Lizzie?' Jenny asked. 'It almost appears like a cowardly way out.'

Lizzie winced at Jenny's criticism. 'That isn't why I'm doing it. Gil's right in the middle of a highly intensive training course that will advance his career no end. It would be most unfair to burden him with my news, because from what he told me before he set off, he'll have more than enough to contend with, so a distraction such as this would be unreasonable.'

Although she had refuted Jenny's allegation of cowardice, Lizzie was too upset to dwell on the personal aspect of her relationship with Gil, and this showed in the distinctly neutral tone of the letter she sat down to compose. Ending the relationship was bad enough, and she had only one tiny crumb of comfort — and even that was a double-edged sword.

How much worse would it have been, she thought, if they had become lovers in the physical sense of the word? Even as she considered it, Lizzie acknowledged that for a long while she had wanted Gil to take her to bed, wanted them to make love over and over again. That hadn't happened, and now she felt certain it never would. It was a long time before she recovered her equilibrium sufficiently to put her decision into words.

She'd wanted to write, *My dearest, darling Gil,* but thought it better not to go down that route. Instead, she began:

Dear Gil,

I hope the course has been successful and will lead to a bright future for you. Perhaps in the years to come your eminence in the field of medicine will be recognized. I would have posted this letter to you, but I feel certain you need to avoid any distractions at the moment.

I am writing to tell you that by the time you receive it, I will have left Scarborough. Over the years, my work has been the most important aspect of my life, and events now call for me to return to the job which has become a vocation.

I have no idea at this point in time where I will end up, or how long I will be away, or even if I will ever be able to return. Although I will be sad to leave the people who have become dear to me, in which I include you, it has now become clear to me that my action is necessary.

So this is farewell, and in saying it, I wish you all the best for the bright, happy and successful future you deserve.

She avoided adding a valedictory message, merely signing her name. She read the text once again, and as she sealed the envelope she felt certain she had done the right thing. Her intention had been to prevent her emotions boiling over into her words, which might cause him further distress. In doing this, Lizzie had forgotten the old saying 'the road to hell is paved with good intentions'.

* * *

Gil Richardson was weary. The intensity of the course he had attended, run by the Royal College of Surgeons, had drained him more than he had anticipated. Although the outcome had been spectacularly successful, Gil was now keen to reach Scarborough, to meet the woman he loved and to hold Lizzie in his arms once again.

As he travelled north, Gil read the newspapers he had bought at the station kiosk to while away the train journey. Such had been the rigorous nature of the tutorials and the long hours involved that he and his colleagues had been unable to follow events occurring in the outside world. One of the course tutors had commented on this, telling the pupils,

'The regime has been designed specifically to mirror the conditions you will face if and when you leave here to pursue your new goals. The long, tiring and back-breaking daily grind of a practising surgeon will test you to the extreme.'

He ignored the papers, preferring instead to concentrate on what was awaiting him when he reached Scarborough. The weeks spent away from Lizzie had convinced him they belonged together, not merely for the present, but for all time. With this in mind, before going to the station to catch the train, he had visited a jeweller's shop, where he purchased a diamond-encrusted engagement ring.

Gil headed straight for Byland Crescent. As he walked from the station through the town, carrying his suitcase in one hand, anyone seeing him would have assumed he was yet another of the mass of tourists who visited the resort during the summer months.

He stood for a moment outside Lizzie's home, then climbed the steps to the front door and rang the bell. The housekeeper opened it, smiled, and invited him in, telling him she would inform Mrs Cowgill he was here.

He put his suitcase down and waited in the hall. He assumed Lizzie must be out or Mary would have directed him to her.

Gil was surprised to see Rachael's normally cheerful expression change to one of wary dismay.

'Oh, Gil, er . . . please, come inside.'

He followed Rachael into the sitting room, surprised and a little confused.

'I . . . er . . . have something for you.' She plucked an envelope from a drawer in the sideboard and gave him it. 'Lizzie left this for you.'

'Left it? I don't understand. Isn't she here?' Noticing from her expression that Rachael obviously knew far more than she had indicated, he was concerned when she told him, 'I think you should read the letter.'

Gil ripped the envelope open and scanned the single sheet of paper. Rachael noticed his hands beginning to tremble as he absorbed the message. After several agonizingly silent moments he looked up, staring at Rachael, or possibly beyond her, before he reached into his pocket. He removed a small, square box and gave it to her.

'You might as well keep this. If you see your daughter again, kindly give it to her. I have no further use for it.' His tone was harsh, at total variance to his usual gentle manner.

With that, he turned abruptly and marched from the room and down the hall. It was as well the front door was constructed from stout oak timber, Rachael thought. A flimsier one would probably have disintegrated from the force with which he slammed it shut.

She looked down at the box in the palm of her hand, then opened the lid and stared at the contents. The diamonds in their gold setting shone brightly. Rachael felt tears welling up and began to weep. She cried for her daughter, who had abandoned her chance of happiness, and for Gil, whose whole world had just come crashing down around him.

A week later, when the family had come to terms with the traumatic event described by Rachael, a letter arrived at Byland Crescent for Lizzie. Although it was addressed to Miss Elizabeth Cowgill, Rachael guessed that it might have come from Gil Richardson — but it was a considerable time before her suspicion was confirmed.

* * *

Although the Cuban missile incident in October attracted attention, certain people who read or heard of the failed invasion had other problems that preoccupied their time. In Australia, the directors of Fisher Springs were struggling to come to terms with the new difficulties arising from the changed economic climate throughout the country. It was the first time in a long number of years that Australia had been faced with a recession, and only a small percentage of the population had experienced such a thing, and knew instinctively how to cope with it.

For the executives charged with steering Fisher Springs' head office through the stormy waters, their business had one great disadvantage compared to their British counterparts. In the Bradford office, Sonny Cowgill, and to a lesser extent Jessica Binks, knew only too well how devastating the effects of a sudden economic downturn could be. In Sonny's case, the Wall Street Crash of 1929 and the Great Depression that resulted from it and dragged through the greater part of the 1930s had posed great difficulties.

As head of the UK sales division of the group back then, Sonny had faced the twin problems of finding clients to sell to, and thereafter ensuring those clients paid for the goods they had bought. The wounds caused by those who failed to make it still remained vivid.

For Jessica, the memory was yet more poignant. Although she had been only fifteen years of age when shares on Wall Street and elsewhere went into free fall, the consequences were highly personal. Overnight, her mother's portfolio of stocks became of no use, save as firelighters. Faced with bankruptcy and with a murder charge hanging over her, Charlotte Tunnicliffe had committed suicide.

Occasionally, when a stray thought or occurrence brought recollection of that grim period in her life, Jessica would have nightmares in which she relived the moment when she walked home from school, and entered the house, to find her lifeless parent hanging from the banister rail.

* * *

As Christmas of 1962 approached, Rachael Cowgill reflected that it would be a far quieter, less exuberant celebration than in the previous year. The reduced number of those sitting down at the festive table was one reason for this, the cause for some of the absentees' desertion being a greater one. Rachael had not heard from Lizzie since she'd returned to her post earlier that year, and there seemed little chance of her joining the family for the festive season.

Neither had any of the family seen or heard from Lizzie's boyfriend, Gil Richardson, since Rachael handed him Lizzie's letter, explaining her actions and attempting to justify them. The image of his haunted expression on reading the letter still troubled Rachael deeply.

She was more than a little surprised, therefore, when she received a phone call from Lizzie. She explained, as best she could, why she had been unable to make contact earlier, adding that she would be working over Christmas, so would be unable to join the family. She had hesitated before asking her mother if she had given the letter to Gil.

On hearing her mother's confirmation, Lizzie asked, 'How is he? Have you seen him recently? Has anyone been in touch with him?'

'I've no idea. We haven't seen hide or hair of him since the day I handed him your letter. I can tell you this, though — he was far from happy.'

'Oh no, I hoped he would have understood why I had to do this. I did write to him again, almost a month ago, asking him to reply via Byland Crescent. Has a letter arrived for me in the past couple of weeks or so?'

'No, there's been nothing for you recently, other than a letter that came at the beginning of June, just after he returned. That might be from Gil.'

'Have you got it handy? Would you open it and read it out to me, please?'

Rachael put the handset down, and opened the drawer beneath the telephone to retrieve the envelope.

Seconds later, Lizzie heard the sound of paper tearing, followed by a long silence that seemed to last for an age. Eventually, impatient as ever, she demanded, 'Is it from Gil? What does it say?'

'Yes, Lizzie, it is from Gil, but I'm not sure you'll want to hear what he's written.'

'Tell me please, Mum. I'm a big girl now. I can stand it.'

'I will if you insist. "*I cannot argue with your decision, because I don't know what prompted it. Even if I did know, you didn't hang around to tell me face-to-face. What I now realize, from the choice you made, coupled with the fact that you didn't have the courage or good manners to tell me it in person, is how little I mean to you. That saddens me, because I know how much I love you.*"'

Rachael paused and said, 'He's crossed the word "love" out and replaced it with "loved". He then goes on, *"Was I nothing more to you than an amusement, a way of passing time and preventing boredom until you were ready to return to whatever it is you do to the exclusion of all else? I cannot write anything further, for I am weary of the topic. I now accept that this is the end for us. Thank you for ruining my life.*"'

Reading the letter had distressed Rachael so much it was several moments before she was sufficiently composed to ask Lizzie what she intended to do. The reply was so disjointed it was almost incomprehensible, from which Rachael guessed Lizzie was in tears. However, she managed to decipher enough to learn that Lizzie's intention was to phone Gil.

'If you are going to call him, I'd better tell you about what he left here for you.'

'What was that?'

'Before he left, he handed me a jeweller's box containing a diamond engagement ring. He told me he had no further use for it. That was just before he attempted to knock the front door off its hinges on his way out.'

The only sound Rachael could hear was that of her daughter sobbing, until, after what seemed an age, the line went dead.

She was even more surprised when, only twenty-four hours later, Lizzie rang again. As she listened, Rachael could tell how upset Lizzie was, and wondered what had passed between her and Gil to cause this. She soon realized that the truth was even more distressing.

'I rang Gil's home number and got a recorded message saying that number had been disconnected, so I tried the hospital. The person on the switchboard said they had nobody by the name of Dr Richardson working there, so I managed to get through to their personnel department and they told me that Gil resigned in early June.'

'Did they say why? Has he got another job elsewhere?'

'I don't know, Mum. I asked if they've received a request for a reference and they said not, and nor do they have a forwarding address for him. He's vanished, Mum, completely and utterly vanished. I need to find him. I need to know he's OK. Everything I did was wrong, I realize that now. I had no idea he'd take it so much to heart. I wish I could go look for him, but as things are at present there's no chance of that.'

Rachael thought for a moment. 'I have an idea, Lizzie. What if I get Mark to go round to Gil's old flat and find out if he's sold it, and if the people there know where he's gone?'

'Thanks, Mum, please do. It might be a while before I can get back to you though. I must go now. Give everyone my love, even Mark.'

The flash of humour in Lizzie's final remark was the only light note in their conversation.

CHAPTER SEVENTEEN

In Bradford, just before Mark left the office, Jessica had taken him to one side, telling him, 'We've been so busy we still haven't finalized who should take on your father's role as Chairman. When he said he'd stay on, I don't think he meant indefinitely. It's almost a year since he announced his intention.'

Mark had told her, 'We can attend to that officially at the next board meeting, but I've already sounded Dad and Paul Sugden out, and I think Harry will agree with the majority. We all think you should be appointed Chairman. With all your background before you joined us, you're the ideal person. That only leaves David to convince, and I feel sure you can think of a way to persuade him.'

'Why, Mark, whatever do you mean?'

He grinned, but declined to answer her question.

Jessica then asked him a couple of questions, the purpose of which baffled him at the time. He'd answered them as best he could, before asking why she wanted the information. 'It's a secret,' she'd replied, 'but hopefully you'll find out soon enough.'

Now, following what was to be Sonny's final meeting, with Jessica, in her new role, she announced, 'Before everyone leaves, I have one other task to perform. Will you all follow me, please?' Although three of them knew what was coming, Sonny and Mark had no idea. She led them all to the general office where Sonny was greeted by all the office staff. A large cake was centrepiece on one of the desks. Jessica signalled to Harry, who walked to the corner of the room and returned with a large box.

She addressed Sonny. 'You have served the group with great distinction for many years, and this is from our colleagues in Australia, as a token of their respect for you.'

Sonny was taken aback at the size of the box, as he delved inside to reveal a beautiful sheepskin rug.

'I am assured this is from one of Fisher Springs' own flock,' Jessica told him. 'And now, this is a token of *our* appreciation for the work, the wisdom, and dedication you have put in. I asked Mark how you intend to spend your retirement years, and he told me you and Rachael have decided to take up walking as a means of keeping fit, and exploring our beautiful county.'

The gathered staff laughed as she explained, 'I had to rely on Mark to give me the sizes. So if these are not suitable, you must blame him. You must also let me know and we will gladly replace them.' With that, she handed two long boxes to Sonny, adding, 'Unwrap this one, and leave the other as a surprise for Rachael.'

Sonny unfastened the paper, to reveal a stout, intricately carved walking cane in the form of a shepherd's crook, with the handle terminating in a ram's head depicted in silver. 'Try it for size,' Jessica urged him as Sonny stared in delight at the cane.

'It's absolutely perfect,' he told them after two circuits of the office. 'Thank you so much, everyone. I will treasure this, and I know Rachael will love hers.'

'Better than a gold watch, Dad?' Mark asked.

'No comparison.'

Following Sonny's emotional farewell to his co-directors and other members of staff, Mark and his father returned to Scarborough.

Mark reflected on the year that was drawing to a close. 'I'll be glad when New Year comes. I won't be at all sorry to see the back of 1962. I don't think next year can be anywhere near as bad as this one's been.'

His words went unheeded, as Sonny was still admiring his retirement gift. His pleasure was echoed by Rachael after he presented her with the other cane.

* * *

On the evening of 12 December, Andy had been sent outside to the coal bunker in order to replenish the empty scuttles and bring in some more logs. When his mother charged him with this errand, he'd protested. 'I filled them this morning before I went to the shop, and I also brought some wood in. Don't tell me you've gone through it already?'

'We have, and that's because the weather has turned much colder. You've been so ensconced with your business that you haven't noticed.'

When Andy returned indoors, his black overcoat he had donned for the task was liberally covered in white blotches, giving him the appearance of a Dalmatian dog that had been turned inside out. He paused on the threshold, put his load to one side, then shook his coat and stamped his feet. This caused most of the white specks to cascade onto the mat.

'I'm sorry I didn't believe you, Mum. I'm not surprised we've gone through a load of fuel today. There's a blizzard raging outside and the path is already an inch deep in snow.'

Although the snow in Scarborough and the surrounding area was relatively light, reports from elsewhere in the country suggested much heavier falls. Even when the snow ceased, the temperature remained close to zero, causing Sonny to remark, 'It looks as if we're in for a long, cold winter, similar perhaps to 1947.' He grimaced as he said it, for it had been during the 1947 snows that his sister Connie had died.

Reflecting on his comment later, Rachael reckoned it had to be one of the biggest understatements of all time, and that perhaps a new career awaited her husband as a weather forecaster. Before long, however, she and the other members of the family had another, far greater priority to deal with.

Late on Saturday afternoon, just three days before Christmas, a passenger emerged from Scarborough station and hailed a taxi for the short journey to Byland Crescent. As the driver stowed the luggage in his car boot, noting two suitcases and a holdall, he reflected that it was an odd time of year for a holidaymaker to visit the resort. After decanting the passenger and luggage outside the address, he drove quickly back to the station, hoping to be in time to pick up another fare.

Rachael was crossing the hallway when the doorbell rang. She opened the door to see her younger daughter standing outside, a look of distress on her face.

'Lizzie darling, what a wonderful surprise.' Rachael stepped forward and hugged her, a long, close embrace. 'Are you here for the holidays, or longer?' she asked, noticing the amount of luggage.

'I'm home for good, Mum, if you'll have me.'

'Don't talk silly, of course we'll have you, darling. Come on in out of the cold.' Still holding Lizzie's hand, she guided her into the hallway. Rachael raised her voice. 'Mark, Andy, come here, I have work for you.'

When they appeared, Rachael ordered them to bring the suitcases inside. Then she took Lizzie into the sitting room. The rapture of her mother's greeting was echoed by the warm welcome from all the other family members. Their pleasure was enhanced when she confirmed that this time she was going to stay and would not be returning to her job, at any price. Their reaction to her news removed the last vestige of doubt in Lizzie's mind that she was welcome here — and always would be.

Before starting to unpack her cases, Lizzie demanded to see her godson. Andy and Consuela escorted her upstairs, where she admired the sleeping infant. 'Look how he's grown. I am so sorry I was unable to be part of all this,' Lizzie told them in a whisper.

'Never mind,' Andy replied, 'just make sure you're available next time.'

'Does that mean . . . ?'

'Not yet,' Consuela told her, 'despite Andy's best efforts.'

They retreated downstairs, as their combined giggles, enhanced by Andy's glare of disapproval, were threatening to wake James.

Even Mark, who had always taken great delight in teasing and tormenting his younger sibling, expressed his pleasure at Lizzie's return, albeit in his own way. 'I think this calls for a celebration,' he announced. 'I'm going down to the nuclear bunker for some bottles of wine.' He winked at Consuela as he told Lizzie, 'For some reason I haven't quite fathomed, my daughter-in-law always insists we buy some stuff called Rioja, and I have to admit it is rather good.'

Over the evening meal, Lizzie explained what had happened to cause her sudden return. 'When I was persuaded to return to work, I agreed because as part of the package, Pointon promised me that when he retired, I would replace him as head of the unit. It turns out that promise wasn't in his remit to make. Had I known that, I probably wouldn't have agreed to go.'

Mark stared at his sister as he recognized the name given to him by Jessica at the time of Lizzie's injury. Now he knew who her boss really was.

Lizzie paused and took a sip of her wine. 'When it became known that he would be leaving at the end of next March, I duly submitted my application for the post. On Wednesday of this week I was called into a meeting. I assumed I was about to undergo an interview, prior to being confirmed for the job. How wrong that assumption was.

'I won't name the three men sitting there, not because of the Official Secrets Act, but because I despise them, and everything they stand for. The chief cretin, who considers himself to be a big noise, started on me as soon as I walked through the door. He held up my letter, between finger and thumb, as if it was something distasteful. The only distasteful part was what he said. "Is this some sort of joke? What possesses you to believe we would entertain appointing a woman to such a high-ranking position? You appear to have got ideas above your station. Kindly return to your post and do whatever it is we pay you for instead of living in a fantasy world". That was pretty much it.'

'What did you do?' Sonny asked.

'I hope you instructed him to stick his job,' Mark suggested.

Lizzie smiled ruefully. 'More or less. I told them I wasn't prepared to work for the likes of them any longer. I asked if they had any prospective candidates in mind, such as their bum chums, Donald Maclean or Guy Burgess.'

'Aren't they alleged Russian spies?' Mark asked.

Lizzie just shrugged her shoulders and gave him a pointed look. 'I finished by telling them there were other traitors lurking in the corridors of Whitehall, but they were obviously too thick to spot them. Then I went back to my desk, wrote a note on an internal memo saying *"I resign"*, signed and dated it, then walked out of the building. I handed my security pass to the guard at the entrance, and went back to the grotty flat I'd been renting and began packing.'

'Was that the end of the matter?' Sonny asked.

'Not quite, Dad. Twenty-four hours later they sent one of their minions as an emissary pleading with me to go back. I sent him away with a flea in his ear. At first I thought he'd come because of what I did before leaving the department, but obviously that hasn't come to light yet. They won't discover it until they need to go into the vaults.'

'I hope you didn't plant a bomb in there?'

Lizzie smiled at Mark's absurd suggestion. 'No, I wouldn't do anything so extreme. What the cretins failed to take into account is that I am one of only three people who know the combination required to gain entry to the vaults, so I simply wandered down there and changed it. The beauty of the system is that if they enter the wrong digits it will trigger an alarm and the whole building will go into lockdown.'

'Bravo,' Mark said approvingly. 'They deserve everything they get for treating someone with your outstanding ability in such a shabby manner.'

Lizzie stared at him, barely able to associate her brother with such complimentary remarks. She was almost in tears, and her mother's next question did little to settle her seething emotions.

'Have you any regrets?'

'About leaving the service? No. My only regret is over the way I treated Gil, but that's something I will have to deal with, if and when I find him.'

Having Lizzie back in the fold added to the contentment of the family, with another setting at the Christmas dinner table.

The warmth of the close-knit family unit was in sharp contrast to the weather outside Byland Crescent and elsewhere in the country. The anticyclone that had brought the earlier cold snap had been replaced with another, centred over Iceland, bringing strong, cold, northerly winds and heavy snowfall. This, although they didn't know it, was merely the preface to one of the coldest winters on record.

* * *

In Australia, Luke and Bella Fisher, their children and extended family sat down to a Christmas dinner menu that was in marked contrast to the one enjoyed in Byland Crescent.

Whereas the turkey that formed the centrepiece was served hot in Scarborough, in the Fisher household the entire meal was cold.

Luke, who had spent several Yuletide seasons in England during his service with the Royal Air Force, commented on the difference, to which Bella replied, 'I can't say I'm surprised. The weather over there is cold even at the best of times, as I recall. In fact I saw a report in one of our newspapers yesterday that suggested they were in for a white Christmas, with sub-zero temperatures for the extent of the forecast. The last thing they'd want is a cold meal. I looked at the thermometer in the garden this morning and it was already registering almost seventy degrees Fahrenheit, and that was before nine o'clock. It could hit ninety later! That doesn't give me much inclination for hot food, or eating indoors for that matter.'

They had been joined for the celebrations by Luke's sister Dottie, along with her husband Elliot and their three children. Also sitting down for the meal with them was Luke's widowed sister-in-law Amelia, together with her daughter Clare, recently promoted to sergeant. Commenting as the throng assembled on the veranda, Luke told Bella, 'I reckon it's as well we're eating outside. I know our dining room's big, but I'm not sure it would cope with so many guests.'

Across town, one of Luke and Bella's co-directors, Josh Jones, was partaking of Christmas dinner in a much smaller, though equally noisy gathering. Alongside Josh were his wife Astrid, their daughter Daisy and the main source of the sound, their second child, Naomi, named after Josh's mother. The principal reason for the infant's racket-making was that she was in the painful process of teething, but her requests for sustenance could prove equally vocal.

In both households, the party spirit was enhanced, if that was needed, by wine from the vineyard owned in part by Luke Fisher. Twenty-five years earlier, prior to the outbreak of World War Two, Luke had purchased the land on which the vineyard stood, going into partnership with his friend Gianni Rocca and Gianni's wife Angelina. The first planting had been destroyed by vandals. Being of Italian ancestry, the couple had met with a good deal of hostility during the war, Gianni even being interned. Their children had been bullied, Angelina had been refused service in the local shops, and it was only when the war ended and Luke came home that life returned to normal and the partners could concentrate on turning the land into a productive vineyard.

The vines were replanted in 1949, an event which coincided with the birth of Gianni and Angelina's youngest child. Because the baby girl was unusually fair-haired, Angelina suggested they name her Flavia, meaning golden in Italian. Flavia's arrival came only six months after Luke and Bella's eldest son Jimmy was born. At the time, Gianni remarked to Luke, 'It would have been nice to celebrate the two events with some wine from our own vineyard, but that might have to wait until their fifth birthday.'

Gianni's and Angelina's families had a combined heritage of viniculture, having lived for several generations in the wine-producing region of Italy. This inherited expertise became apparent as the couple tackled the long, arduous and labour-intensive process of rearing the small plants, tending them as they grew into mature vines, and waiting for them to produce fruit.

Four years had passed before the vines they had so lovingly cultivated produced full, deliciously tasty bunches of grapes. Not that Gianni, Angelina or the small workforce they employed had been idle during that waiting period. Protective measures to guard the vines and their fruit had to be put in place if they were to have any hope of success.

The process involved construction of canopies stretching over and surrounding the crops, to shield them from predators, both land-based and avian. During this, the couple's reputation increased locally, as their workers reported their willingness to tackle even the most menial, back-breaking tasks alongside their employees. Eventually, Gianni had been able to telephone Luke to inform him that fruit was now of suitable quality to harvest for production. He was due to begin, and had invited him to observe the event.

Luke and Bella had driven to the vineyard to inspect the first crop, and had been surprised to see a new sign outside the gate. From there they could see the acres of netting stretching up the slope as far as the horizon. Gianni, who had been watching for their arrival, greeted them, and in response to Bella's question, explained the meaning of the sign. 'Now we are able to produce grapes suitable to make wine, we thought it important to give the vineyard a name, so that people will remember it when they buy the bottles.'

'What does it mean?' Bella had asked.

'Angelina and I talked it over and decided it was the most appropriate we could think of. Because the vineyard is on a slope, we thought the name *Luca Collina*, which is Italian for Luke's Hill, would be best.'

Luke was touched by this, and Bella had responded, 'It certainly rolls off the tongue. Let's hope a lot of tongues soon get to taste the produce.'

Now, nine years down the line, the wine produced under the label *Luca Collina* was beginning to earn a good reputation, and when it came to Christmas celebrations, Luke and Bella were happy to share the cases Gianni and Angelina had delivered personally a couple of weeks earlier.

During the party that had ensued on their visit to deliver wine to the Fisher house, Luke and Bella's son Jimmy, approaching his fourteenth birthday, had taken his seat at the dining table alongside an outstandingly pretty girl of about his own age. She introduced herself as Flavia. Jimmy, who had been attracted to one or two girls in his school, knew that none of them could hold a candle to this stunning blonde bombshell. His sister Robyn, and younger brother Saul, aged twelve and ten respectively, dug each other in the ribs, and grinned at their big brother. Jimmy ignored them, and within minutes of getting into conversation with Flavia, he was smitten. Sadly, once the visitors left for the long journey home, he realized there was little or no chance of him being able to further the relationship at such a distance.

PART THREE: 1963–1969

Two roads diverged in a yellow wood,
And sorry I could not travel both
And be one traveler, long I stood
And looked down one as far as I could
To where it bent in the undergrowth;

Then took the other, as just as fair,
And having perhaps the better claim,
Because it was grassy and wanted wear;
Though as for that the passing there
Had worn them really about the same,

And both that morning equally lay
In leaves no step had trodden black.
Oh, I kept the first for another day!
Yet knowing how way leads on to way,
I doubted if I should ever come back.

I shall be telling this with a sigh
Somewhere ages and ages hence:
Two roads diverged in a wood, and I—
I took the one less traveled by,
And that has made all the difference.

The Road Not Taken
Robert Frost

CHAPTER EIGHTEEN

Once the Christmas and New Year festivities were over, the priorities of Fisher Springs' executives, both in Australia and Britain, were broadly similar, as they attempted to stave off or minimise the negative effects of the recession and accompanying credit squeeze.

There was an additional concern facing the UK directors. This stemmed mainly from the consequences of the prolonged, extremely harsh weather, and succession of heavy snowfalls, that left large swathes of the less accessible countryside completely cut off for several weeks.

In Byland Crescent, Lizzie Cowgill, now unemployed, had another, deeper, more personal problem to face, one she hoped to overcome. She was desperate to find Gil Richardson. The desire to face him, to apologize for having deserted him, and to attempt reconciliation occupied her every waking moment, plus many of the snatched dreams in her succession of largely sleepless nights.

It was barely a week into the New Year when a letter arrived for Lizzie. Although she was tempted to ignore the contents, after some consideration, she wondered if the sender might provide a potential solution to her dilemma.

The letter was from her former superior, Edrith Pointon. He had written, he explained, to express his regret and understanding of her decision to quit the service, and to do so in such an abrupt manner. He added that if there was any way he could be of assistance in her chosen future, she had only to ask. Implicit in all this was his disagreement with the decision made by the committee who had rejected Lizzie's application for promotion. That gave Lizzie the spark of inspiration as to how to tackle her problem.

It was a while before Lizzie formulated her plan, and even longer before she was able to act on it. Before she was able to do so, however, the family at Byland Crescent received some extremely sad news.

Jenny took the phone call, and walked into the sitting room, where the rest of the family was gathered. One glance at her face told Mark something was wrong, but before he was able to ask the cause of her distress, Jenny told them, 'That was George's sister on the phone. I'm afraid it's bad news. George passed away in his sleep last night.'

George Mills had been an invaluable member of the staff at Byland Crescent for many years. He had been employed from the time Albert and Hannah bought the house, when Sonny was only an infant. He had served first in the role of general factotum. Following his service during World War One, he progressed to the role of butler. He had occupied that position until his retirement only a few years ago.

A week later, the family visited the recently opened crematorium to pay their last respects to the man who had devoted all his adult life to ensuring their comfort and tending their needs. For Sonny in particular, it was particularly distressing as he bade farewell to his old friend. To many, the role of a butler would have been nothing more than a servant, albeit a senior one, but in Sonny's eyes, plus that of the rest of the family, George was a close and trusted comrade and friend.

* * *

Lizzie waited for a couple of weeks before finally plucking up courage to enlist Edrith Pointon's help. When she eventually called him, she was able to circumvent the lengthy route via the switchboard. As his former deputy, Lizzie was one of the very few people who knew his direct phone number.

By the time she was ready to make the call, Lizzie had an additional question to ask her former chief. This came courtesy of a conversation she had with her brother shortly after her return home.

'I know you quit your job in a fit of temper,' Mark had said, his smile robbing the statement of any offence, 'but by my reckoning you've worked for that outfit going on twenty years, give or take a month or two.'

'What of it?'

'I don't know how such things work in the murky world of counter-espionage, but if you'd been employed by a commercial undertaking, you would have qualified for some form of annuity or pension. I guess such considerations didn't enter your mind while you were throwing a tantrum, but wouldn't it make sense to follow up on that?'

'You're dead right, Mark, and I have to admit I was so outraged it never crossed my mind,' she'd replied.

When she did speak to Pointon, she discovered immediately that this facet of their conversation had already been dealt with.

'I'm glad you've phoned, because it's saved me having to write to you. I've instructed our payroll department to implement your graduated pension in line with your original contract. They tried to resist, given the manner of your departure, but I overruled them. You should be receiving a confirmation statement from them in a few weeks' time. Was that why you called me?'

'Actually, that was only part of the reason. I wanted to take you up on your offer to help me with regard to my future.'

'I should warn you that we don't provide references for anyone seeking employment, but I thought you already knew that.'

'That has nothing to do with it. The help I need is in trying to trace someone. It's a person I care very deeply about, and I had to sacrifice our friendship when you persuaded me to return to work for the department. Soon after I left Scarborough he resigned from his job, moved out of his flat and disappeared, leaving no forwarding address. The manner of his departure, and the note he left for me, shows how much I upset him, and although I've tried every means I can think of to trace him, I've had absolutely no success. I hoped you might do better with the resources at your disposal, if you're willing to do as you promised.'

'I'll do what I can.'

'Will you have time? You're scheduled to retire soon.'

'Slight change of plan on that score — my assistant walked out and hasn't been replaced yet.'

As he spoke, Lizzie heard the laughter in his voice. She was about to tell him the name, former address and occupation of the person she was seeking. But Pointon forestalled her, surprising her into the bargain by saying, 'Can I assume the person in question is Dr Gilbert Richardson?'

There was a moment of stunned silence before Lizzie acknowledged the accuracy of Pointon's guess.

'Leave it to me. I'll get a couple of my people on it immediately.' Pointon chuckled. 'I was about to say "our people" but sadly, that's no longer so. I'll get back to you as soon as I know anything.'

With little else to occupy her, Lizzie found the time dragging as she waited, with increasing impatience, for Pointon to report success — or failure. The tedium wasn't helped by her inability to leave the house on an errand to distract her mind. She couldn't go shopping, or even for a walk through the town or along the sea front. This was in part due to her unwillingness to miss a vital call, but also the weather conditions. Prolonged bouts of heavy snow and freezing temperatures had left both roads and pavements like skating rinks. The treacherous conditions underfoot had already led to a number of casualties, with broken arms or legs being the most prevalent injuries.

Lizzie wasn't the only family member to have such restrictions forced on her. Aware of the potential for disaster, Andy, supported by his parents and grandparents, had forbidden Consuela from venturing forth. Her attempt to argue the point had failed, the clinching argument coming from Rachael.

'It's much different for other members of the family, because we're all accustomed to such weather conditions, but having spent all your life in Ibiza, I'm fairly certain you haven't seen much snow or ice, except perhaps on Christmas cards. Besides which,' she added with a smile, 'you mustn't take risks in your condition.'

Consuela stared at Rachael for a second, and then turned accusingly to Andy. 'Did you tell her?' she demanded.

'Certainly not! I was waiting for you to give me the go-ahead.'

'How did you find out?' Consuela asked.

Rachael smiled. 'Remember, I was a nurse before I married Sonny. You get used to noticing these things.' She paused before adding, 'Pregnancy wasn't one of the issues when I was nursing wounded soldiers, though.'

* * *

Luke and Bella had been away all day. They had taken the opportunity to visit the vineyard, their stated reason to check the new season's produce. A secondary, equally important motive was to bring a sizeable quantity of that produce home. One of the advantages of owning a vineyard is you have first chance to taste the wine.

It was late when they arrived home, but they had hardly pulled the car to a halt, ready to offload their precious cargo, when their housekeeper opened the front door. 'Your sister-in-law has been on the phone several times,' she told Luke. 'She wants you to call her as soon as you return. There's been a terrible incident. Clare has shot a man dead.'

Luke made the call, but Amelia was so close to hysterics he could hardly make sense of what she was saying.

After a moment he said, 'Don't worry, we'll come straight over.'

Within twenty minutes Luke and Bella were seated in Amelia's lounge as Clare told her story. Unlike her mother, Clare was reasonably calm. 'I've been suspended,' she told them.

'What?' Luke said.

'You must be aware of the rapes and killings over the past months? The bush telegraph has been full of it.' Luke and Bella nodded. 'Last night I was undercover along with two other female officers patrolling different parts of the town.' She threw her hands up. 'Patrolling! Basically we were bait. That drongo of an inspector insisted, thought it was a good idea. He's a hypocritical bully. He only got his rank based on other officers' successes — and he's never wrong! At least that's his opinion. We were sent out armed and looking for the killer. I won't go into all the details, but instead, he found me. He had a knife and dragged me into a yard. There was a struggle before I managed to free myself and I shot him, three times.'

'So why are you suspended? You should be awarded a medal,' Bella said.

'There's one problem — they can't find the knife.' She lifted her chin so they could see the cut across her throat. 'I didn't get that shaving. I saw the glint of steel as he tried to stick me with it. I heard it clatter on the ground. But at the station, nobody believed me. They all think I'm lying, that I panicked when a man approached me and I'm trying to cover it up.'

Luke was furious. 'This is bloody ridiculous. Leave it with me. I'll see what I can do. I believe you, I know lying isn't part of your nature, Clare.' He smiled and then added, 'And neither is panicking.'

Strangely, it was this show of support that finally caused Clare to break down. In an instant, Amelia and Bella were at her side, consoling arms about her.

'Now see what you've done, Luke,' Bella accused him. 'A fine sort of uncle you are.'

* * *

Next morning, the gutter press was verging on slanderous. They named Clare, accusing her of Wild West tactics, calling for her dismissal, and to be charged with manslaughter, if not murder.

Luke Fisher reached his office earlier than normal. As he passed his secretary, he asked her to summon Elliot and Josh immediately they arrived. Having read that news article, she didn't argue. Minutes later, Luke's co-directors entered his office. One glance at the newspaper in Elliot's hand was enough. 'I can guess what that's about.' Luke said. 'Given the identity of that rag's editor, I guess it won't be sympathetic.'

Elliot nodded. 'How is Clare? Have you spoken to her?'

'She's at her mother's. Bella and I went round last night. She's coping quite well, considering what she's been through, better than her mother in fact.' He explained the situation, before instructing them, 'I want you both to ditch whatever plans you have for the next few days and concentrate on this. Elliot, I want you to head up the media campaign defending Clare as strongly as possible. Use as many of our media division's resources as necessary. Josh, I want you to revisit the crime scene, use your previous expertise and check it out carefully. Clare said the man was wielding a knife and actually cut her with it. However, that weapon seems to have vanished. I want you to cast a professional eye on the area and see where it might have gone.'

Elliot suggested Clare should be interviewed, and a photograph taken of the wound, then there would be a permanent record.

'Brilliant idea, Elliot, I'll leave you to put it in motion. She's staying with her mother until this is all over.'

Sadly, although the Fisher Springs newspapers refuted the allegations with some force, even to the extent of publishing photos of Clare's wound, all other media outlets delighted in the chance to embarrass one of their major rivals. In this, they received further assistance via a statement from the head of the inquiry. His response to questions from reporters added fuel to the fire. He might have believed his statement would prove successful in protecting his back, but in so doing he had thrown Clare Fisher to the wolves.

Few officers believed her actions had been justified. There was one notable exception. Ben Lawson had worked with Clare on many occasions. Although they were good friends, he had for some time wanted to take that friendship to another level. He refused to believe the scurrilous stories that were rapidly gaining credence.

He found out she was at her mother's and called round that evening. 'I'd like to wring the neck of that drongo who wrote those foul things about you in that rag,' he fumed. 'Anyone who knows you well would have realized you would only have acted that way if you were being threatened.'

Clare was grateful for Ben's support, told him so, and squeezed his hand in thanks.

Forty-eight hours later, Josh brought Luke news. 'I know where that knife went.'

'You do? Where is it?'

'I went for a walk past the yard where Clare was attacked. There's a drainage channel in the road with openings to catch flood water. One of those gaps is close to where she shot that man. There were too many people about, so I went back at two o'clock this morning, lifted the grille, and shone my torch inside. The knife is lying on the bottom.'

'You didn't remove it, I hope?'

'Certainly not! I don't want anyone saying we planted evidence. Here's what I suggest . . .'

The following day, the police inspector received a visit from his deputy. 'I have good news — at least it's good news for Sergeant Fisher. Earlier, we got a call from the council. Their operatives were doing their routine check of the drainage system to ensure they're free from blockages before the wet season.'

The inspector appreciated this information, knowing the trouble that could ensue from the heavy rains, known locally as 'the wet', but failed to see the relevance.

His deputy continued, 'In the area where Fisher says she was attacked, they found a knife. I sent a couple of our guys to collect it. They dusted it for prints and got a match to the man Fisher shot.'

The inspector thought about this for a few moments. His public condemnation of Clare Fisher had backfired. Now he would be ridiculed, with potentially devastating effect on his career. 'I think that information needs to remain inside this office. Don't mention it to anyone. Can we trust the men you sent to keep silent?'

'I'll make sure they do, if they know what's good for them.'

At the same time, Luke Fisher was receiving a report from Elliot. 'I stationed a photographer across the street from that yard. He used his telephoto lens to pick up some brilliant shots. The one I like best is the guy in State Police uniform putting the knife into an evidence bag, it's an absolute beaut.'

'Great, now we'll sit on them for a day or two.'

Elliot was puzzled. 'I thought you'd want them published immediately because they back up Clare's story.'

'I do want them published. But first I want to see how that idiot in charge reacts to that. Let's give him a bit of rope and see if he hangs himself.'

Later that evening, Ben Lawson was alone in his city centre flat. He was a little puzzled that his flatmate hadn't yet returned. Admittedly, as a fellow policeman, he could be excused for keeping irregular hours, but he was a fingerprint specialist, not a frontline officer.

When the door opened, Ben could tell immediately his colleague had important news. 'I'm glad you're still here. It looks like Clare Fisher's going to be a heroine,' he announced. 'We retrieved a knife from a drain near where she did her Annie Oakley act. It has traces of blood, plus the dead man's prints on it. Then I got called out to go to the cricket ground.'

'What on earth for? You can't bat, and any self-respecting eight-year-old can bowl better than you.'

'I went to retrieve a handbag. It was hidden under the covers, so it wasn't found at the time. It belonged to one of the recent victims. I'm testing it in the morning.'

The next evening, Ben's flatmate said, 'That handbag yielded a load of prints. Not only the dead woman's, but also those belonging to the guy Clare Fisher turned into a colander.' Then he added, 'But I don't want you to repeat what I just told you, not to anyone, understand?'

'Why not? I thought it would be all over the news.'

'I've been given strict orders not to reveal anything about the knife, or the handbag. It was made clear that if I did I could look for work elsewhere.'

'That sounds crook. I bet that dipstick running the investigation is behind this. He's probably galloping to the dunny every five minutes in case the truth comes out. We'll see about that.'

Ben Lawson didn't sleep well to begin with that night, but around three o'clock he came to a decision. Once he'd settled on his plan, he drifted off, to dream about Clare.

CHAPTER NINETEEN

Luke Fisher was surprised to find a young man waiting for him in reception. His secretary introduced the stranger, 'This is Constable Lawson from the State Police. He wants to have a word with you about your niece.'

Luke signalled for Lawson to follow him. He noticed that the young man seemed nervous. 'What's this about?' he asked, as he closed the office door.

He listened intently to what Lawson told him and then said, 'Take a seat while I get some help on this.' He buzzed through on the intercom and asked his secretary to summon Elliot and Josh.

Luke asked, 'Isn't this a bit risky for you? Once they learn it was you who spilled the beans it could damage your career prospects beyond recall.'

'Maybe it will, Mr Fisher, but I don't care whether I've still got a career in the force or not after this comes out. I do care about justice, and I couldn't stand by and let Clare suffer. Doing nothing isn't an option.'

'I think Clare is extremely fortunate to have a colleague as supportive as you. Unless, of course, it's a bit more personal than just colleagues?'

'I think a lot of Clare,' he admitted. 'We're good friends, but we come from different worlds. My family are farmers. I can't compete with people in Clare's social circle.'

Luke smiled. 'That's nonsense, young man. When my mother and father came here from England they had nothing. They became sheep farmers and were lucky their land contained valuable mineral deposits. We're not much different from your folks. Besides which, don't you think you're being rather selfish?'

'Selfish, why am I being selfish?'

'What if Clare thinks the same about you? She might be waiting for you to say something. You should tell her how you feel.'

Luke's co-directors entered the room at that moment. Having introduced them, Luke said, 'I want you to listen to what Ben has to say.'

Once Lawson had departed, Luke gave his instructions. 'Elliot, I want you to put all our media outlets on high alert for a major news story.'

Two days later, the news broke. The radio, then the TV channels, and later the newspapers all carried the same lead story. 'Police Officer's Heroic Action Nails Killer'. Those in charge of the inquiry strongly refuted allegations of a cover-up, going so far as to cast doubt on the existence of any proof. The next editions carrying photographs of the knife being removed from the drain, plus even more damning information revealing the killer's fingerprints on the handbag, was too much for the police inspector. When he attempted to contact the Fisher Springs media department to try and disprove the insinuations with the articles, all his enquiries were directed to Luke Fisher. His secretary said he was unavailable and she would ask Mr Fisher to phone him back.

An hour later, Luke made the call and refused to reveal his sources, before asking, 'Are you trying to imply this story isn't true? I thought fingerprints were infallible.'

'That's for us to decide. Your niece still has serious charges to answer, and I intend to ensure she pays the penalty for bringing the force into disrepute.'

'Really? And how will you do that? I mean, how can you exert any influence within the police force when you've been dismissed and are facing corruption charges?'

The inspector laughed. 'That isn't going to happen.'

'Believe me, it is. If I were you I'd start clearing my desk now, because you'll be out by tomorrow.'

'You're living in a fantasy world.' With that, the inspector slammed the phone down.

Luke Fisher turned off the speakerphone and the recorder. He looked at the man seated opposite him. 'Well, Commissioner, the ball's in your court now.'

The senior police officer smiled wryly. 'Thanks a bunch, Mr Fisher. Sometimes being at the head of an organization involves making tough decisions, as you're no doubt aware.' He gestured to the phone. 'What I've just heard, however, confirms this is the right one. I'll go dictate the dismissal notice now.'

Once the police commissioner had left, Luke picked up the phone and dialled Amelia's number. After a brief conversation, she put her daughter on the line. Clare attempted to thank Luke for everything he'd done, but he would have none of it. 'That's what family is for. Besides, it wasn't my doing. It was your boyfriend who provided all the information — I simply ensured it became public.'

'What boyfriend? I don't have a boyfriend.'

'I'm talking about Ben. Or have you so many boyfriends you've lost count?'

There was a long silence, which more or less confirmed Luke's suspicion.

Eventually, Clare said, 'Ben did all that for me? That's wonderful of him. I do hope he doesn't get in bother over it.'

'Ben wasn't worried whether he got in trouble or not. His only concern was for you.'

'I don't know how I'll be able to thank him.'

'Oh, I'm sure you'll think of a way.'

* * *

That evening, Ben answered his phone.

'Ben, I want to thank you for going in to bat for me. My uncle Luke told me what you did. I really appreciate it, and I only hope it doesn't make trouble for you.' Clare paused. 'I also wondered if you'd do me another favour?'

'Just say the word, and I'll do whatever you ask.'

'I can't impose on Mother forever. I have to return to my flat, but I'm concerned there might be hordes of reporters hanging around. I hoped you might escort me and fend them off if necessary?'

'Of course I will, whenever you say.'

'Will later this evening be too much of an inconvenience? Otherwise tomorrow will do if you're not on shift, though I appreciate it's the weekend.'

'This evening works just fine.'

'That's really kind, and thanks once again. You're an angel.'

There was nobody in sight when they pulled up outside Clare's apartment block. As he took her bag from the boot, Ben stared admiringly at the building. 'I've always thought this place looks real posh. How do you afford it?'

Clare laughed. 'Didn't I tell you I live here rent free? Uncle Luke is my landlord,' she explained. 'Come on up.'

Ben had been in the apartment many times and was happy to stay until Clare was settled. She vanished into the kitchen and returned with two coffees. They chatted for a while and Ben was about to bid her goodnight when she reached out and took his hand. 'I'll never be able to repay you for what you did for me, Ben. You risked your career.'

'Clare, it was nothing. I was just trying to help. You know I'd do anything for you.'

She smiled. 'Anything?'

'Anything,' he agreed.

'Well, there is one thing,' she said, as she pulled him to his feet and stood in front of him, so close their bodies were touching. 'It's something only you can do.'

Ben couldn't resist. He slipped his arms around her and kissed her, gently at first, before passion took over. Clare led him to the bedroom and ushered him inside.

* * *

Clare Fisher and Ben's idyllic weekend had been interrupted twice. The first came when Clare's mother rang to ask if she had everything she wanted. Something in her daughter's enthusiastic tone as she replied that she had all she needed puzzled Amelia. It was a few days later before she worked out the reason.

The second interruption came from Clare's immediate superior, who informed her that her suspension from duty had been lifted, and that she should report for work on Monday. The officer refrained from imparting the second segment of his news. He preferred to deliver the good tidings in person.

Clare and Ben discussed living together in her apartment. 'We have to consider things like you giving notice on your flat.'

'My mate, the fingerprint expert, will continue living there, and probably move his girlfriend in as soon as he can. I'll tell him I'm leaving, although he'll probably have already guessed it. He already knew how I felt about you, even before this trouble.'

'There are other people you'll need to inform, surely. Your family should know, and your bank will need your new address.'

'Oh Lord!' Ben exclaimed, clearly dismayed. 'I shall have to tell personnel department my new address and telephone number. If they put two and two together, word will soon get out at work. If we're not extremely careful, people will know we're living together.'

'Why is that going to be a problem?'

'I was thinking about you. People might get the wrong idea about you, if they think we're living in sin.'

Clare was indignant. 'Do you think I care two hoots what people's opinion of me is?' She giggled, before adding, 'Living in sin sounds positively Victorian. I'm OK with it though, because I enjoy sinning with you.'

* * *

On Monday morning the new inspector greeted them, noting their closeness. He smiled, and hastened to assure them he had nothing but good news to impart. 'Sergeant Fisher, you will shortly be receiving a commendation for your courageous action in taking down a vicious killer. You acted with great bravery, regardless of the danger. You then faced outrageous repercussions owing to the deficiencies of other officers. You demonstrated the sort of conduct this force needs to encourage. You are an inspiration to your colleagues.'

He turned to Ben and smiled again. 'As for you, Constable Lawson, the commissioner was so impressed by your conduct in defence of your fellow officer, and your determination to expose the truth, that he has instructed you should be placed on a fast-track promotion course. If you pass muster, you will be awarded the rank of sergeant. Now, if the two of you can get your heads out of the clouds for a few hours, your duty shift has already begun.'

Later that day, once they had handed over to the night shift, Clare and Ben left the station arm in arm. Outside, however, instead of turning right towards Clare's apartment, Ben steered her in the opposite direction.

'Where are we going?'

'There's something I need to check out, and I thought it would be better if you came along with me.'

Clare agreed, still completely mystified, until Ben led her to the shops in the town centre. There, he paused in front of a jeweller's shop window and pointed to a series of stands displaying a wide assortment of rings.

'Do you see anything there you like?' Ben's voice was tight with nervous tension.

'Ben, these are engagement rings.' Clare stopped suddenly, the significance of Ben's question suddenly dawning on her. 'Is this a roundabout way of asking me to marry you?'

'Er . . . yes, Clare. I've loved you for ages. Will you?'

'Of course I will, Ben darling. Any girl would be a fool to refuse a man like you. And I don't need fancy jewellery. A curtain ring would do.'

If their fellow officers had been left in any doubt as to the nature of their relationship, the same could not be said for the early evening shoppers, who saw the young couple locked in a passionate embrace.

On Sunday afternoon, they visited Luke and Bella to offer their grateful thanks for all that he had done for them. Amelia had already phoned Luke and told him of her delight at the engagement. While Bella admired the ring on Clare's finger, Luke took Ben aside for a quiet word. 'You told her then?' he asked.

'No.' Ben laughed. 'She told me!'

CHAPTER TWENTY

In England, it was March before winter showed signs of relaxing its grip and even then it was an extremely slow process. As Lizzie continued to wait for news, she was intrigued by an article in one of the daily papers.

The piece described a statement made to the House of Commons by the Secretary of State for War, John Profumo. In his speech, Profumo had refuted insinuations about the nature of his friendship with a woman named Christine Keeler, who he had been introduced to at a party some two years before, stating that she was nothing more than an acquaintance and denying that theirs was a sexual relationship.

Mark, who glanced over her shoulder and saw what she was reading, asked her opinion of the report. When Lizzie replied, he was surprised by the emphatic nature of her rebuttal.

'Why do you think it's a load of bullshit?' he asked.

'I don't think so, Mark, I know without doubt that it's a pack of lies. What I also know is there is far more to this story than what's written here. And I think the shit will soon hit the fan, big style.' She smiled as she added, 'Please keep that between us for the time being, will you? But I don't think you'll have to keep quiet for long.'

Less than a week after their conversation, Lizzie received the phone call she had been waiting for, but the result was not what she had hoped it would be. 'This is only a progress report,' Pointon told her. 'Or to be more accurate I should call it a lack-of-progress report. My people have been unable to trace Dr Richardson yet. We've tried almost everything we can think of in the normal way of things, but come up with nothing. We know he hasn't left the country, if he had, I can't say I'd blame him, given the winter we've just had. The alternative is he's living in isolation somewhere.'

'What do you mean by that?'

'If he's in rented accommodation without a telephone, that would make him difficult to trace. And if he's determined to remain hidden, that makes the task even harder. There is one last trick up our sleeves, which is related to his occupation, but if that fails, I'm afraid it will be a lost cause. I realize none of this is what you were hoping to hear, and we're running out of time. I'm scheduled to quit soon, and there's no way my successor will be as cooperative.' There was a slight pause before Pointon switched to another topic. 'I guess you'll have read that your suspicions regarding a certain matter have now become public knowledge. As you know, that's not the end of it by any means, and when the rest comes into the open you'll realize everything you reported was absolutely correct.'

* * *

The Cowgill family were enthralled, horrified and intrigued by two headline-grabbing events in quick succession. As what became labelled by the media as either 'The Profumo Affair' or 'The Christine Keeler Affair' continued to make sensational news, serious developments unfolded. What had begun as a sordid sex scandal took a more sinister turn, with the revelation that in addition to her involvement with the British cabinet minister, Christine Keeler had also been sleeping with the Soviet naval attaché stationed at the Russian Embassy in London.

When the trial of Keeler's pimp, an osteopath named Stephen Ward, took place at the Old Bailey, news of the relationships caused Profumo to resign, admitting to the House of Commons that he had lied to them.

More sensation followed when, on the eve of the final day of his trial for living off immoral earnings, Stephen Ward committed suicide. Shocking as this was, it soon had to compete for headline space with an event that took place during the early hours of August the eighth, in the county of Buckinghamshire.

After tampering with the railway signals, a gang of fifteen men brought the Glasgow to London mail train to a halt. Once the locomotive was stationary, the intruders entered the cab and attacked the driver, rendering him unconscious, and overpowering the second crew member.

Inside information led them to the second carriage behind the engine. Having overpowered the staff in what was known as the high value compartment, the robbers removed over one hundred mail sacks. The monetary value of the haul was estimated at around £2.6 million, making it the biggest robbery in British history.

These exciting events took a back seat in Byland Crescent during the early days of August, giving precedence to the arrival home of Consuela, accompanied by her daughter Angela, a baby sister for James.

Soon afterwards, Lizzie Cowgill received the news she had been waiting and hoping for all year.

Pointon's phone call came during the afternoon of the last Friday in August, and his opening announcement signalled the end of an era. 'I thought you should know I'm leaving my office for the final time in a couple of hours or so, but before then I wanted to tell you we've finally located your man. Here are the details you wanted so desperately . . .'

Minutes later, Lizzie burst into the sitting room, where Jenny was nursing Angela while Consuela snatched a welcome nap. 'They've found him,' Lizzie announced dramatically, her excitement evident.

'Shush, don't wake the little one. It's taken me ages to get her to sleep. What do you mean, they've found him? Who has found who?'

'Do you remember me asking my old boss for one last favour, when I asked him to try and track down Gil? It's taken months, but at last they've traced him.'

'Oh, that is good news! Has he gone abroad as you suspected?'

'No, not unless Wensleydale has declared independence. I'm not sure how long he's been there, but apparently he's renting a cottage in a village called Hardraw, which is close to Hawes, and has been working as a locum for a couple of GP practices in the area.'

'I wonder how they managed to track him down to somewhere like that? It sounds really remote,' Jenny commented.

'I'm not sure of the details, but I think it has something to do with prescriptions he's written. Obviously pharmacists will have to check that the issuer is entitled to write them up.'

'What are you planning to do? Now you know where he is.'

'I'm not certain. I haven't had time to think about it yet. But please, don't tell the others.'

Hours later, Jenny realized Lizzie was no slouch when it came to decision-making. Either that or her swift reaction demonstrated her desperation to meet up with Gil. The subject arose as they were sitting down for dinner, although Lizzie approached it in a roundabout fashion.

'Andy, I wondered if I could ask a favour. If you have a moment, would you check out the Beetle for me, please? Make sure it's roadworthy as it hasn't been driven for a good while.'

'You mean the tin box on wheels? Why would you want to lower yourself by being seen in an object like that?'

'Please, Andy, I need transport. It's very important. If I book it in at the garage, it could take ages.'

'Where are you going in such a hurry?'

'I'm hoping to drive to Wensleydale.'

Andy relented from teasing his aunt. 'OK, I can take a look over the weekend. Grandpa might help if I have a problem.'

Sonny gave him a questioning look, and advised Lizzie, 'Your road tax is up to date, but you'll need to sort out your insurance before you can use it. If the broker isn't open on Saturdays, it's a non-starter. Remember, it's a bank holiday weekend, so there might not be anyone in the offices.'

In the middle of the conversation, Mark had glanced across the table at Jenny, and noticing her smile, resolved to ask her later what had amused her. He tackled her about it as they were preparing to go to bed.

'I'll tell you, but she doesn't want everyone to know. The reason she's so keen to get to Wensleydale is that she's just found out that's where Gil is living. It's a village called Hardraw.'

'I see! From memory, I think Hardraw is pretty isolated — it's no wonder he couldn't be found. Well, good luck to her, I say. Lizzie deserves some happiness after the way those idiots in Whitehall treated her.'

* * *

Lizzie was fortunate in two respects. The first came the following morning, when she phoned the broker who handled all the family's insurance requirements. The office was manned, and Lizzie's insurance was renewed.

As things transpired, her other piece of good fortune came via Andy's report that the car was drivable. 'I checked the oil and kicked the tyres, everything is fine.'

Sonny, who was in the room, stifled a chuckle. He knew Andy had been outside for a considerable time and been very thorough.

Late that morning, Lizzie set off on the long drive to Upper Wensleydale. Where her luck deserted her was in the weather. As the wipers fought to keep the windscreen clear of the incessant rain, Lizzie remembered her father's comment regarding a similar downpour. 'Typical bank holiday weather,' Sonny had remarked. 'It seems to happen every year, especially in Scarborough.'

With a journey of close to a hundred miles ahead of her, plus the strong possibility of a similar return journey should her mission fail, the last thing Lizzie needed was inclement weather. She had taken discreet measures should her visit have the desired effect. Evidence of these came via the overnight bag she had smuggled out of the house, and secreted in the boot of her car. The last thing she wanted was her brother to see it, and come up with some risqué comment designed to tease and embarrass her.

A combination of the lack of driving, Lizzie's unfamiliarity with the narrow, winding roads that formed the bulk of her journey, plus the adverse weather conditions meant that it was well over four hours later when she reached the village that was her objective. Thankfully, finding the cottage was easy enough, because there were few to choose from.

Lizzie pulled the Beetle to a halt alongside the dry-stone wall that bordered the trio of stone-built cottages. She climbed wearily out of the driving seat and stood alongside the car, stretching to release the stiffness in her back, her arms and legs. Then she turned and headed for the middle cottage in the row.

As she approached the house, Lizzie's nervousness increased, her confidence as to the reception she would get ebbing with every stride. At one point, her courage almost deserted her, the temptation to turn and run almost overwhelming her resolve. She paused, gritted her teeth, squared her shoulders and strode forward. She hadn't come all this way to fall at the final hurdle. Come what may, Lizzie knew she had to come face-to-face with Gil. Anything else would merely compound the mistreatment he had already suffered at her hands.

She beat a tattoo on the door and waited — and waited — and waited. Getting no response, she tried a second, then a third time, but without success. Desperation caused her to reach for the handle, confidently expecting the door to be locked. To her surprise, it turned easily and the door swung open. Without considering that her action could be construed as trespassing, Lizzie stepped inside.

CHAPTER TWENTY-ONE

Gil Richardson was beyond weary. He'd been called out to assist in an emergency. Although the outcome had been successful, the task he'd been asked to perform had been a prolonged one.

The expectant mother had gone into labour in the early hours, but seemed reluctant to part with her offspring. Until beyond lunchtime, Gil had struggled to help her. Now, having been denied some sleep, and with his only food being a hastily snatched bacon sandwich washed down with a mug of tea, supplied by the proud father, his only desire was to get home, climb into bed and sleep — hopefully until the next day.

He was dwelling on the diversity of the work a rural GP was asked to perform when he pulled up outside the cottage. He noticed the car parked nearby and assumed one of his neighbours must have visitors, because he couldn't believe for one minute anyone would be calling on him.

One of the advantages of living in so remote a hamlet was that locking the house door was unnecessary. Gil walked into the cottage and stopped dead. He stared in astonishment at the woman seated in the armchair alongside the fireplace, and for a moment thought he was hallucinating, through exhaustion. 'What are you doing here?' he demanded.

Lizzie got to her feet slowly, walked across the room and stood in front of him.

'Gil, I had to come. I had to see you, to tell you how sorry I am for what I did. I know I hurt you deeply, and that distresses me beyond belief. Even if you can find it in your heart to accept my apology, and I wouldn't blame you if you can't, I will never be able to forgive myself for the distress I caused you.'

Gil almost laughed. 'Is that the only reason you came? To say you're sorry?'

Lizzie winced at the sarcasm in his voice and shook her head. 'No, no, that was only part of it. I wondered, or hoped, there might be some way I could make amends. Anything I can do.' She bit her lip, scared that the tears she could feel welling behind her eyes might fall, and at the hopelessness she was beginning to feel.

Gil stared at the woman he had loved so deeply, and shrugged his shoulders. 'Look . . .' He shook his head. 'Look, can we talk about this later? I'm dog tired. I've been up most of the night tending to a mother in labour.'

'You must be exhausted. Was it a good outcome?'

'Yes, she eventually gave birth to twins. Now I really must go to bed.' He looked at her and saw the look of hope on her face, the tears in her eyes, and his attitude softened. 'Will you wait until I've had a rest and we can talk then?'

'Of course I'll wait, Gil, I'll be here for as long as you want me to be.'

'The kitchen is through there.' He pointed to a door at the far side of the room. 'Help yourself.'

Lizzie saw his slight smile, which encouraged her greatly. She watched as he trudged up the stairs which led off the lounge to the bedrooms above.

* * *

Despite his weariness, Gil was finding it difficult to get to sleep. Out of nowhere, Lizzie had walked back into his life.

He wondered where this might lead. He'd been so angry — angry at her desertion, her dismissal of his love, and now? There had been something about her attitude that gave him cause to wonder if things might take the direction he'd always wanted. He tossed and turned, until he was facing the wall, still pondering this when he felt the bedsprings move as Lizzie got in alongside him. As she snuggled close to him, he could tell she was naked. She put her arm around him and whispered, 'Go to sleep, darling, and I will be here for you when you wake up. And if you want me, I'll be here for you always.'

Gil was dreaming. It was a recurrence of a dream he'd had many times before. In it, Lizzie was alongside him, holding him as they made love. Every time, the rapture had been followed by bitter disappointment when he awoke to find he was alone.

As if disturbed by the memory penetrating his subconscious, Gil turned over, only to encounter an obstacle.

He was instantly awake, blinking to clear his vision as his memory returned.

Lizzie smiled, a trifle nervously, as she said, 'We need to talk.'

Gil put his arm around her waist, pulling her closer until their bodies touched.

'OK,' she said, as if answering something he'd said, 'maybe we can talk later.'

A long while afterwards, Gil asked, 'Did you mean it? Are you really here to stay?'

'Too right I am. I'll be alongside you always. I was fairly sure it was the right thing before I came here. The last few hours have convinced me. And to show I'm serious,' — she reached across and handed him the box she'd placed on the bedside table — 'I brought this with me.'

He took the ring out of the box, and as he slipped it on her finger, she whispered, 'Say it, Gil, say the magic words, please?'

'Will you marry me, Lizzie darling?'

'I will.' They kissed and then Lizzie whispered, 'Now we've got that sorted, let's return to the main topic on the agenda.' As she was speaking, Lizzie moved closer, her smile cat-like at his reaction.

Over the next few hours, they talked, and Gil heard about developments at Byland Crescent. Lizzie also explained as much as she was allowed to about her reasons for deserting him.

'There were lots of things happening internationally, and in addition to everything else there was trouble at home, within the intelligence service. The whole system was as leaky as a sieve, with outside sources penetrating our defences. One development in particular was so disturbing, and although I didn't want to, I knew I had to go back. Even though I loved you so much, I couldn't explain. Put it this way, I was aware we were on the brink of something awful, and I allowed my boss to convince me I should return and do my bit to help avoid a catastrophe. Once I knew that wasn't going to happen, I resigned, because by then I was sick and tired of everything about my old life. The only thing I wanted was to find you, and to be with you, if you'd have me. That awful letter I wrote almost broke my heart, because I knew it would hurt you, I just didn't appreciate how much.'

She paused and Gil could see her distress as she explained, 'The problem is all mine, because of my work. For so many years I've trained myself to subdue my feelings, and not allow them to colour my judgement. If I'd written what was really in my heart that day, I'd never have been able to leave. I was also terrified that there would be no future, not only for you and me, but for everyone.'

'Let's forget about the past, shall we?'

'I'm happy with that.' Lizzie smiled impishly. 'Apart from the last few hours — I definitely don't want to forget that.'

'I'm starving, we should eat,' Gil said.

'Yes, I haven't eaten since breakfast either. But could you do something for me first?'

'What? Again?'

Lizzie laughed. 'I have an overnight bag in the boot of the car. Do you think you could get it for me, please? The car keys are on the table.'

She watched from the bedroom window, laughing, as Gil went to the rear of the Beetle and opened what he assumed to be the boot, and stared at the engine for a moment before he realized his mistake.

* * *

Lizzie and Gil had decided to go for a walk now the weather had improved, when he asked, 'Won't you have to go back to Scarborough soon?'

'There's no need to hurry. I suppose we should go, if only to reassure them and tell them our wonderful news. What about you, though, aren't you supposed to be on duty?'

'As of today, fortunately, I'm on leave. I've been covering for one of the partners in the practice for the past three weeks while he and his family went on holiday, so I'm not scheduled to go back until next week. We could go tomorrow if you like.'

'If you don't have to work, why don't we leave it a day or two longer?'

'Is that because you think the roads will be busy with bank holiday traffic?'

Lizzie smiled again, and she realized she was doing that a lot, something she'd rarely done previously. 'Bank holiday has nothing to do with it. I just don't want to leave here.'

They discussed the future — their future — the one they hadn't believed was going to happen. 'Are you going to remain here, or would you prefer to work somewhere else?' Lizzie asked.

'I haven't given it a lot of thought, to be honest.' Gil chuckled. 'I've had other things on my mind, not that I object to that. You can distract me whenever you want. I really like it here, although I've not thought of it as a permanent place to live. When I came here I was marking time, I suppose. I was originally hired as a locum for a twelve-month stint because one of the doctors in the practice has been taken ill. Last week, we heard he is going to take early retirement because of his ongoing health issues, so they've offered me a partnership, but I haven't made a decision yet. I'd be sorry to leave, but now I don't just have myself to consider, I also want what's best for you. Where would you like to live?'

'I don't care where we are, as long as we're together,' Lizzie replied instantly.

After wandering alongside Hardraw Beck they took the footpath towards Bellow Hill. Having found a convenient resting place they paused, and as Lizzie looked back at the pretty hamlet of stone-built cottages, she could appreciate Gil's reluctance to leave.

'I think this area is lovely, from what I've seen of the outside. I think it's worth considering living here full time, if that's what you want.'

'That's a great idea as far as I'm concerned, but what about you?'

'I don't much care what I do, but I could always revert to what I intended, by becoming a language teacher. Even if I didn't get a job, we'd have your salary, plus my pension and savings, so I don't think we'd be hard up.'

'Do you think that would be sufficient?'

'I'm fairly sure we'd have enough, but if we run short of capital, I can always borrow some from the old folks.'

'I wouldn't want to be in debt to them.'

'We wouldn't be, not really. All it would be is an advance against the money coming to me when they pop their clogs.' Realizing what she had said she laughed. 'Not that I want that to happen.'

'I've never given that side of things any thought, but I guess your parents must have a fair amount of money to be able to afford a house like Byland Crescent.'

'You're right, and neither of them are what you'd call extravagant. The only big speculation my dad makes is the string of Bentley cars he's had over the years. I think the current one is number four or five, but I might be wrong. As to what they have in the piggy bank, my guess is it must be well into seven figures by now, maybe even more.'

'Good heavens, I never imagined I'd end up marrying a wealthy heiress.'

'Don't get too excited. It might sound like a lot of money, but it would have to be split several ways.'

'There are lots of things about you that get me excited, Lizzie, but I can assure you, money isn't one of them.'

'In that case, why don't we go back to the cottage and see if I can get you excited again.'

* * *

It was Thursday before the lovebirds, with extreme reluctance, decided to fly the nest. With their plans for the immediate future in place, they formed a two-car convoy for the journey to Scarborough. With Lizzie at the wheel of her car, Gil followed in the Land Rover he had bought following his move to Wensleydale.

When Lizzie questioned what she thought of as an odd purchase, Gil explained, 'A Land Rover is about the only vehicle capable of tackling the extreme weather we get up here, apart from a farm tractor. Even those weren't sufficient in a winter like the one we've just been through. The four-wheel drive is great for tackling slippery road surfaces, and the height of the axle from the ground is very useful when there are deep snowdrifts or muddy farmyards.'

They arrived at Byland Crescent shortly after lunchtime. As they wandered into the sitting room, where the family were gathered, Jenny noticed they were holding hands and nudged her husband, and whispered, 'You got it wrong, Mark. Gil didn't strangle Lizzie and dump her in a ditch.'

The only member of the family who seemed unimpressed by the new arrivals was Angela, who remained fast asleep. Before anyone asked questions, Gil forestalled them, lifting Lizzie's left hand so they could see the diamond-encrusted engagement ring on her finger.

In view of the excellent news, it was decided that the couple should stay the night. 'That way we can celebrate properly,' Mark commented. 'But it will mean making up a bed in another room for Gil.'

'You can if you wish,' Lizzie retorted, 'but it seems like a wasted effort.'

'You're more like your brother than you know,' Rachael replied, recalling the day she found Mark and Jenny in the same room celebrating their engagement.

She told Mark to behave, beating Jenny to it by a split second. 'Naturally they'll want to be together.'

'You don't object, Mum?'

'Of course not, Lizzie. You're quite old enough to know your own mind. We're all delighted for you both, and who knows, you might be able to add to my tally of grandchildren.'

Susan, always eager to embarrass her brother, told Lizzie, 'At least you'll be on a different floor to me. That's good, because I won't be kept awake like I was when Andy and Consuela were at it half the night. That's stopped now, but instead I've got to put up with the miniature Banshee their bonking produced.'

'Suzie!' Jenny exclaimed, but gave up the attempted reprimand in face of the competing laughter.

'Have you made any plans for the future,' Mark asked, 'or have you been too busy playing doctors and nurses?'

'Shouldn't you be at the office?' Lizzie countered.

'I gave myself the day off,' he responded.

Lizzie ignored her brother and told them, 'We're going to live in Wensleydale, permanently. Gil's been offered a partnership in a local practice, and I will either find a job or become a full-time housewife.'

CHAPTER TWENTY-TWO

As life at home returned to normal, it appeared there was every chance of a brighter future, both in Britain and elsewhere. Any complacency people might have felt was rudely shattered three months later by a horrific event in Texas.

Andy and Consuela had built a radio set from scratch, as part of their earlier course work in electrical engineering. Andy had finished his meal and was in their room, turning the radio dial to pick up one station after another. He was happy with the clarity of all but one, where the announcer had broken into a music programme with a newsflash. As he listened with dawning horror, Andy realized it was the distress in the man's voice that had given the false impression of the set being out of tune.

Seconds later, Andy careered downstairs, entering the dining room at high speed. Rachael, Sonny, Jenny and Consuela were still seated at the table when Andy announced, 'President Kennedy's been shot!'

They looked at him, stunned and disbelieving until he explained. 'It happened in Dallas. He was travelling in an open car, part of a motorcade.'

'Is he dead?'

‘I don’t know. Details are very scarce. All they said on the radio was he’d been rushed to hospital with a head wound, which doesn’t sound at all good.’

The assassination of an American president was not unique, but the repercussions throughout the United States and beyond would be of a scale unprecedented since the outbreak of World War II. That was the situation until another alarming event, if not so dramatic as the one in Dallas, took centre stage.

After the French failure to re-colonise what was then known as Indo-China in 1954 had ended ignominiously, America had become involved in the ongoing conflict. Their financial and military support for South Vietnam had led to a guerrilla war waged by irregulars labelled the Viet Cong. The insurgents were directed, and funded by, the communist regime of North Vietnam, who had also invaded the neighbouring country of Laos. There was also covert support from China, whose political affiliations were similar to those of the North Vietnamese.

Ten years on, the conflict showed no sign of abating. On the contrary, the war was escalating, and along with it, American involvement was also increasing. During August of 1964, the confrontation between a US destroyer and a North Vietnamese attack boat provoked the Americans, under their new president, Lyndon Johnson, into action.

Soon, over 180,000 American troops were stationed in South Vietnam. Concern over the deteriorating situation was expressed in Australia, where Luke Fisher told Bella he was worried that Australian forces might be dragged into the war. ‘We’ve had to face this situation twice in the past fifty years, and I’m scared witless the same thing might happen again.’

‘Do you really believe we might become involved? It hardly seems to be any of our business.’

‘It isn’t simply a local skirmish we’re talking about, Bella. North Vietnam has backing from China, for one, and I’m willing to bet there are plenty of people in and around the Kremlin who are anxious to put one over on America for what they see as Russian humiliation during the Cuban Missile Crisis.'

Similar worries were expressed in the Cowgill household. In Byland Crescent, the family turned to Lizzie for an expert opinion. Given her former career, they accepted her summary, which did little to appease their foreboding.

'Like it or not,' she told her father when he phoned her, 'the Americans will do their utmost to involve as many of their allies as possible in the affair. By the same token, the North Vietnamese, with China's overt or covert backing, will be trying to put pressure on Russia and other Eastern Bloc countries to rally to their cause. I've no idea where it will all end, but I don't like the way it's heading.'

* * *

Despite the troubling world events, in 1964 the Cowgill family were more content than they had been for a long time. That wasn't to say the house in Byland Crescent was a haven of peace and quiet — far from it. Susan Cowgill, who had tormented her family for long enough by playing her favourite music at maximum volume, had switched her musical allegiance. But any relief they might have felt when she abandoned her long-term devotion to Elvis Presley was short-lived. Susan, in common with millions of teenagers in Britain and elsewhere, had become addicted to the sound produced by four young men from Liverpool. She was afflicted by the phenomenon known as Beatlemania.

Despite their best efforts, the Fab Four had strong competition within Byland Crescent. This came from the most junior residents. Angela Cowgill was now teething, and given the slightest provocation, could do her best to raise the roof. Determined not to be outdone by his younger sibling, James was, if anything, possessed of an even more penetrating voice, as he ran though the house, screaming loudly as he played with his toys.

As they competed for the higher volume, their great-grandfather remarked that they seemed to have inherited the extremely powerful Cowgill lungs. 'James could match any of the others, but I think Angela might be on course to outdo her brother,' he told their mother. 'I seem to remember their granddad could scream louder, usually if he was in need of food.'

The gentleman in question, Mark Cowgill, who had just arrived home, didn't attempt to refute this allegation.

Other matters within the Cowgill family were on their way to being resolved. Chief amongst these was the plan being finalized for the wedding, due to take place later that summer between Lizzie and her fiancé Gil Richardson. When their engagement had been announced in the local paper, the editor asked that he be informed of the wedding date, so he could send a photographer along. As they discussed the forthcoming nuptials, Sonny and Rachael talked about their own plans for the near future. 'I had an idea, but I wasn't sure if you'd be happy to go along with it,' Sonny told her. 'I thought it might be good to escape the worst of our climate and go somewhere warmer over winter, returning in spring. Apart from other considerations, my old bones are beginning to protest when the temperature drops below zero.'

Although Rachael agreed in principle, she was shocked at Sonny's response to her question, 'Where are you thinking of, Spain or Italy, or further afield?'

'No, I thought I'd like to return to Crete. We were made so welcome by the people there, and we have a special reason to go back.'

Rachael thought about it for a long time, before giving her cautious approval to the plan. 'I'm up for it, providing the family are all OK.'

* * *

In Australia, Luke Fisher and Bella were pleased and relieved that the business they ran had weathered the recession gripping the country with nothing more than minor setbacks. At home too, family life seemed settled. Although they were blissfully unaware of it, their eldest son Jimmy was preoccupied with the fairer sex, and he concentrated his feelings on one girl in particular.

His interest had been roused on their first meeting, but now it was heightened considerably. It was nearing the end of the spring term when a conversation between his parents provided Jimmy with the opportunity to renew his brief acquaintance with the girl who had been the subject of many of his dreams.

Jimmy listened as his parents discussed a problem that had only come to light that day. 'I was talking to Gianni this morning,' Luke told Bella, 'and he's very concerned over a potential manpower shortage at the vineyard, and it's come at a most inconvenient time.'

'Why has that happened? Gianni usually has all the workers he needs.'

'Apparently the crop is later than usual this year, owing to the weather at the back end of last year. That means the grapes won't be ready for harvesting until bang in the middle of the Easter break, when a lot of the pickers will want to spend time with their families. Gianni reckons he's got most of it covered, but it's the two weeks following the end of the school term that's got him worried.'

As his father was speaking, Jimmy, who was seated nearby, conjured up the delectable vision of Flavia, Gianni Rocca's daughter. Their one and only meeting was still fresh in his mind.

Bella was pondering the difficulty Luke had described when her son interrupted her thought process.

'I could help, if things are bad,' Jimmy volunteered. 'After ten weeks stuck inside a classroom day in, day out, a fortnight spent in the open air would be very welcome, especially if I'm being paid to do something. I could travel to the vineyard on the bus, if that helps, and bunk there, if Mr Rocca agrees.'

When they had recovered from their surprise, Luke promised to phone Gianni and put Jimmy's offer of assistance to him.

Left alone, Luke and Bella discussed their son's idea. 'I think it would be good for him. He's never had to work before, so the experience will be useful,' Bella suggested. 'And I think it would be good for Jimmy and Saul to be separated for a while. Those two are forever squabbling. I don't know why it is, but they seem to be constantly sniping at each other.'

Luke was also concerned over their sons' perpetual disagreements, which occasionally flared up into open hostility. 'I worry about it sometimes, and wonder where it's heading. I don't want history to repeat itself.'

'You mean you don't want it to end up like your rows with your brother Philip?'

'Exactly, because that's something I will always have to live with.'

'I understand that, and although Phil died during the war before you could make peace with him, at least his wife Amelia doesn't hold a grudge. With Jimmy and Saul, it's probably just brotherly rivalry. Luckily they haven't involved their sister in their arguments, and she seems oblivious to the rows, or she believes they'll soon blow over. Perhaps that's because she's the middle child — and obviously, a girl!'

The following evening, Luke informed Jimmy that Gianni had accepted the offer of assistance. But in doing so, he couldn't resist teasing his son. 'Gianni told me you'd be on the same pay scale as all the other pickers for the time you spend there. I told him that was good, because if you were paid value for money you'd probably end up owing them.'

Despite his father's snide remark, Jimmy impressed Gianni with his work ethic during his short stint at the *Luca Collina* vineyard. The teenager was also delighted to meet Flavia again. One look at her confirmed Jimmy's memory as being correct, and that time hadn't detracted from her beauty. Flavia was, Jimmy knew, the loveliest girl he'd ever seen. He stayed with the family in their home, and chatted to her on several occasions, adding to his impression that not only was she extremely beautiful, but she also had a delightful personality.

Before he left, with deep regret, at the end of his sojourn at the vineyard, Jimmy told Gianni he'd be more than willing to return for the next harvest, if required. Not only that, but he'd be happy to undertake any other work Gianni felt he was capable of, providing that school didn't intrude.

As he returned to the Fisher family mansion, Jimmy was warmed by Gianni's praise, but even more so by Flavia's smile as she bade him farewell. Now, at the age of fifteen, he acknowledged that he was head over heels in love, but would not admit the fact to anyone.

* * *

Elsewhere, Luke and Bella's co-directors were also enjoying a period of contentment. Bella's brother Elliot, married to Luke's sister Dottie, had three children, whose progress gave their parents pride and happiness. Their two daughters, Jane and Hazel, had received excellent reports from their teachers, who had been lavish in their praise for their academic progress. The girls' elder brother Lance, at fifteen years of age, was already showing talent with both a cricket bat and ball. This was an inherited skill-set derived from his maternal grandfather, James Fisher, founder of Fisher Springs, although Elliot and Dottie were unaware of that. The fact that Lance's cousin Saul was also a budding cricketer might have given them a clue, but they didn't think the matter through deeply enough.

The other main board director at Fisher Springs' head office, Josh Jones, and his wife Astrid, were equally proud of their offspring. Their daughters Daisy, now five years old, and Naomi, three, were smaller editions of their mother in appearance, Josh thought, although Astrid couldn't see the likeness. They were different to many sisters, in that they never quarrelled and would play together happily, sometimes for hours on end.

CHAPTER TWENTY-THREE

As Gil and Lizzie's wedding day approached, Sonny and Rachael announced to the family their intention to go abroad. 'Once the wedding is over we're going away for the winter,' Sonny told them. 'We're wanting somewhere warmer, with less snow and ice than we had last year. We're returning to Crete, and we might stay there until after Easter next year. That's their Easter, not ours. They work on a different calendar to us, and apparently the Easter festival is considered more important than Christmas.'

'Won't you be bored, being away for so long?' Jenny asked.

'I don't think so. We're taking up some new hobbies,' Rachael replied. 'Apart from that there are many places of great historical interest to visit. I for one am keen to see some of the remains of the Minoan civilisation, like the palace of King Minos at Knossos that I've read so much about, the one with the labyrinth and mythical monster.'

'So you're going on a Minotaur of Crete?' Andy suggested.

'I'll hold him if you hit him,' Jenny told Consuela as the others groaned at Andy's dreadful pun.

Returning to the subject, Sonny continued, 'We're also going to do some touring. There are some splendid scenic places, including three magnificent gorges leading to the south coast. If we take short walks, the exercise will help offset the mountains of food Cretan tavernas and restaurants provide. We're also going armed with cameras, so we'll be able to bore you silly with reams of holiday snaps when we return.'

'That all sounds wonderful when the sun's shining,' Mark told them, 'but what about when you're trapped indoors? I have heard it rains in Greece, not just here.'

'We've some indoor pastimes to entertain us,' Rachael replied.

'What are those, or is that an indelicate question?' Mark asked.

Sonny smiled at the risqué suggestion, but told him, 'We are both keen to do a lot of reading, so we are taking a stock of books with us. We are also packing a chess set, because we both enjoy it, and we can sharpen our skills. There is another board game we learned, one that is very popular in Crete. That's backgammon, and we saw lots of locals playing it in the evenings over a glass of something in the tavernas, so we had to try.'

'*Tavli*,' Andy said, startling everyone.

'What did you say?' his mother asked, fearing another diabolical joke.

'*Tavli*, Mum, it's the Greek name for backgammon.'

* * *

Although Lizzie tried to refuse her mother's offer, stating that there was no need as she could afford everything, Rachael had insisted she pay for the wedding dress and for Lizzie's trousseau. 'And why not?' Rachael had asked. 'It's my privilege — your father's paying for the wedding.'

Along with Jenny, they met up in York and spent hours touring the shops, looking for suitable attire, not just for the bride. It seemed that for weeks, bags and boxes were constantly being delivered to Byland Crescent.

When the bright summer's day dawned, Lizzie looked wonderful in her bridal gown for the ceremony at St Mary's Church. Susan was her bridesmaid, with Andy as groomsman.

Gil, dressed in a morning suit, admired the sight as Lizzie walked up the aisle on Sonny's arm. The best man, a friend and fellow doctor Gil had worked with at the hospital, nudged the groom. 'I can see why you gave up your career as a surgeon. You lucky devil.'

As Gil had no relatives, the wedding numbers were deliberately kept small, but his side of the church was filled with colleagues, mostly off-duty nurses, wanting one final glimpse of the handsome doctor.

At the back of the church sat an elderly figure, watching the proceedings. As the bridal party headed back down the aisle, Edrith Pointon rose to his feet, smiled and nodded at the bride, slipped discreetly from the pew, and exited the church.

Outside the church, with sea views behind the happy couple, the family gathered for the photographs to commemorate the occasion. The press cameraman fought for position to get the best image that would satisfy his editor, with the photographer employed by Sonny, before dashing back to the office to meet his deadline.

Following the reception, when asked where they were to spend the honeymoon, Gil replied, 'I'm taking her to Norway — it's one place she hasn't been!'

* * *

Towards the middle of October, Mark drove his parents to York, where they were to board the train on the first leg of their journey, described by Andy as a modern-day odyssey. Given the complete lack of urgency, they had decided to spend a couple of weeks in London, before heading onwards.

'What are you planning to do while you're in the big city?' Mark asked as they drove along the A64.

'We're going to do a lot of sightseeing,' Sonny replied, 'using London to get in practice for gawping at ancient buildings. Neither of us has spent any time in the capital, so we thought this would be the ideal opportunity.'

'It's a shame you didn't go in summer, then you could have watched some Test cricket,' Mark replied, with a provocative glance in the rear-view mirror. He grinned, as his mother gave him a disdainful look.

'Hardly worth it. The only match that ended with a positive result was at Headingley, and that went the wrong way,' Sonny muttered.

'Besides which,' Rachael added, 'your father would only get agitated, because he reckons most of the current English batsmen aren't as good as he was.'

'True,' was all Sonny could respond.

Rachael continued, 'As well as sightseeing, we've been lucky enough to get tickets for some West End shows, thanks to your sister.'

'Lizzie got them for you?'

'Yes, when I mentioned the idea to her, during one of our phone calls, I bemoaned the fact that all the best ones were booked solid months in advance, she told me she had a contact who might be able to help. A fortnight later, she sent a letter containing tickets for *Camelot* and *The Mousetrap.*'

Mark whistled with surprise. 'Her contact must be pretty influential, getting tickets for both of those. I find it staggering that *The Mousetrap* is still attracting full houses given that it's been running for twelve years already.'

'I didn't realize you'd developed such a keen interest in thespian matters,' Sonny commented.

'I haven't really, but I read an article in one of the papers last week all about what's on in the West End and it gave all sorts of statistics about the Agatha Christie play and the records its long run has broken.' Mark paused, before asking, 'Once you've wallowed in the fleshpots of London are you heading straight for Crete?'

'Don't you ever talk to your wife?' Rachael teased him. 'I gave Jenny a detailed itinerary a few days ago. We're spending time in Athens first. After our previous visit, we know there are lots more sights to take in. Then we'll take a ferry from Piraeus to Crete, and Sifis, our taxi driver, has promised that if we phone him beforehand he'll meet us from the boat.'

'It certainly doesn't sound as if you'll be bored,' Mark told them, adding with a grimace, 'and at least you'll be away from the wailing infants.'

CHAPTER TWENTY-FOUR

Seated in the office they shared at Fisher Springs, Bella announced, 'I'm worried about Jimmy.'

Luke stared at his wife, surprised by her statement. He glanced round, a reflex action because there was no chance of them being overheard. 'Why? What has he done wrong?'

'Nothing, and that's the point.'

'I must be thick, because whatever the point is, I've missed it.'

'I've kept a close eye on him and I've seen no evidence of him showing the slightest interest in girls. He'll be seventeen soon, so don't tell me that's natural.'

'Perhaps he's decided to steer clear of them until he's older. If that's all you're worried about, I'd say you can relax.'

'I suppose you're right, but he doesn't seem interested in much else either. When I asked him the other day if he'd any plans or ideas for the future, he didn't seem to know, or care. He doesn't even seem interested in joining the business.'

'That's by no means unique in a lad of his age, though. I'm sure he'll find something that appeals to him before long. He's certainly not afraid of hard work, which is a good sign.'

'How do you know that?'

'He's been helping out at the vineyard since he was fifteen, spending a chunk of every holiday there. Gianni reckons he works harder than some of the full-time employees.'

'That's good to know, so perhaps if he's so interested in it, his future might be in viniculture. I wonder what it is about the vineyard that's caused him to be so keen on going back there?'

Although they puzzled it over, neither parent came up with the solution to Bella's question.

'One good thing about Jimmy spending so much time at the vineyard is that it keeps him and Saul separate. I thought things had calmed down between those two, but I've realized recently that something about Jimmy gets Saul's back up. Jimmy does nothing to provoke it. I almost think Saul is deliberately trying to goad him, but why is a complete mystery.'

'Maybe it's simply a clash of personalities.' Luke chuckled and then told her, 'If you want something to worry about, I'd concentrate on Saul rather than Jimmy. He certainly isn't disinterested when it comes to girls, and by the sound of it, the interest is mutual.'

'How did you find that out?'

'Robyn let something slip when I was driving her to violin practice yesterday.'

'What did she say?'

'We were passing two girls wearing school uniform. Robyn recognized them, and said, "They're members of Saul's fan club". I asked what she meant and she told me Saul's got quite a few admirers. By the sound of it, I don't think the girls are devoted because of his skill as a batsman.'

'Oh, thanks, Luke, he's not yet fourteen, that's even more to worry about. I just hope Robyn doesn't get fascinated by the conductor of her orchestra waving his baton.'

Luke grinned at Bella's salacious comment, but told her, 'I don't think that's at all likely. Of the three, Robyn is the only one we've never had to be concerned about. Even if she does start to get ideas about boys, I don't believe she would behave improperly. Anyway, I think she'll prefer not to settle for just one lad.'

'Why?'

Luke grinned. 'She's a violinist, remember, she'll want more than one string to her bow.'

He moved sideways swiftly enough to avoid the scrunched-up ball of paper Bella hurled at him.

Although Bella's bewilderment over her son's apparent disinterest in girls remained, the question over his path in life was seemingly answered following his next, and final, school term. Jimmy had begged his parents to allow him to leave school. They knew his reports were always as expected, and he had a good head on his shoulders. Knowing if they insisted he continued with his education it would possibly build resentment, they conceded with one proviso — they insisted he should find decent employment.

On leaving the academic life behind, Jimmy had headed, as in all previous breaks, to the vineyard. When his time there was over, he returned home, being ferried there by his employers, Gianni and Angelina, who used the journey for a social visit, and to put forward a proposition to Luke and Bella.

Gianni began by telling them, 'We would like to take Jimmy on as a permanent employee. Our idea is not simply to use Jimmy as a manual worker, but to train him in all the aspects of viniculture.' He glanced at Angelina, who explained in more detail.

'There will come a time when we are no longer able to run the vineyard, attending to all the finer details, and there have been some aspects we have overlooked in the development of the business. We think Jimmy has great potential for a management position, and might also be successful in marketing the wines throughout the country.'

'He's already demonstrated his diligence, in fact I'd say he's one of the best workers among all our employees,' Gianni added. 'And I know from experience he can be trusted to tackle a job without the need for supervision. Obviously he would start as a trainee, but Angelina and I will tutor him on the technical side. Above all we like and trust him, and he is very popular with the other members of staff. We think the vineyard's future would be safe in his hands.'

'Does Jimmy know what your plans for him are?' Bella asked.

'He knows some of it, but not all. We certainly didn't tell him how much we value him, because we didn't want the praise going to his head,' Angelina told her.

'What was his reaction when you mentioned it?'

'He seemed very keen, but he told us you'd have to agree.'

'I think we need to talk it over, both between ourselves and with Jimmy. But we'll be sure to let you know our decision in a couple of days or so,' Luke told them.

Once Gianni and Angelina had left, Luke and Bella discussed their offer, which had come as a complete surprise. 'Above all, we need to make absolutely certain this is what he really wants to do,' Bella suggested, 'or whether he was merely being polite to them.'

'That's an extremely good point, Bella, and I agree it's certainly an unusual career choice for a seventeen-year-old. However, the evidence would tend to support his interest in it. He seems as keen as ever to return whenever the opportunity arises.'

'I'm beginning to wonder if there's another attraction, apart from being paid to spend his time in the fresh air, and if so, what that attraction is?'

Having thought it over, Luke said, 'Maybe you're reading too much into it, and it is purely the chance to work in the open air, at a job that doesn't test him too much intellectually. After all, his school grades have always been average, never exceptional. He's not dim, but he's certainly no rocket scientist.'

'Would you be upset if he decides to go down that route, rather than following in your footsteps and those of your parents at Fisher Springs?'

'No, not really, because it's his future that matters, and I've never seen Fisher Springs as a dynastic operation. Let's be fair, although we don't know the exact circumstances, Mum and Dad left England for a completely new life here, so I can't really hold a grudge if Jimmy wants to do something similar.'

'OK, let's put it to him and see how he reacts.'

* * *

Before that meeting took place, however, Jimmy was involved in another confrontation, one that resolved a difficulty that had been troubling him and his parents. He was in his bedroom, sorting out clothing that required washing, as instructed by his mother, when there was a knock on the door. He opened it to find his younger brother standing outside.

'What do you want?' Jimmy demanded.

For some reason he couldn't fathom, Saul appeared nervous, which was totally unlike him. 'Could I have a word in private, Jimmy?'

He opened the door wider, allowing Saul to enter. 'OK, what's this about? What have I done to offend you this time?' He'd been troubled by their differences, which seemed to be escalating, so he was surprised by Saul's response.

'I . . . er . . . came to say sorry. I know I've been a pain, and taken it out on you, but I now know I was being totally unfair. The thing is . . .' Saul hesitated, unsure of how to phrase the next part of his apology. 'Over a year ago I was told you'd been slanging me off at school. Some guys said you'd told them you knew I was a queer, that you'd seen me kissing a boy.'

Jimmy gasped with surprise, but listened as Saul continued. 'I've taken a lot of abuse, but kept quiet. It was only last week, when I overheard two of them laughing and talking in the changing rooms about how one of them had invented it, all because the girl he had the hots for was interested in me, not him. That's when I realized the whole thing was a set-up. Today, I got him on one side, and had a quiet word. He won't do anything like that again.' As he spoke he rubbed his bruised knuckles, subconsciously.

'So you dealt with the mongrel?'

'Er, yes, he could be singing treble for a while. Look, Jimmy, I'm truly sorry, because I should have trusted you not to do, or say, anything that bad.' Saul looked at his brother, still uncertain of his reaction.

'No worries. I've been trying for ages to work out why you'd suddenly turned nasty on me. I couldn't understand what I'd done that was so offensive.'

The meeting ended with the brothers shaking hands. 'I'd give you a hug,' Jimmy told him as he opened the door, 'but I don't want anybody to think we're both queer.'

Their laughter echoed through the building, causing Luke and Bella to stare at each other in surprise.

* * *

Next morning, Luke and Bella summoned Jimmy into the sitting room, having made it clear to Saul and Robyn that they were not to be disturbed. As he entered the room, Jimmy saw that both his parents looked serious, and wondered if he'd done something to upset them. He was surprised, however, when they explained what the meeting was about.

If Jimmy was uncertain about their motive for seeing him, Luke and Bella were astonished by his enthusiastic response when they asked him if he would truly wish to continue working at the vineyard full-time. This was before they revealed the extent of Gianni and Angelina's plans for his future. As they were unaware of Jimmy's secret agenda, they were puzzled by his positivity. Had they known what was behind it, they would have been relieved to learn he had an interest in girls. Whether they would have approved is a different matter.

As Jimmy left the room he recalled his most recent tour of duty at the vineyard. He had worked alongside Flavia, the first time they had been paired up as a team. During one of their rest periods, they had discussed their respective futures.

'I'm fortunate, because my path in life is already set out for me, and it's the one I want more than anything,' Flavia told him. 'I suppose it's genetic, but I couldn't think of anything better than being here, working in the family business, producing something that brings immense pleasure to a lot of people.'

'That's great. I must admit, I envy you for having such a clear idea about the future.'

'What about you? Have you made any plans?'

'Not really. Although I've really enjoyed working here, I don't know whether I'd be considered good enough to be employed full-time. So I suppose I ought to start looking elsewhere.'

'That would be a shame, having gained so much experience. Perhaps you should ask my parents if they'd take you on.'

Jimmy stared at the row of vines stretching into the distance and sighed. 'They might think I was being pushy, taking advantage of my parents' interest in the vineyard. I will regret it, because I've really enjoyed being here.' He glanced at the girl seated alongside him and added, 'Particularly this time, working alongside you.' He stopped, aghast at his temerity, almost trembling in fear at her reaction to his bold declaration of interest.

Flavia smiled gently, and said, 'I'm glad about that, because I've enjoyed it too.'

Now, as Jimmy listened to the offer made by Gianni and Angelina, and remembered that conversation, he knew it provided promise for his developing friendship with Flavia.

When he signalled his delight in accepting the deal, neither he nor his parents could envisage where that decision would lead.

CHAPTER TWENTY-FIVE

Resting at home after a long day, Luke and Bella were talking over family matters.

'Robyn only seems interested in her music. If she isn't attending violin or piano lessons, it's only because they clash with choir practice,' Bella said.

'Talking of Robyn, I've got some really exciting news. When I dropped her and Saul at school this morning, Robyn's music teacher was waiting by the gate to speak to me. As you know, the school is giving a big concert and Robyn has been selected to perform a violin solo.'

'That's great, what does Robyn think about it?'

'She's very excited, and more than a bit nervous, I think. Anyway, that wasn't all the teacher told me. He went on to say that although he's been teaching music for over twenty years, he's never had a pupil with Robyn's outstanding talent, her ear for music, or her ability to interpret a particular melody. He said there is very little he can do to improve her technique, so all he concentrates on are one or two minor points of her performance. The rest of the time he sits back and enjoys listening to her playing. His final comment was that if she wants to follow music as a profession, he sees no reason for her not to become a first-class violinist, either as a soloist or in an orchestra. He also said if she doesn't continue, it would be a great loss.'

'Wow, that really is good news. Do you think Robyn will choose to go down that path?'

'I'm not sure, but one thing I do know is that we must make no attempt to try and persuade her one way or the other. She has to make the decision alone, and whatever she chooses, we must back her all the way.'

* * *

The day was hot, the skies clear, ideal for the occasion. The concert in which Robyn Fisher was to play her violin solo was scheduled to take place in the park alongside her school, so the weather came as a relief to the organizers. Admission to the event was free, the purpose being to provide entertainment, and to showcase the burgeoning talent of the pupils.

Many of the town's residents attended, along with family members and guests visiting for the holiday. Alongside Robyn's parents and siblings in the audience were Luke and Bella's co-directors, with their children, plus Gianni and Angelina Rocca, accompanied by Flavia.

The family, together with the other members of the audience, listened with awe, mixed, in Luke and Bella's case, with pride, as Robyn played the piece she and her music teacher had suggested, the hauntingly beautiful 'Romance' from *The Gadfly*, composed by Dmitri Shostakovich. Although they were unaware of it, Robyn's interpretation of this moving work would have a lasting effect on her future.

The concert also gave Bella an inkling as to the reason for her eldest son's eagerness to embrace a career in viniculture. Having noticed the tender expression on Jimmy's face as he was talking to Flavia between acts, their hands touching occasionally, Bella was convinced he had more than a passing interest in the girl. She waited until the visitors were bidding their farewells and then seized the opportunity for a private word with him.

'I do hope you're behaving yourself. Please remember that Gianni and Angelina are not only our business partners, they are also close friends. I do not want that friendship undermined because you're behaving inappropriately towards their daughter.'

Jimmy looked at his mother and could tell by her expression as much as her words that his secret was no longer a secret. 'I certainly won't do anything wrong, Mum. I think far too much of Flavia to behave badly.'

'Is Flavia the reason you've been returning to the vineyard time after time? And is she the reason you've accepted the offer to work there in future?'

'Partly, Mum, but even if I didn't care for Flavia like I do, I'd still enjoy working there. I think it suits me.'

'OK, just remember, you're both only seventeen, and you've lots of time ahead of you.' Bella paused and asked, 'Do you know if Flavia feels the same about you?'

'I don't know, but I certainly hope so.'

Bella left it at that, but later, she pondered long and hard before revealing what she'd discovered to Luke. When she did, his reaction was immediate. 'That shows what good taste he's got. Flavia's not only a very nice girl, she's also extremely pretty.'

* * *

There was a further pleasant surprise awaiting Luke and Bella when they returned from work a fortnight later. Bella opened an envelope addressed simply to Mr and Mrs Fisher. She had to read the contents three times before the full realization dawned on her.

'Luke, listen to this. Robyn's been selected to audition for the Melbourne Symphony Orchestra. Apparently one of their people was in the audience at the concert and was so impressed with her performance of that Shostakovich piece he recommended her to their music director.'

If the early part of 1966 had brought exciting news to the Fisher household, there was more to come that year, for them and their extended family. The first item came via the mail and was no surprise to the recipients. Bella opened the envelope, scanned the contents before passing the card to Luke. He read the opening line, which was addressed to the whole family. '*Mrs Amelia Fisher requests your company to celebrate the wedding of her daughter Clare to Benjamin Lawson.*'

'That's great news. We haven't been to a decent party for ages.' Luke paused, smiled slyly at Bella, then added, 'I wonder if Clare will follow the Fisher family tradition? If she does, we might soon have a christening to attend before long.'

'Don't judge everyone by yourself,' Bella chided him. 'Just because you were as randy as a goat doesn't mean everyone acts like you.'

'Hah, I didn't hear you complaining. In fact you were the one desperate to get me into bed. In any case, it wasn't just me. Amelia was expecting when she and Phil got married, and after my parents left England they got married here. You can work out Mum must have been pregnant by the dates.'

The ceremony and reception that followed were splendid, organized right down to the last detail. On leaving the church, the happy couple passed a guard of honour formed by their fellow police officers. They stood rigidly to attention with truncheons held high, until the bride and groom reached halfway along their line, before the lawmen broke ranks and began pelting them with shower after shower of confetti and rice.

Once they had run the gauntlet, the bride and groom climbed into the limousine provided for the occasion for the short drive to the hotel restaurant where the reception was to be held. Although the officers attending the event were mostly of similar rank to Ben and Clare, Luke was pleased to see several senior members of the force there, including the commissioner.

One of the couple's colleagues, deserting the guests seated at his table, spent a fair amount of time talking to Luke and Bella's younger son, Saul. Later, Bella asked what the conversation was about. 'You haven't been getting into trouble, I hope?' she asked, only half-joking.

'No, it's nothing like that. Geoff is captain of the local cricket team. He's been hearing about my batting and wants me to attend one of their net practice sessions so he can judge for himself. If he rates me as good enough, he wants to give me a try-out.'

'How did he get to know about you?'

'Apparently my school cricket coach mentioned me, and quoted some statistics which got Geoff interested. With a bit of luck, I might get into the club's squad for next season, which is unusual for someone my age.'

Saul's older brother Jimmy was also at the wedding, having taken a weekend leave of absence from the vineyard. Although many of the younger guests took full advantage of the music provided during the evening by the DJ to demonstrate their dancing skills — or in some cases their lack of skill — Jimmy took no part in this.

Bella noticed Jimmy's unwillingness to be dragged onto the dance floor, despite the availability of several undoubtedly pretty potential partners, and correctly identified the reason for his reluctance. In an aside to Luke, Bella suggested, 'We should have asked Amelia to extend the invitation to Flavia Rocca, because Jimmy is obviously pining for her.'

'You don't think that's cooled off, then?'

'Certainly not as far as Jimmy is concerned, judging by his downcast expression. Looking at him, you'd think he was at a wake rather than a wedding. What we don't know yet is whether Flavia is as interested in Jimmy. If that's so, we might have another wedding to attend before too long.'

'They're a bit young to be tying the knot, though, don't you think?'

Bella shook her head, and laughed. 'Getting forgetful are we, Luke? I was almost sixteen when you went away to war, otherwise we'd have got married after my birthday. And those two won't be getting into any trouble before they do. I warned Jimmy to behave properly, and he promised me he would. He insisted that he thinks far too highly of Flavia to do anything like that. He also respects Gianni and Angelina and would not want to risk offending them.'

CHAPTER TWENTY-SIX

When Jimmy returned to the vineyard, he was given new instructions from Gianni. 'I need you to inspect the vines before we harvest, and also remove any weeds from the soil surrounding them. You must pay particularly close attention to any signs of aphid activity or blight on the plants. You will not be alone — this task requires two people working together. Because of the size of the vineyard, all the crews will be given a specific area to cover.' Gianni smiled. 'I have given you the most remote section of land, because you and your co-worker are younger and fitter than the others, and therefore able to walk further, and cope with the steeper gradients. For that reason you will be working with Flavia.'

Given the detailed nature of the task, Jimmy realized it would take a while to complete the section allotted to him. Far from being daunted by this, he relished the prospect, knowing it would give him extended time alone with Flavia.

When they met up the following morning, Flavia presented him with a small package plus three bottles of water. 'My mother made up some sandwiches for our lunch,' she explained.

Although Jimmy desperately wanted to tell Flavia what was in his heart, it was lunchtime before the opportunity, and his courage, arose. They had paused for their snack which they took while sitting at the perimeter, leaning back against the stanchions supporting the covering net that protected the vines from avian assault.

'How was the wedding?' Flavia asked.

'All right, I suppose. The happy couple seemed happy enough.'

Flavia was puzzled by his following remark.

'Everybody looked to be enjoying the reception and disco, so I suppose it was a great success.'

'Did you have a good time? Were there lots of pretty girls to dance with?'

'There were a few girls there, and I guess some of them were pretty enough, but I wasn't interested.'

'Why not?'

Jimmy took a deep breath. It was now or never, do or die. 'I didn't enjoy the party because you weren't there, Flavia. None of those girls could hold a candle to you. I'm sorry if this offends you, but the plain fact is I love you. I have done for years. That's the reason I kept coming back here every chance I could get.'

'Why have you not spoken of this before now?'

Jimmy looked abashed. 'Because I was scared of how you would react. I was afraid of rejection, afraid of getting my heart broken, afraid of the loneliness of not being close to you.'

She smiled. 'I understand, and I believe it is important for you not to be afraid. So please do not worry, Jimmy. I'm glad you told me. It makes all my efforts worthwhile.'

'Efforts? What efforts?'

'The effort of pushing my father into offering you a full-time job, plus the effort of telling my parents I wanted to work alongside you and nobody else, and persuading them to ensure we were together.'

'You did all that?' He reached out and took her hand, pulled her close, and kissed her gently. He could feel the warmth of Flavia's body against his. He kissed her again, and this time there was nothing gentle about it. He backed away. 'I cannot do this, Flavia. I mustn't. I made a promise, a solemn one. My mother found out how I feel about you, and I vowed I wouldn't do anything your parents would disapprove of, or which would upset them.'

'That's very sweet of you, but my mother knows I love you, and she suspects you feel the same.' Her smile widened as she added, 'Her advice to me was to get you and keep you, because men of your calibre don't grow on trees.' Flavia giggled, and added, 'Or even on vines.'

It was much later, when he had recovered his breath, that Jimmy whispered, 'I have a question to ask you.'

'Tell me.'

'Will you marry me, Flavia? If we got married, nobody could stop us from being together.'

'Of course I will. But we must follow tradition. You should go to my father and ask his permission.'

Jimmy looked panic-stricken. 'What if he says no, or tells me we're too young?'

'If he does, he will have to answer to my mother.'

There was a long silence as they celebrated the engagement with a kiss that outranked the previous ones for passion. Then, with extreme reluctance, the couple returned to work.

* * *

Late that afternoon, Gianni and Angelina were seated on their veranda, as they received the reports from the workers returning from their day's toil. The last to arrive were Jimmy and Flavia, which was hardly surprising, as they had the furthest to travel. The time between the previous returning workers and the youngsters was sufficient for Gianni to comment.

'No doubt they have their reasons,' Angelina replied.

Eventually, when the absentees came into sight, Angelina nudged her husband and pointed out that they were holding hands. 'I said that would happen, didn't I? I guessed ages ago that Jimmy had fallen in love with her, and I know Flavia is keen on him.'

'But they're only seventeen. Are you not concerned?'

'Gianni, they are in love. Do you not remember what that feeling was like?' She looked at him, quizzically.

Gianni nodded and squeezed her hand, smiling. 'Yes, my dear, I do.'

'I also think Jimmy is soon going to ask you a question.'

'You reckon he is going to seek my approval for them to marry?'

'I do, and the fact they are holding hands in public convinces me.'

Angelina's prediction came true within minutes of the couple's arrival at the house.

Having gained the approval of Flavia's parents, Jimmy phoned his mother and told her the news. Flavia, who was standing close to him, listening to the conversation, blushed slightly when Bella told her son she was delighted, and impressed by the wisdom of his choice.

Once Bella put the phone down, she dashed through to the sitting room, where Luke was watching cricket on TV. 'I was right,' she announced triumphantly. 'We'll soon have another party to attend.'

Luke smiled. 'Does that mean Clare's—'

'No, it means that our son has just become engaged to Flavia Rocca.'

'Good for him — that's terrific news.' Luke gestured to the TV screen, where off-spinner Bob Cowper was about to bowl. 'I'll just wait until the end of this over and then I'll put some champagne in the fridge.'

* * *

Three months later, Flavia told Jimmy, 'I think we should visit your parents.'

'OK, any special reason?'

Flavia hesitated before she explained.

Jimmy looked concerned. 'I'm not sure how my mother will react.'

When the harvest was almost over, on a Saturday morning the young couple arrived at the Fisher house. Bella expressed her surprise. 'I thought you'd be too busy,' she told them.

'We've been given time off,' Jimmy replied. 'So we could come and visit, and, er, tell you we've decided to move the wedding date forward' — he glanced at Flavia — 'by a couple of years.'

'I think I can guess the reason for that.' Bella was furious. She looked directly at her son. 'You idiot. I assume this means you've disobeyed me. I ordered you not to misbehave with Flavia,' she said, sternly. 'And now, we're supposed to be happy about this?'

'I'm sorry. I really am. I didn't mean to let it happen, it just did. But we love each other, Mum.' Jimmy hung his head.

'Disobeying your mother is not what we expect from our family,' Luke said.

The young couple looked at each other in dismay.

'You'd better sit down, Flavia, while we discuss this.' Luke indicated the sofa, before leading Jimmy, along with Bella, to his study.

Flavia waited, her hands clenched tightly, unshed tears in her eyes. After what seemed an eternity, the trio returned and Flavia noticed Jimmy looked more relaxed. He sat alongside her, gripping her hand.

Luke looked directly at Flavia. 'Now we've both got over the shock, I have telephoned your father and, for some reason I can't quite fathom, he seems to like Jimmy. As he is already aware of, and accepts, the situation, we have concluded that as you were intending to marry, there is no reason why the ceremony cannot be brought forward. It doesn't mean any of us are happy about this, but what is done is done, so we better get this wedding arranged as soon as possible. I've told your father that although it's usual for the bride's parents to cover the cost, on this occasion it will be mine. And I'll take no argument on that.' Luke sank into a chair.

There was a long silence before Bella spoke. 'I've just realized — I'm going to be a grandma! Luke, you're going to be a grandpa!' she exclaimed. She stepped forward and hugged Flavia. 'We really are glad to welcome you into our family. Now for the important part — when is the baby due?'

'I . . . er . . . we're not sure. Sometime in October, we think.'

Six weeks later, the lavish wedding took place. 'Remind you of something?' Luke asked Bella as they danced at the reception.

'What are you thinking of?'

'December, 1948.' He held her closer as they waltzed round the room. 'You looked wonderful, my darling, and you still do.'

Bella, always known to be outspoken, responded, 'Yes, well you don't look too bad yourself, for an old geezer.' With that she looked into his eyes, smiled, then kissed him.

As Flavia had forecast, early in October of 1966, their daughter, Alice Lucia Fisher, was born. Luke was particularly pleased that Jimmy and Flavia had chosen to name their first child after his mother.

CHAPTER TWENTY-SEVEN

As Christmas 1966 approached, Susan Cowgill returned home following her first term at Leeds University, where she had begun the long process of studying to become a barrister.

On the train journey home, as she stared out of the window of the first-class carriage, she was reflecting on the time when she had told her parents of her intention to enter the legal profession.

She was approaching her fourteenth birthday, and it would soon be time for her to make choices in the subjects she needed to prioritize in her schoolwork. That decision had become a foregone conclusion after she had become addicted to television, to one genre in particular. Crime dramas such as *Maigret* and *No Hiding Place* fascinated her, but it was the cut and thrust of legal arguments in the American show *Perry Mason* that she found irresistible. The courtroom drama appealed far more than the police procedural shows.

As far as she was concerned, the arguments, and counter arguments, put forward by prosecution and defence counsels enabled her to come to a decision.

Although she was aware that the career she wanted to pursue would involve several additional years of intense study, at university and beyond, her mind was made up.

She had informed her parents and the careers master at her school of her ultimate goal of becoming a barrister.

Her father had cautioned her. 'That could prove harder than merely the studying aspect. It's a bit of a closed shop. If your face doesn't fit, you'd stand little or no chance of making it to the top. And you have an additional disadvantage, being female. As far as I know, women barristers are scarcer than hen's teeth.'

'I don't care. It's what I want to do, so I'm going for it, come what may. OK, I might fail, but at least I'll have given it a shot,' she'd told him.

At the time, her stubborn refusal to be deterred had impressed her parents. Jenny told Mark, 'Suzie wasn't put off by your dire warnings. In fact, if anything, I'd say they made her even more determined.'

'I know, and that's one of the reasons I said what I did. Her obstinacy will ensure she refuses to take no for an answer, so woe betide anyone who tries to stand in her way.'

Jenny stared at him. 'You said that just to test her resolve, didn't you? There are times when I think you could give Machiavelli lessons in deviousness.'

When Suzie had discussed this plan further with her parents, Mark had begun by commending her on the wisdom of her choice, then added, 'If you need help with any history research, you can always ask your grandpa, he's lived through a fair amount of it.'

Jenny had ignored her husband's attempt at humour, and asked, 'Does that mean you'll be at university longer than normal undergraduates?'

'Yes, in all, I'll need at least five or six years to get where I want to be. I plan to get a job to help with the finances.' Suzie wasn't often shocked, but her surprise when her father burst out laughing was obvious.

'You don't need to worry about the money, Suzie. We have more than enough to pay for your accommodation, course fees, reading material and a living allowance for you, even if it takes longer than six years.'

'Yes,' her mother had added, with laughter, 'it will also enable you to buy suitable clothing. Something that will keep you warmer than that deep belt you are wearing that you allege is a skirt.'

Now, on the train home, Suzie smiled recalling her mother's reference to her new miniskirt, the tears she had shed at their acceptance, and their generosity that enabled her to study, working even harder to make them proud.

* * *

It was during the Christmas celebrations, with the entire family resident, that a plot was hatched. Rachael Cowgill recruited her conspirators in the strictest secrecy. While Sonny was in his study, Rachael called Lizzie, her husband Gil, plus Andy, his wife Consuela, and Susan into the lounge and outlined her plan. 'Sonny will be seventy-five next year, and both Mark and Jenny will be fifty. I propose we hold a joint birthday celebration for them. If any of you can help with suggestions, I'd be grateful. But none of them must find out — it must be a total surprise. Phone me during the day while Sonny's likely to be on the golf course if you think of anything.'

When they were back home in Wensleydale, Lizzie and Gil discussed the plot and dwelt on the importance of the year ahead. 'Mum would have excluded me from our little secret society, but I'd already told her I didn't want any fuss for my fortieth birthday. I said that like most women I'd prefer to remain thirty-nine years old for the next ten years. Besides, I'll have enough to do.' She patted her expanding waistline as she spoke.

Gil laughed, but told her, 'Let's be fair, there have been a considerable number of momentous events over the past few years — some of them good, others terrible. So I think 1967 will be a great year for the household to celebrate.'

The news that she was pregnant had stunned her family, and even surprised her husband. There was concern, mainly because of Lizzie's age, expressed by her father. However,

Rachael was able to reassure Sonny, and the other family members. 'Lizzie is only thirty-nine,' she pointed out. 'There have been many instances of women conceiving and giving birth when they are over the age of fifty.'

Some weeks later, Lizzie struggled to her feet to continue packing suitcases for the journey to Scarborough. Her mother had insisted they stay in Byland Crescent in preparation for the birth, to be closer to a larger facility than the local cottage hospital. Gil had arranged locum cover for the surgery so he could accompany her.

As she worked, Lizzie reflected on Gil's earlier comment. It was certainly true that both nationally and internationally there had been plenty of reasons to celebrate, and equally to mourn.

In the latter category, 1965 had marked the death of the man deemed by many to be the greatest Englishman of all time, Sir Winston Churchill. His passing had plunged the nation into mourning, relegating other events. There was also light and dark in 1966, with England's triumph over West Germany in the football World Cup being cause for national rejoicing. However, the landslide that destroyed the village school in Aberfan, causing the deaths of 116 children and twenty-eight adults shocked, horrified and saddened the whole of the United Kingdom and many people worldwide.

All in all, Lizzie thought, there was much to remember — and equally, much to regret. Her musing was rudely interrupted by a kick beneath her ribcage, reminding her of the impending arrival of their first child in a couple of weeks.

Two weeks later in the summer's evening, Gil Richardson bounded through the sitting-room door at Byland Crescent with momentous news. His beaming smile told the family he was bearing good tidings, even before he spoke.

'Lizzie is OK, but extremely tired. In the end, everything went well. We've decided to call our daughter Heloise, after my mother, who was French.' Gil paused, grinning even wider, then added, 'And we've decided to call our son William.'

There was a stunned silence, broken eventually by Mark. 'She's had twins, is that what you're telling us?'

'That's right, and both of them were a healthy weight and are doing fine. That explains why she's been so exhausted these last few weeks.'

'How absolutely typical of Lizzie, she never does anything by halves,' Mark said.

'Why didn't you tell us she was expecting twins?' Jenny asked.

'Because we didn't know.' Gil sank onto the sofa, shaking his head.

'I thought you were a doctor,' Mark retorted.

'Mark!' Rachael said.

Gil laughed. 'It's all right. I am not my wife's doctor, Mark. I don't believe it would be ethical for me to be so. My colleague told her she was carrying a lot of water. But it does explain why I had so many kicks in my back during the night.'

'I didn't know there were any twins in the family,' Jenny said.

'Oh, but there are,' Sonny told them. 'My aunt Bessie on my father's side had twins, Ephraim and Jessie. Their elder brother was the notorious Clarence Barker.'

Andy turned to Consuela. 'He's the one that got hanged.'

'Well, enough of that,' Sonny said. 'I think this calls for a celebration.'

* * *

1967 was drawing to a close, and Sonny and Rachael were discussing the memorable events the year had brought to the Cowgill family. 'So much has happened, it's difficult to know which has been the most exciting,' Rachael commented.

Sonny couldn't resist teasing her. 'I'd have thought that as a grandmother, the birth of Lizzie's twins would have topped your list. They certainly got your maternal juices flowing.'

Rachael smiled. 'They're a couple of adorable little cuties, that's for sure. I just wish I could see them more often.' She paused before switching topics slightly. 'Apart from them, we've had a fair amount on our plates this year. There's been James' first term at primary school, the twins' christening, and Suzie finishing her first year at university. That's been a lot to contend with.'

'You've forgotten one major event,' Sonny pointed out, 'which surprises me, as you were its instigator.'

He smiled as he saw Rachael's puzzled expression. 'I'm talking about the party to end all parties. That has to be classed as the social event of the decade.'

It was true the two-day celebration that had taken place over the August bank holiday weekend had been a great success. It had been planned to mark significant birthday anniversaries for three family members, but these had been augmented by the birth of Lizzie's twins, Heloise and William. The weather had been kind to them, unusually so for a holiday weekend.

This had enabled the family, along with a contingent from Bradford of the directors of Fisher Springs UK and their families, plus other friends, to enjoy the outdoor feasts provided by Sarah, the cook, with the help of the housekeeper, Mary. Under normal circumstances, caterers would have been employed, but Rachael did not wish to offend Sarah, who was not to be dissuaded.

On the Saturday the guests had been able to tuck into an outdoor buffet and grill. The main component of which was enough steaks and sausages for Mark to comment that their butcher would be able to take his wife on a luxury cruise on the proceeds. If his takings had been swollen by the Saturday order, the fishmonger would have benefitted similarly from Sunday's menu. This comprised a giant paella, prepared and cooked under the direction of Consuela.

At one point during the planning, Rachael had wondered why Lizzie was determined to make it a two-day event. It was only on the Sunday, when she and Sonny stepped into the large garden in the centre of the Byland Crescent that the reason became clear.

Their family and friends were gathered again, and as Rachael linked Sonny's arm and led him into the throng, she glanced round. Rachael saw the balloons and streamers commemorating their golden wedding, and she realized she'd been upstaged by her daughter and co-conspirators.

'It's certainly been an epic year,' Sonny concluded, 'and I doubt if next year will be able to match it. Perhaps that's no bad thing, particularly for us old folks. There comes a point in life when too much excitement is bad for you.'

'Don't you start acting like a geriatric! It's bad enough coping with the younger end of the family without having to worry about a doddery old man.'

'I'm fine. You don't have to fret about me.' Sonny grinned and added, 'I've still got all my teeth as well, as I could demonstrate later if you want.'

The love bite reference had become a standing joke between them, but definitely not one they shared with other family members.

* * *

Many thousands of miles from Scarborough, Luke Fisher was also taking stock of an exciting year's events, along with Bella.

'They've all done really well this year,' Bella commented. 'Jimmy and Flavia have a lovely daughter and seem really contented. Robyn's been offered the chance to study at Melbourne University. Not only that, but her music teacher believes she's good enough to be considered for acceptance by the Yehudi Menuhin School in England, which is apparently the highest honour available for any budding violinist.'

'I agree, although I know as much about classical music as I do astrophysics. Nor has it been a bad year for our budding Bradman, and that is a subject I do understand. Not that I believe our Saul will ever be good enough to emulate the great Sir Donald, but for someone as young as him to score four centuries in club cricket has to be an outstanding achievement. Having watched a couple of those games I was impressed with the way Saul handled some very good, sometimes hostile, bowling.'

'I don't know as much about cricket as you by any means, so what was it in particular that pleased you?'

'The way he played the quick bowlers. He wasn't fazed when they dropped the ball short and I think the method he adopted for dealing with bouncers is by far the best.' Noticing Bella's puzzled frown, Luke explained, 'Fast bowlers drop the ball short of a length to make it rise around chest or head height. It's a way of intimidating the batsman, by attempting to make him play a false shot. Saul simply got inside the line of the ball every time it was short of a length and hit it out of the park. Nothing annoys a bowler more than being hit for six, so his shots made them reluctant to repeat the tactic.'

'It isn't only our immediate family who have much to be pleased about though,' Bella suggested. 'Remember, Clare and Ben have announced they are expecting.'

'That's true, and I'm really happy for them. They've had more than enough adversity to contend with, one way or another, so this will be really good for them.'

CHAPTER TWENTY-EIGHT

For the Cowgill family in Scarborough and their hidden relatives, the Fisher clan in Western Australia, the new year lived up to the promise they had both anticipated.

In Byland Crescent, the good news centred round Sonny and Rachael's children and great-grandchildren. Principal among the good tidings was the successful birth of Andrew and Consuela's third child, a baby sister to accompany, or to annoy, her older siblings, James and Angela.

The new arrival's great-grandmother was particularly touched, her pride evident when they told her the name they had decided on for the infant. 'We're going to call the little one Raquel,' Andy informed the family. 'That's the Spanish equivalent of Rachael.'

'Wow, I'd never have guessed that if you hadn't told me,' Andrew's father commented.

Sonny glanced across the room to where Rachael was seated nursing the baby, and saw she was close to tears. He decided to lighten the moment and divert his wife from the emotion that threatened to overcome her. 'Is that because you've always fancied Raquel Welch?' he teased Andy. The glare he got from Rachael, accompanied by Andy's strenuous denial, achieved its objective by distracting them from becoming too emotional.

The pregnancy meant that Consuela had to retire temporarily from her job. The management of the appliance shop she owned along with Andrew had to take second place to caring for her baby. Nora Watts, who worked part-time in the shop, had agreed to increase her hours to help cover her absence, while Andy considered employing another technician.

Meanwhile, in Australia there was also plenty for the Fisher family to celebrate. The first big occasion they attended was the christening ceremony for Clare and Ben Lawson's first child. Clare gave birth during April, and two months later, her uncle and aunt, Luke and Bella Fisher, were honoured to stand alongside the proud parents as they promised to care for baby Charlotte as her godparents.

There were mixed blessings in the other good news they received that year, when Luke and Bella learned that their daughter Robyn had now been accepted as a student at the prestigious violin school in England. They were naturally delighted at this honour, but at the same time saddened when they realized this would mean separation from their daughter for long periods of time. It was heartening to know that Robyn's undoubted talent was becoming recognized, but the thought that their seventeen-year-old daughter would be thousands of miles away was of immense concern, particularly for her mother.

They received a measure of reassurance via her music tutor, who told the anxious parents, 'Robyn will be in a totally safe environment, there is a housemother to ensure all pupils' welfare. The administrators of the school have invested a good deal of time and resources in their pupils' advancement, and will not allow anything to distract the students from that purpose. In fact, I'd say the school is almost like a seminary — as if they had entered a nunnery, but without the religious aspect.'

In Luke's sister's household, there was also satisfaction at the continuing progress of the three children at school. The trio's talents lay in completely different directions. Lance, allied to his cricketing skills, had shown developing talent in an area that demonstrated the power of heredity. His father Elliot had been a proficient artist as a young man, but had forfeited his artistic career to concentrate on a more stable occupation at Fisher Springs that would enable him to provide for his wife and family. Throughout his school years, Lance's art teacher was lavish in her praise for the pupil's work.

Jane, the eldest daughter, was an avid reader, her favourite subjects being history, be it fact or fiction, plus adventure stories. She was also no mean writer, as some of her school essays proved. By contrast, her sister Hazel was attracted by science, her attention being focussed on physics and chemistry, subjects in which she excelled, gaining highly positive reports from her teachers in those fields.

As Christmas approached, both wings of the Cowgill/Fisher clan knew there was much to celebrate and give thanks for.

* * *

In America, 1968 was marked by two horrific events. In early April, Martin Luther King, the prominent civil rights activist, was assassinated in Memphis, Tennessee. The American public and people throughout the world were still coming to terms with this appalling crime when a second, equally brutal murder took place.

Only two months later, in early June, Robert F Kennedy, younger brother of the assassinated president, entered the Ambassador Hotel in Los Angeles. Kennedy, one of the Democratic candidates being considered for the forthcoming presidential election, had just won a prestigious primary. Shortly after midnight, those aspirations were blown away by an assassin's bullets.

When the evening paper arrived in Byland Crescent, the entire family were shocked at the headline. For two siblings, both potentially great leaders of their country, to be struck down in this manner was almost beyond belief.

* * *

Five-year-old Angela Cowgill was unhappy, and took the grievance to her father, aware that she would get more sympathy from him than from her mother. The source of Angela's tribulation was her younger sibling Raquel. When Raquel was born, Angela had been excited and pleased, looking forward to the companionship her sister would provide. This optimistic viewpoint had continued for several months, but now Angela had become aware that her sister had several anti-social habits. Chief among these was the noise she made.

'Why does Raquel scream all night?' Angela demanded.

'That's because she's in pain,' her father replied. 'It's known as teething. When a baby's teeth begin to push through their gums it can be agonizing for them.'

Angela's grandmother, who was also in the room, added, 'Everyone goes through this stage, it won't last forever. You did the same, and so did your brother, your father, and your aunt Suzie. In fact I remember your dad complaining about Suzie in much the same way.'

'It's true,' Andy confirmed. 'Why do you think I call Aunt Suzie "Noise box"? I gave her the nickname. It was long before she started playing loud music.'

'I see,' Angela conceded. 'But why is it when I'm asleep?'

'That we can't answer,' Jenny told her. 'But if it's any comfort to you, she should soon have all her milk teeth and then she'll quieten down and you'll be able to get a good night's sleep again.' Jenny couldn't resist teasing her granddaughter a little, so she added, 'Unless your mum and dad decide to have another little brother or sister for you.'

Angela stamped her foot and glared at the adults. 'If that happens, I'm going to live with Auntie Lizzie and Uncle Gil. The twins have got teeth!'

* * *

In 1969 a telephone call from the family's solicitor gave Sonny cause for thought. After agreeing to what their legal representative proposed, Sonny went in search of Rachael. He found her in the nursery. Rachael was nursing her little namesake in an attempt to soothe her teething pains, and allow the child to have some much-needed sleep.

His voice barely more than a whisper, he said, 'We need to talk. But only when the little one has settled down.'

Rachael nodded her agreement and Sonny tiptoed quietly from the room. When she joined him in his study, she asked what was troubling him.

'Not troubling exactly, just something I think we ought to attend to without delay. I think we need to visit our solicitor and have new wills drafted. The ones we signed before we made our first visit to Crete are now way out of date. We made no provision for Lizzie, because at the time we had no idea where she was, or even if she was alive. Not only that, but since we made those wills there have been substantial additions to the family.'

'That is an extremely good point, but have you any idea how we should dispose of our assets?'

'Not as yet, because I haven't had much time to think it over. Apart from that, I think it would be unwise to rush into making such big decisions. I think it needs careful consideration to ensure everyone gets treated fairly and equally. That way there should be no grounds for recrimination between family members when we're no longer here to do anything about it.'

Having thought over Sonny's final statement for a few minutes, Rachael replied, 'I agree with your thoughts generally, but I believe the bricks and mortar side of things will be straightforward enough to sort out. As to the liquid assets, perhaps we should think about setting up an open-ended trust for the grandchildren and great-grandchildren. I'm not sure if that's legally practicable, so maybe we need to have a word with our solicitor first. It's no use making detailed plans for something that in the end isn't a feasible proposition.'

'What exactly do you mean by "open-ended"?' Sonny asked.

'There's no saying that Lizzie and Gil won't have more children, and the way Andrew and Consuela are carrying on, I think further additions to their little brood are highly likely.'

'That's a very good thought, Rachael. Perhaps we should make notes of things as we go along, that way we'll ensure we don't miss anything important out. There are other considerations too, things we haven't touched on, such as your jewellery, my father's gold fob watch and similar personal items. And of course there's the Bentley. In the meantime, I'll have a word with our solicitor and run your open-ended trust idea past him.'

CHAPTER TWENTY-NINE

One problem neither Andrew nor Consuela had anticipated when they opened the appliance sales and service venture eight years ago was the space it would occupy — space that they didn't have much of. As their reputation grew, the dilemma they faced was created by the need for more room to expand the business. The question was one that troubled both partners.

'Have you seen that vacant property on the high street?' Consuela asked.

'Yes, it would be ideal. But we need to think this through carefully.'

An opportunity to resolve the problem came about when Andrew's grandfather overheard a snippet of conversation on the subject, a discussion that was intended to be private. 'The space issue is becoming worse and worse,' Andrew told Consuela. 'In fact as things stand today it's nearly impossible to move, either in the shop, the stockroom or the workshop. I've had enquiries about washing machines and a range cooker this morning, which we can't supply. There's a demand for larger goods, along with our normal stock, but everywhere is crammed from floor to ceiling — the storeroom can't take anymore. If that wasn't bad enough, we also took in a vacuum cleaner, a record player and a TV set all in need of repair. Storing them is bad enough, trying to work on the repairs is well nigh impossible. Heaven help us if more items come in.'

Sonny didn't say anything, or reveal his presence, but later, after having spoken to Rachael, he managed to get Consuela alone. She had just finished putting the baby in her cot when Sonny called her into his study and asked her to close the door. He was well aware that approaching his grandson would not be an option, knowing Andy would undoubtedly refuse any further financial assistance from him.

'I understand there's a bit of a problem with the shop,' Sonny began. He saw she was about to protest, so he held his hand up. 'Don't deny it, Consuela, I overheard Andrew talking to you earlier, and I know it's true. I have a suggestion for you. I think you're right, what the business needs is a larger building to act as a shop, service centre, and warehouse combined. Like that one on the high street.' He smiled. 'In a more prominent position it would be a better sales outlet. I also think it would be a good idea to buy a van so you can make deliveries instead of relying on local couriers.'

'These are very good ideas, but we don't have the money for such expenditure yet. The business is making good progress, but we think it would be foolish to put that at risk by spending what little spare cash we have. Andy's father has taught us it's better to do it without borrowing money. At present almost all our takings are put to good use by replacing stock items and introducing new ones, so further expenditure isn't an option. Nor would it be fair to ask Mark and Jenny.'

'I wasn't for one minute suggesting you should borrow the money, or approach Mark and Jenny for it. They aren't the only family members with money to spare, you know. Since I retired, I have very little to spend my cash on, apart from a new Bentley every now and then. I've talked this through with Grandma Rachael and she's agreed my plan. We'll put up the money to enable you to buy the high-street building if it's suitable. We can also fund the purchase of a delivery vehicle. The sum we have in mind will also be sufficient to allow you to increase stock levels and widen your range of products much quicker.'

Consuela stared at Sonny, her face registering a range of emotions. 'Talk this over with Andy,' he continued, 'and when he raises objections, as he definitely will, tell him we're determined to help and won't take no for an answer. If that doesn't persuade him, tell him Grandma Rachael says he has to do as he's told. If all else fails, I'm sure you can think of another way to convince him.'

He waited for a few seconds, before adding what he believed would be a decisive statement. 'Let me explain our wider plan, and when you know it, you should be able to make the right decision. At the same time as we are doing this for you, we intend to make similar gratuities to other family members. That means we're not playing favourites. There is a sound reason for doing this,' Sonny paused, 'in fact there are two good reasons. The first is that it's important to have the money available when it's needed rather than having to wait until we're dead and gone. The other reason is that if we make these gifts now, they will become tax free, as long as we don't pop our clogs for a few years yet.'

Seeing Consuela was dumbfounded, and close to tears, Sonny told her, 'We're planning on having a celebratory meal at the weekend, when Suzie is home from university. We'll use that occasion to make the grand announcement.'

Eventually, when Consuela had recovered sufficiently, she asked Sonny the question that was puzzling her. 'What does "pop our clogs" mean?'

The room echoed to the sound of Sonny's laughter before he could explain. 'It means when we are no longer here.'

* * *

As the family members gathered for Sunday lunch the following weekend, they had no inkling of what the special occasion they were to celebrate was. Sonny guided them into the sitting room and asked them to sit down. Once they were settled, with Lizzie and Gil holding a twin each and Consuela cradling Raquel, Sonny looked at them and smiled. 'OK, here's the big announcement,' he began. 'As soon as the paperwork has been completed, which will hopefully happen within the next week or ten days, Rachael and I intend to make one-off payments in the sum of £50,000 each to everyone in this room. That includes those who are minors, for whom we are in the process of establishing trust funds. Furthermore, the trust we establish will be open-ended, to provide for any great-grandchildren who are yet to make an appearance.'

Sonny paused to let this news sink in, and into the stunned silence, continued, 'The reason we are doing this now is to avoid you having to pay tax on these sums as a legacy. In addition, subject to the agreement of all parties concerned, we intend to sign new wills next week, and in those documents we have decided to bequeath this house jointly to Mark, Jenny and their family. We have made separate bequests to our other children to match the value of the property. One thing we would ask of you is that you all consider what I have told you at great length, and if there is anything you are uncertain or unhappy about, you should come and talk to Rachael or me. What we want to avoid at all costs is for anyone to feel let down or cheated by this arrangement. As we see it, these provisions go as far as we can think of to avoid any potential bickering when we are no longer here to take preventative measures. We've seen too many family squabbles over the provisions made by the deceased for us to want you to endure that.'

* * *

Some weeks later, Consuela entered into a conversation with Andy's grandfather that led to her hearing a fascinating, deeply moving, and romantic part of the Cowgill family history of which she had previously been unaware.

A Welsh dresser that had once been situated in the hallway had been moved into Sonny's study, where there was much less passing traffic. Its shelves were a repository for a selection of family photographs, the subject of many of these being younger editions of people Consuela knew.

'Checking out the rogues' gallery?' Sonny asked, with a smile.

'I was actually wondering who the people were.'

Sonny identified each of the family members, relating what had happened to them, leaving one person until last. 'That,' he said, pointing to a handsome young man Consuela guessed to be in his late teens, 'is my older brother James, the black sheep of the family. His bedroom was the one you and Andrew now occupy. That's where he got up to mischief.'

'I don't understand what "black sheep of the family" means.'

'It means a person who is in disgrace.'

'What happened to him? Why do you call him black sheep?'

'James was eighteen years old when my parents took my sister Cissie to a sanatorium in Switzerland, hoping to cure her of consumption. They took me along, and as my sisters were away at school, the house was all but empty, save for a few staff. While they were away, James came home from school unexpectedly, and became romantically involved with Alice, the housemaid. As I recall she was an outstandingly pretty girl. Anyway, the upshot of their misbehaviour was that Alice became pregnant, and when my father was told this he threw them out, giving them no time to argue. They went away and we never saw them again.'

'Yes, Andy told me a little of this,' Consuela said.

Sonny nodded. 'What Andy won't know is James kept in touch occasionally with my sister Connie, by letters via a solicitor friend of his in London, though he wouldn't say where he was. Where the lovebirds ended up is still a mystery, although I suspect they were in Australia.'

'Why do you say that?'

'Because I believe I might have met their eldest son during the First World War. He was serving with ANZAC.' He saw Consuela's confusion. 'The Australian and New Zealand Army Corps.'

She nodded. 'I understand.'

'We'd got talking, and he said I reminded him of his father who spoke the same as me. But soon after, there was an attack, and I suffered severe shell shock, so my memory of events and people from that time is very blurred. In some ways that's no bad thing.'

'So you never knew for certain what happened to your brother?'

Sonny shrugged. 'No idea.'

Consuela was entranced by this romantic story. She stared at the photo again. 'He's a gorgeous-looking young man.'

'Thank you, that's kind of you to say.' Sonny laughed at her puzzled expression and explained, 'People used to tell me I looked just like a younger edition of James.'

PART FOUR: 1973–1982

How can I live without thee, how forego
Thy sweet converse, and love so dearly joined,
To live again in these wild woods forlorn?
Should God create another Eve, and I
Another rib afford, yet loss of thee
Would never from my heart, no, no, I feel
The link of nature draw me: flesh of flesh,
Bone of my bone thou art, and from thy state
Mine never shall be parted, bliss or woe.

Paradise Lost
John Milton

CHAPTER THIRTY

In Australia, 1973 began with sadness that touched the Fisher arm of the family deeply.

Gianni Rocca, close friend and business partner of Luke and Bella Fisher, had managed the vineyard on the land Luke had bought since planting the first vines. He had been hands-on since day one. Gianni's close personal involvement covered all aspects of viniculture, including protection of the plants and their valuable fruit from every type of predation.

This involved the use of pesticides, and at that time little was known of the possible dangers of such products. It was only later that people came to realize chemicals designed to dispose of pests could have seriously damaging effects on people who used them.

Gianni's first symptoms took the form of persistent, recurring headaches, sometimes accompanied by nausea and dizziness. He ignored these for long enough, ascribing them to his advancing age. Likewise, he attributed the sweating to the high temperatures in that region, and dismissed the occasional respiratory secretions.

Although Gianni ignored the signs, his wife Angelina picked up on them, and also noticed the muscle twitches, his seemingly constant weariness and lack of coordination.

She pleaded with him to seek medical advice, but it was only when he began vomiting and suffering abdominal cramps that he consulted a doctor.

Within days, he was admitted to hospital for investigation, but before a diagnosis could be made, let alone treatment begun, a severe bout of vomiting and dysentery put an intolerable strain on his heart. The first attack left him in a weakened state, too febrile to withstand a second, and on the day before his seventieth birthday, Gianni Rocca, co-founder of the *Luca Collina* vineyard, passed away.

* * *

Gianni's widow Angelina was astonished by the huge turnout for her husband's funeral. As the family and close friends gathered following the interment, her daughter Flavia remarked on this.

'I'm not in the least bit surprised,' Luke Fisher told her. 'Gianni was immensely popular. Once he and your mother overcame the wartime prejudice due to their Italian origins, he rapidly became well-liked in the community. Evidence of that is clear from the number of local people who came to pay their respects.'

'That's true,' Bella added. 'I recognized a fair number of council members, from the mayor downwards, plus other dignitaries.'

This prompted Angelina to make her first contribution since returning from the cemetery. 'It wasn't just local people. There were representatives from our suppliers, plus the stores and wholesalers we sell to. Even the man who supplied and installed the bottling plant travelled all the way from the other side of the country to be present. That's a measure of how respected Gianni was.' Her final words were muffled by the handkerchief she was using to mop away her tears.

Seeing her distress, Bella and Flavia went to comfort her. It was later, as much in an attempt to divert the grieving widow as to seek clarification that Luke, with some hesitation, broached the subject of the vineyard's future. 'Now that Gianni's half of the business has passed to you, have you given any thought as to who will run the operation? Let's be fair, although Bella and I are partners, we know little about how it works. More important, though, this is Gianni's legacy, and for that reason alone I'd want it to prosper.'

Jimmy and his wife Flavia looked at one another, uncertain whether to put forward their idea. Before they could decide, Angelina interceded on their behalf. 'I think we should entrust full management of the vineyard to Jimmy and Flavia. I am confident they will do well. That way, we are simply handing the enterprise to the next generation of the Fisher and Rocca families.'

'Are you certain they're ready to shoulder such a big responsibility?' Bella asked. 'It's a huge undertaking.'

'They have worked in the vineyard since they were teenagers. Gianni spent a lot of time with Jimmy, teaching him, and if they need advice, I can guide them,' Angelina reassured her.

Luke smiled wryly. 'That's the problem with being a parent. You tend to forget your child is twenty-four years old, not fourteen. The only reservation I have is the vineyard might occupy too much of their time, limiting their duties as parents. If they're working non-stop, who will look after Alice?'

'Don't worry about her, Alice is more than capable of looking after herself, and I will be on hand to help. That's what grandmothers are for, and the advantage is you can give them back at the end of the day.'

As she was speaking the young lady in question entered the room, her pace little short of a gallop. Her aunt and uncle had sought to divert the child with an impromptu game of cricket in the yard alongside the house. 'Uncle Saul's a cheat,' Alice told them.

'How come?' Bella asked.

'He was batting and he hit the ball in the air. It bounced off Auntie Robyn's shoulder and I caught it. But he says he's not out, because it struck someone else.'

Luke grinned at his granddaughter. 'Tell him to read the *Laws of Cricket* again. As long as the ball didn't hit the ground, he's out — he should know that.'

Alice turned and marched triumphantly from the room.

'What did I tell you?' Angelina said, when Alice was out of earshot. 'She's more than capable of sticking up for herself.'

Later, as they were driving home, Bella asked Luke if he felt comfortable with the proposed arrangement. 'Actually, I think it will work OK. I had a chat with one of the long-term vineyard employees and he told me Jimmy has been more or less controlling operations for the past twelve months.'

Bella noticed his smile and asked what was amusing him. 'The guy also said, "Of course, Flavia controls Jimmy, just as she has done since the day they met". That gave me confidence, even before Angelina added her blessing to the arrangement.'

* * *

As Luke and Bella Fisher celebrated Christmas with their extended family, they reflected on the pride and delight their offspring had brought them. Joining them at the dinner table were their son Jimmy, his wife Flavia and granddaughter Alice. Also in attendance was their other son, Saul, home from university, where he was studying accountancy. Luke had joked that the course was merely a way for Saul to fill in his time when he wasn't on the cricket field, an accusation Saul strongly denied.

Angelina had also come for Christmas. Her eldest daughter was now married and living in New Zealand, while her son Roberto was working in California, where he was learning more about viniculture.

The sole absentee from the festive table was Robyn. Although they missed her, the reason for this was also a source of pride to her parents. Robyn was in the middle of a tour of North America along with the other members of the renowned orchestra and was now lead violinist.

With some difficulty, given the difference in time zones, Robyn touched base with her kinfolk, using the phone in her hotel room in Toronto. The contact had to be truncated — not because of the cost, which was to be borne by the orchestra — but because Robyn had fitted the call in between rehearsals and performing in the televised Christmas carol concert.

News delivered by Jimmy, Flavia and Angelina merely added to Luke and Bella's happiness. The vineyard was now showing a handsome profit, and this was likely to increase dramatically in a few years' time. As Angelina pointed out, 'At present, our range is limited, but Jimmy and Flavia want to introduce new wines. Selling them won't be a problem. The *Luca Collina* label is already proving very popular, and we're hoping to pick up an award or two for this season's crop. They have put together a plan which involves buying a few hundred hectares of land close to the existing vineyard, giving us ample growing capacity.'

Later, when they were alone, Luke and Bella reflected on what they had been told. 'I think the responsibility of running the business, combined with marriage and parenthood, has done Jimmy the world of good,' Bella suggested.

'I agree, he's much more confident, focussed and cheerful. Mind you, I think having Flavia alongside him has been the biggest factor.'

'True, she's a delightful girl, and together they've given us a beautiful granddaughter.'

Luke smiled. 'Alice is certainly beautiful, but woe betide anyone who crosses her, or upsets her in any way. She doesn't suffer fools gladly and she certainly doesn't take prisoners.'

Several years later, Bella remembered Luke's appraisal of their granddaughter, and the accuracy of his prophecy, but by then much had changed for all of them.

* * *

In Byland Crescent, Mark and Jenny Cowgill were reflecting on the first three years of the new decade. 'We've already had to get used to decimalisation,' Mark said. 'Which seemed to be designed to help people too dense to learn the twelve times table, and also enable retailers to put their prices up.'

Jenny smiled at this cynical appraisal of the change, but pointed out, 'That's not the worst of it, though. There was last year's miners' strike, and now we're facing an economic crisis, judging by what the papers tell us. I'm not sure whether joining the European Economic Community was a good thing or not.'

'The EEC can hardly be blamed for our financial woes,' Mark objected. 'The real problem lies with the coal strike, added to rising oil prices. And things must be pretty bad, because they're already talking about a three-day working week to conserve energy supplies.'

'Do you think it's wise making the alterations to the house that we've talked about, given so much uncertainty?'

'Yes, in fact I think it's long overdue. If we convert the old servants' quarters in the attic, it will give three additional large bedrooms, plus, if we plan it carefully, a room where the children can go to do their homework in peace and quiet. That will free up space for when we have visitors, which is at a premium currently. I'm thinking of when Lizzie and Gil bring their brood to visit, and what if Fran and Hank come over from the States with their two?'

'In that case, I think we should put two single beds in one room. It will give us more sleeping space. But do you think a study for the children is necessary?'

'I do, because they'd have no excuse, such as being disturbed by the noise. Remember how annoyed Suzie got when she was trying to study.' Mark grinned as he mentioned their daughter. 'Perhaps it was to get revenge that she used to play her radio at maximum volume. I vote we speak to the family. We need to get the old fogeys on board — that way they can foot the bill.'

'You shouldn't speak about your mother and father like that,' Jenny chided him.

Over dinner that evening, Mark put forward the plan he and Jenny had dreamed up for renovating the attic rooms, and gained the approval of Sonny and Rachael, backed up by Andy and Consuela.

'It will be a messy job,' Andy said. 'Have you told Mary about this?'

'Not yet, we wanted to see what you all thought first,' Jenny replied.

'Mary's the one who does the housework, I hope she likes the idea of more rooms to clean,' Andy said, jokingly. 'You'll have to give her a pay rise.'

Much to the laughter of the others, he then began counting on his fingers, pretending to calculate the cost per room in the house.

* * *

When Rachael wasn't attending one of her new-found committees or the WI, she was able to accompany Sonny on his daily fitness walks, either around Scarborough or further afield. This enabled them to explore areas of the county they had never visited before. The only limitation to the locations they selected was the need for the Bentley to navigate some of the winding lanes. The luxury car was too big to cope with the narrower ones.

Jenny, however, having been the biggest performer of the household chores for several years, was now virtually redundant. With Sarah in the kitchen, and Mary running the house like clockwork, in contrast with her mother-in-law, Jenny found herself at a loose end now the grandchildren were all at school. She was only needed on their return at the end of the day. This situation soon changed, because when she mentioned the fact at dinner one evening, her son offered a potential solution. Given the rapid growth of their business, Andy and Consuela were considering employing another member of staff. 'We need someone to take charge of the office, on a part-time basis,' Andy told his mother. 'That would involve dealing with the mountain of paperwork we create, plus answering the phone, and booking repairs in.

Occasionally, it might also be necessary to help Katy, Nora's new assistant, on the shop floor while Nora is on her lunch break, or when she's away on holiday.' He explained further, 'At the moment one of us has to stop what we're doing and go to the sales floor, which can be tricky if we're dealing with a complicated issue. Would you be interested, Mum? The wage is quite good, and I know you and Dad are always skint.'

Ignoring her husband's expression, Jenny told Andy, 'I'll have to think about it. Dad and I are going to Leeds to attend your sister's graduation ceremony next week. Then we're helping her move into the new flat she's rented. Suzie wants to get settled in before she starts work in the law chambers — they headhunted her before she'd taken her finals, which is almost unheard of, I understand. Apparently, Suzie is highly thought of from the time she worked there as an intern.'

'Hang on, Mum, are we talking about the same person? Is this the one who spent every leisure moment tormenting us with pop music played at maximum volume, when she wasn't watching hour upon hour of cop shows on telly? Or has she got a twin you've kept secret from us?'

Jenny smiled. 'When we've got your *only* sister settled I'll have to think about the job.'

There was one proviso to Jenny's acceptance of Andy's offer. 'Much as I think I'd like to help out at the shop,' she told Consuela, 'I'll need to be here to supervise the renovation work in the attic. It wouldn't be fair to ask Rachael to deal with it on her own, nor would I put the burden on Mary.'

'I don't see that being a problem,' Consuela replied. 'Andy was thinking of it as a long-term solution, so we can manage for a while longer, until you're available.'

'In that case, I'll give it a shot.'

* * *

Although Rachael and Jenny had made a fleeting visit to the attic prior to putting forward the renovation scheme, neither they nor other family members had inspected the area closely. Having contacted a reputable local builder, they explained what was required when he arrived at Byland Crescent, before taking him upstairs to examine the project.

After giving the larger rooms a once-over, he spent a much longer time in the next, where he paused in the doorway, sniffing the air for several seconds prior to entering. Once inside, he concentrated his attention on the far corner, towards the end of the side wall, alongside the sash window.

Curious as to what had sparked his interest, which extended to opening a small cupboard beneath the window and peering inside, sniffing audibly as he did so, Jenny asked if there was something wrong.

'This window frame's rotten.' As he spoke, the builder removed a penknife from his pocket and thrust it into the wooden windowsill. When he removed the blade, both women saw the flakes of paint and sawdust that drifted to the floor. He pressed the frame with his thumb in several places, and they were shocked to see the action penetrated the wood to a significant depth. He repeated the action at the top of the frame, but without such dramatic results.

He then turned his attention to the cupboard, removing several musty, damp parcels of paperwork all tied with string, which he passed to Jenny. His next action was to peel back the linoleum. Having peered at the exposed floorboards, the builder repeated his surgical operation, examining the knife blade closely before delivering his verdict.

'The window needs replacing, and so will the floorboards in this corner of the room. The cupboard needs removing too. I'm not sure of the exact source yet, but they are all rotten. Damp has got in, probably over a long number of years, but luckily it seems to have been limited to this area. It might have been down to the window being badly fitted when the house was built. Alternatively, when the room ceased to be used, the window might have been left unsecured, and slightly open. I can't tell if that's so or not, but I'm fairly sure that's the cause. The wood on the frame and the sill has swollen, and the latch is in the open position, which does make it likely.'

He indicated the parcels Jenny was clutching and made a joke. 'I hope what's inside there isn't valuable, like the deeds to the property, or a map revealing the location of buried treasure, because it's now an illegible heap of pulp.'

'If they have been up here all these years, I very much doubt if they are at all important,' Rachael replied.

The builder left, promising to supply a quotation for the renovation work, the price to include remedial work for the damp.

* * *

Their curiosity aroused, Jenny and Rachael attempted to investigate the parcels retrieved from the attic. Jenny cut the string and opened one of the packets, but the contents were stuck together, the writing blurred and faded beyond recognition. Gently, they peeled the pages apart.

'Some of these look like old invoices,' Jenny said, holding a sheet of paper up to the light.

'Yes, and some appear to be lists of some sort. Look here,' Rachael said. 'I can make out a name — George, George something or other. I wish I had my spectacles on.'

'Let me see.' She stared at the point indicated. 'You're right, it is George. Oh my goodness.'

'What is it?'

'It says Mills — our old butler, George Mills, but it says factotum.'

The women looked at each other, dumbfounded.

'Of course,' Rachael explained, 'George was employed in that position when the family bought Byland Crescent — these are the household accounts from over the years. Hannah, Mark's grandmother, was a stickler for record-keeping.'

Neither woman was aware that almost half a century earlier, Hannah Cowgill had concealed letters sent by her son, now James Fisher. When James, under the guise of

Fisher Springs Pty, bought Haigh Ackroyd & Cowgill, and others, to bail out his family, Hannah had worked out a connection from the name Fisher, the surname of the housemaid James had gone away with. She wrote a letter, using the London solicitor, the only point of contact, and received a reply from James admitting he had wished to help the family, but would not want his identity or whereabouts revealed. When Hannah knew of her son's family, her grandchildren, and their happiness, she was content and put the letters away, hidden in her meticulous household accounts, never to reveal their existence.

Rachael and Jenny carried them to the kitchen where they could be burned in the range. Sitting on the top of the pile were the accounts for 1897. Had they chosen that parcel to examine, and the contents still been legible, they may have uncovered family secrets that had been puzzled over on many occasions.

CHAPTER THIRTY-ONE

Luke Fisher gave his approval to the proposed purchase of further acreage at the vineyard. Late in 1974, he and Bella travelled there for him to sign the purchase agreement for the new land. This was in part business, but equally a chance to see and catch up with the family.

As they drove home, Bella noticed how quiet Luke was. 'Something is concerning you, isn't it?' she asked.

'I was just reflecting on the way things have developed. My parents started Fisher Springs and when Philip and I joined the company it became a family outfit. That will end with us, because none of the kids are interested. I could be upset about it, but then I thought of Mum and Dad. They left England, changed their lives completely, so why should I worry if our children want to do something similar?'

'I get your point. I thought it was something else you were worried about.'

'Such as?'

'I didn't know if you'd noticed, but when I saw Angelina I was surprised by how much weight she's lost, which concerns me.'

'What do you think the reason for that is?'

'It could be she's grieving more than she's prepared to let on. She and Gianni had been married a long time. Alternatively, it could be the strain of looking after Alice. Your granddaughter is becoming a real handful.'

Angelina, Alice's maternal grandmother, had assumed the role of childminder, acting in loco parentis while Jimmy and Flavia concentrated on running the vineyard.

'Hang on, she's your granddaughter as well, so don't go putting all the blame on me.'

'So you didn't see how much Angelina's changed over the past few months?'

'I didn't pay attention, because I know how much you dislike me looking at other women.'

Bella smiled, but returned to the subject matter. 'I didn't want to say anything in front of the others, but as soon as I get chance I'm going to have a quiet word with Angelina when there's no chance of us being overheard.'

A further two weeks passed before Bella related the shocking news to Luke. 'I was right,' she began. 'I've spoken to Angelina, and there is something wrong, dreadfully wrong. When we visited the vineyard, Angelina was awaiting an appointment with a specialist, an oncologist. The prognosis is as bad as can be. We're talking a matter of months, not years.'

Sadly, the medical opinion was correct, and four months later, Angelina passed away. Her funeral was well attended, further proof, as Luke pointed out, of the respect and popularity both she, and her husband, had acquired.

After she had been laid to rest alongside Gianni, the family gathered for a private meeting, with the exception of Alice, who had retired to her room. Although reluctant to bring up such a topic at so emotional a time, Bella eventually asked Jimmy and Flavia how they would cope without Angelina's help and guidance.

Roberto, Flavia's older brother, home for his mother's funeral, volunteered to help. 'I'd come back from the States if you want, although from what I've seen while I've been here, things seem pretty much under control.'

'What he really means,' Flavia retorted, 'is there's a girl in California he's got the hots for, and he's hoping to get lucky.'

Roberto smiled ruefully and conceded defeat, while Bella elaborated on her earlier question. 'I wasn't concerned about the running of the vineyard — I was thinking more about Alice.'

'We should be OK with that,' Jimmy told his mother, 'except if we both have to go away. That's extremely unlikely, but if and when it happens we hoped you might have Alice to stay with you.'

'You know that's never going to be a problem,' Bella reassured them.

'And in the meantime, Flavia and I are going to take it in turns after school to watch her. Once Alice starts secondary school it will be even easier.'

* * *

In Byland Crescent, as the family gathered for their meal one evening, Jenny told them what she had learned earlier that day. 'I have some interesting news,' she began. 'When I went into town this morning I visited the greengrocer to place an order for Sarah.'

'Wow, that's bound to make national headlines,' her husband interjected. 'I'm surprised it wasn't on the TV bulletins.'

Jenny gave Mark a withering look. 'As I was about to say before being so rudely interrupted, the greengrocer told me something he'd heard about in the pub a couple of nights ago. You know number six, along from us, is up for sale? Apparently it's been bought by a couple from Leeds. Not only have they bought that, but they've also bought number seven, next door. Old Mrs Harris has been considering moving for a while, the house is far too big for one person, and she wants to live nearer her family in Bridlington. So when the chance came to sell, she jumped at it.'

'Why are these people buying two houses, have they got a large family?' Rachael asked.

'No, and that's where it gets really interesting. Rumour has it they plan to knock down some walls and create one property. They will open it as a superior B & B. The talk is it will be a fully licensed guest house, more like a small hotel, with its own bar and restaurant. They want to attract a wealthier clientele than some of the competitors, who can't offer those facilities.'

'That's quite a bold scheme,' Mark commented, then frowned. 'Am I correct in thinking there was some sort of scandal attached to number six?'

The younger members of the family hadn't been paying much attention up to that point, considering the conversation to be boring. What followed, however, caught and held their interest. Sonny's reply to his son's question began the process.

'I don't think there's much wrong with your memory, Mark, and you were only little at the time you heard of it. As I recall, the owner of the house committed suicide, but that was years earlier. Your grandmother, Hannah, told me about it,' Sonny added. 'But that was only part of the scandal. The police found a packet of letters addressed to the wife from her lover. Apparently, she had eloped with him and the couple were never seen again. The husband left a suicide note, and if I remember correctly, he said he couldn't live without her, and begged her forgiveness.'

'If the wife was never traced, what happened about the house?' Andy asked.

'There was one other relative, a nephew of the husband, but he was killed during World War One, so eventually the building society foreclosed on the mortgage and it was sold at auction.' Sonny paused, then added, 'If you believe a building can be cursed, number six would be a prime candidate. Nobody seemed able to settle there, and I can't even guess how many times the property has changed hands over the past fifty years, but I reckon it would be close to double figures.'

'If nobody stays there long that would make it ideal as a guest house,' Andy said.

Once the groans at the dreadful joke died away, Mark commented, 'I'm not sure I like the idea of a guest house in the crescent, I think it would lower the tone of the neighbourhood. Not that I've anything against such hospitality venues, but I've seen the way a lot of tourists behave — or misbehave when they hit town.'

'Don't be such a snob,' Jenny reprimanded him.

'You're forgetting something,' Sonny added. 'It wouldn't be the first time there's been a guest house in the crescent. My parents moved in here in 1897, when I was only five years old. Byland Crescent had just been built, and number eight, the last property on the street, was opened as a guest house. I remember the first time my grandma and grandpa came to visit, they stayed at number eight because this house was still being decorated and furnished. When the couple who ran it died, back in the 1920s, their son wasn't interested in continuing the business. What he was interested in was making money from it, so he had it converted into flats, and later, when he passed away, his daughter sold it to the company who are the current landlords.'

'One thing's for certain,' Andy commented, 'they won't be opening for business any time soon. First of all, they'll have to get planning permission and that's a lengthy enough process, even if there are no objections. Added to that, if the rumours regarding the work they plan to do are correct, that'll take a good while to complete. I reckon you're talking two or three years, maybe even longer.'

* * *

As Christmas of 1976 approached, Sonny and Rachael's daily walk had been prevented by the slanting heavy rain that had enveloped Scarborough all day. This was further evidence that the drought affecting Britain during the hottest summer for two hundred years had finally ended. Restrictions on the use of hosepipes had now been lifted, and although the nation breathed a collective sigh of relief, Sonny emphasized the change, telling Rachael, 'Only an idiot would want to water the garden, or go outside to wash his car in weather like this.'

Inside the house, with the renovations to the former servants' quarters now complete, the space had been commandeered by the two most junior residents. Angela and Raquel were delighted to have their own bedrooms, a shared bathroom, and even a reading room to further their studies. At least that was the stated intention. How much time the children actually spent on homework was open to question. Other, less educational matters sometimes took priority for the girls.

No such distractions troubled their older brother. Having celebrated his fifteenth birthday during the summer, James Cowgill was fully committed to the work necessary for him to pass his GCE O-level examination. In his mind, the Ordinary level was merely a forerunner to the main event. Two years down the line, his ambition was to achieve sufficiently high results at Advanced level, ones good enough to enable him to gain entry to university and follow his dream. Visits to the electrical hardware store run by his parents, a business which extended to the fledgling electronics industry, gave the teenager ample opportunity to indulge his passion. By the time he was thirteen, he could strip down, repair and reassemble many of the products sent to the shop for repair or service.

Heredity, as his great-grandmother told him, formed part of his interest. 'Not only are your parents in electronics, but my father, your great-great-grandfather, was a highly talented engineer with his own company.'

Andy and Consuela were justifiably proud of their son's talent, but recognized such ability was too great to be frittered away on repairing domestic appliances. 'I think James wants to get involved with computers,' Consuela told her husband. 'He seems bent on becoming proficient enough to design programs as well as building the hardware on which to run them.'

'It seems a bit chancy, though, because from what I can gather there's no certainty such things will ever become viable. Much of what I've read about them centres around some big firms in America.'

'That might be true at present, Andy, but think how far our industry has developed over the past two decades. I was talking to your grandmother a few days ago, and she said she never expected to see black and white television, let alone colour sets. She reminded me colour only became available less than ten years ago, and now almost every household has a colour TV set. I made her laugh, because I said how good that was for our business.'

Even as they were talking, Andy and Consuela knew nothing about a fledgling company set up a year earlier in America. The brainchild of Bill Gates, Microsoft would lead a revolution that would have a far-reaching effect.

* * *

1977 brought much to celebrate — and also to mourn. In Britain and elsewhere, there was prolonged festivity as the nation rejoiced during the Silver Jubilee of Her Majesty Queen Elizabeth II. With only eight properties in Byland Crescent, the idea of a street party was not practical, so it was decided to hold a formal dinner. Rachael insisted, much to the amusement of the younger members of the family, that everyone wore evening dress to mark the occasion to toast Her Majesty's health.

Following the Queen's earlier tour of Australia in March, in December the entire Fisher family gathered to watch the parades of serving personnel held across the entire country.

Another event brought a sadder note. The shocking death of the legendary rock-and-roll singer Elvis Presley — allegedly from an overdose of drugs. Millions of fans worldwide went into deep mourning for the man who had risen to fame only two decades earlier, becoming arguably the biggest icon in the history of pop music.

Mark had phoned Suzie to ask if she had heard the news and was surprised at her reply.

'Thank goodness it wasn't Paul McCartney.'

CHAPTER THIRTY-TWO

Any complacency the senior members of the Cowgill family might have felt regarding the opening of a nearby guest house was shattered in spring of 1978, when details of the planning application, together with that for a liquor licence, were published. If the word 'bar' in the change-of-use section wasn't bad enough, 'disco', certainly troubled them.

Their dismay was only partly assuaged by the reassuring passage referring to sound-proofing. This would be required, the applicants stated, not only to avoid troubling residents of nearby properties, but also for the benefit of guests who did not want to avail themselves of the in-house entertainment.

'That's all very well,' Mark told the family, 'but we'd still have late-night revellers wandering into the crescent, probably worse for wear, and maybe trying to mimic the songs they've just heard in the disco.'

'At least they won't be passing our door,' Jenny pointed out.

'That's by no means all they'll get up to. There is the private garden in the middle of the crescent to consider — I doubt if they will heed the notice on the gate.' He glanced towards the children and tempered his last statement by adding, 'If you get my meaning.'

The grins exchanged by James and his sisters showed that Mark's attempt at tactfulness had been unsuccessful.

Despite their reservations and the objections raised by fellow residents of the crescent, the plans were approved, and during early spring of 1979, renovation work commenced. The building firm awarded the contract had a momentous task ahead of them. Change of use would require extensive, and expensive, alterations carried out by a wide range of skilled craftsmen.

All their work would have to wait, however, until the engineers removed the dividing walls without endangering the stability of the structure. The divisions were to be removed on two levels, the basement and the ground floor. None of the other alterations could get the go-ahead until the demolition work was deemed safe.

One of the labourers involved was puzzled by a section of the plaster covering part of the wall, the material varying in colour from the remainder. Having chiselled this away, he and his colleague attacked the bricks.

One of them paused to remove debris via the wheelbarrow supplied, as his colleague wielded his crowbar to remove another section. Once the bricks were clear, he stared at the gap he had just created in disbelief, which changed rapidly to horror. 'Jack,' he called to the man with the barrow. 'Jack, go fetch the foreman. He's got to see this.'

Jack lowered the barrow and wandered along to see what his mate had found. He took one glance, before turning and racing towards the stairwell, his pace as near a gallop as possible.

* * *

It was late afternoon, and James Cowgill was returning from sixth form. He glanced along the crescent before stepping off the kerb, conscious of the recent increase in vehicles at the start of and along the normally quiet road. The way was clear, the only obstruction being a temporary eyesore, the builders' portacabin. His interest was caught when he noticed one of the construction workers emerge from the house, haring across the road like the Olympic hopeful Sebastian Coe, before diving into the hut. James wondered what the panic was about.

Once the foreman had inspected the scene, he returned to the portacabin. He would have to make some phone calls. One was to his employers, the other to their clients, who had asked to be kept *au fait* with developments. But taking immediate priority was his phone call to the police.

Angela Cowgill would normally have accompanied her brother on the walk home from school, but she was a member of the school choir, and that afternoon was one of their regular practice sessions. She entered the house via the back door an hour after James, and immediately encountered her grandmother and Sarah in the kitchen.

'Is the front door locked?' Jenny asked.

'No, I couldn't get by, there's something going on across the road,' Angela told Jenny, her voice reflecting her excitement. 'There are lots of policemen standing around, plus a couple of panda cars by the building site, blocking the access from the main road. If I hadn't come round the back, I couldn't have got home.'

'I wonder what that's about? I do hope none of the workers has been injured. I'd better phone the shop and warn your parents.'

The following day, the sensational news broke. 'Workmen's Grim Find' read the headline in the *Scarborough Evening News*. There was little in the way of detail, merely a short report of human remains being discovered in a house undergoing renovation. The article gave no indication of the property's location, but members of the Cowgill family were convinced they knew.

* * *

The officer leading the investigation, having established the skeletons had been murdered, only had one piece of evidence

— a highly distinctive necklace taken from the female. He sent officers to speak to the other residents, in the hope that someone might come up with something useful. He knew it was a long shot.

Sonny Cowgill was meandering towards the kitchen in search of a mid-morning cup of tea when he was distracted by the pounding of the door knocker. Mary appeared at the kitchen doorway. 'Don't worry, Mary, I'll get it, if you can provide me with a cuppa, please?' He opened the front door to be confronted by two uniformed police officers.

'Good morning,' one of them greeted him. 'We're looking for someone to help with our enquiries.' He smiled slightly and added, 'Sorry, I didn't mean that the way it sounds. As you're probably aware by now, the builders up the road found a couple of skeletons. We're hoping to find someone who may have been a resident for some time, and might give us a clue as to their identities.' In looking at the older gentleman, the officer was tempted to cross his fingers.

'I think I might be able to assist,' Sonny told them. 'Why don't you come in and I'll tell you what I know.'

He ushered them into the sitting room and asked them to take a seat. Moments later Mary appeared, smiling, with a tray containing three cups of tea.

Sonny thanked her, before telling the officers all he could remember of the events from years ago. The officers glanced at each other, knowing this could be the answer they were seeking. 'After the wife disappeared, the homeowner committed suicide, but there was one thing which didn't make sense at the time. I recall hearing that the husband left a note, in which he begged his wife's forgiveness. It always puzzled me as to why he would do that, if she had betrayed him?'

Two cups of tea later, as they were about to leave, Sonny remembered something else. 'I don't know if this is of any use, but after the husband's suicide I seem to recall they published an appeal in the papers, along with the wife's photo, asking for anyone who knew her whereabouts to contact the police. I don't know if there was any success.'

Some days later, after hours spent in the archives of the local newspaper, officers found the article, including a photograph which showed the wife wearing the distinctive necklace. The lead detective reported the successful closure of the case. The local press had a field day with the outcome. Headlines read, 'Walled up in the Cellar', telling the story in gruesome detail.

* * *

Knowing the inside story behind the sparse details released to the press by the police, James Cowgill was keen to share the scandal with his girlfriend, Christine Morris. The day after Sonny revealed the facts to the officers, James was about to walk through the school gates when he heard someone call his name.

He looked round and smiled. Christine was walking towards him. 'Hold on a minute, James,' she called as she struggled to catch up.

As far as James was concerned, she was the best-looking girl in the sixth form, if not the entire school. She was tall, blonde and, according to James, had the most beautiful blue eyes. They had been classmates throughout their years at the school and had been going out together for over a year. They were both competitive at sports, from which their relationship had grown — that was until Christine's accident. One weekend she was out horse riding, when the horse, startled by a pheasant, reared and threw Christine to the ground. Thankfully, she recovered well from her injuries, but was left with a limp, ending her future sporting career.

'I've been reading about those bodies,' she began, 'and I saw a lot of police activity in Byland Crescent last week, so I wondered if it was there they were found. You didn't say anything.'

James glanced back and saw a group of other pupils heading their way. 'I know the whole story,' he replied, 'and I'll tell you everything, but not here.'

Christine nodded her understanding. 'OK, meet me at the end of the day in our usual spot, and you can tell me then.'

They sat side by side on a bench, holding hands, as he revealed the story of the errant wife, her lover and the husband who had committed suicide.

'How long had they been there, do you know?'

'My great-grandpa was only a boy back then. But according to him, they must have been there somewhere around seventy years.'

Christine shuddered at the thought, but after a few moments told him, 'I know it was a horrible thing the husband did, but his wife's misbehaviour can't be excused either. I have no time for anyone who enters a relationship and then plays away.'

'That almost sounds as if you're speaking from experience,' James responded, half-jokingly.

'You're right, I am. Before you and I became an item, when I was sixteen, I thought I was in love. We'd been going out together for a few months before I had my accident. As you know, I was in hospital and a therapy clinic for a while recovering and getting fit again. I already knew I would have to give up my athletics career, but when I was discharged I discovered my boyfriend had moved on, found someone else, and ditched me. He hadn't even the nerve to tell me.'

'He's a prize idiot. He wasn't worthy of someone as lovely as you.'

Christine smiled. 'That's very nice of you to say.'

James squeezed her hand. 'I mean it, you know I do.'

He listened as she continued, 'When my treatment finished and I came home to my grandmother's, I was lonely. As you know, my parents died years ago, and I have no siblings. Being without anyone to turn to is a really desolate feeling. My grandmother is a wonderful lady, but she doesn't understand what it is to be young, to want music and light in my life. It was only after I came back to school the feeling of loneliness began to lessen. Being with you meant the sunshine came back into my life.'

James put his arm around her shoulders and held her tight.

Christine changed the subject. 'We've only a couple of weeks left before the end of term, then, before we know it, you'll be heading off to university. Have you any plans for the summer break, like jetting off to foreign parts?'

'Absolutely none. I'll be kicking my heels at home, trying not to get too bored, or helping Mum and Dad at the shop. What about you? Are you looking forward to university?'

'I'm not going, James. I'm sorry. I've been meaning to tell you, but didn't know how.'

James was shocked. 'You're not going? But we were going to be together.'

'My grandmother's decided she can't afford it. So, I have to start looking for a job.'

James tried to hide his disappointment. 'What will you do?'

'I've no idea, but something will turn up, I'm sure. In the meantime, I'm going to be busy attempting to redecorate the flat. It's looking a bit tired. The problem is, since my accident I can't go up ladders without putting myself at risk, so repainting is going to be difficult, and the ceilings will be impossible.'

'I could give you a hand,' he volunteered, which was just what Christine was hoping he would say. 'I don't mind heights, so ceilings wouldn't be a problem for me.'

'I really would appreciate the help. I'm sure Grandmother would see you're rewarded.'

James laughed. 'If it stops me from being bored and I get to spend more time with you, I'll be glad to help — I certainly wouldn't expect any reward. When do you want to make a start?'

'Straight after the end of term, then we'll have the rest of the holiday free.'

James leaned forward and kissed her.

CHAPTER THIRTY-THREE

On the Monday after leaving school for the last time, James arrived at the block of flats and rang the bell alongside the ornate carved door. He believed the large property had been converted from what had been home to a former mill owner, as were many along the impressive row of properties. Christine opened the door and greeted him with a smile, before she grabbed his hand, led him through the big vestibule, and escorted him up a wide staircase to the first floor. They entered the hallway of the flat and she asked if he'd like a drink of tea or coffee before starting work.

'Let's get on with it. We can take a break later.'

'Let me show you what you're up against.'

James looked confused.

'Didn't I mention I plan to paint every room, except Grandmother's bedroom?'

'I don't believe you did,' James answered, shaking his head. 'Isn't it convenient we have the entire summer?' he added, sarcastically. 'And where is your grandmother? I thought she'd be here to supervise — or chaperone,' he added, with a grin.

'She goes to the "old-biddies" club, most days. If not, she keeps an eye on the old lady in the flat below. The fact that she's younger than Gran doesn't seem to come into it. At the moment Gran's gone on one of the club's organized trips. She left this morning, and will be away two weeks.'

The apartment was large. The sitting room was almost the size of the one in Byland Crescent, giving a view of the sea from the large bay window. There were two bedrooms, a dining room and kitchen, plus a bathroom. 'I thought we should make a start in the lounge,' Christine suggested.

'I sort of guessed that by the dust sheets covering the carpet and furniture, plus the ladder, rollers and pots of paint.'

The painting took most of the day, during which Christine explained, 'We didn't want to go to the expense of buying rolls of wallpaper simply to leave for other people if Grandmother decides to move in the future. It could be too big for her on her own, once I've left the nest, and the stairs might become an issue.'

Once they'd finished, James helped her fold the protective sheeting and take it to her bedroom, ready for the following day. She stood to one side for James to enter, and he placed it on the floor. He turned to face her, and stepped closer. His arm slid over her shoulder, gently pulling her forward until their bodies were touching. 'I think it's time to claim the reward I was promised,' he whispered. He kissed her. 'I've wanted this for such a long time. You know how much I want you?'

Much later, as they were relaxing against the pillows, his arm around her shoulders, James said, 'I've made a decision. I'll have to tell my folks I'm not going to university.'

Christine stared at him. 'Why ever not?'

'Because that would mean leaving you, and I'm not prepared to do that.'

'I can't let you ruin your future for me.'

'You won't ruin it, you'll perfect it.' He smiled and kissed her gently.

'But what will you do if you drop your studies?'

'I'll work for my parents in their electrical business. They're desperately in need of another full-time technician.

I've been helping out during school breaks, but we still can't cope with the demand. That way, I'll be earning money, and best of all, I'll be close to you.'

'Are you telling me you're prepared to forego your future just so we can be together?'

'Too damned right I am. You are the most precious thing in my life now, and I want us to be together — always.'

* * *

Later that evening, James returned to Byland Crescent, his visit a fleeting one, as he explained to his parents, 'Christine is feeling a little wary on her own. So to ensure her safety, I suggested I stay over until her grandmother returns. I've just popped home for some clothes and a razor.'

Andy accepted the statement at face value, but Consuela was not convinced. After their son had departed, she voiced her doubts. 'I think there's far more to this relationship than mere friendship.'

Andy lowered his newspaper. 'He's just being a gentleman, quite the right thing to do.'

Consuela looked at him and shook her head. 'A gentleman, is that what you call it?'

'You think they're . . . er . . .'

'I certainly do. They're always together at weekends and any evening they can. She's forever popping round here.'

Andy was shocked. 'Do you think they were involved while they were at school?'

'I think they've been more than friends for a long while, but for one thing, James is too well behaved to do that sort of thing. Now, despite the paint splashes on his clothing, I'm wondering how much decorating got done today.'

'What makes you say that?'

'His hair was slightly damp, as if he'd recently taken a bath, and the soap he used has a distinctly feminine aroma. Add that to the smell of Chanel Number Five on his clothing and I'm sure I'm right.'

'Is that all?'

'Well, there was also the same smug expression on his face, which reminded me of you when you've had your wicked way with me, plus the speed with which he wanted to return to the flat. I guess they'll be back in bed by now.'

'Accepting all that, if you're right, my hope is she makes him as happy as you do me.' He returned to reading the news.

* * *

Christine's grandmother had returned from holiday and James had moved back home. Now, the lovers finally plucked up courage to face James' parents. He'd warned Andy and Consuela in advance that he had something extremely important to discuss with them, in strict privacy.

'This will be the big announcement,' Consuela predicted. 'Leave it to me to do the talking.'

'I'm happy with that,' Andy agreed. 'You're rather good at it.'

It was mid-afternoon when the young couple entered the sitting room, nervously holding hands.

Consuela told them, 'Sit down, and tell me what I haven't already guessed.'

James looked at his mother. 'What do you mean?'

'I guessed you and Christine are more than friends.' She looked at her son accusingly. 'And you are forfeiting the chance to go to university so you can be together. Is there anything I've missed?' she asked, sternly.

'Er, no, I think that just about covers it,' James said, as he glanced at his father, unsure of his reaction.

Andy looked at his wife, wondering why she hadn't warned him of this possibility. He jumped to his feet. 'Is this right? You're prepared to pass up your remaining education, and potential career, because you think you're in love?'

James stared at his father. 'Er, yes, Dad.'

Andy turned to Consuela. 'Would you take Christine out of the room, please? And see that we're not disturbed.'

Consuela led Christine into the library at the rear of the hall, and told the girl to sit down.

It was at that moment Sonny and Rachael returned from their walk. They entered the hall to be met by raised voices from the sitting room. 'What on earth?' Sonny exclaimed.

Mary dashed from the kitchen, looking very flustered. 'I'm just making some tea. Can I suggest you take it in the drawing room?' she said, pointing to the other side of the hall. 'I'm afraid the library is also occupied?'

Unaware of what was happening they agreed, and began removing their outer clothing. As the sound emanating through the hall continued, Consuela hurried past them. She opened the door to the sitting room. 'Andy, your grandparents are home, noise — and language!' she said, pointedly. She went back to the library, casting an apologetic glance at the bemused couple.

Sarah the cook, and her sister Mary, had been given use of Lizzie's old lounge where they could take their breaks, or rest, if so required. They were now both seated on the sofa, cup of tea in hand, wondering what had caused such uproar in this normally peaceful residence.

Christine was in tears.

'Do you love my son?' Consuela asked.

Between sobs, Christine said, 'Yes, and I promise you my feelings for James will never change, no matter what life throws at us. I want to be with him always, and I promise to be faithful and loving.' Wiping the tears from her face with the back of her hand, she looked directly at Consuela. 'We desperately need your approval for our plan.'

Looking at the girl, Consuela's memory stirred, recalling how she and Andy had met, the tears she had shed, and how easy it had been to fall in love.

There was a short silence when Christine finished speaking, before Consuela asked, 'Have you made any plans for the future, or have you been too busy — decorating? Come to think of it, have you actually done any decorating?'

'We've finished it,' Christine protested.

Andy appeared at the door. 'Would you come back, please?'

The atmosphere was tense — but at least it was quieter.

Christine was ushered back into the sitting room, and Andy closed the door behind her, remaining in the hall to speak to his wife.

Rachael appeared in the doorway of the drawing room, concern all over her face. 'Is everything all right?' she asked.

'Please, Grandmama, I'll explain later.'

Rachael nodded and closed the door.

In the sitting room, James was trying to console Christine, who had taken a seat alongside him, and was again in floods of tears. This was certainly not the reaction either of them had expected from his parents.

Five minutes later, Andy and Consuela re-entered. Together they faced James.

'Tell your mother what you have just told me,' Andy instructed him.

James glanced at Christine, before he spoke. 'I, that is, *we* were hoping you might take me on full-time in the business. You're forever complaining about the workload. That way we can be together.' He reached out and took Christine's hand. 'If that isn't to your liking, I *will* go to university, and Christine will get a job nearby. Her pay will support us until I qualify and get a job, perhaps in America, where the computer industry is beginning to take off.'

Andy looked at Consuela, who nodded imperceptibly.

'You're quite right, we do need an extra pair of hands,' he said. 'And at least we wouldn't have to go through the procedure of interviewing applicants.' Andy sighed. 'If you're absolutely set on this, before we go along with it I want to suggest a modification to your plan.'

James and Christine looked mildly apprehensive until Andy explained. 'With the lack of a university education, you will continue your studies at the technical college. You will enrol for evening classes, or even a day course.'

'If I do that, then you'll agree to my marrying Christine?' James asked.

'Marriage? Who mentioned marriage?' Andy asked.

Consuela took Andy by the arm, leading him towards the hall. 'That's a conversation for another time. I think you ought to rescue your grandparents and apologize, not just for the noise, but also your vocabulary. Tell them what has transpired, and later we can tell the rest of the family the news.'

'If that doesn't put the girl off, nothing will,' Andy muttered.

The day ended with Christine staying for dinner. By the time they sat down to eat, she had been introduced to the members of the Cowgill clan she had not met previously, who were immensely impressed by her lively, happy nature.

Later, after James had escorted her home, he reflected that his happiness was now complete. He was deeply in love. He had his girl, and felt certain nothing could change that.

CHAPTER THIRTY-FOUR

It was the Friday before Christmas, 1979. A day dreaded by police officers serving in towns and cities throughout the UK. Once offices and factories closed for the festivities, employees took the opportunity to celebrate. Some were even encouraged to do so by their employers, who organized staff parties to entertain them. Pubs, clubs, hotels, restaurants and taxi companies did a roaring trade as they indulged the needs of a mass of people in party mood.

One person definitely not tempted by the lure of alcoholic refreshment was Christine Morris. She was working in an office which had closed early that day, allowing the staff to join the celebrations, should they wish. Christine declined the invitation from her colleagues as they headed for the nearest public house and went shopping before she headed home, clutching the fancy ornament, her gift from the office Secret Santa. As she returned to the flat she now shared with her fiancé James since the death of her much-loved grandmother, Christine wondered what his reaction would be to the surprise Christmas present she was also carrying. Hopefully, he would be as delighted as she was.

Leaving the town centre, she was almost level with a barber's shop, unaware of a vehicle being driven erratically behind her. The men's hairdressing salon was on the corner of a quiet side street. As Christine stepped off the kerb, the driver suddenly realized he had almost missed his turning. His reflexes dulled by the excessive amount of alcohol he had consumed, he completely failed to notice the pedestrian until it was far too late.

The car was travelling too fast to control, the street too narrow to take evasive action. There was a loud bang as the nearside wing hit Christine, hurling her backwards with great force. A split second later, there was a resounding crash as she collided with the side glass wall of the barber's shop, which exploded under the extreme force of the impact as her body hurled through it like a jet-propelled projectile.

The terrified car driver accelerated away from the carnage, his sole objective to get as far from the mayhem he had created as possible. The vehicle soon disappeared into the maze of small side streets.

* * *

It had been a long, tiring day, as James and his parents tried to complete as many of the repairs and servicing tasks as possible prior to the holiday. As he reached the block of flats, James noticed a police panda car parked outside the front entrance, but dismissed it as having nothing to do with him. Glancing up at the first floor, he was puzzled to notice there were no lights on, despite it being after 7 p.m. There was little reason for Christine to go out.

Then he remembered her telling him she had planned some shopping when the office closed. James laughed to himself, noting the time, thinking she could have changed her mind and be in the pub with the others. He had only been inside the apartment a couple of minutes when the doorbell rang. 'I'll bet she's forgotten her key,' he muttered with a grin.

He opened the door and blinked with surprise at the sight of two police officers, one male, one female, who were standing outside. For some reason they looked nervous, which puzzled him. The policewoman spoke first. 'Does Christine Morris live here?'

A cold frisson of fear ran through James' body. 'Yes, she does,' he agreed. 'Is something wrong?'

'Who are you, sir?' the male officer asked.

'I'm James, James Cowgill, Christine's fiancé.'

'May we come inside, sir? I'm afraid we've got some bad news for you. Is there anyone you can call to be with you at this time?'

'Why would I need someone? Please tell me what's happened? Is Christine hurt, or in trouble?'

The woman took over again. 'It might be better if you sat down, James.'

'I don't want to sit down. Just tell me what's going on.'

The officer took a deep breath. 'There was an accident late this afternoon, what we refer to as a hit-and-run. Christine was hit by a car that failed to stop. She was thrown through a shop window by the force of the collision. I'm extremely sorry, James, Christine died instantly.'

Fifteen minutes later, the officers took James to their car for the short journey to Byland Crescent, where they imparted the dreadful news to his parents. 'We thought it better for James not to be alone,' the policewoman told them before they left.

Back in the car, the two officers agreed that this would undoubtedly be the worst job they had ever been given. The female officer took a handkerchief from her pocket to wipe her tears, saying, 'They've been planning their wedding for next summer — this should have been their best Christmas ever. Instead of which, he's going to spend it grieving and thinking of what might have been.' The male officer simply nodded and patted her arm.

There was little in the way of celebration in the Cowgill household that Christmas. Even the traditional exchange of presents was a muted affair, with James a noted absentee. The meal on Christmas Day contained all the usual ingredients, but the diners, while doing justice to the chef's ability, did little to mark the festive occasion. There were no party hats, or crackers with appalling jokes inside, merely a formal dinner such as would have been eaten on any Sunday throughout the year.

New Year was also noted for its lack of riotous enjoyment. Usually, marking the end of a decade and the start of a new one would have been cause for reflection and optimism, but there was little of that in Byland Crescent, where almost all the residents were in bed long before the beginning of 1980 was signalled by church bells, fireworks and the striking of Big Ben as seen on television.

Having already undergone the ordeal of formally identifying Christine's body, in early January James attended the coroner's inquest. As he listened to the pathologist deliver his report, another layer of horror was added to his suffering as he heard him say, 'Although this has no bearing on the cause of death, the victim was in the early stages of pregnancy.'

With that, James blundered from the courtroom, just managing to reach the men's toilets before he was violently sick.

* * *

Although Christmas of 1979 was a far happier occasion for the Fisher family than in the Cowgill household, Bella noticed that one of them appeared somewhat discontented. Concerned about her granddaughter, Bella had taken her son to one side. 'What's bothering Alice?' she asked. 'She's normally the life and soul of the party, but today she doesn't seem at all happy.'

Jimmy shrugged. 'She probably didn't get the present she was looking for — either that, or she doesn't relish the prospect of having a younger sibling who will have all the attention lavished on them.'

Bella blinked with surprise. 'You didn't tell me Flavia was pregnant.'

'We only found out for definite a couple of days ago. We were waiting until we were all together to make the grand announcement.'

Bella was mildly perturbed at how easily her son had dismissed Alice's obvious disenchantment, and resolved to keep a watchful eye on her. In the euphoria following the news, she noticed that Alice, far from being upset by the prospect of having a baby brother or sister, took the family reaction in her stride. Dismissing Jimmy's other explanation, the lack of a suitable present, as not being in Alice's nature, Bella was keen to establish the true cause of her dissatisfaction.

Alice had begun her secondary education two years earlier. Such was her resolute character that the challenge had failed to cause trepidation. She had the iron determination to meet the consequences head on. Quite how bad they would turn out to be, even Alice's wildest dreams — or nightmares — couldn't have envisaged.

Alice had begun to suspect the love her parents had for their only child took second place to their primary interest, the vineyard. Jimmy and Flavia were so committed to their work they barely seemed to notice the development of their daughter. Being treated and spoken to like a six-year-old when you were more than twice that age was galling, to put it mildly.

Alice had the notion they lived by the old maxim 'if it ain't broke, don't fix it'. Her parents failed to take into account that some breakages can stem from outside sources. Having said that, they could not have foreseen the chain of circumstances that would lead to a family crisis.

Later, as the adults gathered on the veranda to enjoy the cooler evening air, Bella took the opportunity to go upstairs to the room Alice was occupying. 'Right, what's wrong?' Bella asked in her usual forthright fashion. 'I can see you're unhappy about something, but your mum and dad don't seem to know why. Is it the thought of a new baby commanding all their attention, as your dad suggested?'

Bella was surprised when Alice, now aged thirteen, laughed, a scornful expression of disbelief lacking much evidence of humour. 'No way, I actually feel sorry for the poor little mite.'

'Why on earth do you say that?'

'You said the baby might grab all the attention, didn't you? Well, if they pay as little attention to the baby as they do to me, it'll probably starve to death when breastfeeding is over.'

'Let me get this straight. Are you saying your mum and dad neglect you?'

'They don't even notice I'm there half the time. I want to talk to them about something important, something that's upsetting me, but I can't get a word in edgeways, 'cause they're too busy spouting on about next year's Pinot bloody Grigio.'

Bella was shocked, as much by the bitterness in Alice's tone as by her words. It was clear by the depth of her feeling that the resentment had been brewing for quite some time. That was part of it, but she was also keen to know what had disturbed Alice to such an extent she'd wanted to tell her parents, but had not been able to.

'You can always talk to me, you know. I will never be too busy to listen to my beloved granddaughter, and neither will Grandpa Luke for that matter. So, come on, out with it, what's really troubling you?'

Alice looked at her grandmother, bit her lip and then told her, 'It didn't matter so much when I was at primary school, because I had a lot of good mates. I liked the teachers and enjoyed the lessons, so Mum and Dad's bee in their bonnet with the vineyard wasn't as bad. Now, since I moved to secondary school, that's all changed. I hate the school, hate most of the teachers, and hate the other pupils. The girls all seem to dislike me — why, I don't know. And one or two of the boys have been trying it on, if you know what I mean, one in particular.'

Bella was alarmed. 'Has anyone touched you?'

'No, it's just the things they say, and the way they look at me, the comments they make.'

'Surely you must have told your mum and dad about this.'

'I have. But it's OK. I don't have to worry because it's all in my imagination.'

'Is that what they said?'

Alice nodded, her expression showing she was close to tears.

'Right,' Bella told her, 'don't forget, I'm always at the end of the phone line, night and day, whenever you need me. In the meantime, I'm going to have a word with your father about this.'

'Good luck, but I think you'll be wasting your breath.'

Although Bella did as she promised, by the end of the conversation, during which Jimmy cited Alice's 'overactive imagination, the dream world created by always having her nose in a book, and her wishful thinking about boys', Bella came to the conclusion that Alice's version of events had been accurate. Within weeks, however, matters were to change dramatically, in a way that would affect all their futures.

CHAPTER THIRTY-FIVE

Alice was walking along the school corridor, having finished her final lesson of the day. Others from her class were heading for the playing fields, but as Alice had recently suffered a head cold, she was excused from sporting activity. She was not concerned as she could spend her free time in her favourite room, the school library.

She had almost reached her destination when the door to the boys' toilets swung open. The youth who stepped out was two years older than Alice, and had been one of her chief tormentors. He was also a good deal stronger and heavier than her. Before Alice could take avoiding action, he grabbed her round the waist from behind and dragged her inside. She struggled to free herself, but he was too strong for her. When he shifted his grip to turn her to face him, she seized the chance.

Alice struck, her knee making contact with his groin. He winced, bent over by the pain. The second blow was delivered with her foot, the toecap of her shoe unerringly accurate, causing him to collapse on the floor, writhing in agony.

Alice's fury was out of control. Twice she stamped down, bringing her full weight to bear on the already damaged groin, until he passed out, a dribble of vomit forming a pool alongside his head.

She turned and ran from the room, almost colliding with another boy as she galloped into the corridor.

* * *

Luke and Bella had just finished their evening meal when the phone rang. With Robyn and Saul away, they were alone. Bella was carrying their plates back into the kitchen, so Luke answered the call. Bella had almost completed the washing up when Luke joined her.

'Who was on the phone?'

'It was Jimmy. Alice has been arrested.'

'Arrested? Whatever for?'

'She's been charged with assault, having attacked one of the boys in her school. Apparently, he's in hospital, quite seriously injured. From what the boy told police, and what they told Jimmy, Alice has been making overtures to him for some time. She followed him into the boys' toilets, and when he refused her advances, she turned vicious and attacked him. She kicked him in the balls time after time, until he passed out.'

'I don't believe a word of it. He's spinning a yarn to excuse what he was trying to do to her. My guess is Alice was merely defending herself. Remember me telling you what she said when I chatted to her at Christmas?'

'I agree, but I think you and I are the only ones who believe her version of events. Alice told it much the same as you guessed, but it seems even Jimmy and Flavia think she did something awful.'

'That's bloody ridiculous — how on earth can they believe such utter codswallop about their own daughter?'

'Jimmy's had to go to the police station. He's furious with her, says they've been concerned about her for some time, because she's been acting weird. He says she never talks about school, or other pupils, or her teachers, and spends all her spare time in her room, barely taking any interest in what's going on around her.'

'That might be their version, but Alice tells it completely differently. She told me they're only interested in the vineyard and never pay attention to her. When we talked at Christmas she mentioned some boys who had been unpleasant, but back then it had only been verbal. It doesn't take much to believe one of them took things a step further. What will happen now, I wonder?'

'Alice has made a statement, along the lines of what you suggested. I can't say for certain, but if there were no eyewitnesses, it would be difficult to prove one way or another.'

As Luke predicted, without eyewitnesses and with two completely diverse accounts of what had taken place, police were unable to proceed, and the charge of assault was dropped, as was her counter-claim of sexual misconduct against the boy. No such restrictions troubled the school authorities. On the recommendation of the headmaster, conveniently a friend of the boy's father, Alice Fisher was expelled, the notice arriving in the post two weeks after the attack, when she was already suspended.

Alice now had to face the full extent of her parents' disapproval. This was summed up by Jimmy, who told her she had brought the family name into disrepute, and that henceforth she would be confined to the house until further notice, without pocket money, and would spend her time doing washing, ironing, house cleaning and other chores.

The day following this angry confrontation, having thought the matter over long and hard, Alice remembered what her grandmother had said at Christmas. 'Time to put up or shut up, Granny Bella,' Alice muttered. Once she was certain her mother and father were otherwise occupied in the vineyard, she picked up the phone and began to dial.

It was early evening when Alice's parents returned to the house after a long, tiring day's work. There was no sign of life, and Flavia noticed the breakfast pots were still in the kitchen sink, unwashed. She dashed upstairs to her daughter's room.

One glance at the empty wardrobe, its doors wide open, the missing suitcase and the empty dresser told her all she needed to know — the note leaning against the dressing-table mirror was merely confirmation.

'I'm leaving,' it read. 'It is clear I'm no longer welcome in this house. If you think I'm a liar and a violent criminal who has embarrassed you by disgracing the family name, you'll be well rid of me. And as you don't believe a word I say, I'm forced to remove myself from people who no longer trust me. I don't expect you to come looking for me, after all, you're far too busy with the vineyard, which is all that matters to you.'

Flavia sank down on the bed, sobbing uncontrollably as she clutched her daughter's farewell diatribe to her breast. Eventually, a measure of calm returned and she stumbled from the room, walking downstairs, clutching the handrail for support as she went to tell Jimmy the terrible news.

She hadn't heard the phone ring, but as she heard his side of the conversation, she realized he was speaking to his mother. Flavia held out the note. Jimmy looked at it and nodded. Suddenly, Flavia thought, he seemed to have aged, looking more like his father. He replaced the handset and told her, 'Alice has gone to Mum and Dad's place. She's asked them if she can live with them, because she doesn't want to return here.'

'Oh, Jimmy, what have we done to our beautiful daughter? Why has everything gone sour? How can we ever put things right?'

'The only way I can see is to beg Alice's forgiveness. I think the action she's taken proves we were wrong. If she's so offended by our mistrust in her, that proves to my mind she was telling the truth all along. Whether she'll overlook our stupidity is another matter.'

'Let's write to her immediately, tell her we're sorry, and that we believe her.'

Alice received the missive, and was about to answer it, when they came to visit her.

* * *

In any school rumours abound, and within days of Alice's dismissal notice, other girls mentioned similar instances of the boy's improper behaviour. Eventually, these came to the attention of the teaching staff, and when several of the victims came forward and repeated much of what Alice had endured, a reassessment of the position was called for. Alice's expulsion notice was rescinded, and her attacker was given his marching orders.

News of this reversal was sent to Alice's parents, so after reading it, Jimmy and Flavia decided to take it to the Fisher homestead. The atmosphere was stilted to begin with, but after reiterating their apology and begging her forgiveness, the tone became much easier.

Then they produced the letter which contained the invitation for Alice to return to the school the following term. She read it through, before tearing it into tiny pieces and depositing it in the waste basket. 'If they think I'm going to set foot in that place, they can think again. I'm glad to have seen the back of it.'

Her grandparents and parents looked on with degrees of approval at her actions. 'That's all very well, but you've the rest of your education to think of,' Bella reminded her.

'Why not look at getting into another school?' her father asked. 'Obviously there's no chance around our way, but if Mum and Dad can manage with you living here during the week, you could come home at weekends. That way we could get you into a school nearby, such as the one Saul, Robyn and I attended.'

'I will need somewhere, because I have to get good exam results if I'm to qualify.'

'Qualify?' her father asked. 'Qualify for what?'

'I want to train to become a vet.'

As they stared at one another in surprise, Luke said, 'I didn't know you liked animals.'

'I always have, and then I read this.' Alice produced a book and told them, 'I went into a bookshop in town and picked this up a long time ago. It's my favourite.'

She handed the volume to Bella, who read the title aloud, '*It Shouldn't Happen to a Vet*, by James Herriot. Hang on, though, this book is set in northern England — does that mean you want to go live there?'

'That wasn't my idea. Judging by the number of sheep alone there must be a great demand for veterinary surgeons here in Australia.'

As they returned home, having given their blessing to the new plan, and been reassured of their daughter's forgiveness, Flavia said, 'This has been a lesson to us. We must learn from it and never make the same mistake again.' She paused, before adding, 'It also shows how much we have misjudged our daughter, both in her iron determination, her strong principles, and her will to succeed.'

CHAPTER THIRTY-SIX

As Easter of 1980 approached, Consuela Cowgill expressed concern about James to her husband. 'He seems to have lost all interest in anything, even the work he used to enjoy so much. A number of times I've watched him sitting at his bench, staring out of the window for ages. The job he'd been working on is in front of him, but he takes no notice, just looks blankly at the wall of the building next door. I don't need to ask what he's dreaming about, his expression says it for him. I thought things would be getting easier for him but I'm beginning to think it would be better if he gave up the flat and moved back home.'

'I agree. But when he was at home he barely spoke to anyone, and as soon as he could he went to his room and stayed there. He doesn't sleep well either. On a couple of occasions, when I needed to go to the bathroom in the early hours, I saw his bedroom light reflected beneath his door, and heard him pacing up and down.'

'What can we do?'

'I don't see there's much we *can* do except to be there for him if, and when, he needs us. Hopefully, sooner or later, the pain will ease and we'll get our son back, the cheerful, happy version, I mean.'

As things transpired, it was a chance encounter in early July that marked the first step on James' road to recovery. He had collected a couple of items for repair and taken them to the shop, when he bumped into a customer entering the showroom.

'James, just the man I was looking for.' It was the captain of the cricket team James had played for over the past three seasons. As they shook hands, the cricketer said, 'I know things must be difficult for you right now, but we're desperately short of players at the club. So bad we're down to just one team, made up from anyone who happens to be available. This season's been a washout so far. I hoped you might see your way to coming back and helping us out. Perhaps taking the anger you must feel out on a cricket ball might prove helpful.'

James was about to refuse, but could see sense in the captain's remark. 'I'll have a think about it,' he promised.

Realizing this was the best he could get, the captain wisely left matters there. Later James told his mother of the encounter. She could tell he was leaning towards accepting the offer, and saw the chance to add some words of encouragement.

'I'm not going to press you into a decision, one way or the other,' she told him. 'But look at it this way, given Christine's cheerful, lively personality, I think the last thing she would want is for you to continue grieving forever. She'd want you to pick up the threads of your old life and maybe add a few more. That way the accident will only have claimed one victim, not two, as it will, if you turn into a recluse.'

'It was two, Mother.'

'Two what?'

'Victims. Christine was pregnant.'

'*Madre de Dios*.' Consuela crossed herself. 'Why didn't you tell us?'

He shrugged. 'Because I didn't know. I only found out at the inquest.'

* * *

Two days later, having given it much thought, James phoned the cricket captain. He told him he would be available for selection, and would attend practice sessions. The decision was greeted with immense relief by his family, their concerns eased by this first positive sign of his recovery. The grief had also been suffered by his nearest and dearest, albeit to a lesser extent. They had all taken Christine to their hearts, won over by her captivating smile, her vibrant personality and the kindness and patience she showed to everyone she met.

'Let's hope James is finally beginning to put all this behind him,' Rachael told Sonny. 'I know how desolate the world seems when you're young and have lost someone you plan to spend all your life alongside. The four years when you were missing, and everyone believed you were dead, were the worst time of my life. You returned to me, and the joy I felt was indescribable. How much worse it must be for James, knowing a miracle such as that cannot happen for him. We've been lucky, as have Mark and Jenny, and also Andy and Consuela. That luck seems to have run out for James. All we can hope is that eventually the tables will turn and he can find the happiness he's been cruelly denied.'

'I think you're absolutely right, but then you usually are,' Sonny replied. 'I only remember fragments of those years. I know I was in hospital somewhere before I started wandering, not knowing why or where I was going, my mind numbed by shell shock. One thing I was convinced of, although at times I wondered if it was purely my imagination, is that I was searching for something, or someone, but I couldn't work out what. It was only when I woke up in hospital here and saw your beautiful face that I knew for certain what I'd been seeking all that time.'

'Who knows, perhaps sooner or later James will see another beautiful face and that will act as an antidote to all his problems,' Rachael said.

Reflecting on this in years to come, Sonny reckoned it had to be one of the most accurate predictions of all time.

* * *

As the year was drawing to a close, Mark Cowgill was taking his daily train journey from Scarborough to Bradford, and hence to the headquarters of Fisher Springs (UK) Ltd. Mark had travelled the route almost every working day for the past twenty years. Until Sonny had relinquished his role as a managing director, they had completed the journey together. It was only after Sonny's retirement that Mark began to recognize that the trip was a chore he could well do without. That came, not so much as a shock, more a gradual realization. Other concerns now added fuel to the growing disenchantment with the way of life he thought was ingrained.

When he had established the synthetic fibres wing of the group, the company was one of the few to embrace what had been groundbreaking technology, giving them a cornerstone in the emerging market for their products.

Over recent years, however, rapidly growing competition, both within the UK and from foreign imports had decimated their profits, resulting in the division posting their first ever loss at the end of the financial year. Nor was that competition likely to cease, in fact it showed every sign of gaining momentum. Asia was the main source of such products. The biggest threats came from the Indian sub-continent and further east, via Japan, China and Taiwan.

There were other concerns regarding the group at the forefront of Mark's mind throughout that journey. He acknowledged that the executives in charge of the UK arm were all approaching retirement age. What had begun as a family business, of which Mark represented the third generation, now had nobody to carry it forward into the future.

Every one of the board members was either over sixty years old, or approaching that landmark. Within a short number of years, they would no longer want to shoulder that responsibility, nor would it be fair to ask them to do so.

As Mark saw it, there were two possible solutions to the problem, either of which required the approval of their Australian parent company. One way out of the dilemma would be to close the UK operation entirely, but that would be a waste, as the pharmaceutical and chemical division, together with the insurance arm, were still recording handsome profits.

The alternative would be to shut down the textile operation and put the remainder of the group up for sale. That would be a better way to end what had been a long-term successful commercial venture. As he dismounted from the train, Mark decided to put his ideas before his fellow board members, but before doing so he would consult with his father, and seek Sonny's opinion. As a former director and chairman, Sonny would undoubtedly have his own views on the best way to resolve the matter. Apart from that, he was still a substantial shareholder, who ought to have advance warning on such a radical development.

When he boarded the train for the return journey late that afternoon, Mark was unaware that three of his colleagues were discussing the same issue. The group's senior executive, Jessica Binks, had been concerned about her partner and fellow director David Lyons' health for several months, and a recent episode had finally caused her to raise the subject.

'When you were gardening at the weekend, you didn't bend down to do the weeding like you used to. I've noticed other occasions when you seem to have problems with your legs, so tell me what's going on, and why you've been trying to hide it from me.'

'It's my knees,' David admitted, abandoning any attempt to conceal the issue. 'They seem to be forever stiff and sore, and at times extremely painful.'

'You should see a doctor then, and do so immediately. There's no point you continuing to suffer if there's a remedy, even if it's only something to ease the discomfort.' Jessica paused, before adding, 'One good thing, as we manufacture them, you should be able to access the painkillers easily enough.'

Although he smiled at her joke, David listened intently as she continued, 'My guess is you might be suffering from some form of arthritis. If that's the case I have a long-term solution that will help ease the pain.' Jessica paused before asking a question that seemed irrelevant. 'Do you know why textile manufacturers chose places like Bradford, Huddersfield and Halifax as the base for their factories?'

'No, I've never given it a thought.'

'They did so because there's a high level of humidity in the atmosphere round here, and that lessens the chance of yarn snapping during the spinning and weaving processes. However, what is good for textiles is bad for someone with problems such as you might have. Once we have a proper diagnosis, it might be worth our while to go and live somewhere with a warmer, drier climate.' She hesitated. 'Somewhere like Spain, for example.'

David stared at her in disbelief, before stammering, 'You would do that, for me?'

'No, David, I would do it for us. You came into my life when I was in distress, and you helped me through that crisis, and took away the sadness that threatened to overwhelm me. You have been my support and mainstay ever since. Now, I think it's time for me to repay the debt I owe you, and if that means quitting our jobs, selling up in the UK and moving to the Costa del Sol, so be it.'

David thought for a moment. 'It would make a good honeymoon.'

'What would?' Jessica looked puzzled.

'The Costa del Sol.'

'David, what are you talking about?'

'Jessica, how many years have we been together?'

'Around thirty,' she responded, wondering where this conversation was going.

'Then don't you think it's time we got married?'

'Married?' She stared at him. 'We've never mentioned marriage. So why now?'

He took her in his arms. 'Quite simply, because we should.' He tightened his grip. 'If you want us to start a new adventure together, that is my condition. We begin as husband and wife.'

Jessica, always forthright and determined, tried to hold him at arm's length, but failed. 'So you're adding conditions, are you? Well, here are mine. Registrar's office, two witnesses, no fuss,' she paused. 'And we have to retire first.'

David laughed. 'I'll take that as a yes, shall I?'

She was trying hard not to grin.

'One more request,' David said. 'Can we at least have a small wedding cake? You know I love a good fruit cake. But not as much as I love you.'

* * *

A few miles away, in their Baildon house, group financial director Paul Sugden and his wife Sally were having a similar conversation, albeit with different reasons to consider a change in lifestyle. 'I've been thinking it over,' Paul began, 'and now that our chicks have flown the nest, I think we deserve some quality time together. I know we work alongside one another, but that's not exactly what I had in mind when we got married. Apart from the occasional few weeks in places like Scarborough or Filey, we've never taken proper holidays together. Now that air travel is more widely available, I reckon we should see the world, visiting places we've only read about. And what's more, I think we should do so while we're still fit and able.'

Sally recovered from her surprise, and said, 'That sounds rather reckless for you, Paul.'

'It isn't, not really. The kids have been provided for, the mortgage has been paid off, and we've a six-figure sum in the bank. Also, when I set up the new group pension fund, I incorporated a sliding scale of benefits for staff members taking early retirement. One way or another we have no financial concerns, not unless three banks and six building societies go into liquidation overnight.'

Paul's last remark puzzled Sally, until he explained, 'I've spread our savings between nine different deposit accounts to lessen the risk, and give us better interest rates.'

The more Sally thought over Paul's idea, the greater it appealed to her. 'There's one thing you didn't enter into the equation,' she said after a while. 'When my mum and dad passed away, I banked the money from the sale of their house, and that has never been touched. My salary has also been paid into that account. That gives us another fifty thousand pounds to spend.'

'Really? Well, before we go any further with the idea, I think we ought to give it some consideration. That way, we might spot something we've failed to take into account. I also believe we should forewarn our colleagues of what we're thinking of doing. That would only be fair, and it will give them chance to find suitable replacements.'

'How long are you planning to put it on the back burner for?'

'Six months. Twelve at the most, depending on how things transpire.'

That, Sally thought, was typical of Paul's prudent, bordering on cautious, nature. 'OK, let's go the whole hog and make it twelve months,' she agreed.

* * *

Although Sonny could see a lot of sense in what Mark had in mind regarding the future, he suggested nothing should be done in a hurry. 'You can't shut down the textile operation based on one set of bad figures. That would be unwise. What if things change rapidly? Let's be fair, the world's a volatile place. When I was growing up, anyone who suggested we'd have two world wars within twenty-five years of one another would have been locked away in a lunatic asylum. More recently, we've faced another potent threat from Russia and nuclear armaments. Who is to say we won't wake up next week to find ourselves involved in a major conflict with China, for instance? That was a strong possibility until recently, during the Vietnam fiasco. OK, that danger might have receded, but there could be others we can't foresee. I'd suggest waiting until you've another set of trading figures to work on before you make any move.'

Sonny paused and then gave voice to another strand of his argument. 'It doesn't have to be anything as dramatic as the scenarios I've outlined. It might be something on the lines of import restrictions, or the exchange rate. If that rate fluctuates wildly, goods from the countries you've mentioned might no longer be competitive.'

CHAPTER THIRTY-SEVEN

It was April of 1981 when Paul Sugden produced the evidence Mark had been waiting for, and the figures were as bad as he'd dreaded. The trading year that had just ended was far worse than the previous one. This was sufficient to establish a downward trend, and Mark knew remedial action had to be taken without delay.

Having shown his father these, Mark presented his idea at the next board meeting, which took place in early May. This produced only mild surprise, and it was Mark who was on the receiving end of several shocks. As his fellow directors spoke in turn, they echoed his thoughts and Mark quickly realized it wasn't merely the textile branch of the group which was facing an uncertain future, and that the dynasty founded by his great-grandfather was coming to an end.

Harry Barnes, head of the insurance division, spoke first, his announcement bringing the first of the startling revelations. 'I want you all to know I've decided to retire. I enjoy working here, but age is catching up with me. The daily commute is getting too much, and now I can't cycle anymore.'

'What will you do?' Jessica asked.

'I'll have my garden to keep me occupied.'

Having sympathized with their insurance supremo, Jessica added her news. 'David and I are also planning to give up our jobs. As David's osteoarthritis worsens, we need a warm dry climate to stave off the pain, so we've decided to buy a permanent home in Spain.'

Her colleagues had barely time to recover from the fresh shock when Paul Sugden signalled his intention to quit, his stated plan being for him and Sally to travel the world.

'I think we should send a telex to Australia and make them au fait with developments here,' Jessica suggested. 'It might mean they'll decide to close the whole of the UK operation. It will not be an easy task, and could take some time to finalize. I need to know if we are all prepared to work through this and stay the course, not just drop out. I'm not certain where that puts us, contractually speaking.'

Everyone agreed they would not leave until the time was right.

Mark thought for a moment. 'It might mean someone having to travel to Australia to sign documents and finalize arrangements. I recall head office representatives have been sent here in the past. I think we may need to reciprocate.'

As they were dispersing, Mark reflected on Jessica's final comment. He waited until the others had gone and then asked her, 'Would you mind delaying that telex for a while? I've had an idea concerning what you just said, but I want to run it past Jenny first. If she's in agreement, we might be able to kill two birds with one stone.'

As he was leaving the office, Mark glanced back at the building. The fine Victorian stone-built edifice had housed the company for over a hundred years. What would become of it if and when they moved out? he wondered. He hoped it wouldn't get torn down to make way for one of the concrete monstrosities, such as those perpetrated on the city as part of the strategy put forward by the engineer and planner Stanley Wardley.

One thought led to another, as Mark considered the equally sturdy buildings, old mills that housed the textile operations, the pharmaceutical and chemical plants. Rather than disposing of them piecemeal, it might be better to have a concerted scheme to put them to the best possible use.

That evening, when they were alone, he told Jenny what he had in mind. She stared at him for a few seconds, stunned speechless by what he was proposing. 'You think we should take a long holiday, go travelling, and include Australia as part of our journey, so we can visit Fisher Springs and wrap up the UK business?'

'That's pretty much it, yes.'

'I suppose there's a minute chance that one day you'll cease to surprise me, Mark Cowgill. Every time I think I've got to know all about you, something happens and I realize I'm nowhere close to fully understanding what makes you tick. OK, if you can make it work, I'm all for it.'

Mark put his arm around her. 'I'll tell you what makes me tick. It's you, Jenny, as it always has been.'

* * *

If May was a time for reflection in England, early in June, Luke and Bella Fisher were also assessing their situation as they adjusted to the new regime required to suit the needs of their granddaughter, who was now a semi-permanent resident in their home. Although Alice had forgiven her parents for their distrust in her, the need to live close to her new school, and her parents' priority with the vineyard and her baby brother, meant she saw less and less of them.

For the first time, Luke saw his granddaughter almost every day, and this evoked feelings and memories from long ago. These caused him deep satisfaction, as he confided to Bella. 'As Alice matures into a young woman, she reminds me more and more of my mother. Alice's dark hair, those brilliant blue eyes and even the shape of her face are just as I remember my mum.'

'Does that upset you?'

'Not in the slightest.' Luke paused and added with a grin, 'But if Alice gets any prettier she might upset a few young men in the near future.'

Although Bella smiled, Luke's final phrase reminded her of something she'd been intending to mention for a while. 'Have you given any more thought to *our* future, and that of the group? We're not getting any younger, and our fellow directors aren't exactly spring chickens either. None of our brood is interested in joining Fisher Springs, and from what I can judge, that applies to Elliot's tribe and Josh's kids.'

'You've got a good point, Bella. I haven't given it much thought. Have you any suggestions?'

'No, I wanted to run it past you first. Then we can put our heads together and see if we can come up with a simple solution. We're going to have enough on our plates looking after Alice, and soon there'll also be baby Richard to consider.'

Luke and Bella's grandson, who bore the anglicized version of Ricardo, was now approaching his first birthday. His parents had decided not to follow the tradition of naming the first son after the parental grandfather as, in Italian, this would have been Lucas. They laughed at the idea that people would assume they had named their son after the vineyard.

The baby was likely to become a regular visitor before long, as his parents continued to manage the vineyard.

A week later, as Luke and Bella were still pondering alternative options, a telex from their UK subsidiary gave an added dimension to the factors they needed to consider.

The day prior to the arrival of the telex, Luke had a meeting with his brother-in-law. Elliot Finnegan was a fellow director of Fisher Springs Pty and, amongst other things, bore responsibility for the maintenance and upkeep of the group's various properties.

'I'm proposing to renovate and redecorate the office building,' Elliot told Luke, 'including the directors' suite. To keep inconvenience to a minimum I'll move everybody one by one into the boardroom until their office has been completed, and then I'll finish off by redecorating the boardroom.'

'It will be quite an undertaking. This is a big building,' Luke said.

'Yes, but at the moment my team have very little on the books, as we haven't bought anything for a while that needs renovation work.'

As he agreed the plan, Luke had a stray thought. If the refurbished premises did nothing else, they might impress a prospective buyer for the group.

The following morning, Luke's secretary brought the UK telex to him. Luke studied the message, which bore the names of Jessica Binks and Mark Cowgill as authors, before passing it across to Bella. After taking in the gist, she looked up.

'It sounds as if our UK colleagues are thinking along the same lines as us, and what's more, they've even told us they have a couple of ideas. But they think it would be best if everything was discussed face to face. Might that mean someone travelling to England to sort it out?' she asked.

'I'm not sure, perhaps we should find out.'

Together they drafted a reply, and waited to see what the UK directors would propose. When the next telex arrived, Luke read it and told Bella, 'It's only signed from Mark. He and Jenny are planning a holiday, and as part of it they want to come here so they can discuss the business.'

'Should I message them back and say that's fine with us?' Bella replied.

'Yes, but before they do come, I think we should have the next year's results first, for both UK and here. Ask them to wait, and if they agree to that, ask them when they'd be thinking of coming.'

Bella thought for a moment. 'And I'll tell them not to book a hotel. If they're travelling all this way they can stay with us.'

After another short wait, Luke reported, 'Mark's suggested a date in mid-July. They're planning to visit his sister in Texas first. He thanks us for the accommodation offer, and says he and Jenny are looking forward to seeing us again.'

'I'm looking forward to seeing them. How long is it since we met them?'

'You don't remember our honeymoon?' Luke teased. '1950!'

'Of course I remember! It was delayed. I just couldn't recall the year.'

He grinned at Bella when she retorted, 'Well, at least Elliot and his merry men will have finished decorating by then. It wouldn't make a good impression with the place reeking like a paint factory.'

* * *

The Easter holiday of 1982 gave rise to the usual celebration, tinged with a little sadness in Byland Crescent. The Cowgill family were greatly relieved that James seemed finally to be overcoming his grief. Evidence of his return to normal was marked by his demeanour, which was more like the cheerful extrovert they loved and thought they had lost.

Conversation centred round the journey Mark and Jenny were planning to undertake. The younger members of the family marked the send-off with their own slant on the travels. Angela asked her grandparents to bring her a boomerang back, while Raquel pleaded with them to smuggle a koala bear in their luggage.

'It's lucky you weren't going a hundred and fifty years ago,' Andy told them, 'because in those days most travellers to Australia were in chains. Mind you,' he added, 'being from Yorkshire that would have one advantage, because at least you wouldn't have had to pay for your passage.'

'That would certainly appeal to our father,' Susan said, having made the journey home to join the party. 'Tell me everything,' she demanded. 'I've missed out on all the details.'

'We've split the journey,' her mother told her. 'We head first for Texas to visit Fran, Hank and their family. They've promised to show us the country, so we'll stay with them for three weeks. We have four days in Hawaii and then Fiji en route to Sydney. We've allocated a week to look around the city and see the famous beach, before moving on to Melbourne, where we'll repeat the process. That part, and the last stage of the journey will be by train, so we'll get to see more of the countryside.'

'Wow, that's some holiday,' Suzie remarked.

'We've very little idea what the interior of the country known as the Outback looks like,' Mark added. 'Although I understand some Aussies call the area the Gaba.'

'What does that mean?' Suzie asked.

'Apparently there are large tracts of barren land, so they refer to it as "the Great Australian Bugger All".'

* * *

It was a day for departures. The Bentley was loaded with luggage and, with his grandfather's permission, Andy was driving his parents to York. As the family stood on the steps of number one Byland Crescent waving goodbye to the parting couple, Sonny reflected that part of their journey would mark the end of an era.

Mark had a copy of the annual accounts in his possession. He had been entrusted by his fellow directors with the task of negotiating the disposal of parts of the UK arm of the Fisher Springs group. Although this saddened Sonny a little, at least it would be an honourable end to the adventure, unlike sixty years earlier, when his despicable cousin Clarence Barker had brought the company to the brink of liquidation, their rescue only achieved by the intervention of the Australian venture.

At no point in his thought process did the expression 'as one door closes, another opens' cross Sonny's mind.

The party waved and returned indoors for Suzie to collect her things and for James to take her to Scarborough station.

'You could have gone with them in the Bentley to York,' Rachael pointed out.

'Of course I could, but where would I have stowed my luggage?' She laughed. 'No Grandmama, I've said my good-byes — in private.' She hugged everyone and headed for the door with James.

Moments later Sonny looked out of the sitting-room window to see another car passing by with Mark's sister Lizzie, and her husband Gil, driving back to Wensleydale.

Lizzie told Gil, 'I think Mark will be only the second member of our family to visit Australia.'

'Who was the other one?' Gil asked.

Lizzie glanced at the back seat where the twins were both asleep. It was a reflex action, brought about by the need for secrecy in her former career, and it brought a rueful expression to her face as she replied, 'I went there in 1956, liaising with our counterparts during the Suez Crisis. So Mark and Jenny will be the second Cowgill visitors.'

Lizzie had no idea just how wrong she was.

CHAPTER THIRTY-EIGHT

Over at the Fisher Springs headquarters, Elliot Finnegan was putting the finishing touches to the entire renovation and redecoration of the building. The process had taken far longer than expected and the boardroom was the final area painted. Now the workmen had departed, and the unmistakeable aroma of their work had gone. All that needed to be done was to replace the furniture and hang the paintings on the walls, along with his surprise for Luke and Bella.

During the reshuffle of the offices, Elliot had needed to empty his late father's desk that he had inherited. Important documents had been removed long ago, and now it stood unused against the wall in Elliot's office. He had put this task off for many years, the emotions it evoked being too much for his sensitive spirit. When he finally had to tackle the job, he discovered something which puzzled him.

In the bottom drawer of the desk, secreted beneath an empty file folder, was an envelope, devoid of any inscription and sealed with tape. He was curious as to what it contained, and why his father had taken such precautions to keep it hidden. Elliot took a paper knife and slit the end, no easy task given the multiple layers of tape holding it firm.

Eventually he freed it, slid his hand inside, and withdrew an old photograph. It was face down, and he could just make out the impression of some handwriting on the reverse, but it had faded with age and was now completely illegible. He held it to the light, but without success. Turning it over, Elliot stared at the image of a large group of about fifteen people, he estimated, some seated, dressed in their finery, others standing behind, some wearing aprons and mob-caps, as they posed in what Elliot assumed to be a garden, or perhaps a park.

The photograph was very old — that much was obvious by the attire of the group members, which suggested the Victorian era or thereabouts. As he stared at the assembly, Elliot felt a memory stirring when his attention was caught by two of the group members. The young man at one side of the photo and the girl at the opposite side had been in another group photo, one he remembered seeing many times. That couple had been present at his parents' wedding, and were in a photograph his mother cherished. For years it had stood on a side-table, and Elliot had been told their names. Although both were younger in the image he held, they were unmistakably James and Alice Fisher.

Elliot had heard many things about them. Not only were they his wife Dottie's parents, they were the founders of Fisher Springs. This photograph should not be hidden away, Elliot decided. It should have pride of place in the boardroom, in honour of their endeavours. There, visitors could see the couple who had begun the great adventure which had become a leading light in the country's commercial sector.

However, the old image was far too small for his intention, so he'd headed across town to the media division. There, he and a friend managed to scan and enlarge the photograph which he then had suitably framed.

As well as allowing the visitors to view it, it would make a pleasant surprise for Luke to see his parents getting the recognition they deserved.

In the boardroom he drove a nail into the wall at head height and hung the large photograph on it. It would be worth seeing the look of surprise on Luke's face. Once he was satisfied it was hanging straight, he headed for Luke and Bella's office and reported the progress of the redecoration. 'We're finished. The paint smell has cleared, as you can tell. Everything will be ready for the showdown.'

Luke grinned at Elliot's description of the meeting with Mark Cowgill, but told him, 'It's a damned shame Josh has had to visit the mineral plant. With luck he'll be back before Mark and Jenny set off back to the Old Country. I know he's keen to see them, as we all are. Now we'd better get home.' He nodded to his wife, before telling Elliot, 'I'd better see what other jobs Bella's got lined up for me besides setting up the barbie. We have to show these Brits how we do it in Oz. Don't forget, we're taking next week to show them the sights before we get down to business. So with Josh away, you're in charge.'

Elliot gave a mock salute. 'Yes, sir! But before you go, I've something in the boardroom I'd like you both to see.'

Luke and Bella followed him, wondering what was making Elliot so excited.

'This is beaut. Where did you find it?' Luke asked, as he gazed at the image.

Elliot explained, and Bella agreed with Luke that Elliot had done the right thing in displaying the photograph. 'Wait till our visitors see this!' she exclaimed.

* * *

Late the following afternoon, the taxi bearing the visitors pulled up outside the Fisher homestead. 'Wow, that's some shack,' Mark exclaimed as he stared at the imposing structure. The vehicle had barely stopped moving when the front door of the building opened and three people stepped forward.

After greeting their long-term friends and business associates with 'G'day' and hugs, Luke and Bella introduced the third member of the welcoming party. 'This is our granddaughter Alice. She's staying with us at present, because it's more convenient for her school.'

Once they had freshened up in the palatial en-suite bedroom, Mark and Jenny joined their hosts downstairs, where refreshments prior to the evening meal awaited them. Luke offered Mark a beer, telling him, 'Sorry this isn't Tetley's bitter, but we don't get that over here.'

Mark smiled. 'I don't think room-temperature beer would work in this climate.'

The conversation turned to their respective families. It was with a good deal of pride that Bella told them of everything Jimmy, Robyn and Saul had achieved, before asking about Mark and Jenny's children.

Luke, Bella and Alice were enthralled by the story of Andy's rescue of Consuela and their romance, leading to a marriage everyone thought was purely a device to get Consuela away from the danger threatening her.

Jenny explained, 'When we saw them together we knew instantly they were deeply in love, and now they've given us three wonderful grandchildren.'

'How are they doing?' Bella asked.

'The girls are still at school, and they're absolutely fine. James was intending to go to university, but that didn't work out. And we were very worried about him for a long time, but he seems well on the road to recovery now.'

'Recovery? Has he been ill?'

'No, but he's been through a dreadful ordeal.'

Luke and Bella listened with horror as they learned of James' burgeoning romance, and the tragic and brutal way it had ended. 'He's always had an outgoing nature,' Jenny said. 'But now it seems he's lost all interest in women.'

Alice, who was seated nearby, felt deep sympathy as she learned of the suffering he had undergone. How strange it was, she reflected, that she should be so moved by the tragedy of a young man she had never met, a man only a few years older than her. She decided that to have recovered from such a cataclysmic event showed considerable strength of character.

This was reinforced as Jenny revealed the final, shocking revelation that nobody had known his fiancée was in the early stages of pregnancy when she died. On hearing this, Alice was startled to find tears forming in her eyes. She mopped them away, hoping nobody had noticed. Alice's troubles had seemed bad enough, she thought, but they were as nothing compared with what Mark and Jenny's grandson had undergone.

The rest of the week was spent giving their visitors a guided tour of the area. On the following Monday morning Luke and Bella drove Mark and Jenny to the headquarters of Fisher Springs to begin the business discussions. There, they were able to renew acquaintanceship with Elliot Finnegan, whom they had met when he'd been seconded to the UK arm of the group many years earlier.

Having shown their visitors around the building, before they headed for their office, Bella said, 'You should see the boardroom and you can tell me what you think.' It wasn't the paintwork she wanted them to see. She was curious about the photograph and thought they might find it interesting.

CHAPTER THIRTY-NINE

'Wow, that's some view,' Mark exclaimed, as he marched across the room to gaze out through the picture window forming almost all the rear wall of the boardroom.

'You think that's beaut,' Bella said. 'Our office is on a corner and has two glass walls. You'll see that later.'

Jenny stepped forward to get a closer look at the panoramic scenery, but as she did so, something on the wall alongside her caught her eye. She looked for a long minute, then turned and grasped her husband's arm. 'Mark, look at this.' She pointed to the photo Elliot had placed there. Mark stepped forward and gasped with astonishment.

'Is something wrong?' Bella asked.

Mark stared at the image. 'Where did you get this photograph?'

'Actually, I found this,' Elliot replied, taking the original small print from inside his jacket. 'It was hidden in my father's old desk. I thought it ought to be on display, so I had it enlarged and framed as a surprise for Luke and Bella.'

Mark was visibly shaken. He turned to Luke. 'Do you know who the people in this photo are?'

'Yes, I recognize two of them,' Luke replied. He pointed to the image of the young man and the pretty girl. 'That's my father and mother, when they were younger, of course. But I don't know where it was taken. It must be back in the Old Country.' He put his arm around Bella and continued, 'I'm so pleased Elliot found it. All our family photos were destroyed in the house fire that killed my parents. This is the only one I have of them.'

Mark and Jenny looked at one another in bewilderment.

'Have you seen the photo before?' Bella asked.

'We certainly have.' Mark reached out for Jenny. 'I need to sit down.'

'Elliot, bring some water,' Bella instructed.

Elliot dashed from the room and returned moments later, handing a glass to Mark.

'Mark, are you OK?' Luke asked, concern etched on his face. 'Do we need to call a doc or an ambo?'

Jenny shook her head. 'No, no, he'll be OK in a minute.' Tears began to run down her face, while Mark, pale-faced, sipped at the water, clutching her hand. They stared at each other for what seemed an eternity to the others in the room, as the silence grew.

After a few minutes Mark managed to pull himself together. 'Please, would you all sit down? Elliot, would you be so good as to take the photo off the wall and place it here, please?' He pointed to a spot on the table in front of him.

Jenny dried her eyes and bit her top lip, worried how they would react to what Mark was about to tell them.

Mark took a deep breath, and rubbed his hand across his face, uncertain where to start. 'Although you only recognized two people in this group, you've met another of them before.' He turned to Jenny, who nodded, her eyes glistening with unshed tears. 'We get to see this photo at home, albeit the smaller version.' He pointed to the image, and the others noticed his hand was shaking slightly. 'If, as you say, that is your father and mother, I have to tell you the little boy standing in the middle, is my father, Mark senior — known to one and all as Sonny Cowgill.'

Luke, Bella and Elliot stared in disbelief, while Mark took another drink of water before he continued, 'We, at Fisher Springs UK, know nothing of the formation, or background, of Fisher Springs. We only had vague information about a reclusive business couple who wished to remain anonymous.'

He paused again, took a deep breath, and said, 'Unless I'm very much mistaken, your father's name was James, and your mother was Alice.'

There was another long silence.

'Am I right?' he asked.

Luke nodded, lost for words. Bella was gripping his hand as she listened, totally puzzled.

Mark watched Luke and Bella as they tried to grasp the meaning. 'Luke . . .' — he hesitated — 'that means your father and mine were brothers.'

He tried to explain. 'I've heard the story of James and Alice many times. My father told me how our grandfather, Albert, threw James out because he'd become romantically involved with the housemaid, Alice, and she was expecting a baby.' He paused for breath. 'One of the greatest regrets of Sonny, *my* father, was losing touch with James, who I believe he hero-worshipped. He has spent decades wondering what happened to both him and Alice.'

Luke and Bella sat stock-still as Mark thought for a moment, and then asked Luke, 'I'm sorry to ask this, but did you have an older brother, named Saul?'

Luke nodded again.

'Did he die during the First World War?'

Luke could do no more than croak agreement.

Mark told him, 'Dad was serving in the trenches with the ANZACs, and he believes he met Saul.' Then he added, 'Saul was the name of our great-grandfather — James' grandfather.'

Luke struggled to his feet and rounded the table to stare at the picture. 'Is this some weird joke? Has someone told you facts and you think this is some kind of British humour?

I got used to the pranks during the war when I was over there. Elliot, you've been there, are you in on this?'

Elliot looked shell-shocked, and shook his head.

Mark got to his feet and put his hands on both of Luke's shoulders. He looked him in the face. 'I'm not joking. No one has fed me any information. Who would? And when could they?'

Luke stared at him, his eyes wet with tears. 'Is this fair dinkum?'

'By that, if you mean is it true? Then yes. Luke, we have just solved an eighty-three-year-old mystery.' Slowly, he nodded and began to smile. 'Luke, you've been to our home. You, Bella and baby Jimmy have been in that garden.'

Luke tried to understand, looking at Bella, who was just as confused.

'That photograph was taken on the day of Queen Victoria's diamond jubilee, in the private garden in the centre of Byland Crescent.'

Mark watched Luke's expression change. 'I remember the garden.' He picked up the photograph, as if some unseen voice would fill in the empty spaces in his memory.

Bella came to his side and looked with him. 'I took the baby in there for fresh air to sit in the sun on a rug.'

'This is unbelievable,' Luke said.

Mark grinned. 'I'm sorry to break the bad news to you, Luke, but it appears that you and I are cousins.'

Luke stepped forward and hugged Mark, an embrace that soon involved Jenny and Bella. In the hubbub of conversation and tears that followed, Elliot slipped from the room to make a phone call. 'Dot,' he told his wife, 'drop whatever you're doing and come to the office — immediately! There's someone here you absolutely have to meet.'

* * *

What was intended to be a business conference soon became a series of family meetings, as Mark and Jenny were introduced to more kinfolk they hadn't known existed. Among these, Luke's sister Dottie and his niece Clare were the most direct, but later in the week, they met up with Jimmy and Saul. Unfortunately, Robyn was away with the orchestra. These meetings involved recounting the tally of relatives on both sides of the world.

As they listened to Mark and Jenny tell everyone about the others in the photograph, and the UK arm of the family, of Billy, Frances and Lizzie, plus their own children and various offspring, Luke gave a wry smile. 'I reckon with all these new rellies, Christmas is going to be a whole lot more expensive from now on.'

Mark eyed his cousin. 'If anyone had any doubts regarding your heritage, that's just proved it. Spoken like a true Yorkshireman.'

When Josh returned from his field trip, they brought him up to date with the revelations. He was as stunned by the news as the others, and speculated if his stepfather, Simon Jones, had known of the connection. 'He worked at Haigh Ackroyd and Cowgill, but I guess not, because I feel sure he'd be duty-bound to tell Sonny.' He took an admiring look at the photo, a puzzled expression on his face, and began to laugh.

'Something funny?' Luke asked.

Josh pointed at the faces in the photo. 'I think I've seen this before, at my grandmother's house. If I'm not mistaken, that lady there is my great-grandmother — she was a Cowgill before she married.'

The only thing they could all do was laugh, as the family history was unravelling before them all.

Elliot said, 'I think my father must have known. And that's probably why he took such pains to conceal the photo.'

'You're right, Elliot,' Bella said. 'He took me and Ma to England when I was very little. I don't remember anything about the trip, but he may have uncovered the connection.'

'I think it's more likely he knew beforehand. Otherwise he might have let something slip. We'll never know the answer to that, but one thing for certain, we're going to have a lot to tell my father when we return to England,' Mark said. 'It'll be like an early birthday present for him.'

'When is his birthday?'

'Next month, August the eighteenth. He'll be ninety years old.'

Bella was about to respond, but then thought better of it. What she had in mind was too important to bring into the open without consulting Luke beforehand. That evening, when they were alone, she put her idea to him.

She could tell the plan appealed, as he asked for clarification. 'You think we should ask Mark and Jenny to keep all this family history under their hats, and we can go to England in time for Sonny's birthday and make the revelation then?'

'That's what I had in mind, but I think you should be more respectful — it's Uncle Sonny now.'

Luke chuckled. 'I'm sure he'll forgive me. I think it's a great idea, but it's a lot to ask. Will Mark and Jenny be able to keep the secret?'

'We can ask. But wouldn't it make the best birthday gift? And I'm glad the birthday's in August — I don't think I could stand a British winter.'

'OK. Let's pitch it to them tomorrow and see what they think.'

Mark and Jenny were equally enthusiastic, and a great deal of time was spent planning the details of the visit. Granddaughter Alice listened to the discussions, and as she thought of the location of the forthcoming visit, she vowed to do her best to be included in the invitation. Alice knew Scarborough was in Yorkshire where her hero, vet James Herriot, who had inspired her choice of career, lived. How far Scarborough was from Darrowby, where the series of books about a vet's life were set, she had no idea, but it was much closer than Australia.

* * *

Eventually, the initial purpose of the trip, the future of Fisher Springs UK, was discussed. Luke and Bella had taken time to study the year-end figures Mark had brought, which made them even more interested in what he had to say.

With them listening intently, Mark put forward the ideas formulated by the board in Bradford. 'The figures show the textile arm is no longer profitable, and we believe it would be better to close this section of the business before it becomes unviable. The other problem we face is that all our senior executives are getting on in years and all have their reasons for wishing to retire.'

Mark listed these and then told Luke and Bella, 'The insurance division, plus the pharmaceutical and chemical manufacturing plants, will all yield handsome profits if we sell them as going concerns, which would only leave the buildings that house the textile mills, plus the offices to be dealt with. Our idea is to sell them to a development company. Now that property prices are beginning to improve, they would make a good investment for refurbishment, converting them to house a department store, or apartments.'

As he listened to Mark outlining the plan for the UK sector, Luke realized that in many ways, their situation mirrored the Australian one. With none of the next generation wanting to take up the reins of running the enterprise, now might be a good time to adopt a similar tactic. Eventually he spoke, responding to Mark's suggestions. 'I think this is an excellent plan, and I want to see if we can adopt something similar here. I will put it to the board. I also think we should announce our intention to visit England to oversee the disposal of our assets. At the same time we will take a holiday. That would mask another reason — to attend Uncle Sonny's birthday party.'

CHAPTER FORTY

Mark and Jenny returned to Byland Crescent. On this occasion, Mark had refused his father's offer to collect them from York for the final leg of their journey. In a phone call from their London hotel, Mark explained, 'Jenny wants to raid the shops. That's her excuse. I think she just wants to go on a spending spree. One way or another, I've no idea which train we'll catch when she eventually wearies of trying to spend the family's wealth.'

'What was all that about?' Jenny asked.

'I thought Dad would use the journey from York to quiz us in depth about every aspect of our trip, the Australian part in particular. He's no fool, and given sufficient chance without distraction he might well spot we're concealing something important. Once we're home we can divert his attention by telling him the business aspect of our Australian visit and then move on to talk about Fran, Hank and the kids. Mum's sure to intervene and demand chapter and verse about their grandchildren, and great-grandchildren. While we're back at work we'll be fine, but we will have to be careful what we say during the evenings. Hopefully Dad will have the television on and that will save us!'

The ploy worked, and Sonny's attention was further diverted by a phone call from his daughter and son-in-law in Texas. On this occasion, however, Fran had exciting news for him and Rachael. 'We're making arrangements to head across the pond. We're booking flights, so we'll be with you in time to join the rave-up for Dad's birthday. Hank junior and his family are running the ranch while we're away. Unfortunately, Maggie and her brood can't get away, so it will just be the two of us.'

When the call was over, Sonny confronted Mark and Jenny. 'You knew what Fran and Hank were planning, didn't you? Ever since you got back, I suspected there was something you were hiding from me, but I couldn't guess what.'

Later, when they were alone, Mark said, 'That was a narrow escape. I told you the old man was shrewd. Luckily, Fran's news sidetracked him.'

* * *

Shortly after their return home, Mark had travelled to Bradford and briefed his colleagues on their parent company's reaction to the disposal plan for the UK branch of the business. As Mark explained, 'Luke Fisher's all in favour of the idea. He and his wife are coming here to oversee the process, very soon.'

After the meeting, in the privacy of Jessica's office, Mark grinned and told her, 'That's the reason we've told Dad, but their real intention is something far deeper, more personal. I'll tell you, as long as you keep it secret.'

'Don't worry about that, Mark. Given my former career, keeping secrets is something I'm used to.'

Her eyes widened with surprise as Mark told her the outcome of his and Jenny's visit to Fisher Springs' headquarters. 'And nobody's known about this all these years?'

'We think Patrick Finnegan knew, but for some reason kept the photo hidden. If his son Elliot hadn't recognized the couple in the photo and hung it in their boardroom, we might never have found out.'

'What a wonderful, sad story,' Jessica replied. 'And I certainly won't spill the beans.'

'You and David are invited, are you coming?'

'Given what you've just told me, I think this party should be family only. But it would be ungracious to decline. We could stay at that new hotel, opposite your house.'

'That's a good idea, but you might be happier had the original bed and breakfast catering for older people still been next door.' Mark laughed.

'One thing I would suggest, though,' Jessica added.

'What's that?'

'I think you should keep a camera handy so you can take another photo, one that shows Sonny's reaction when all is revealed.'

Later, at the office, Mark collected a telex from Luke Fisher, confirming details of their trip, and where they would be staying, first in Bradford and then in Scarborough. Mark smiled as he read the final line of the message. He'd noted Luke and Bella's granddaughter's determination to be included in the visiting party. It seemed her grandparents had been unable to resist her pleas.

* * *

The Cowgill family concentrated on preparations for the forthcoming party. Planning was necessary, owing to the importance of the event, and the number of people who would need catering for. Rachael, assisted by Jenny, Consuela, Sarah their cook, and Mary the housekeeper, formed the organizing group, with occasional input from Mark. Before he and Jenny went away, he had suggested a garden party, providing the weather didn't spoil things. The central garden would be ideal. He had organized the hiring of a gazebo, suitable seating, and serving staff.

Now Sarah needed numbers for the catering.

His mother took command. 'If we take the permanent residents, including Susan, that makes ten. Add to that Fran and Hank, plus Lizzie, Gil and the twins, and we're looking at a total of sixteen people staying in the house.' Rachael looked at Sarah. 'That's a lot of mouths to feed with all the other work you have for the party. How do you suggest we tackle it?'

Sarah smiled. 'I've cooked for far more than that — just let me know how many days they will all be here and it won't be a problem. As for the actual day, I think the best way would be to set up a buffet.' She tapped Rachael's arm reassuringly. 'Leave it to me.'

'That sounds fine,' Rachael agreed, quite relieved. 'On the day, there will be five more guests coming over from the Bradford office, and a couple of our neighbours, so you have carte blanche on the menu and dining arrangements, Sarah. How are things on the accommodation side, Mary?'

'We can cope with everyone. The four adults will have the guest rooms on the top floor and I'll make up the extra bed for Heloise in with Angela and Raquel. William can have James' old room.'

'One thing nobody's thought to mention,' Consuela pointed out, 'is the liquid refreshment. Given the celebration, we'll need plenty of that.'

'Don't worry about that,' Jenny reassured her. 'Mark's got it all in hand.'

Once the meeting was over, Jenny had a quiet word with Sarah. 'When you're planning the buffet for the party, there are three more guests, but it has to be a surprise for Sonny and Rachael. I don't want a word of it to reach them before Mark and I have the opportunity to tell them nearer the time.'

Sarah promised. 'Don't worry. I'm used to keeping secrets. Fortunately, there's plenty of room inside a toque.'

'What's a toque?'

'It's one of those white chef's hats. The one I'm delighted I no longer need to wear.'

* * *

In the Bradford boardroom, there was a sense of anticipation as they awaited the arrival of Mark. He had gone to the hotel to bring Luke and Bella Fisher to the meeting. Of those present, only Harry Barnes had not met them on Luke's previous visit on a fact-finding tour in 1950.

On their arrival, Luke, as owner of the company, was invited to take the chair. He declined, telling Jessica, 'We don't stand on ceremony in Oz, and I sure aren't going to start now.'

Luke asked for more in-depth details regarding each division of the company than those he already knew. Everyone realized this meeting could last for several days.

When the meeting broke for lunch, Mark asked Luke what Alice was doing during this time. 'Oh, that's an easy one,' he replied. 'Reading! She spotted a book shop and has bought more of those vet books she's so keen on.'

'Don't you think she might get a little bored alone in her hotel room while you're here?'

'Bella can miss out, if necessary, take her shopping or something. Alice is not used to city life and knows not to leave the hotel alone.'

'Excuse me,' Bella, standing alongside, said. 'Don't I get a say in this? I should be here. But I must admit this didn't occur to us when she begged to come with us.'

Mark thought for a moment. 'Why don't I take her to Scarborough with me? I have two teenage granddaughters there with nothing to do now it's the summer break. They could keep her company.'

'That would be ripper,' Bella said. 'I think she would like that. But are you sure the family won't mind?'

'Why would they? I'll just go and phone Jenny.'

That evening, there were two travellers heading for Scarborough. Alice had been warned by Bella to be on her best behaviour and to be careful what she said. There was to be no mention of the family connection. Both Alice's grandparents were sure she could be relied on to maintain her silence.

As the train headed though the countryside, Mark told Alice of the places they were passing through, and was surprised when she asked, 'Where's Darrowby?'

'Darrowby? I don't know of Darrowby.'

'You must do.' She reached into her bag and pulled out the latest James Herriot books she had bought. 'It's in here.'

'Oh, I understand. Unfortunately, Alice, it's a made-up name.'

Alice looked disappointed. 'I thought it was real. I was hoping to visit the town and see everything that's mentioned in the books.'

'Well, I'm sorry, but I'm sure, knowing my granddaughters, you'll find plenty to do in Scarborough.'

* * *

At Byland Crescent, there was a reception committee when Mark and Alice arrived. Jenny hugged Alice, welcoming her, before she introduced her to Angela and Raquel. Alice was startled as the girls grabbed her by the hands and headed for the stairs. 'This way,' Raquel cried.

Obviously primed by their grandmother, Angela said, 'Come on, Alice, we'll show you the bedroom. Gran said you could sleep in with us if that's OK with you? If not, you can have one of the guest rooms, but you'll be on your own.'

'And that won't be much fun,' Raquel added. 'Mum and Dad will be home from work soon and Dad can bring your bags up. When you've unpacked we'll give you a tour and you can meet the others.'

'Others?' Alice asked.

'Yes, there are four generations living in the house,' Angela told her.

'Well, it looks big enough.' Alice laughed. 'And this is really kind of you,' she said as she eyed the girls' room. 'I'll sleep in here with you, if you don't mind. I spend a lot of time on my own when I'm not at school. It will be beaut to have someone to chat to.' She admired the bedroom, the walls decorated with posters of pop stars. In the corner stood a Decca record player, on the floor a heap of records.

'Want some music?' Angela asked.

'Yes, who have you got?'

'Loads. There's Wham, Elton John, and some old Buddy Holly and Beatles stuff Aunt Suzie gave us. Have a dig through and see what you want.'

A short while later there was a knock at the bedroom door, barely heard through the noise from within.

A voice called, 'Room service.'

Angela and Raquel giggled. 'Come in, Dad,' they called, in unison.

The door swung open to reveal Andy, clutching Alice's luggage. Behind him stood a dark-haired woman with tanned skin, smiling directly at Alice. She was carrying a tray bearing three glasses of orange juice.

'Turn it down,' Andy ordered. 'We can hear that racket downstairs.' The girls grinned and obeyed their father. When the introductions were over, Consuela hugged Alice. 'This is a pleasant surprise. I'm so happy you've come to stay. It will keep my girls busy looking after you.' She turned to her daughters. 'See that Alice has anything she needs. And don't be late down for dinner,' she added as a warning.

After the door closed, the girls grinned. 'Leave the unpacking, we can help you later. We want to show you round the house before we eat,' Raquel said, and led Alice to the hallway. She indicated the guestrooms and the bathroom, before they came to the study area. 'This is where we're supposed to do our homework.'

'Well, some of us do,' Angela, five years older than Raquel, said pointedly. 'I have exams next term, and I for one don't want to flunk them.'

One floor down, Angela pointed to one of several doors and said, 'That room belonged to our brother James, but he has a flat now. That's a bathroom, and the other rooms are where the old folks sleep. The smaller room at the back is the office. We're not allowed in there.'

'Under pain of death,' Raquel said, in macabre tones.

'This house is big,' Alice said, 'almost as big as Grandma's. And I thought all houses in England were small.' She laughed.

Angela shrugged. 'Wait till you see downstairs.'

In the main hallway the girls indicated several doors. 'This,' Angela said, with an arm-waving gesture, 'is the drawing room.' She opened the double door to reveal a formal room, beautifully furnished. 'We only use this for special occasions.'

Raquel took Alice's hand. 'This way.' She led her down the hall. 'This is the kitchen, and this is Sarah, our cook. Well, actually, she's a chef, but that doesn't seem to matter anymore. This other lady is our housekeeper, Mary.'

Angela asked, 'Do you mind if we show her Lizzie's old room?'

'Be my guest,' Mary laughed.

'Who's Lizzie?' Alice wanted to know.

'She's Grandpa's sister,' Raquel said. 'She had a terrible accident that left her unable to walk for a long time. These rooms were originally called the butler's pantry, but as there wasn't a butler anymore, they were converted for Aunt Lizzie to use.'

'And this is the wine cellar.' Alice was led down the steps to where racks of wine were lying along a short wall. Alice began to laugh.

'What's so funny?'

Alice grinned. 'Don't you know my family own a vineyard? You should see our racks.'

The girls shook their heads, and Alice explained the volume of bottles at her home.

The tour continued outside to the old stables, housing the family cars and Sonny's carpentry workshop. Back indoors, Alice saw the library, the dining room, and was at last shown the sitting room where she met Sonny and Rachael.

They were delighted to meet Alice, and asked her about her life at the vineyard, and her prospects at school. They were surprised to discover how confident she felt about achieving her goals.

‘I have exams soon, but they won’t be a problem since I changed school. I’ll have time for cramming when we get home. I had to get permission to visit as it’s term time. I just want to discover about life here in England while I can. And Scarborough is so different from Bradford. Angela and Raquel are showing me the town tomorrow, and I’m looking forward to the funfair.’

Raquel was confused. ‘But it’s the summer holidays, why should you be in school?’

‘Because at home it’s the middle of winter. The summer break doesn’t start until mid-October.’

‘I’ll explain later,’ Sonny said. ‘Geography isn’t one of her best subjects.’

Over dinner, the chatter continued, and when the meal was over, Angela and Raquel cleared the plates to the kitchen and began the washing up. Alice, used to her grandparents’ live-in housekeeper, wondered where the staff were.

‘They don’t live in,’ Angela told her. ‘When dinner has been served, they leave the tableware for us to wash.’

‘Yes, every night,’ Raquel muttered.

‘Stop moaning — you want your pocket money, don’t you?’

CHAPTER FORTY-ONE

Next morning the girls took Alice on a sightseeing tour. They headed into town, walking slowly downhill towards the sea in the South Bay, while Alice admired the architecture of the older buildings. Angela assured her they would take in the shops another day, but the plan was to have some fun. Angela and Raquel were in sleeveless summer dresses, enjoying the warmth of the sun. Alongside them, wearing a thick cardigan over hers, Alice shivered in the light breeze coming from the sea.

'Is it always this cold?' she asked.

'This is a glorious summer day, it's hot!' Angela told her.

'Really, well, I suppose it's not as bad as the Fremantle Doctor.' Seeing their confused expressions, Alice explained about the Australian sea breeze that helps to keep temperatures lower in the summer months, but can be a strong wind on the coast.

At the funfair, following several rides, the next thing on the agenda was ice cream, before they began the climb back up the hill through the town. The girls stopped outside an electrical store.

'We need to pop in here for a minute. I want to see Mum, I missed her this morning before she left,' Angela said.

'Does your mother work in a shop?' Alice was confused. She believed the people who worked in the English arm of Fisher Springs were as wealthy as her family.

'No, silly. Mum and Dad own the shop. Come on, we'll show you.' They walked through onto the sales floor where Alice was surprised at the wide range of goods available. At the counter stood an older woman who was busy serving a customer. Angela waited until she was free, then said, 'Hi, Nora. This is Alice from Australia.'

The woman smiled. 'Hello, Alice.' She turned to the girls. 'They're both in the back, go on through.'

Alice was led through to the rear into a large workshop full of electrical goods in various states of repair. At a long workbench sat Consuela and Andy, who looked up and smiled at the teenage group. 'And what can we do for you, ladies?' Andy asked.

'Can we go to the cinema tonight, please, Dad?' Angela asked.

'Why would you want to sit in a stuffy cinema in the height of summer?'

'Please, Dad,' Raquel said. 'There's this fantastic new musical called *Annie*. It's about an orphan who needs a home. She gets adopted by a millionaire.'

'If you know the entire plot, you don't really need to see it, do you?' Andy asked, trying to hide his smile, while teasing his daughters.

Raquel stared at her father and folded her arms. 'Fine, we'll just go for a walk and show Alice the North Bay. We want to be home before it gets dark, so we'll ask Sarah if we can eat early. That means you'll have to clear the dining table tonight as we won't be there,' she said smugly.

'Won't you need to eat early if you're to get to the cinema on time?'

Raquel looked to her sister for help.

'And if you do,' her father continued, 'I'll have to clear the table in your place anyway.'

'Andy, stop teasing them. Of course you can go if that's what you want,' their mother said. 'Just make sure Sarah is in agreement for an early meal, or you'll have to go tomorrow.'

The chattering girls turned to leave as at that moment the connecting door swung open and a young man backed through carrying a television set. As he put the set down, he glanced in their direction, spotting the attractive, dark-haired young woman in the company of his sisters.

Alice stared at him as he turned to face them. Before she had chance to ask the girls who this good-looking stranger was, he approached them.

He stepped forward and held out his hand. 'A pleasure to meet you, Alice.'

'How do you know my name?' she asked as she shook his hand.

'You would be surprised at what I know.' He bowed slightly, a gesture that sent his sisters into fits of giggles.

'Your name is Alice Fisher, and you've travelled to England with your grandparents on business.' He smiled. 'Don't worry, I'm not clairvoyant. I recognized your accent when I heard you speak as I came in.'

Alice realized he was still holding her hand.

He gazed into her deep blue eyes, smiled, and said, 'My name is James Cowgill, and Australians are as rare as rocking horse droppings here in Scarborough, so I worked the rest out.'

Alice smiled at his joke, but listened as he continued, 'After my grandparents, Mark and Jenny, visited you in Australia, they told me all about you.' He paused, and then added, 'But they failed to mention how beautiful you are.'

She blushed at the compliment, and the obvious sincerity in his voice. His sisters were wide-eyed. At the other side of the room, his parents paused in their work, and listened.

'It's lovely to meet you, Alice. If there's anything you need while you're here, you only have to ask. And I suggest you ask me — not my little sisters.' He smiled, released her hand, and returned to his work.

Alice watched him go and smiled. So that's what an English gentleman is like, she mused.

'We'd better say hello to Gran while we're here, or she'll never forgive us,' Angela directed Alice to a door over in the corner.

'Does Jenny work here too?'

'Only part-time. She does the office work so Mum, Dad and James can get more done.'

* * *

That evening James arrived at Byland Crescent after work, having arranged with his mother to join the family for dinner. At the table he sat next to Alice, interested in finding out more about life in Australia.

'You're not thinking of emigrating, are you?' his grandfather asked.

'Not specifically. From what you told us on your return it just sounds so different there. I'm curious, that's all.'

In the sitting room after the meal, the conversation continued. Alice, who they all expected would work in the family vineyard, surprised them when she told them of her desire to become a vet. 'It was the book *It Shouldn't Happen to a Vet* by James Herriot that convinced me,' she said. 'I was hoping to be able to visit Darrowby, but I've been told it doesn't exist.

'But the surgery is real. I could take you to see where it is, if you like?' James told her.

'We could do that?'

'If it's OK with the family we could. What do you think, Dad? Can I have a day or two off to show Alice the sights?'

'I suppose we could manage. Are there any outstanding pick-ups to do, Jenny?'

'Not that I'm aware of. But I do feel we should do this correctly. We don't want to offend anyone, especially Luke and Bella. If Alice is to go with James, there should be a chaperone.'

'Oh, Gran,' Angela said. 'Don't be so old-fashioned.'

Jenny turned to her granddaughter and gave her a fixed stare. 'Old-fashioned or not, if someone doesn't go with them, then they don't go.'

'Jenny is quite right,' Rachael said. 'With the business in the middle of such important discussions, we will not allow anything that will cause offence. Alice, I suggest you phone your grandparents at their hotel and ask their permission before anything is agreed. The number is alongside the phone.'

Alice left the room and the discussion continued in her absence. 'Well, I'm sorry, but I have some studying to do, so count me out,' Angela said. 'I can't miss a whole day.'

Consuela knew this to be true and, raising her eyebrows, glanced at Raquel, who was sitting quietly at one end of the sofa.

Raquel saw her mother's expression, knew she was being asked. 'I'll go. As long as we get fed,' she added.

Aware that Alice would have to return to her grandparents when the Bradford meetings were finalized, and she may not be with them in Scarborough for much longer, arrangements were made for the next day.

* * *

At nine o'clock, James drew his Mini to a halt in Byland Crescent and tooted his horn. The front door opened and Alice and Raquel came down the steps.

'Wow,' Alice cried, 'you've got a Mini, it's beaut.'

Behind them was Mary, carrying a picnic hamper and rug.

'Sarah thought this might be useful,' she told James. 'This way you'll not need to find somewhere to have lunch.' She looked at Raquel. 'And Miss Greedy Guts here won't think she's being starved. I think this should go in the boot, otherwise it may be empty before you reach your destination.'

James opened the passenger door and turned to his sister, to find her standing, arms crossed, on the pavement. 'Well, are you coming? Get in.'

'Why am I in the back? I'm your sister.'

'Exactly! Alice is our guest and it's a much better view in the front. Come on, Squirt, get in.'

Raquel clambered in, and James replaced the passenger seat. Signifying that Alice should get in, he announced, 'Advance Australia Fair.'

Alice climbed in, laughing. 'When did you learn our national anthem?'

James was laughing too. 'I must have read about it somewhere.'

Alice was struggling, looking round the car. 'Where's the belt?'

'Belt? Oh, you mean the seatbelt. I haven't had them fitted yet. Thanks for reminding me, they will be compulsory after next January.'

'They're mandatory at home. It will feel strange without one.'

'Well, settle back and enjoy the ride.'

En route to Thirsk, Alice marvelled at the villages they drove through. 'This is much better than the train journey on the way here. That seemed to be all fields — this way is far prettier. Do we go through York?'

'Sorry, not today. The places we're going are all this side of York. If you want to visit the city, you should speak to your grandfather. I understand he was stationed in England during the war and he might like to go there. He may have already been since then, when he was here on business before.'

It wasn't long before they passed through the market town of Pickering. James drove round the town and continued the journey onwards.

'Why didn't we stop?' Raquel asked.

'We can stretch our legs when we get to Helmsley.'

'Good, because I'm squashed in here.'

'Ignore her,' James told Alice. 'She's always moaning about something.'

In Helmsley market square, James parked the car and the trio had a walk round the small town, with Alice admiring the cottages. From her bag she produced a camera and began snapping. 'I want to show these to my mates back home. They'll be so jealous. Can we go in the castle?'

'Not if you want to see the veterinary surgery. There won't be time.'

'No contest,' Alice said, putting the camera away.

The drive continued, and after a short while, as James approached a bend in the road, he said, 'Hold on to your hats!'

Alice's eyes were wide as they began the descent of Sutton Bank, a steep winding road. 'Wow, that is some hill,' she said.

'You can recover soon, we're nearly in Thirsk.'

They left the car in the market place and headed across the cobbles to Kirkgate. There, James indicated a door, alongside which was a brass plaque bearing the name *Mr D V Sinclair, MRCVS*. Beneath it, a second wooden nameplate was engraved, *Mr J A Wight, MRCVS*. 'There you are, Alice, the vet's.'

'I can see that, but I want to see James Herriot's place.'

Raquel giggled. 'This is it! The vet here, Alf Wight, is who writes books as James Herriot.'

'Mr Herriot isn't a real person?' Alice looked deflated.

'Come on, Alice, take a photograph and then we'll go. In fact, give me the camera and stand by the door — I'll take one of you, then I'll explain about Mr Wight as we drive. At least the countryside we're passing through is where the books are set.'

James led them back to the car, saying, 'Knowing your interest in animals, I'm now going to show you the biggest horse you've ever seen.'

Throughout the drive James and Alice chatted as they drove through Kilburn and saw the workshop of the carpenter Mousey Thompson. Up the steep White Horse Bank, they saw the limestone horse, before they parked at the top of Sutton Bank for their picnic.

'Food, at last,' Raquel said. 'I'm beginning to think you two had forgotten I'm here.'

'How could we forget you, Squirt?' James said. 'You're my favourite sister.'

Raquel, two years younger than Alice, was certainly not as worldly wise. 'I am?' She was now eager to help when they found a flat area of grass and set out the food on the picnic rug.

'Why didn't I notice this view on the way here?' Alice asked.

Raquel, with her mouth full of cake, said, 'Probably because you had your eyes shut as we went down the hill.'

James laughed. 'My driving is not that bad. And you were the one in the back, squealing.'

The banter continued as they made one last call on the return journey to Scarborough. James turned the car off the main road and pulled to a halt outside a graveyard containing a small church.

'This is bonzer,' Alice said, grabbing her camera again. 'What is this place?'

'St Gregory Minster. It was built in 1060 on land that once held a church dedicated to Pope Gregory.'

'How do you know all that?' Raquel asked.

'Because, unlike you, I happened to like history in school. Come on, we should be heading back.'

When they reached Byland Crescent, James let Raquel out of the car, asking her to tell Sarah he would bring the picnic hamper inside.

He opened the passenger door for Alice.

'Thank you, kind sir,' she said as they went to the boot. 'Let me help. I'll get the rug.' She reached inside and her hand brushed against James' as he was lifting the hamper. She pulled back quickly. 'Oh, I'm sorry,' she said, a slight blush on her cheeks.

'That's not a problem, Alice, you can touch my hand anytime you like,' he teased.

'I, er, have to thank you for today,' Alice said, hurriedly. 'You've been really kind taking me all these places. I've really enjoyed it.'

'There's always tomorrow. Dad said I could have half a day off. If you want, I'll take you up to the castle. You'll be able to get some great photos from the headland.'

'Are you sure? There must be lots of other things you could do with your time off.'

'Perhaps there are, but none of them are as interesting as you.'

Alice blushed again, wondering if he was still teasing her.

CHAPTER FORTY-TWO

James stayed for dinner again and that evening, following the meal, Alice was asked about her day. Before she could answer, Raquel said loudly, 'She and James talked all the time. They forgot I was there.'

'I'm sure they didn't,' her mother said, sympathetically.

'Yes, they did. I'm not sure what a chaperone's supposed to do, but whatever it is I didn't do it. All they could talk about was Australia, life here, and the places we passed.'

'Didn't you find that interesting?' her mother asked.

'I wasn't listening.'

When the laughter subsided, Angela nudged her sister. 'Idiot, how do you know what they were saying if you weren't listening?'

'There must have been something you liked?' Rachael asked.

'The picnic was good, oh, and the little church, I liked that.'

'Which church was this?' Sonny asked.

'I took them to St Gregory Minster on the way back,' James replied.

'Lovely place. Do you know about Kirkdale Cave, near there?'

'That's a new one on me,' James said.

'It's an ancient site discovered years ago, where fossils were found. Would you believe some of them were hippos, rhinos and elephants?'

'You are joking,' James said.

'Come into the library and I'll find the book it's mentioned in.'

* * *

The following morning when James called for Alice, he spoke to his great-grandmother. 'I don't think we need a chaperone today, do we? It will be a quick trip to the castle, and we're on foot, walking through crowds in the town.'

'I'm sure Alice will be quite safe with you. Enjoy yourselves,' Rachael said.

Ensuring Alice had her camera, they set off across town to the headland and climbed the slope to the ruin. Within the walls, Alice marvelled at the view and took shot after shot, grateful she had remembered to put a spare film in her bag. All the time she and James chatted as if they had known each other for years.

Alice remembered the tragic loss James had suffered, and the comment his grandmother, during her visit to Australia, had made about him having lost all interest in girls after the death of his fiancée. Judging by the warmth of his smile when he looked at her, perhaps that was about to change.

As they exited the castle, Alice spotted St Mary's Church. 'Do we have time for a quick look?' she asked.

'Make it quick,' James said. 'You can see the grave of Anne Bronte in the churchyard. There's a shortcut back to the foreshore we can take from there.'

A short while later, following more photography, James led Alice to an archway in the wall of the graveyard. He reached out and took her hand, to assist her down steps leading to a path to the old town.

When they reached the promenade, Alice realized James was still holding her hand. She looked at him, then at the clasped hands.

He smiled at her. 'You don't mind, do you? I should hate for you to get lost.'

'No, James, I don't mind at all.'

All too soon for Alice's liking they reached the door at Byland Crescent, where they were greeted by Rachael. 'I've had a call from your grandmother,' she told her. 'They will be arriving in Scarborough to collect you. I've got their hotel details and have been asked to deliver you to them tomorrow.'

'Oh. So soon.' Alice glanced at James.

Rachael didn't seem to notice, and continued, 'She said she has missed you and is looking forward to you showing them round. She seems to think things will have changed since they were last here, but I don't think they have.'

Later, when Sonny heard that Luke and Bella were planning to visit Scarborough, he asked, 'Are they coming to my party?'

Mark grinned at his father. 'When we told you Luke Fisher was coming to England to oversee the disposal of the business, that was only half the story. We had mentioned your birthday bash when we were at their place, and Luke said he and Bella would like to come. So I hope you don't mind, but we invited them.'

Sonny replied, 'That will be wonderful. I like Luke and Bella, but I never thought I'd see them again. It will be really good to catch up.'

* * *

Three days prior to the event, a delivery van arrived at the rear of the house. The driver and his assistant began offloading cases of wine, which Mark, assisted by Andy and James, stacked on the ground floor, before forming a chain to take them to the basement wine cellar.

Sonny, who was watching the operation, examined the stack of cases. 'I've never heard of this brand before. The name *Luca Collina* suggests it's from Italy.'

'I think the vineyard might belong to someone with Italian ancestry,' Mark replied, 'but the wine is Australian. Jenny and I got introduced to it on our visit and it's really nice. Luckily, they've just started exporting to the UK, so I ordered some.'

'How long is this party going on for? There's enough here to last a month.'

'I wanted to ensure we have sufficient. There would be nothing worse than running out of booze halfway through the celebrations.'

'I don't think there's much chance of that happening. But, tell me something. Why are you carrying them to the cellar when you'll have to bring them up again?' He raised his eyebrows, turned, and walked away, leaving the others looking at each other in confusion.

On the day before the party, Sonny and Rachael were further distracted by the arrival of their daughter Frances, along with her husband Hank. Moments later, Lizzie, Gil and the twins arrived. They had only been in the house an hour when Mark and Jenny's daughter Suzie also returned. Suzie, now an up-and-coming barrister, had a few days to spare before she needed to begin preparing for two cases where she would be acting for the defence. There was no way she would miss the opportunity to attend her grandfather's party.

* * *

As the big day dawned, activity in Byland Crescent went into overdrive. Out of courtesy, notice of the family's intentions to use the garden on the day had been made to the other properties in the crescent. As the area was now little used, unlike the earlier years, Mark believed there would be no objections — not that it would make any difference if they did.

The gazebo had been erected and, under the direction of Jenny, the seating was being arranged by Andy and the serving staff employed to assist Sarah. Long trestle tables with large white tablecloths were ready for the delicious food, currently filling every available space in the kitchen. Given the time of year, the temperature outside was already beginning to warm up, promising a sunlit, cloudless sky.

Sarah was glad she'd opted for a buffet. The tables would bear a heavy load of salads, sandwiches, delicacies and desserts spread out alongside the main attraction, a large birthday cake to mark the occasion. Made in secret by Sarah, for Sonny, for whom she had the utmost respect.

Sonny watched the activity with interest from the sitting-room window. He turned to Rachael. 'Do we have to make such a fuss? It's only a birthday. I have had them before.'

Rachael linked her arm through his and hugged him tight. 'Don't be such an old fusspot,' she chided him. 'You've got a wonderful family who are doing this for you. And don't forget your special guests from Australia.'

* * *

At the appointed time, the front door of number one Byland Crescent was opened wide and the family, with the exception of Sonny and Rachael, began to assemble in the garden. The Bradford contingent arrived together, ringing the doorbell and presenting Sonny with gifts and congratulations.

Rachael had her cue and led Sonny, sporting his walking cane, down to the garden as a taxi was pulling to a halt. The car door opened and out stepped Luke and Bella, followed by Alice. Exiting behind her stood a man and woman.

'Sonny!' Luke cried. 'Congratulations! It's so good to see you again after all these years.'

'And you too, Luke. But shouldn't that be "g'day"? I've been practising since I heard you were coming.'

Amid the laughter, Sonny hugged Bella, and turned to their granddaughter. 'Welcome back, Alice.'

A voice behind him said, 'G'day, Sonny.'

He turned round, staring in disbelief at the man. 'Elliot? Elliot, is that you?'

'Sure is. I wouldn't miss a trip when the boss is paying.'

'My word, what a surprise this is turning out to be. And who is this lovely lady?'

'This is my wife Dorothy, or as we call her, Dottie.'

Dottie reached out her hand. 'G'day, Mr Cowgill. Good to meet you. Happy birthday.'

Sonny smiled. 'Thank you. But please, call me Sonny. How are you enjoying England?'

'Bloody ripper — and there's no mozzies.'

Seeing the expression on Sonny's face, Elliot stepped in. 'Sorry, Sonny. What Dot means is she's having a great time, and there are no mosquitoes.'

'Ah, yes, mosquitoes. Rachael and I encountered them when we were in Greece.'

Jenny took Alice by the hand as the formal introductions continued, saying, 'Let me introduce you to some more of the younger members of the family you haven't met.'

Alice smiled. 'Thank you, Jenny. I didn't know there would be so many people here.'

'Now you know what it was like for me and Mark at your place!'

Alice laughed, and began to relax as she was led towards a small group.

'This is Alice,' Jenny stated, 'and I want you all to look after her.' She turned to the boy nearest to her. 'This is my nephew William, and this is his twin sister Heloise. They are cousins of Angela and Raquel. And James is around somewhere.'

William, being of similar age to Alice, smiled, appreciating the good looks of the striking young woman standing before him. Before he could think of something to say, the girls surrounded her, insisting she sat with them.

James appeared, having been to the cellar for yet another case of wine. This was his second trip and he wished the cases had been stored in a more convenient place, as his great-grandfather had implied. He approached his sisters, where he could see they were entertaining Alice. He paused and listened to the girlish chatter for a moment before he stepped forward.

He turned to his cousin. 'William, fetch Alice some lemonade, please.'

Consuela was watching, standing with Lizzie, as William headed for the drinks, scowling at James.

'If I'm not mistaken, I think young William has just been thwarted by my son,' Consuela said.

'Good,' Lizzie replied. 'William's far too young to be thinking about girls.'

'I wonder if James is far too old to be thinking about Alice?'

'Oh, I don't think so,' a voice from behind them said. Jenny had noticed her grandson rejoin the party, his mission to the wine cellar complete. She'd watched with interest, and a degree of pleasure, as James threaded his way between his relatives to reach his goal. She could tell James was attracted to Alice and, judging by the girl's reaction, that attraction could well be mutual. 'This,' she told Consuela, 'could be just what your son needs.'

* * *

James smiled at Alice. 'It's good to see you again. Are you glad to be back?'

'I've only been gone just over a week.' She laughed. 'But yes, I am really happy to be back. I've missed our chats.'

'So have I, but I've missed you more. When do you go back to Australia?'

Was he teasing her again? Alice wondered, replying, 'Two weeks. I'll be sorry to go. I've enjoyed my time here in Scarborough.'

'Not as much as I've enjoyed your company,' James said, as he smiled again and indicated two chairs away from the teenagers.

Alice sat down. 'I've been happier here than I have for the past few years. I'd like to write to you when I'm home. If you agree?' she said, hesitantly.

'You can write as often as you like, and who knows, I might even write back. I may even come for a visit one day. If you don't mind?'

'That would be ripper. When could you come?'

'Hold your horses, you haven't left yet.'

They were both laughing, when Jenny turned away to hide a smile as her grandson's little finger entwined with that of their visitor. Little did she know what the future held — that in eighteen months' time, when Alice had left school, James would visit Australia. There, he would remain for two years working as a technician before, as in a previous generation, James Cowgill would marry Alice Fisher.

CHAPTER FORTY-THREE

The party progressed well into the afternoon, the wine flowed freely, and the buffet was replenished constantly by the servers. There was much laughter and reminiscence as tales were told, many of which were new to the guests. The one subject certainly not mentioned was business.

Once the party was in full swing, and after he had managed to call for silence, Mark, who had elected himself master of ceremonies, began to speak. 'Friends and family, we are gathered here to celebrate my father's life on the occasion of his ninetieth birthday. Please raise your glasses and toast my father, Mark Albert Cowgill. Happy birthday, Sonny.'

As the cheers rang out, Sonny got to his feet, but Mark signalled to him to be seated and continued, 'I have to tell you all a story.'

There were light-hearted groans from the guests, while Mark attempted to call for silence again, by tapping a spoon against his wine glass.

'When he was a small boy, Sonny lost touch with his brother, who left this house' — he gestured to the building — 'along with his pregnant girlfriend, never to return. Sonny frequently tells the story, and over the eighty-some years that have passed, he has always wondered what became of them.

Now, I'm going to hand over to Luke, who I understand has brought Sonny a very special birthday present.'

Luke stepped forward and passed Sonny a flat, oblong parcel wrapped in gift paper. 'We brought this from home, Sonny. We hope you like it.' He and Bella watched anxiously as he unfastened the paper and slid the contents out.

As Sonny stared in astonishment at the framed photo, Rachael and several others crowded round, keen to see what had rendered him speechless.

Eventually, Sonny asked, 'Where on earth did you get this?'

'The one you're holding is actually a copy taken from the original which was hidden in Patrick Finnegan's desk.'

'I'm completely baffled. How did Patrick obtain it? And why did he keep it?'

'I take it you recognize everyone in that group?'

Sonny nodded, confused and wondering where this was leading.

Luke continued, 'When Mark and Jenny visited us, they recognized this photograph immediately. It's an enlarged duplicate of one you keep in your study, I believe?'

Sonny nodded.

'Mark told me the small boy in the centre is you, correct?'

Sonny nodded again.

'He also told us you'd pointed out many times that the handsome young man at one end, and the very pretty girl at the other end of the group, are your brother James and his sweetheart Alice, the housemaid he eloped with.'

'Yes, that's right.'

'What none of you know is that photo hangs with honour in the boardroom of Fisher Springs.' Luke looked at Bella, who nodded encouragement. 'It hangs there . . . because they founded the company.'

'What? James founded Fisher Springs? Is that right?' Sonny looked at Rachael, thoroughly confused. She stood behind him and placed her hands on his shoulders, trying to provide reassurance.

'So did you know James and Alice?' Sonny asked.

Luke nodded. 'After their marriage, James and Alice had a large family. Although, sadly, most of them are dead, two are still alive.' He reached out for Dottie, who came and stood alongside him, as tears began running down her cheeks.

'My sister Dorothy Finnegan, nee Fisher, is one.' He tried to contain himself. 'And I am the other.' He paused, allowing the importance of his words to register. 'James, formally Cowgill, and Alice Fisher, were our father and mother.'

There were gasps from those listening.

Luke continued, 'When I learned of the connection,'— he raised a glass towards Mark — 'for which Mark and Jenny must be thankful has now been revealed,' — there was a murmur of laughter — 'Bella and I simply had to come to wish you a very happy birthday — Uncle Sonny.'

While those who hadn't been in on the secret recovered from the shock revelations, and eyes were dried from the happy tears shed, Sonny called Mark and Jenny over. 'You knew about this,' he accused them.

Mark's expression was that of a schoolboy being reprimanded. 'Er, yes, we did. Luke asked us to keep it under wraps, he wanted to surprise you. It hasn't been easy to do.'

Sonny smiled. 'I should think it hasn't. But it certainly was a wonderful surprise.' He hugged them both. 'Thank you, thank you both so much. If you hadn't been to Australia, I never would have known what happened to James.'

Sonny, leaning on his walking cane, took the floor, raised his glass, and told everyone, 'Thank you to all of you for coming today. I have reached the evening of my life, but I could not have wished for a more glorious sunset than today has brought, with *all* my family around me.'

THE END

ACKNOWLEDGEMENTS

When you have lived through what are now the historical events you are writing about, your judgement can become clouded as you recall instances from your own past. Recollection is a strange thing; it presents a distorted picture of your understanding of the time. Research and fact-checking have been the role of my in-house editor, my wife, Val. Without her support, this fourth, and final, book of the Cowgill Family Saga would not have been written.

I am extremely grateful to my reader, Wendy McPhee, who knows the characters from the earlier books, and without her input I feel sure my editor could have been very busy.

I must also thank Emma and Steph at Joffe Books for their guidance after the first draft, and all the Joffe crew, from design to advertising. Without them this saga would never have been concluded.

THE JOFFE BOOKS STORY

We began in 2014 when Jasper agreed to publish his mum's much-rejected romance novel and it became a bestseller.

Since then we've grown into the largest independent publisher in the UK. We're extremely proud to publish some of the very best writers in the world, including Joy Ellis, Faith Martin, Caro Ramsay, Helen Forrester, Simon Brett and Robert Goddard. Everyone at Joffe Books loves reading and we never forget that it all begins with the magic of an author telling a story.

We are proud to publish talented first-time authors, as well as established writers whose books we love introducing to a new generation of readers.

We have been shortlisted for Independent Publisher of the Year at the British Book Awards three times, in 2020, 2021 and 2022, and for the Diversity and Inclusivity Award at the Independent Publishing Awards in 2022.

We built this company with your help, and we love to hear from you, so please email us about absolutely anything bookish at: feedback@joffebooks.com.

If you want to receive free books every Friday and hear about all our new releases, join our mailing list here: www.joffebooks.com/contact

And when you tell your friends about us, just remember: it's pronounced Joffe as in coffee or toffee!

ALSO BY BILL KITSON

THE COWGILL FAMILY SAGA

Book 1: BROTHERS AND SISTERS OF BYLAND CRESCENT

Book 2: STORM CLOUDS OVER BYLAND CRESCENT

Book 3: COMING HOME TO BYLAND CRESCENT

Book 4: NEW ARRIVALS IN BYLAND CRESCENT

Made in United States
North Haven, CT
12 January 2024